A Yellow Cotton Dress

by H. L. Osteen

only one love survived the Cuban revolution...

A Yellow Cotton Dress

by H. L. Osteen

OZ PUBLISHING
SACRAMENTO, CALIFORNIA

A Yellow Cotton Dress
By H. L. Osteen

First paperback edition, 2005

ISBN 0-9716437-5-X (trade paperback)

Library of Congress Control Number: 2003095657

Cover Art by Karen Mandell
www.karenmandell.com

To order copies of this book, contact:
  OZ Publishing
  P. O. Box 1349
  Sacramento, CA 95812-1349
  lewosteen@aol.com
  Toll-free (888) 668-0744

Printed in the United States of America

Dedication

To the Osteens: Mrytis Ginn, Heyward Lewis Sr., David Milton, Harriett Carter, David Christian, Gabrielle Patrice, and my grandson Joseph Lewis Tobin. Thanks to my editors: Carol Minard, Francisco Javier Adame Jr. and John Schaff. To those who believed: Ann Camille Spilman, Lou and Dorathy Zalar, Roz, Barbara Watson, Fozzie, Kelly Wynn, King Willian Walter Smith, Bill Walsh, and the loyal members of the Wednesday Night Literary Guild.

A Special Dedication

To Marie Ruth, the gentle soul who was my
surrogate mother. In the slang of the times she was
referred to as a "Black Mammy." In appearance
she was a look-alike for Hattie McDaniel. In
reality she was always there for me though I often
took her for granted and doubt I ever appreciated
her true worth. The character of Sarah in the text
of this novel was patterned after her. I hope I have
been faithful to her memory and she will forgive
me for any slights my youth and ignorance may
have caused her.

Book One

A Lady of Elegance

"Thou art Black but beautiful as the cedars of Lebanon, as the curtains of Solomon . . . tell me, O Thou whom my soul loveth . . . did you know not that thou are the fairest among women . . ."

—Song of Solomon

Chapter One

Charleston, South Carolina—Spring 1950

IT WAS THE FIRST THING THAT CHRISTI HAD EVER OWNED ALL BY HERself and the first thing she didn't have to share with anyone. Not that Christi was selfish—she wasn't. Christi shared everything with her extended family, from her meager meals to her small bedroom. But the dress would fit no one else, so it belonged, solely and completely, to Christi.

To people of means, the dress would have meant little. To those with closets great and tall enough to stroll within, the dress would have been relegated to a dark and dusty corner. To most people, all except Christi Jones, the dress was plain and ordinary as the cotton staple from which it was spun and would not rate a second look.

But to Christi it was the most beautiful thing she had ever seen. The dress was yellow but in differing patterns of light it took on varying shades. In morning light, it was the shimmering saffron color of a Tibetan monk's robe.

In bright sunlight, it was the color of lemon blossoms the first morning of spring. In twilight, it was the color of soft amber caught by a stained glass window in the church on the hill.

The bright yellow cloth was cut from premium flour sacks bought with money that should have been used for medicine or coal. Sarah, Christi's mother, had used all her sewing skills to cut the rough cloth into a serviceable form. It had been a labor of love that, Sarah believed, was her finest work. Her only concern was that it would not fit her lovely daughter.

To Sarah, Christi was everything she had longed to be and Sarah was determined, despite grinding poverty, to raise Christi to be a lady of elegance. Sarah loved her daughter so much it bordered on worship and, at times, was stifling to Christi's free spirit.

South Charleston of the late forties and early fifties was not the storied Charleston of romance and grandeur, gossamer parasols, lemon-flavored tea, and polite conversation. South Charleston, this spring of 1950, was a world of leeward leaning shanties, with rusty, leaky, tin roofs, fatback, Fast Eddies, and collard greens. It was also a sometimes deadly, often dangerous, seamy world of flashy hustlers, con men, and the daily fight for survival.

Sarah was the queen of a kingdom of decent hard-working people, surrounded by flimflam men, jive ass hustlers, and professional ne'er-do-wells. Despite her long hours of desperate labor sewing, washing, and ironing, she never made it across the tracks to the storybook Charleston except to work as a domestic—a domestic in a great house where she had once been most grievously shamed.

It was a bitter pill for Sarah to swallow, doing "house nigger duties" in a household that held painful memories and a dark secret—a secret that Sarah would tell no one until the proper time.

"Thanks, Momma! It's gorgeous!" Christi bubbled as she stood before the cracked full-length mirror and tried on the dress. Christi knew it was not just any dress. It had a warmth about it. It made her feel good. Christi knew she wasn't ugly, but the yellow cotton dress made her feel beautiful and unashamed of that beauty. It also made her feel the equal of everyone. Christi had no idea how much the dress would mean to her during the terrible times to come.

"It's a simple enough dress, but you make it elegant, chile. Lordy! How you do shine!"

"She certainly does," Mrs. White, Christi's diction teacher, agreed.

Mrs. White was an extravagance that Sarah really could not afford, but was damn well determined to afford. It was important to Sarah that Christi not talk Geechy or low-life slang, or any of the other dialects associated with her economic station in life. Sarah knew that because Mrs. White liked Christi, she worked for less than she could have made prepping debutantes in the niceties of proper manners and diction.

"Momma, it's the best thing you've ever given me and I will take such good care of it." Christi paused as Lucius, her stepfather, walked into the room.

"Lordy mercy, woman! Is this little Christi all grown up?" Lucius's eyes were barely able to control his desire.

Christobel "Christi" Harriet Jones was cute at birth, attractive at the age of eleven, a lovely young lady at fourteen and was now, on her seventeenth birthday, a voluptuous woman with the heart and soul of an innocent maiden.

Physically, she had matured fast. Much too fast for her own good. Her curvaceous body was the object of men's lustful eyes long before she understood what their long, hungry looks implied.

Sarah looked hard at Lucius and stepped in between him and Christi. "Ain't you supposed to be over at the warehouse talking with The Man about that job?"

"Ain't no use in doing that. You know as well as I do it's gonna be a white man what gets it!" Lucius pulled on a long-necked bottle of beer.

"No, I don't know that! Mr. Thomas told me he'd give you fair consideration. Mr. Thomas is a man of his word," Sarah insisted.

"Well, you believe what you want but I'm not wasting my time," Lucius said through beer bubbles.

Sarah hated herself for being so weak as to put up with a no-count man like Lucius. He was everything she hated in the world, but he did have his charms and she had a fatal weakness for them. "Well, you're wasting our time. This is women folks' talk, so you just go on about what you were doing and leave us be," Sarah said firmly.

Lucius took a quick, hungry look at Christi. He smiled wryly, then turned and left the room. His parting long, lewd stares made Christi's skin crawl.

Christi stayed out of his way as much as possible. She shivered slightly then turned back to the mirror and smiled. "I'm going to save up and buy me a pair of bright yellow shoes to go with this here dress."

"What did you say?" Sarah snapped.

"I said . . ."

"You said this 'here' dress, Christi," Mrs. White corrected.

"I'm sorry. I slip sometimes. I meant this—this very special dress."

Sarah and Mrs. White nodded approval.

"She is doing well, Sarah. She is the fastest learner I have ever tutored. There are times when she's speaking and I'm not watching that I swear she is English royalty," Mrs. White beamed.

"You have done good, Mrs. White."

"Done well," Christi chided.

Sarah smiled and looked fondly at her lovely daughter. The sunlight coming through the window cast an aura around her that gave her an angelic glow of innocence. Sarah hoped she could find a way to preserve that glow of innocence and keep Christi from all the low-life mean things in the world. Sarah wasn't naive. She knew what treacherous things waited just outside their door. Sarah had no illusions about stopping the world—she only hoped to slow it as much as possible.

"I'm ready, Momma. Where are we going?" Christi smiled.

Sarah looked at Mrs. White.

"That's for us to know and for you to find out. A surprise isn't a surprise if you know all about it," Sarah said.

"Then can I go over to Lucy's and show her my dress?"

"Yes. If you're back here by five o'clock sharp. Not a minute one way or the other. You hear me?"

"Yes, ma'am." Christi gave Sarah a hurried kiss and skipped out of the door.

Sarah watched her go then turned to look at Mrs. White.

"All my life I wanted a dress like that. Now I'm way past too old to look good enough in it to be wearing one anyhow."

"Now, Sarah. You know you aren't that old. I say you could wear anything you care to wear."

"Mrs. White, please save your flattery for the white folks. As long as Christi is happy, I'm happy. Besides, it would take more flour sacks than Rockefeller himself could afford to get enough cloth to make up a dress to fit me."

"Oh, Sarah. Now don't berate yourself." Mrs. White started to disagree until Sarah started laughing.

The laughter was infectious and she joined in until they were both laughing loud and hard and long.

Christi skipped down the street oblivious to the leering eyes that followed her. It was a bright spring day, and she felt pretty, so looks were welcome. Looks that, to her innocent heart, she believed were innocent as well.

She skipped through a small park and stopped at a big oak tree with a swing. She plopped down in the swing, pushed herself off and began to swing to and fro. As she did, her dress lifted softly in the slight spring breeze. Unashamedly, she kicked out with her long legs, exposing her perfect thighs to her panty line. Christi was swinging higher and higher, lost in happy thoughts, when she felt the strong hands on her waist that held her until the swing came to a stop. She smelled old whiskey and stale body odor. She turned to see Lucius standing behind her grinning from ear to ear.

"Let me push you up, girl. Like I used to when you was a tiny thing!" Lucius started to push her.

Christi jumped out of the swing. She took several hurried steps away from Lucius. "No! No, thank you, Lucius. I have to be going now. I really do! Mother wants me home."

"What the hell, gal! That surprise party ain't 'til six o'clock. It's only 'bout two now. We got plenty of time to swing . . . or anything else you got in mind."

"I don't have anything in mind except going home. Please let me go."

"You know you think you're a high-faluting bitch, don't cha?"

"I never said that, Lucius."

"It ain't what you say. It's the snotty way you been acting. That white woman's got you trying to talk like white folks when you're just a nigger like the rest of us. You ain't no better than anybody, bitch!"

"I never said I was . . ."

"Hell, you're not even anybody who can claim to belong to anybody. You're whiter than they are but they ain't gonna let you forget you got black blood. You can talk and walk that white shit but when it comes to something close to home, you're still just another nigger."

"I don't like that kind of talk, Lucius. I really do have to go." Christi tried to push by him.

He grabbed her arm and held it firmly. "You think you're better than me!"

"I never . . ."

"I seen you look down that high-yellow nose at me. Well, maybe I oughta teach you to have respect for your stepfather. I ain't never took the belt to you and maybe that's my mistake!"

Lucius started to unbuckle his belt.

Christi pulled away from him.

Lucius reached out and grabbed her harder.

"Leave me alone, Lucius. Sarah won't like this!"

"Oh? You think I'm scared of Sarah? You think I'm some kind of candy ass? I'm a man, woman! A man! You understand that? Do you? You white bitch!" Lucius shook her hard.

"White bitch? I'm not white, Lucius!" Christi was hurt by the words.

"You shore as hell ain't black! But that don't matter. What matters is how much you be knowin' 'bout how to treat a man!"

Christi did not like the look in this eye. "I'm going home now, Lucius. Now let me go. I mean it!"

"Oh? You gonna hurt me? You got me so scared. I'm shakin' in my boots," Lucius laughed.

As he laughed, Christi pushed away from him. She started to run but tripped and fell. As she fell, her dress hiked up to the middle of her thighs. Quickly, she pulled the dress down, but not before Lucius looked at her with heightened lust.

Christi got to her feet and started to run.

Lucius grabbed her by the arm and spun her around. "You turned your back on me for the last time, bitch!"

"Leave me alone!" Christi clawed at him.

Lucius slapped her hard across the face.

Christi was stunned only a moment. "Sarah's going to fix you for this, Lucius!"

Lucius's reply was to force his mouth on hers. His mean hands dug their way into her hair. His hot spit tried to force its way past her clenched teeth. The feel and taste of it made her ill. She wanted to vomit. Instead, she summoned the courage to bite his lip.

Lucius pushed her away. As he did, he held onto her dress and tore her sleeve. "Damn you, bitch!" Lucius spit blood.

Christi looked at the tear on the sleeve of her dress. "You tore my dress? I don't believe it! You TORE my dress!"

"Yeah! So I tore your damn dress! And now I'm gonna tear off somethin' else!" Lucius started toward her.

"You tore my dress!" Christi repeated as she looked at him in disbelief.

"Hell, gal! It's just an old cotton dress what ain't even that pretty. You give me what I want and I'll buy you lots of real dresses."

Lucius grabbed her arms and tried to pull her close.

As he did, something snapped inside Christi. She had suffered many indignities quietly and patiently as she had been taught a lady should. But there was something about this man's manner, the tear in her dress, and his foul breath that released a torrent of pent-up rage.

Christi broke his grip. "Don't touch me ever again!"

Lucius studied the look of defiance in her eyes. It only made him more determined. "Come here, woman! I'm past tired of playing games!"

As if she had done it many times before, Christi bared her claws and leaped toward his face. Her fingernails found his eyes and dug in.

Lucius was stunned for a moment before he screamed in pain and dropped to his knees. "I can't see! Damn you, bitch! You done clawed my eyes out. What in the hell is wrong with you? Are you crazy?"

"You tore my dress," Christi kept repeating as she picked up a large rock and hit him on the head until he stopped moving. Then she dropped the rock and examined the tear on her dress. She did not see Mrs. White approach from behind.

Mrs. White reeled back in horror at the sight of Lucius's bloody head. "Oh God! Oh God!" Mrs. White looked at the blood on Christi's hands "Oh God! Christi, what have you done?

Christi looked at Mrs. White with a look of rage unlike any Mrs. White had ever seen. "He tore it. He tore my dress!"

The look terrified Mrs. White into silence. She wanted to reach out to Christi but Christi backed away looking defiant.

Lucius moaned and Christi turned to look at him.

"No, Christi! No!"

Christi started to ignore Mrs. White. Then just as quickly burst into tears. She hugged Mrs. White around the waist and sobbed uncontrollably.

Mrs. White almost fainted.

Chapter Two

SARAH SHOOK HER HEAD AS SHE CHECKED THE REPAIR JOB SHE HAD done on the tear in the sleeve of Christi's dress. "Good God almighty, chile! You could of got yourself killed. I swear, I'm so sorry I had anything to do with that no-count man! I'm so sorry," Sarah chided herself.

It was three weeks after the attack but Christi still shivered at the thought of it. Sarah had held back giving her the repaired dress, knowing it would bring up bad memories.

Christi had begged to have it back and Sarah had finally agreed. "Momma, don't go blaming yourself. It's okay. It's over," Christi soothed.

"Over? I'm afraid you don't know much about that man. He ain't likely to forget this anytime soon. Not with that scar you put on his right eye. But don't you worry none, I'll take care of his sorry ass. You just tell me if you see him anywhere near where you want to be. Don't you do anything by yourself. Understand?"

"Yes, ma'am."

"You okay, honey chile?"

"Yes, Momma. I'm fine. Thanks for the lovely party."

Sarah responded with eyes brimming with love. "Well, three weeks late is better than never. Happy late birthday." Sarah chuckled.

Christi gave Sarah a big hug. "Momma? Momma, he called me a 'white bitch'!"

Sarah looked into Christi's mysterious sienna eyes. They glowed with a light from within that made them both compelling and alarming. "He said that?"

"Yes, ma'am."

"Well, I say you consider who was saying it. He's a no-count man with a no-count mouth."

Christi smiled. She walked over to a table holding a family picture album. Slowly, she turned the pages until she found a family photograph. She studied the photograph of Sarah, an almost full-blooded African woman of Nubian countenance. She looked at Etta May, her stepsister, a light-skinned, doe-eyed young woman. She looked at Little Eddie's bronze face and striking Masai features.

She pondered how her white face shone out in that black and white rainbow spectrum.

"Who am I, Momma?" Christi looked sad.

"I don't understand." Sarah dodged.

"I can't deny what I see in the mirror. It's not what I feel inside. I walk into stores and use the colored fountain and people who don't know who I am look at me like I was crazy." Christi paused and sighed hard. "I could go across town and pass for a hotsy-totsy debutante at one of those fancy cotillions."

"You just hush, chile! I don't like that kind of talk. That ain't our world."

"But, Momma, Mrs. White has me talking like them. You said once, I look like better than them."

"You ain't them! You are flesh of my flesh and bone of my bone and I'm as black as they come!"

Christi looked at Sarah and started to reply. Sarah's stern look made her keep silent.

Christi sighed hard. "It's so hard sometimes, Momma."

"I know, honey chile. But you just trust me and I'll help you through it."

"Yes, ma'am," Christi paused. "Momma, you said my father died in the war?"

"You know that."

"But I thought Blacks were mostly cooks and things like that."

"You know I don't like talking about it, Christi." Sarah moved over and shut the album.

"I just wish we had kept just one picture of him."

Sarah tried to look sad. She failed. "You know they were all burnt up in the fire. Now let's just go on to something else."

"Yes, ma'am." Christi had to swallow hard. Out of respect for Sarah, Christi had never pressed her mother for the identity of her father.

Everyone told Christi that Sarah had made up the lie about her father being killed in the war.

The rumor was that her real father was a powerful white man who paid Sarah to keep her mouth shut. Christi always wondered why, if that were true, they didn't have more money. She also knew every time she looked in the mirror that he was nobody from this side of town.

"Momma, can I ask you one more question? Then I won't ask you anymore. Please?"

"Of course you can. You know you can ask me most anything."

Christi knew the "most" in Sarah's reply meant anything but questions about her father. But this day Christi was going to push a little. "I don't care what white folks think of me, but why do some black people hate me?"

Sarah looked irritated for a moment.

"That's 'cause you remind some people of things they'd just as soon forget. Then there's some people that are just plain jealous of pretty things. And maybe there's a lot of people who don't like themselves so they don't want to like nobody else."

"I think it's because I'm TOO white."

"I told you I don't want to hear that kind of talk."

"Why? Everybody we know says it?"

"What has gotten into you, chile?"

"I think I'm old enough to know the truth about my father."

Sarah's face was flushed with anger mixed with shame as she stared at Christi before she replied. "You saying your Momma's been lying to you?"

There were times when Christi didn't know if she loved her mother or feared her.

This was one of those times.

At this moment, the hunger to know the truth overcame her need for love and her fear of Sarah's wrath. "He was a white man, wasn't he?"

"What?"

"God, Momma! Look at me! It's so obvious!"

"You believing all them rumors over what your Momma done said?"

"I'm seventeen. It's time you told me the truth!"

Sarah was visibly shaken by Christi's probing. She had to take a moment to gather herself. "This bad thing with Lucius has made you a little crazy. I understand."

"No, Momma!"

"No?"

"I want to know who he is and where he lives!"

"Good Lord, chile! I give you some slack because of what had happened but this is unbecoming of what all I done taught you."

Christi felt a little sorry for Sarah. It was plain it was a secret that hurt her deeply. Only a few days ago, Christi would not have dared take it further.

"Then you don't intend to ever tell me the truth?"

Sarah rose up to slap Christi. Her eyes brimmed with tears as she dropped the dress to the floor and stormed from the room.

Christi started to follow. She thought better of it. Instead she put on the yellow cotton dress and stood before the full-length mirror. She checked it out from every angle.

Her mother had done a splendid repair job.

As Christi looked at herself in the mirror she felt guilty she had made Sarah feel bad. She started to move from the room. She turned to see her mother staring at her.

"Did I sew it up good?" Sarah asked.

Christi could tell her mother had been crying and that made her feel even more guilty. "I'm sorry, Momma."

"You got nothing to be sorry about. Them was honest questions."

Christi waited hoping for Sarah to tell her more.

The look on Sarah's face told her Sarah would say no more.

"You did a good job, Momma. Thank you."

"That sure enough is your color." Sarah moved up and stood beside her.

They both stared at Christi's starkly white image contrasted with Sarah's ebony features.

"You give me some time, chile. I knows what you want to know and there be a time for telling it."

"Soon, Momma?"

"I expect so."

"I hope so."

"Don't think I don't know what you're worrying on. I say don't you be caring what other folks say. You respect yourself first, Christi. You begin deep inside where God put your immortal soul. You keep it pure and clean and it's easy to respect yourself. That's what you do before you can love anybody else."

"But isn't that the sin of pride?"

"I didn't say you should be dotin' on yourself in the looking glass. I said you take care of your soul. You keep it pure and you'll like yourself. When you like yourself it's mighty easy to like other people."

"Momma, I wish I understood the world like you do!"

"Maybe I put on a good show."

"It's the best show I know of," Christi said as she looked at Sarah with respect.

Sarah sat down in her chair and sighed hard.

Christi kneeled down by the chair and lay her head on Sarah's ample lap. "I love you, Momma!" Christi said as Sarah put some finishing touches on the repairs to the yellow cotton dress.

Sarah stroked her daughter's shiny dark hair and swallowed her secret bitterness. ". . . and, God knows, I love you, honey chile," Sarah said before they fell silent and delighted in the quiet warmth of each others' embrace.

Chapter Three

LUCIUS COULD NOT GET THOUGHTS OF CHRISTI OUT OF HIS HEAD. He was torn between lust and an anger that cried out for revenge. Sarah had thrown him into the street and he had a scar on his eye from Christi's scratches. He figured he owed Christi and Sarah. It was in his mind to pay his debt to them both at the same time.

For almost nine years Lucius James had been Christi's stepfather. All those years he had looked upon Christi's uncommon beauty with ever-increasing desire and ever-diminishing control.

Lucius had never liked Sarah. It was always Christi he wanted. Lucius had never seen Christi as his stepdaughter. To Lucius, Christi was a woman of great beauty to be had somehow, someway, sometime.

Lucius could not bear the thought of any other man having her. He knew she was a full-grown woman at seventeen and he had seen how the young men watched her as she walked, dressed in the simplest dresses. He knew some man would have her sometime real soon.

Why shouldn't it be him? After all, she wasn't a blood relative. He had married her mother to escape the unemployment lines. Sarah's house was just a place to hide out until the cops got off their morality kick and he could go back to running parlay cards and numbers.

Lucius was still thin and trim at thirty-one. He was a dapper dresser and conked his hair in the style of the times.

He thought of himself as irresistible and had convinced himself that Christi's most innocent flirtations were but well-concealed acts of lust. In his twisted mind, the scars on his face from her scratches were only visible reminders of her secret passion for him.

It had been almost six months now since the incident with her. In that time, not a single night had gone by when Lucius had not plotted to have Christi first beg his forgiveness, then submit to his most carnal desires.

This stormy late summer night, Lucius had been drinking heavily and his whiskey-soaked brain told him that Christi wanted him. The lusty fire in his blood said that he should go to her and remind her of that fact. He truly believed that she avoided him only to make her mother happy and would swing her bedroom door open as soon as Sarah was out of the way.

Lucius took a quick drink of whiskey. As most of the liquid poured out of the sides of his mouth, he gurgled with self-delight. His overheated brain was alive with the prospect of a night of passion that would follow an hour of torture and humiliation.

Lucius meant to hurt Christi, then have her beg for his favors. In his twisted mind he truly believed that Christi was lying in the darkness making herself hot for him.

Lucius visualized her bright, young eyes dancing with joy as he exposed what, to his mind, was a magnificent manhood. He could almost hear her girlish giggles turn to passionate sighs as he slapped her until she parted her legs. His swollen tongue panted as he saw himself climbing in between her thighs while she begged for him to enter her.

He gargled more and more whiskey until he drowned out the last small whisper of reason.

All his life he had teetered on the borders of sanity. Now he was a crazed, frothing, mindless beast all teeth and appetite. A self-made monster who would devour as he pleased this night and who would have his way with her—willingly or unwillingly.

The blood-lust in his dark soul hoped she would resist.

The warm summer rain poured down on the leaky tin roof, steaming the already humid air. Lucius stood beneath Christi's window, oblivious to the hard rain. He strained to hear any sound from the small room where the lovely, young, polished Christi Jones lay sleeping.

As suddenly as the thunderstorm had appeared, it vanished, leaving behind a heavy humidity that made Lucius take an extra breath before taking each long pull on the whiskey bottle. He moved cautiously until he stood under Sarah's bedroom window and listened for her familiar snoring. When he was satisfied Sarah was sleeping, he moved to a back window and crawled inside the house. He had done his share of burglaries, so, as drunk as he was, he felt he could still sneak around inside undetected.

Carefully, he made his way to Christi's bedroom.

He stood in the doorway watching her breathe for half an hour while the crickets chattered and an old bullfrog croaked. Lucius watched her intently as he studied every exposed part of her body. He was no stranger

to rape. After all, that was how he had lost his virginity. His other rapes had been brutal things, over in a few minutes with the victim so terrorized they never spoke of it.

Lucius wanted this one to be much slower and he hoped Christi would talk about it. He delighted in thinking of how he would brag to Sammy Moore and his other cronies about this one.

His dilated eyes followed the bright Carolina moonbeams that sent a million silver arrows through each rip in the tattered croaka-sack window curtains. He watched with delight as they fell gently on the partially nude body of Christi Jones. Nervously, Lucius took two more long pulls on the pint of cheap booze and gulped down the fiery liquid. On tiptoes, he moved back to Sarah's small bedroom and looked at Sarah who was sprawled across the small, undersized mattress, sleeping.

Quickly, Lucius pulled down another two swallows of the bourbon and moved back toward the room where Christi slept.

While he was gone, Christi had turned over and in the process spilled the sheet off her body. Now she lay in the moonlight, with her legs partially opened and her arms back in an innocent, but to Lucius inviting, position.

Lucius looked at the young body before him and quickly swallowed the remaining five ounces of whiskey. He wiped the residue from his stiff moustache and pulled at the buckle of his belt as he crept across the clapboard floor that creaked under his slightest tiptoe. Several times he hesitated, fearful that the loud groans of the tired old wood creaking under his feet had aroused Sarah. He was equally concerned it had awakened the sleeping beauty before him. Finally, Lucius crept ahead until he now stood over the peacefully sleeping Christi. He fought off a lusty burp, as he wrested his stubborn belt from its reluctant buckle.

He took three hurried breaths before he pulled the belt out of his pants and let them fall to the floor about his feet. Awkwardly, he stepped out of his pants and wobbled to and fro.

It took several long moments before he steadied himself and sighed. Lucius could smell the traces of the alluring perfume Christi wore against her mother's wishes.

Lucius almost felt faint as he felt the wonderful sensation of the swelling in his groin. He panicked as he watched Christi sense something in her dreams and wrinkle her lovely forehead. For an instant, he started to leave. Then she sighed herself back to sleep.

Lucius was mad at himself for backing off. He curled his lip in anger and stumbled forward. He wobbled then knelt by the bedside, only inches from her left thigh. Slowly, he reached out his shaky hand and started to stroke her thigh as he watched her face to see if she would awaken.

Christi stirred slightly and Lucius withdrew his hand for an instant. Then he tired of subtleties.

With one violent motion, he drove his face in between her legs as he grabbed for her firm young breasts.

Christi rose up in the bed screaming. "What? Who is that? Lucius? Lucius! God! Sarah! Help! Sarah!"

Christi's scream almost scared Lucius away. But the alcohol-induced madness made him more determined than smart. With an angry snarl, he jumped on her with his heavy body and shoved her head back down into the pillow with his big hand.

Christi tried to bite his hand and gasp for breath at the same time. With his free hand, Lucius tried to shove apart Christi's thighs, while she fought desperately to hold them together.

Lucius gathered strength from her resistance. He felt like Superman as he delighted in the fear in her eyes.

With one forceful push of his arms, he shoved her legs apart.

Christi clawed at him with her fingernails.

Lucius enjoyed the feel of them tearing at his skin. Thin streams of blood trickled down his face as he slapped her until she stopped fighting him. He paused, smiling perversely, as he eased down between her legs and prepared to enter her.

Christi shoved him backwards as she slid out from under him.

Lucius balled his fist and started to hit her.

He never heard the shotgun blast that blew him against the wall of the old shack. He clawed at the splintered wood for support before he fell over on the floor in a pool of thick blood and chunks of his flesh. He tried to cry out but was mute as he shivered and wretched, struggling for life.

Moments after the last echo of the gun blast had faded into the oppressive darkness of the humid night, Sarah let the gun drop to the floor and reeled backwards, falling hard against the door.

Christi watched Sarah with an eerie, detached fascination.

It all seemed so unreal.

For an instant Christi thought she was dreaming some terrible nightmare that would go away like all the others. She resisted reality with all her psyche. She groped for the pillow she often used to cover her eyes and hide from evil things.

The pillow was soaked with Lucius's blood.

The still-warm thickness of the blood oozed through Christi's fingers. She held her hand out in front of her face and stared in disbelief. The moonlight made the blood glisten a bright red.

Christi leaped from the bed, screaming, and ran toward the door. She would have run blindly into the night had she not tripped over Little Eddie.

Little Eddie had been panicked by the gun blast and was rushing to his mother for safety.

Christi tripped over him and fell hard on the rough, wooden floor. A large splinter of wood pieced Christi's skin, but she felt no pain.

Christi's stepsister, Etta May, a big girl at thirteen, came down the short hallway rubbing her eyes. She stopped and looked down at Christi, her eyes opening wide as she saw the blood on Christi's hands and nightgown.

Etta May looked around and saw the shotgun lying on the floor near Sarah, who had slumped to the floor.

Finally, Etta May saw Lucius, lying in pieces on the bedroom floor. "Oh, my God! Christi's done gone crazy and killed everyone. Oh, my God!" Etta May screamed. Then she picked up Little Eddie and held him tight to her chest as she ran screaming into the night. Little Eddie's yelps of protest echoed behind Etta May's screams.

As the initial shock passed, Christi's thoughts turned to her mother. She crawled over to Sarah's side. Gently, Christi took her mother's hand and patted it.

Slowly, Sarah turned her eyes toward Christi and opened her arms.

Christi welcomed the embrace as she lay her head on her mother's ample bosom and felt Sarah's arms close around her. She shivered with fear and rage before she began to cry softly.

Sarah stroked her hair and sang her favorite gospel song rocking her as if she were a child.

It was not long before Christi's shivers eased and her sobbing went away.

Chapter Four

CHRISTI LIVED IN THE WORST SECTION OF THE POOREST PART OF South Charleston, South Carolina. This October of 1950, almost one hundred years after the Civil War and the Emancipation Proclamation, she and her people lived in squalor only a few small steps up from slavery. As a child, she often climbed a big oak tree in front of her house and stared lovingly at Charleston Harbor where the opening rounds of the Civil War were fired. She could also see the Battery with its lovely antebellum homes overlooking the harbor that seemed to stare mockingly at her.

Christi loved and hated Charleston.

It was both a beautiful and an ugly place.

Its beauty lay in its rich history. History that predated the American Revolution and could be found around any street corner. It was a quiet beauty that could be seen inside any of the hallowed churches or the majesty of the well-preserved old mansions nestled under ancient oaks, gracefully hung with Spanish moss.

Charleston, a lovely town steeped in history, was ugly in the way it treated Christi's people. The clapboard house Christi lived in was built to house slaves and was only a short carriage ride from lovely homes inhabited by descendants of the slave traders who had once owned her people. She swore to herself that one day she would own one of those houses.

She had felt the pain of hunger and she had been cold many winter nights. But there had been laughter in the summertime and lots of fun when all the relatives came to visit. There were good whites as well as the rednecks who still treated her people like slaves a hundred years after slavery had ended.

Yet, for all its faults, Charleston was home, and Christi was very much a homebody.

As she stood on the dock in the shadow of a huge old ship, Christi's head was still dizzy from the rapidity of events. The police had come to investigate Lucius's death, but since it was just "niggers killing niggers" they filed a report in a back drawer somewhere.

It wasn't the police that Christi and her mother were afraid of anyway.

It was Lucius's friends.

Lucius's friends were as mean a bunch of riffraff as ever walked the earth.

Christi understood that well enough. She didn't understand why she had to go all the way to Cuba just to get away from them. Christi had been visited by her Cuban aunts many times, but she had never thought she would ever go there. Things had moved so fast she had not had time to realize exactly what Sarah was planning. As she looked up at the hideous old tramp steamer, she could not make herself believe her mother would ever put her aboard such a ship.

Christi took comfort in the notion it had to be some kind of a ruse to fool Lucius's evil friends. She looked over at Sarah who was talking to Sammy Moore, her new "friend."

Christi thought Sammy Moore was no better than Lucius. Even though Sammy was a part-time preacher she had heard bad things about him. Sarah said they were all rumors and Sammy was a good man.

That's what Sarah had said about Lucius.

Christi felt a sudden urge to bolt and run as Sarah approached her.

"Sammy has it all arranged, Christi," Sarah said.

"What, Momma?" Christi asked.

"You will have your own cabin and free meals. All you have to do is a little housekeeping work."

All Christi could do was stare at Sarah in stunned disbelief.

"You okay, chile?"

Christi looked past Sarah towards Sammy who was standing in the shadows looking pleased with himself.

"What's really going on, Momma?"

"Now, Christi we done talked about this. You know you can't stay around here. You said you would go stay with Aunt Gladys and she's ready for you."

"Yes! But not on a ship . . . a ship like this!"

Sarah looked a little embarrassed. "I'm sorry about that but I just can't afford much else."

"Then I'll find a job and save until we can."

"Christi, you know we don't have time for that."

"You really mean this? You really mean to put me on this ship?"

Sarah nodded slowly. "I wish to God it didn't have to be done but you know it has to be."

The sting of betrayal gave Christi a feeling of bitterness toward Sarah she had never felt before. She had to suppress outright hatred as she backed away. "If you make me do this I will hate you forever!"

Sarah looked stunned by Christi's words. "What did you say, chile?"

Christi's anger abated as she saw the pain in Sarah's eyes. "I'm sorry, Momma but you can't make me do this. Please?"

Sarah was visibly shaken. "You think your Momma would do something she thought would hurt you?"

"What about Aunt June's house in Georgia?"

"Lucius's brother and his friends know all about her place. You know that, Christi."

Christi looked up at the dirty old tramp steamer then back at Sarah. "Well, I'm not going on board this ship!" Christi insisted as she dropped her old cardboard suitcase and started to back away.

Sarah looked deep into Christi's sparkling eyes. "Christi, you know how much your Momma loves you. You ain't staying one more minute around here where all this devilment is going on. Now they done got your testimony and that's all they'll be needing. You get on down to Aunt Gladys and you stay there until I get things settled down. This trouble will soon be over. Now I done got this all arranged. Sammy Moore done helped fix it up for you to earn your way. You can come home when everybody's forgotten all this mess."

Sarah was a physically imposing woman and her size along with her intense eyes usually intimidated Christi into silence. This time they did not.

"No, Momma!" Christi was defiant.

"No?" Sarah looked dumbfounded.

Christi shook her head and looked unafraid. She loved Sarah, but she knew Sarah thought of her as some fragile piece of china that was easily shattered. Sarah had worked day and night at any job she could find to send Christi to special schools where she was taught poise and bearing. Christi appreciated Sarah's efforts, but she resented being put in a special place. She had lived all her life being overprotected from whatever Sarah considered a threat.

This day she was weary of it.

"I'm not afraid of Lucius's friends, Momma."

"Oh Lord, Christi! Why are you acting like this?"

"If they try something we can go to the police."

"Good Lord, chile! You know to them it's just 'niggers killing other niggers.' Ain't no police around here going to get excited about that." Sarah grimaced.

"But I'm scared, Momma. I don't know anything about Cuba. I only met Aunt Gladys twice. I don't even remember what she looks like!" Christi shuddered.

Sarah smiled understanding. "Well, that ain't no never mind. All you need to know is Aunt Gladys will leave Havana in time to be waiting for you when this boat gets to Santiago."

"Santiago? I don't know anything about Santiago!"

"Aunt Gladys will be waiting and watching. You just hold onto her picture, this letter, and that little bit of money. And don't worry none, honey chile. You got lots of kin in Cuba who can look after you and who I can trust not to be messing around."

Christi was desperate to avoid boarding this ship. She looked at Sammy Moore and thought she had an out. "What about him? Can't he protect us?"

Sarah looked at Sammy then back at Christi. "Sammy Moore? He's mostly a man of the cloth. He won't match up good with Lucius's brother Alex. You know Alex is bringing lots of bad men when he comes down here from Detroit city and he'll be here soon."

"Well, you sure found Sammy Moore fast enough. Maybe you can find another one who can really protect us!" Christi smirked.

Sarah looked at Christi as if she was staring at a stranger. "What has gotten into you, chile?"

"Nothing! All these problems are because you keep picking these poor excuses for men. Why should I have to suffer for that?"

Sarah took her daughter firmly by the arms and shook her.

"You listen to me, Christobel Jones. Everything was sacrificed to make you a lady. Nobody got no schooling but you. You're the prettiest thing I've ever seen among all the ugly misery in this whole shanty town. I ain't gonna lose you. You can do good for all of us, but you ain't going to do no good for nobody by staying around here and getting killed. You gotta live, my darling. You gotta live to be a lady of elegance so you can make us all proud," Sarah Jones said sternly.

Christi tried to break away.

Sarah held her even more tightly. "Everything I done was so you don't talk and act like no riffraff and no white trash. I don't never want nobody calling you the names I heard all my life. I took all that for you so you might be free of it."

"You're hurting my arms, Momma!" Christi said as she tried to break Sarah's grip. "I'm not afraid of names, Momma!"

"Well, you damn well should be! Ain't nobody going to make you fold up inside when they use them names 'cause you know you ain't one, ain't never been one, ain't never gonna be one!"

Christi finally broke Sarah's grip.

"Okay! I understand," Christi said, rubbing her arms where Sarah had gripped them.

"I hope you do, chile! All I ever wanted was for you to take a piece of me and show everybody out there that black people ain't niggers. Now, that's what you going to do chile. You hear?" Sarah insisted.

"How can I do that in Cuba?" Christi challenged.

"Don't you worry none about that now. Someday when it's time, then you'll know. You just keep working hard on them books and don't you never miss no opportunity to learn something."

Christi had tried everything she could think of to stop this madness except the one thing Sarah had never been able to resist. She took a deep breath and blew it out hard. She shivered as if she were cold. She forced huge tears from her eyes.

"Oh Lord, chile! I know you're scared. I know that. But it'll be alright. There's no way I would let it be if I didn't know that for sure." Sarah took Christi into her arms and held her gently.

Christi broke free of Sarah's hug and looked up at the dark shadow of the old steamer that seemed to blot out the morning sun.

She felt an overwhelming sense of guilt as she saw Sarah was crying also.

"Momma! It's okay. I'm sorry. Maybe I could do it." Christi offered, hoping to quell Sarah's tears.

They were interrupted by a tall man clothed in the dress blues of a

Merchant Marine Captain. He had a neatly trimmed beard and an eye patch over his left eye. He held out a handkerchief to Sarah and smiled at Christi.

"May I be of assistance, ladies?" he asked.

Sarah took the handkerchief and dabbed her tears.

"I'm Captain Harry Hornecker. I do not mean to intrude but Reverend Moore told me you might have some questions about passage aboard my vessel."

Christi liked his polite manner but was wary of anything to do with this ship.

"It is understandable that, on first glance, my ship is not much to look at but I assure you she is very seaworthy and our accommodations are comfortable."

Sarah dried her eyes and tried to look dignified. "Thank you, Captain," she said as she handed his handkerchief back. "This is my daughter Miss Christobel Jones. She will be your passenger."

Christi thought it over a long moment. More tired than sure, she nodded.

"Nice to meet you, Miss Jones," Captain Hornecker said.

Christi half-smiled as a reply.

"I would be glad to answer any questions you might have. I know this is quite an adventure for someone who has never been at sea," Captain Hornecker said with an upper class British accent.

Christi sensed his accent and manner were phony but, for Sarah's sake, she relaxed a little. "Where will I be sleeping?"

"Yes! A very good question. You will have a nice cabin all to yourself. If you like, you and your mother may inspect it now." He stopped as he was interrupted by the blowing of the ship's loud horn. "My! It seems we will are preparing to cast off. I suppose you will have to take my word for it."

Sarah and Christi looked at each other and waited for the other one to speak first.

"Whatever your decision, you will have to make it in the next few minutes. We must sail with the tide," he paused. "I hope to see you on board, Miss Jones." Captain Hornecker tipped his cap then turned and walked briskly up the gangway.

"I believe this Captain will watch over you, Christi. If he doesn't he knows who he has to deal with!" Sarah insisted.

Christi sighed hard as she looked at Sarah's determined stare.

The fact that very few people dared cross her mother gave Christi some small comfort.

The ship's horn blew a loud long blast that told Christi it was time to either board or run. The only thing that stopped her from running was the wounded but still intact respect she held for Sarah.

"Do I really have to go, Momma?"

"I want you to live, my darlin'. I'll have it all set straight when you get back."

Christi heaved a long sigh.

In her sigh was respectful obedience now tinged with a sense of betrayal that bordered on hatred.

Christi and her mother hesitated then gave each other a long embrace.

Christi broke the embrace. She turned and picked up the old cardboard suitcase. Without a backward glance, she began walking up the splintered old gangway toward the ship's deck.

Halfway up the gangplank Christi paused and looked back at Etta May Jones and Little Eddie who stood in the shadows and watched Christi. Christi waved to them.

Little Eddie waved back.

Etta May half-smiled.

Christi understood Etta May's barely concealed joy. Now Etta May would have a room to herself.

Christi hesitated.

She moved back down the gangway to within earshot of Sarah. "When can I come home and be like everyone else, Momma?"

Sarah's eyes were brimming with tears as she replied. "You can't be like nobody else, my darlin' because you ain't like nobody else that ever was. Now, you go on to see your Aunt Gladys. She's chief of housekeeping in that big hotel in Havana and she'll see to it you get the best. I got her promise in writing. Now, you go on and do good!"

"But when can I come home, Momma?" Christi repeated.

The ship's loud horn blew as Sarah spoke and Christi could not hear her reply. When it was quiet once more Christi spoke. "When? When did you say I could come home?"

Sarah backed away as the horn blew once more.

"Hurry, Christi. Hurry on now!" Sarah waved as the ship's horn blew one final long blast.

Christi paused. She started to demand that Sarah give her a more definite answer. She was interrupted by Captain Hornecker who took her suitcase. "I'm sorry, Miss Jones. We must cast off now."

Christi almost took the suitcase back. Her impulse was to run away as fast as she could.

She looked back at Sarah who had turned her back and was walking away holding Little Eddie's hand.

Little Eddie was the only one waving goodbye.

Christi closed her eyes tight as they filled with tears. She quietly vowed to never open them again. She could not bear to look at the world she was leaving behind nor the shadows of the world she was yet to know.

Chapter Five

THE ROTTING GANGPLANK SWAYED BENEATH HER FEET AS CHRISTI, hesitantly, walked upward toward the ship's deck. A dozen grizzled-looking seamen leaned over the guardrail and smiled gap-toothed grins at her. She turned and looked back at Sarah hoping that Sarah would beckon her to leave the ship and come home. Instead Sarah backed deeper into the shadows until Christi could no longer see her face.

Christi had never felt so alone and betrayed in her life.

Slowly she turned and made her way onto the ship's deck. As she did, she looked up directly into the face of the ugliest man she had ever seen. He was a stranger but there was something familiar about him. He was dressed in a common sailor's uniform with a grease-stained t-shirt. He had a horrid scar beneath his right eye. His right eye was pale blue and had the dull appearance of cut marble.

His left eye was dark orange and slightly cocked. Neither of them would look directly at her.

"We meet again, Miss Jones. Welcome aboard."

Christi thought it over a moment then stepped back in shock as she realized it was Captain Hornecker without his eye patch and dress uniform. The transformation was breathtakingly hideous.

"Oh, no!" Christi started to turn and flee. She found her way blocked by two unsavory looking seamen.

"Come now, Miss Jones. Don't be wasting my time. We got to be getting underway. Time is money! Time is money," Captain Hornecker repeated. Then he took Christi's cardboard suitcase and motioned her to follow him.

Christi felt like running away, but anyway she turned she was blocked by menacing-looking seamen. "Captain Hornecker?"

"What?"

"This isn't right. It's all wrong now. I need to talk to Momma. This isn't how you said it was supposed to be."

"Not right? You mean my working clothes? Or my pretty face?"

"I just can't go now. It's a bad mistake. I need to talk to Momma!"

"Momma?" He looked over the side at the empty dock. "You can write later. We have to go below now. This is a merchant ship, young lady, not a cruise liner. Now let's move it!"

Christi bolted to jump overboard.

Two burly sailors stopped her. In trying to avoid them, she fell to the deck and hit her head hard. When she got to her feet she was dizzy.

Captain Hornecker grabbed her arm and pulled her along

She was too disoriented to resist. Reluctantly, she let Captain Hornecker lead her through a small hatch, all the while under the leering taunts of the deckhands. Once inside the door, she found herself in a narrow passageway that caused her to bend her back to keep from bumping her head.

"You are tall for a lady. Move carefully on board. I'm afraid the doorways are small."

"My head hurts. I still need to talk . . ." Christi stopped as she ducked to miss a low beam.

Captain Hornecker stopped in the dark passageway. A small shaft of sunlight glistened off his orange eye. His foul breath almost made Christi sick. He turned away and pointed to another small doorway. "You will be staying in this cabin. It is close to the galley where you will be working. We go to Port-au-Prince, then Kingston, then to Cuba. It is a hot journey but you are to dress in heavy men's clothing. You understand?" He insisted as his eyes traveled the length of her curvaceous body.

Christi had to think about it for a moment. She smiled and felt a little relieved that he was thinking of her welfare. "Yes. I understand." Christi replied as she looked for a heavy lock on the cabin door. There was one and she began to feel less afraid.

"You have just a short while before you begin to prepare our meals. The galley is down this corridor down the stairs on the lower deck." Captain Hornecker motioned toward the dark corridor.

"Captain, I don't know what Sammy Moore told you but I'm not a cook," Christi said.

Captain Hornecker looked irritated. "You signed on as a galley swab. If you do not cook then there will be dishes to wash and floors to scrub, as well as cleaning out the grease trap and whatever else is required."

"I didn't sign anything, Captain."

"Oh? We are almost under way and this woman wants to make trouble. I have all the papers in my office with your mother's signature."

Christi was having a hard time dealing with Sarah's betrayal. She felt more ill than angry. "Can I see them?"

"Later! There's no time for that now."

"No! Now! Now or I get off this ship!"

Captain Hornecker turned and looked at her hard. "That mouth! It is a bad thing for you. It should be shut as much as possible to avoid trouble. Understand?"

"Let me off this ship or I'll charge you with kidnaping at the first place we stop." Christi turned and started for the main deck but stumbled as the ship moved beneath her feet.

Captain Hornecker caught her in his arms and held on longer than necessary.

Christi pulled away.

He smelled awful and his mouth-foam wet the shoulders of her dress. Christi started to run away again, but the ship was rolling slightly, and she could hear feet scurrying around on the decks above her.

She knew it was too late.

"Toot! Toot! We are underway, madam. If you wish to leave it will be a nice swim. Can you swim?"

Christi shook her head, sadly.

"I see. Then what do you suggest I do?"

"You have a contract and it was signed by Sarah Jones?"

Captain Hornecker shrugged.

"I just want to read it. Okay?"

"Of course you do. Now move along!"

"I'm well-read, you know. I've even done some basic reading on maritime law."

"Just shut the fuck up, woman!" Captain Hornecker snapped.

Christi was not intimidated. She glared at him. "I just want you to know I know my rights. I want them respected."

Captain Hornecker shrugged. "What you want is of no concern to me or anyone on this ship. You will soon learn that. Educated nigger or not!"

"What did you say?" Christi bristled.

"You heard me. Now stow your stuff and get ready to work!"

Christi started to bare her claws. She felt the ship picking up speed and thought better of it. Instead, she decided it was time to use a little charm. Christi was very charming when she knew she was cornered— and she was very much cornered right now.

"I just want you and your men to help me. I'm not a veteran sailor like you. This is all new to me. I'm very frightened, like I imagine your daughter would be frightened. This is like another world to me. I'll really need your help and kindness to do well." Christi tried to be endearing without being sexy.

Captain Hornecker licked his lips. He was as crude as spit-soaked bilge and he delighted in it. He looked at her for a long moment, with a stare from a face so ugly that it would have turned Medusa to stone. He put an old cigar in his mouth. He chewed on it for a minute before he replied. "Galley swabs don't have many rights around here. They don't go telling anyone how to do anything! Now, if you think you're somethin' special . . . well, there's two or three lonely seamen who will like to know that right now."

He paused and grinned.

"I never said I was special. I just want fair treatment."

"Where the hell do you think you are? Jesus!" he snarled as he put a mop handle in her hand. "Get used to the feel, swab! You have four hours to rest. Sleep well and dream of accepting your fate. Now I must attend my ship!"

Christi despised this grubby little shadow of a man, but she knew she was in foreign territory and she could not survive without his favor, or at least his indifference. "I'm sorry, Captain. I didn't mean you. I just know there are certain elements that might try to take advantage of a young lady in my position," Christi used the formal tone that Mrs. White had taught her and which Sarah had loved to hear her speak.

"You speak mighty nice for a nigger."

"I won't be called that! You hear!"

"You don't get it, do you? You make no demands. Period!"

Christi started to reply until her eyes fell on the Nazi tattoo on his right arm.

Captain Hornecker followed her eyes and felt his arm where his SS tattoo had been proudly etched so many years ago. "If you are so well-read you understand what this symbol stands for. Most of the men on this ship are former comrades in arms. They do not suffer foolishness well. Be in the galley in four hours and steel yourself to say little and move in the shadows."

Christi let the mop fall to the floor and glared at him. "I still want to see that contract."

Captain Hornecker looked at her with a hint of admiration. "In time. For now your roommate has the early call so he is sleeping. I would not disturb him if I were you. You have the hammock on the far wall. Each morning you will be awakened at 3 A.M. by the boson's whistle. You will be on time. Oversleeping is a dollar fine a minute."

Christi frowned with displeasure for a moment before she regained her composure. "He? I have a he roommate?" Christi whispered nervously.

Captain Hornecker took great delight in her discomfort. "We have only so many cabins for the swabs. What can I do? You are last on board. The assignments are made," he grinned.

"I don't believe maritime rules permit such berthing," Christi challenged.

"Maritime rules? There are rules?"

"That's what I said. Now look, I want to get along, but I'm not bunking with any man," Christi insisted.

Captain Hornecker chewed hard on the already over-chewed cigar for a minute before replying. "I believe maritime rules have emergency clauses for captains at sea," he mimicked Christi.

"Maybe they do, if you're at sea you are empowered to make judicious decisions, but we are not at sea and there is no emergency," Christi declared.

The Captain smiled as he put a hand to his ear and cocked it toward the open door at the end of the passageway.

"Ah, but I hear the screws turning and the foghorn calling. I believe we are already some miles at sea."

"You've met my mother, Captain?"

Captain Hornecker frowned. He thought it over and seemed to get the point. "Yes."

"She and ten more like her will come after you if I'm harmed!" Christi insisted, more scared than threatening.

"Oh? I believe the Reverend Moore can handle Miss Sarah Jones."

"Not if I'm harmed."

Captain Hornecker smirked. "You're here, aren't you?"

His words were a cold slap in the face and he enjoyed her look of pain. This was all Sammy Moore's doing but Sarah had gone along with it. At that moment Christi felt the hot bile of resentment and betrayal for her mother well up in her throat. She felt cold all over for she knew that now she was all alone.

Christi would not let Hornecker have the pleasure of seeing her fear. She put on a brave face as she peered through the shadows into the small gray cabin she was to share with some sailor. "Could I please talk to this sailor first. Maybe he doesn't want a roommate." She hoped.

"Cosmo C. Collins? Not want a roommate? I think not. I understand he has been without a woman for many months now. So I would sleep with one eye open." Captain Hornecker pointed to his dead eye and beamed with perverse delight. "Be at the galley at three-fifteen. Forget about your mother. You may not ever see her again. Be pleasant and do as you are told quickly and with little comment. Do as I tell you and perhaps you will survive to see Cuba," Captain Hornecker snapped as he turned and walked away.

"I don't care what you or that Sammy Moore say. My mother will hold you responsible for anything that happens to me! She will! You better believe it!" Christi yelled after him, trying to convince herself.

The only reply was a hundred mocking echoes and then an oppressive darkness.

Chapter Six

THE SINGLE NAKED LIGHT BULB IN THE PASSAGEWAY CAST A WAVER-ing, ghostly, pale amber light over the small cabin. The light was too weak to illuminate the shadows.

Instead it made them more ominous.

Slowly, Christi moved through the eerie darkness toward the torn and patched hammock that was to be her bunk for the journey. She took a deep breath and blew it out as she pondered her situation. It was hard to hate her mother but easy to feel bitterness. Christi blamed Sammy Moore and her mother's weakness for smooth-talking men. Christi never doubted Sarah's love except when her judgement was clouded by con men like Sammy Moore.

Christi could not understand why Sarah couldn't see through them as easily as she did. Christi vowed that no man would ever make such a fool of her. There was no doubt in her mind that Sammy Moore had sold her out and she was on a ship that would take her to some harem in some faraway land after she had been raped by every sailor on board.

Christi could sense the presence of someone in the room, but she was too frightened to look around to see who it might be. She knew that close by there was a man. She could not see him but her senses said he was there somewhere in the darkness—and he was not sleeping.

She could feel his eyes watching her.

The ship was now at full speed and rolling slightly as Christi moved to lift herself into her small hammock. She was so nervous she kept slipping and almost falling to the floor each time she tried to mount the hammock gracefully. She was tempted to leap into it with a single tomboy bound. The thought of missing and falling flat on the back before those prying eyes stopped her.

She thought of turning to confront whoever was watching her but could not summon the courage to look in the direction of his scent—a scent she had grown to loathe.

It was the smell all men had when not masking it with oceans of cologne. A heady, alluring yet repulsive musky mix of stale cigarettes, un-washed underarms, and last night's whiskey. It filled the cabin and made her want to puke.

Slowly, she kicked off her shoes and tried to lift herself into the elusive hammock, keeping her tight-fitting cotton dress about her as modestly as she could and tried not to show fear.

The hammock rolled away from her and she cursed it under her breath. Once more, she pulled it to her body and tried to mount it, and once again it moved and she fell to the floor. Finally, she decided there was no way to get into the hammock in a ladylike manner. She was more mad than afraid as she took a very unladylike leap. She was proud of herself as it put her safely on her back in the hammock that now swung freely back and forth.

She had only a moment to be pleased with herself as she saw that her dress was hiked above her thighs and her silk panties were spotlighted by a small beam of light.

Quickly, she pulled her dress down and lay stiff in the hammock, slowly dying of embarrassment.

"There is something about a lady in a pretty frock," a deep male voice said.

Christi did not dare look his way.

"Hammocks are a bitch! That's why I took the bed," the voice offered sympathetically from the darkest corner of the room. "I fell out of one once in Singapore. Damn near broke my back."

The Irish accent somehow relieved the heavy atmosphere of the small room.

Christi sighed in relief that the voice sounded friendly and rational. There was something about the lilting tones of an Irish accent that tended to put her at ease.

The room fell quiet as the ship turned to the port side, swinging Christi to and fro.

The rocking motion made her already queasy stomach even more upset. She wanted to stick her head out of the porthole and throw up. Yet for some strange reason she did not want to embarrass herself in front of this stranger. His voice was so soothing and welcome she wanted to ask for his help. She dismissed the thought as a panic-stricken attempt to find a friend. "Discipline! Discipline! Discipline!" She repeated the words Mrs. White had said to her each morning of class for four years. "You are class, Christi. You were born to be a lady of substance, of bearing, of elegance. A lady doesn't talk to strangers."

Christi turned those words over quietly in her mind. They were of small comfort now.

"Appeal to their sense of honor, Christi. When all else fails make men feel guilty by appealing to their sense of honor." Mrs. White's voice suddenly made sense. It didn't work on Captain Hornecker, but maybe this was a more honorable man.

"Sir, I'm a very frightened young girl in a dark place, far from home. Please forgive me if I'm not as friendly as I should be. You understand that under normal circumstances I am as civil as anyone. I'm sorry if I have intruded upon your space. It was not my doing that I am here," Christi offered solemnly.

There was no response as the ship now turned starboard and picked up speed.

Christi waited for a reply with nervous anticipation.

"My God, what a mouthful. A beautiful young woman with an Oxford English accent and a face that has no business aboard this ship. Are you sure you didn't miss the Charleston Library on your way here?" The voice was now a little cynical.

Christi was feverish and shivering at the same time. "Breathe deep! Breathe very deep!" Mrs. White had advised for tension. Christi was too scared to breathe deep. "Beautiful? How can you see me in this darkness? I can just barely see you."

He was quiet for a long moment before he spoke. "That yellow cotton dress has a glow all of its own. I advise getting rid of it right away."

"No! I could never do that!"

"Well, you suit yourself. But if you like, there are seaman's clothes piled in the corner over by you."

"You won't catch me wearing any men's clothes!"

The room fell quiet once more as Christi lay still until she finally found the courage to look his way. When she did, all she saw was a huge shadow moving toward her.

"Oh God! Here it comes!" Christi thought as she closed her eyes and gritted her teeth. "Please just make it quick and don't hit me!" Christi pleaded.

"What?" he asked.

"If you have to do it just don't hurt me!"

"Good Lord! What has Hornecker sent me this time?"

"I'm Christi Jones and my mother is Sarah Jones. She killed a man that once tried to hurt me!"

His reply was a cynical chuckle then quiet. Finally the silence was broken by a masculine sigh of frustration. Moments later the man moved out of the shadows and stood before her.

He was breathtaking.

Christi had done her share of flirting and stealing admiring glances at handsome men. But she had the power to take them or leave them. No one she had ever seen had the raw masculine beauty that stood before her now. He was gorgeous with dark wavy hair that parted in the middle and piercing blue eyes that were almost hypnotic. His muscles pushed against his white t-shirt in all the right places. His tight seaman's jeans bulged with raw power yet his countenance was almost angelic. As she looked at him she found she could not look away. For the first time in her life she was not in control of her emotions and did not care to be.

"Now, Christi, if you don't mind, can you tell me what the hell you're doing here?"

"I'm . . . I'm working my way to Cuba."

"Cuba? On this ship?"

"It was not my idea."

"I see." He paused and shook his head in dismay. His dark wavy locks bounced to and fro like silken ribbons on a summer breeze. His piercing eyes looked at her with interest and concern.

Christi sat up and offered her hand. "As I said, I'm Christi. What's your name?"

He thought it over a long moment. "I'm Cosmo C. Collins." He stopped as he got a closer look at her. "My God! You're all of fourteen!"

"I am seventeen going on eighteen!"

"Of course. And this is the Queen Mary, Captain Hornecker is a real captain, and I'm the March Hare!"

Christi thought it over a moment. "I see. Hi, Mr. March Hare. I'm Alice. Do you know the way out of this wonderland?"

For a brief moment, Cosmo looked impressed. "Whoever the idiot was that put you here did you a disservice. This is no wonderland."

"The 'idiot' was my mother. No! I take that back. It was her friend

Sammy Moore."

"Sammy Moore? Jesus! Your mother has friends like that?"

"Look! My mother is a good woman. Okay?"

"If you say so. Would you be mad if I asked you to bunk somewhere else?"

For a long moment Christi was speechless. She was used to men falling over themselves to be near her.

She couldn't believe Cosmo wanted her to leave. "Leave? Just like that?"

"Yes!"

"Well, I don't want to be anywhere I'm not wanted, mister! I'll be glad to bunk somewhere else!" Christi started to leave.

He grabbed her arm and held her back. "Not tonight. It's too late tonight."

"Get your hands off of me!" Christi shook loose from his grip.

"I'm sorry, miss, but there really is nowhere else to go tonight. We'll work it out tomorrow. Okay?"

Christi moved away from him without replying. She stood in the shadows and fumed with anger. "You make sure you stay on your side of the room, mister. I'm not as fragile as I look."

Cosmo chuckled.

"You think I'm funny? Well, you just try something, you'll see how funny I am. Lucius James didn't respect me and you know where he is? He's dead, that's what!" Christi stopped as Cosmo stood towering above her.

"Lucius James and Sammy Moore? This is the company you keep? Maybe I was in too much of a hurry to kick you out. You might be fun after all." Cosmo's tone was playful but there was a hint of the devil in his eyes.

"They are the low-life men my mother finds attractive for some stupid reason. You just stay away from me!"

Cosmo fought off a condescending smirk. "I take it your mother was the lady that shot him?"

"Yes, she was, and she will shoot you if you bother me!" Christi insisted.

"I see. Then I will step back and show you the respect you deserve. You didn't by any chance get the hundred he owes me?"

"No, I didn't. And if you knew him and Sammy Moore, maybe I don't want to know you."

"Touché! Good point. Piss-poor character references."

"Your friends?"

Cosmo looked insulted by Christi's inference. He turned away from her before he replied.

"I played the parlay cards like a lot of people. Not that it matters, but I knew his brother Alex in Detroit better. I wish your mother had shot Alex. Now there is a man who deserves killing."

"Not as much as Lucius did!" Christi grimaced.

Cosmo looked sympathetic for only a brief moment then he smiled and laughed.

"It's not funny, mister."

"You're right. There is absolutely nothing funny about your situation." Cosmo looked serious. "You understand that I couldn't care less except if I'm in the way when the bulls stampede, then I might get trampled."

"I'll take care of myself just fine, thank you!"

"If you're the lady that got Lucius killed, maybe you're right. Maybe you can take care of yourself."

"You better believe it!" Christi bluffed.

Cosmo smiled then looked deadly serious. "Lucius on his worst day was not as bad as the men on this boat."

That was much too frightening a thought for Christi to let herself believe. "Oh? So why are you here if it's so bad?"

"I signed on for personal reasons."

"You're most probably running from the law."

"You're not as intelligent as I think you are, Christi, if you believe being a smart-ass here is a cool thing to do."

"You just mind your business and I'll mind mine."

"Fine! Just don't come running to me for help when they come knocking on the door." Cosmo grumbled under his breath. He lit a match and used it to light a small lamp on the wall by his bed. As he adjusted the lamp for maximum light Christi shot a very unladylike look at him. He was a very tall and muscular young man. He had broad shoulders and when he turned his back toward her, she could not help but admire his cute ass.

He was the most handsome man she had ever known. At a time when everything seemed to be going wrong, Cosmo seemed to be a godsend. Christi hoped he was as pretty on the inside as he was on the outside.

She looked across the room at Cosmo's bed. "I have ten dollars cash. I'll give it to you for your bed," Christi offered, nervously.

Cosmo did not reply for a long time. "You mean you want to give me a ten spot for a swap of beds?" he chuckled.

"Yes, please. This hammock rolls too much."

"Now, Miss Jones . . ."

"Christi. Please, Cosmo."

Cosmo smiled as he thought it over.

"Now, Christi, that's a right fair offer but I'm in my twilights about now and don't feel much like moving. Ask me tomorrow night and maybe we can work it out." Cosmo laughed.

Christi liked the way he laughed. His laughter had a way of easing her fears. So much bad had happened to her, she had a silly hope he might be a good friend. "Goodnight, sir."

"Cosmo."

". . . Cosmo."

"That's better. Goodnight, Christi. You'd better get to sleep. It will be three o'clock in the morning very soon and they will come calling, *'Cosmo, venga! Rápidamente!' Habla español?* Do you speak Spanish?"

"*Sí, un poco.* But I'm much better at French. I'm sorry. I didn't mean to sound haughty."

Cosmo moved closer and looked more sad than lustful. His presence made Christi want to unfold and reach out to him. It made her want to back into a corner and hide. She was a mess of contradictory feelings that, as he approached ever closer, dissolved into one secret desire.

Suddenly, she had an overwhelming wish to reach out for his strength. She wanted to grab Cosmo around his muscular neck and hold onto him for dear life. She wanted him to nestle her in his arms and keep her safe from the world outside. Instead she made small talk.

"Do I have the privacy of a bath?" Christi asked.

"There's one down the hall. You lock the door when it's your turn. I get up at two-thirty on days when I want to shower. I shower maybe twice in the four weeks it takes to get to Havana."

"Four weeks! I was told three?"

"Three? Four? It took almost two months one time. This ship is not very reliable. Not in any way."

"Well, I won't spend four weeks aboard this garbage scow," Christi swore as she fought her way out of the tricky hammock. She almost fell to the floor but righted herself quickly and walked away from him. As she did, the lamplight outlined the silhouette of her curvaceous figure against the thin cotton of the dress.

Cosmo thought himself a man of the world who had seen it all and was calloused by it, but the outline of Christi's perfect body beneath that yellow cotton dress made him gasp for air.

"Are you okay, Mr. Collins?" Christi turned and looked a little worried until she caught him staring. "Oh, no! You're just like all the others! Aren't you?"

Cosmo tried to shrug it off. He ended up looking like a schoolboy with his hand caught in the cookie jar. "For your sake, I hope the trip is only three weeks this time." Cosmo sighed hard.

Christi was crushed. He was her last hope for a safe journey. She had desperately wanted to trust him. "Is it safe for me to go to sleep now?" she replied curtly.

Cosmo looked sheepish then bold. "Ah, you fear I'm after your bones. Is that it?"

"You're a man, aren't you?"

"As to that, I have not been caught dropping the soap in the shower as yet. But perhaps before I'm off this ship, who knows? I was a long time in the African bush and the water buffalo began to take on the appearance of women I had known and loved. . ."

". . . some months later they began to take on the appearance of women I had known only in dreams. In the end they were just warm and friendly, if you get my meaning."

"Mr. Collins, I don't care to hear about your disgusting habits, whatever they are."

Cosmo stood directly under the small cabin lamp and began to take off his shirt slowly. Then he turned away from Christi in an almost boyish display of modesty.

Christi thought it was cute he was so modest. She felt much more comfortable in that knowledge.

Once his shirt was off, Cosmo turned toward her and paused to let his muscular chest and arms catch the flattering light. The pale amber light lit every ripple in his many muscles as if they had been massaged with baby oil. Cosmo smiled mischievously as Christi's eyes gawked then turned away.

She hated herself for having stared but knew she would keep the erotic image of his rugged masculinity forever in her memory.

"This is your first time really going anywhere isn't it?" Cosmo asked.

"Well, I've been around . . . some."

"Where is that, miss?"

"Jacksonville and Atlanta, and places like that."

"Oh?"

"I know that's not England or Ireland, but at least I didn't look at buffalo and think they were people."

Cosmo laughed. "Good point, miss." He smiled a moment before his face turned deadly serious.

He moved to a corner of the cabin and picked up some clothes. He threw them on Christi's hammock. They landed by her feet and she could smell the burnt diesel oil that saturated them. "Miss, you wear these clothes. Do not wear that yellow cotton dress again. Don't put on any makeup. Don't so much as smile at a crewman. I don't know how you came to be aboard this garbage scow, but it's all wrong. Understand?"

"Ugh! I'll never wear those!" Christi said as she threw the smelly clothes off her hammock.

"Then God help you. Just keep me out of it!"

"I'll try not to be a burden to you, Mr. Collins," Christi mocked him.

Cosmo shook his head in dismay.

A small sliver of moonlight fought its way through the greasy porthole and illuminated Cosmo's face. Christi watched him out of the corner of her eye. The soft moonlight made his pleasant features even more attractive. His face was strong with a chiseled masculinity that told, instantly, of his strength. Yet there was an unspoken gentleness that shone through his eyes and put her at ease.

"I thank you for treating me with respect, Mr. Collins."

"That's all well and good, but you remember, young lady, a hundred miles at sea Hornecker is God and his motley crew is about as undisciplined a bunch of misfits as I've ever seen. You stay alive by staying the hell out of their way." Cosmo grimaced and paused. "I was raised to be a gentleman but I'm not a fool, Christi. I'm no knight in shining armor. I'm more likely to be the first man to the lifeboats. Understand?"

Christi did not want to acknowledge his words with a reply. She would cling to his image as her knight until he proved otherwise.

She started to get up to go to the bathroom. As she got to her feet the seas began to get rougher and the floor seemed to begin to fall and rise sharply. Christi put her hands over her eyes but it did not stop the onrushing feeling of sickness.

"Oh God, Mr. Collins! Please! I'm so sick!" Christi choked falling to her knees.

Quickly, Cosmo moved beside her. He looked down at Christi and looked frustrated before a look of understanding crossed his face. "Haven't seen anyone as green as you since I heaved my guts out on my first trip." Cosmo placed his arms underneath her and lifted her gently.

Cosmo's arms were strong and his warmth felt good as he carried her out the cabin door and up the stairway to the deck.

The wind was refreshing and Christi took long deep breaths as Cosmo sat her down beside the aft rail. The old ship took a beating in the smallest swells, and listed sharply as twenty-foot waves hit the ship broadside.

"Oh, Mr. Collins. I just want to go home!" Christi coughed, fighting back the urge to heave.

Cosmo stepped back out of the line of fire. He looked at her with some sympathy. "Well, lassie, if I could I would take you there, but I'm afraid, for you and me, home is not a possibility at the moment. Keep taking deep breaths." Cosmo urged.

"Mr. Collins?"

"Cosmo."

"Cosmo, please help me get to Cuba safely. Please!" Christi pleaded.

Cosmo backed away. "I told you, miss! Don't put any responsibility on me. That's why I'm on this damn ship! I don't want that responsibility ever again."

Christi grabbed the rail and took many deep breaths of the refreshing air. "Okay, I'll handle it alone, Mr. Collins. I do have to tell you that you have failed the Christi Jones test of courage. Thanks for your help tonight but you were right. You're no hero!" Christi coughed as she wobbled against the rail.

Cosmo turned and looked out at the turbulent sea.

"I love storms. They have a majesty about them. Men die quickly in storms. Women kill you slowly. Many times you don't see it coming. Yes! I'm no hero, Miss Jones. There are none aboard this vessel," he said sadly.

Christi gripped the rail tightly.

She stared out to sea with him. The cool wind drove a distant bank of storm clouds toward them.

"Leave it to Hornecker to ship out with a storm in the forecast. If this turns into a hurricane, we won't have to worry about anything," Cosmo said quietly.

Christi gave him a worried look.

"Do you feel a little better?"

"Yes," Christi nodded.

"Then we'd better get you some rest. It's hell pulling a shift in the cooker if you're tired." Cosmo offered his hand.

Christi hesitated then took it. She enjoyed its warmth and strength. "Thank you, Cosmo," she said sincerely.

Cosmo shrugged as he led her back to the cabin. Once inside he released her hand. He started toward his bed and paused, took one look at the hammock and leaped into it.

"What the hell, so you owe me a ten spot!" he said.

"Cosmo, you don't have to . . ."

"Christi, just get to sleep. Please!" he insisted.

Christi nodded and lay down in his bed.

"Cosmo! Thank you. I really mean it. Thank you," she said softly. "I'm really glad you're here. I really don't expect anything. I really just want you to help whenever you can. Nothing real heavy. I wouldn't want you to get really involved or hurt because of me but I do consider you a friend, you know, if you want to be . . . I don't mean you have to be . . . but if you would be then . . . well then I . . ." Christi stopped prattling as her ears picked up the sound of Cosmo snoring.

She sighed a worried smile as she lay back on the small, hard pillow and tried to sleep.

Chapter Seven

CHRISTI COULD NOT SLEEP. AS THE SHIP ROLLED BEFORE EACH SMALL wave and rattled with each small wind gust, she lay awake and tried to keep her mind off the reality of her predicament. She wondered how Cosmo could sleep so soundly.

She reminded herself it wasn't he who had the problem.

The hours passed painfully slow, and she toyed with the idea of waking Cosmo to keep her company. She was mad at herself for such a stupid idea. At last, her eyes began to tire. She started to close them when a large fat man carrying a lantern and wearing a cook's apron and hat entered the cabin.

"I am Diego. I am chief cook. You come to work for me. This Cosmo, he is no good as the alarm clock. It is already past six. *Ándale!* Very fast! You get ready and come to the galley. *Es mucho* very hard work," he paused to grin. "But I am easy. For *las señoritas bonitas* I am always easy!" Diego smiled.

Christi eyed Diego with suspicion as she eased out of bed. She resented the way his eyes watched her.

"Maybe you think you are too pretty for this work?"

Diego looked critical.

Although Christi understood Spanish, she pretended not to understand Diego.

"Please show me where the shower is. May I have a shower before I go to work?"

Diego looked very unhappy with her question for a moment. "A shower the first day at sea? I do not think the showers they are ready for many more days. Maybe not at all."

"But I really need to wash up. Please?"

"Maybe this is possible but the water if it is on it is *muy frío* . . . very cold!"

"That's okay. I'm very much in need of soap and water, no matter how cold the water. Please, Mr. Diego?"

Diego looked uncomfortable at the word "soap." He frowned, then looked puzzled. He gave her a sarcastic grin. "You are the *señorita* . . .

the woman. I do not want the woman aboard but you are here and already we must make the special favors." He looked worried. "To take this shower very fast! I will have to go get a gun and watch outside. There is no time for this."

"You will watch?"

"I am a grandfather with a bad heart. I do not need these troubles. I think we go work now!"

Cosmo stirred. He rubbed his eyes and sat up in the hammock. The early morning sun was weak, but strong enough for Christi to see Cosmo's golden tan glisten in the soft light. He was even more handsome than Christi remembered. He looked at Diego with his sparkling yet hard blue eyes.

"Dammit, Diego! You're a half hour early. Now that's not sporting," Cosmo insisted.

Diego turned and glared at Cosmo before he replied.

"No. As always, you are some hours late, Señor Collins. You do not like it, you go jump overboard." Diego laughed a loud, hearty laugh that turned into a cynical one Cosmo ignored.

Christi looked at Cosmo and their eyes locked for a brief, uncomfortable moment.

"Will you put her on the kettles with me, cookie?" Cosmo asked through a series of yawns.

Diego looked displeased as he replied, "*La señorita* wants to take the shower and it is only the first day out. You are not on the kettles. The Captain, he wants you on deck. You have the new job." Diego paused. "Me too. I am now the shower guard. *Ándale, señorita!* The shower must be quick!" Diego's voice was deadly serious.

Christi looked at Cosmo for guidance.

Cosmo was angry. "What the hell do you mean I'm on deck! I'm no goddamn sailor! What's Hornecker up to?"

Cosmo paused as Diego was joined by a tall thin man, who smiled at Christi with a toothless grin.

"Pinkus, what's going on? Is this true?" Cosmo addressed the tall man.

Pinkus looked intimidated by Cosmo but more intimidated by Diego. Pinkus stepped back, his eyes downcast, grumbling under his breath.

"You think I am the liar, Señor Collins?" Diego paused and looked sinister. "You are the deck hand now, Señor Collins. You will not work with the pretty lady. Only Pinkus and me," Diego grinned.

Pinkus looked up to eye Christi with vacuous, hungry eyes before he looked down again.

Christi moved behind Cosmo. "You can't do that! That's not right. Cosmo is supposed to work with me. I demand . . ."

"You demand, *señorita?*" Diego smirked.

"Yes! I've already been pushed around too much on this ship. I'm not working at all if I don't work with Mr. Collins!" Christi insisted.

Cosmo grabbed her elbow and turned her around to face him. Christi looked up at the strength in his eyes. She had never believed in love at first sight before now. She was thrilled that Cosmo was going to be her hero and show these men his love for her.

Cosmo bent close to her and spoke quietly but firmly.

"This is not some prep school field trip. You don't insist on anything. Understand? Your best course is just to keep quiet and go do your job! Forget the friggin' shower!" Cosmo tightened his firm grip on her arm.

She did not feel anything but hurt that he was not on her side. Christi wanted to reply but Cosmo's manner and tone made that impossible. Slowly, she nodded agreement.

Cosmo released her and turned back toward Diego and Pinkus. "So, what do I do on deck?"

"I do not know. I am not *el capitan.* But you? Are you not the protector of *la señorita,* Cosmo?" Diego laughed.

Pinkus grinned sardonically.

"Not me, Diego! I'm like you. I believe women are unlucky on ships. Topside is fine with me. The air is much better than in the galley," Cosmo said sincerely.

Christi could not believe what had happened.

She had broken Sarah and Mrs. White's rules and fallen for the first real man she had ever met. They had warned her such emotional infatuations always ended in betrayal. Cosmo was betraying her moments after she had opened her heart to him. She could not understand how he could do that. Christi was so confused she did not hear the rest of the exchange between Cosmo and Diego. Cosmo, Diego, and Pinkus were like surrealistic characters talking to each other on a distant dock in some heavy ocean fog.

"Christi! Christi!" Cosmo finally broke into her consciousness. "Wake up and get with it, woman!"

"Yes? What? 'Woman'? Don't call me 'woman'!" Christi snapped back.

"Jesus! Whatever! Just get your butt to that kitchen before Hornecker checks on us!" Cosmo glared.

Christi did not like this dark side of Cosmo. She decided that he was not a hero after all and not to be loved or relied on. If she had been a man she would have punched him. "Okay! I'm going. But I will have my shower."

Cosmo moved between her and Diego. He looked at her with a steady gaze mixed with anger and concern. "You must go with them, now! Work hard. Say nothing. Forget about the damn shower! Just go along and try to look ugly and think ugly. Understand?"

Christi turned away from him in a smoldering pout.

"Aieee! Cosmo he has gone crazy to tell this pretty woman to look ugly!" Diego huffed.

Pinkus nodded as a small trickle of lustful spit oozed out of the corner of his mouth.

Christi looked at Pinkus's hideous face and backed into the shadows. Suddenly she felt cornered and the urge to break away was overwhelming. She looked around, then broke into a run.

Cosmo watched her disappear into the darkness and grimaced.

"Go and bring her to us! Now!" Diego ordered Pinkus.

Pinkus started to go but Cosmo stood in his way.

Pinkus looked at the towering Cosmo and backed off.

"You must go on deck, Señor Collins. We will take care of this problem." Diego stepped up.

"Look, Diego, this young woman is scared to death. You have a daughter. You understand, right? Give me five minutes and maybe I can make her less afraid. The ship is not approaching an iceberg. We won't go down in the next five minutes. Now you and Pinkus just back off and I'll have her in the kitchen in a few minutes. Okay?"

Diego hesitated and looked cynical.

"Maybe you want to tell Hornecker and the crew breakfast will be delayed?" Cosmo added.

The blood drained from Diego's face.

"*Cinco minutos!* You have this crazy woman in my galley in five minutes!" Diego motioned Pinkus away.

Cosmo gave them one last intimidating look and turned to find Christi. He did not have to go far because the doors leading to the ship's aft were locked. The contraband they carried was not meant for prying eyes.

Christi had made it only a few yards to the first door where she huddled in the darkness and looked defiant—though her shaking belied that pose.

Cosmo stood in the shadows and looked at her with censure that only hinted of concern.

"Do you want to get us both killed?" Cosmo snarled as he grabbed her firmly by the shoulders and shook her.

"You don't think they're going to do it anyway?" she snapped back.

"I don't know, but I sure as hell am not going to make it easy for them!" Cosmo paused as he felt her shivering beneath his touch. "Jesus! You're a frightened little puppy, aren't you?"

"No, I'm not!" Christi replied with the hoarseness of doubt.

Cosmo shook his head in dismay as he wondered what to do. For an instant, he let his eyes show deep concern. In that instant, Christi put her arms around his waist and drove her face hard into his masculine chest. The smell of his musky maleness and the firmness of his muscular chest gave her instant relief from her fears.

Moments later, when he let his strong arms fall around her shoulders, she allowed herself to sob uncontrollably.

Cosmo held her, not in a lover's embrace but more as one holds a friend in need of comfort. He did not offer sympathetic strokes or pats but a powerful aura of much needed security.

As they stood quietly in the darkness she sobbed until she felt more embarrassed for crying than the need for his strength.

Quickly, she pulled away and hung her head in shame.

"I'm sorry. I'm so stupid sometimes," Christi said as she regained her composure.

"No need to apologize. I cried at Paddy's funeral."

"A friend of yours?"

"No. As smart a sheep dog as there ever was."

"A dog?"

"Hey! Paddy was more than a mere dog! He was the best friend I ever had."

Christi chuckled.

"Now that's much more like it. But a bit too good." Cosmo paused and looked around.

"Too good?"

Cosmo did not reply until he found some grease on a nearby pipe. He wiped it off with his fingers and smudged Christi's face before she could stop him.

"What are you doing?" Christi backed off and tried to wipe the grease off her face.

Cosmo held her hands and shook his head. "That's ugly. That's good!"

Christi thought it over.

"Oh! 'Think ugly.' I see." She paused and wiped some more grease from the pipe and smudged her face. "Thanks, Cosmo. I understand."

Cosmo sighed with relief before he regained his composure.

"No showers until we reach Jamaica. Lots of grease and dirt and the worse you smell the better."

"I'm sorry I was so dense," Christi stopped and looked embarrassed. "I'm sorry I hugged you so tight."

"My pleasure." He stopped and looked deadly serious.

"But one we will not share again. You understand this?"

Christi started to object before she reluctantly agreed.

"Good. Only one more thing."

"Yes?"

"Never let them see fear," Cosmo insisted.

Christi took a deep breath and blew it out hard. "Never again, Mr. Collins. Never again!"

"Yes. Well, I'm afraid they are waiting."

"Will you be okay?"

Cosmo shrugged. "I expect we will not be seeing much of each other, so go along carefully, lassie. I'll try to be somewhere behind you."

"Somewhere behind me? You will be there tonight?"

Cosmo thought that over as he looked at Christi's radiant face. Even through the grease and dirt it had a shine that made him behold it. "I expect not."

"My God! Then where? Who?"

"Don't lose it now. Buck up! Whatever happens don't show weakness. Act the role of a nasty fish wife. No smiles. No winks. Only pissing and moaning and much ado about nothing!"

"And lots of grease?"

"Yes. Also you must wear the most baggy seaman's clothes."

Christi grimaced then nodded.

They fell silent for a long moment before Cosmo looked at her with some embarrassment.

"You won't be helping me again?"

"I'm afraid there are no knights in shining armor on this ship. Me least of all. I'm sorry, Christi."

The thought of not seeing Cosmo again was almost as scary as thoughts about what might be waiting for her. "I think I stopped believing in knights in shining armor the same day I stopped believing in Santa Claus," Christi sighed.

"What? There is no Santa Claus? Damn!"

They laughed sardonically together.

"Thanks for your help, Cosmo. There's really a nice guy beneath all that pretense."

"Now I know I've really muffed it. So I'm just a little pussy cat? My, the boys in the dragoons would love to hear that!"

They fell quiet once again and their eyes met in a long look of admiration and respect.

"*Rápidamente!*" Diego interrupted them with a growl.

Christi looked deep into Cosmo's eyes. He looked back at her with concern then feigned indifference.

"Go ahead, Diego. I'll have her along in two minutes." Cosmo flexed his muscles at the squat Diego.

"No! *Uno minuto!* You have her there, Cosmo. You are nobody special here!" Diego snarled as he pushed Pinkus along before him.

Christi and Cosmo looked away from each other. They remained quiet for a moment after Diego had gone.

"I suppose I'd better go," Christi started to move away.

"Yeah! I suppose."

Cosmo moved over beside her like a high school boy on his first date.

It was funny, but he seemed to be embarrassed around her. "Christi, you are most probably going to get me killed."

"No, Cosmo. I wouldn't want that."

Christi almost reached out to touch him.

"Then after today don't ever speak to me again. Is that a promise?" Cosmo said as he backed away.

"What?"

"Don't look my way. Don't act as if we've ever spoken."

"No! You're my only friend!"

"Wrong! I'm just another member of a very nasty crew."

"But we're roommates. Can't we just talk as friends? Please? Please! I really want you as a friend," Christi pleaded.

Cosmo disappeared without replying.

Christi stood and stared into the darkness. She did not move a muscle until Diego came along some moments later. She did not respond to his screaming orders so he pulled her along through the damp, dark corridors past the rusty shower toward the ship's galley.

Chapter Eight

IN THE LONG DAYS THAT FOLLOWED, CHRISTI WENT ABOUT HER MENIAL duties with one eye on Diego and Pinkus and one eye on her work. Covered in grease and dressed like a tramp, she did every chore quickly and with the least amount of talk necessary.

Diego treated her well the first ten days. During that time, he was overprotective and called her his "pretty little daughter." Nevertheless, whenever he was near, Christi got a creepy feeling that ended just short of nausea. She wore so much grease and let her appearance deteriorate to the point she no longer thought of herself as pretty.

In that knowledge she felt less vulnerable.

Her hopes had been buoyed by the fact that Cosmo remained her cabin mate even though he said little and discouraged any but the briefest of conversations. But Christi's hunger for his friendship and protection made her swallow her pride and keep trying to gain his good-will.

As the long hot nights passed, Christi talked herself to sleep wondering if he ever listened.

Cosmo was a secretive man, but she believed he had a warm side he tried his best to keep hidden. It was funny that although he said little, he became less and less modest as they began to make adjustments in order to live comfortably in their small compartment.

Christi was no voyeur but she could not resist taking many long peeks at his beautiful male form as he began to dress and undress less in the shadows and more in the light.

Diego had told her that Cosmo had traveled the world and had countless death-defying adventures. Yet for all his bravado there was a wonderful aspect of boyishness in him that delighted Christi. During this time, she came to love Cosmo without knowing him. She felt a love for him deeper than the love she felt for Sarah or anyone she had ever known. She would never dare tell him that. At least not before he took her away from this awful place and pledged his love to her. She dreamed of telling him how much she loved him some romantic, moonlit night as he knelt before her and placed a diamond on her finger. Of course she would make him wait for an answer and maybe beg a little before she said "yes."

As she looked in the mirror at her grease-smeared face and her matted hair, she despaired that it would ever happen.

On the morning of the eleventh day at sea, Christi worked at her duties in the galley with a light heart. She even dared to hum a favorite tune. Her initial fears were somewhat allayed by the nice treatment so far accorded her by the crew. Cosmo's grease paint had worked. She had noticed at the breakfast meal that Diego was unusually short with her and in turns, unusually attentive. She thought little of it as she served breakfast and lunch. It was shortly after she finished serving lunch that things began to happen that rekindled her old fears.

Christi was tired from the heat of the galley, so she took a small break and sat down on an old orange crate. She had spent all her life in the South. She clearly remembered how hot the cracked cement sidewalks and gooey-tar streets felt beneath her bare feet.

She could easily recall how it seemed to get hotter some nights after the sun went down and Charleston Harbor let off the heat it had gathered during the day. It was a heat that floated inland driven by a weak, even hotter breeze that almost had the stifling intensity of steam.

Yet Christi had never felt a heat like the one in the small ship's galley.

The galley was deep in the ship's noisy old bowels and there was only one small fan for ventilation. The fan worked, like Diego, whenever it felt like it and at its own pace.

Christi did not mind hard work. Sarah had tried to shield her from hard work, but Christi always did things when Sarah wasn't looking to make sure she was pulling her own weight. It was important to Christi not to feel special. It had been hard to avoid this feeling living with Sarah. Sarah always singled her out as something special and Christi always had to work that much harder to feel normal, to feel accepted by others her age. In a way, it was a relief to get away from Sarah's "plan." Christi was never comfortable with Sarah's plan to make her a lady of elegance. She was almost always embarrassed by Sarah's announced hopes.

Christi hoped her mother would forget the "plan" by the time Christi returned home. If she ever did.

These thoughts passed through Christi's tired mind as she sat on the crate and tried to relax. Thinking she was alone, she unbuttoned her shirt to cool herself. The small fan blew the loose-fitting shirt open exposing her cleavage. She was so intent on enjoying the small breeze she did not notice Diego standing above her.

"Ah, *señorita*. You still keep the *mucha bonita* in this ugly, sweaty place. We have to use the hot, steamy water so the sail boys don't get the germs." Diego sighed hard.

Christi smelled him before she saw him.

Diego loomed above Christi, so close she could feel his hot breath. Huge beads of sweat rolled off his brow. He swiped at them with a handkerchief soaked with sweat. He paused and laughed. "But they go ashore and get the germs anyway." Diego winked, coughed, then his eyes fell on her exposed cleavage. Instantly they narrowed their focus and his tongue found his lips.

Quickly, Christi pulled the shirt together and fumbled to button it. She got up and walked over to the sink. She found a semi-clean cloth, soaked it in cold water, and dabbed at her face. She tried to get her breath. She felt faint.

Diego stood back and stared at her.

Christi did not like the look in his beady eyes. She tried to force the last button into the buttonhole but broke it off instead. As the button fell to the floor the shirt opened wide and her unrestrained breasts spilled out. Quickly, she pulled the shirt together and held it with both fists.

It was too late. Diego's eyes were mean with lust. His breath began to come in short gasps. He moved even closer. His grubby hands reached out for her.

Christi picked up a large iron skillet and moved into a corner. She held the skillet at arm's length.

"*Señorita?* Why do we have all these games? Now you do not have to work the pots and pans. Maybe if you are nice to me I can let you plan the menus. For this you can take all day because I have already planned them! I have sent Pinkus away so we are alone all day." Diego's eyes were as cold as his hands were sweaty.

Christi raised the skillet above her head.

"*Señorita?* You do not want to cause the trouble. I am a friend. We should be *amigos*. I help you. You help me. Okay?"

"Diego, I just want to do my job and be left alone. Please leave me alone. If you come any closer I'll hit you with this. I mean it!" Christi's voice revealed her fear.

Diego covered his head with his hands and shied away in mock fear. "*Por favor*. Do not hit me! I am a poor defenseless man. Oh, please?" Diego cackled.

"Leave me alone, Diego!" Christi shivered.

Diego's eyes grew smaller. His breath came in long determined draws. He picked up a meat cleaver and ran the blade the length of one of his calloused thumbs. It cut into his thumb and drew blood.

"You want to hit me, yes? You hit me and I will cut you a little but not so much that I cannot take you many times!"

Diego chortled.

Christi's knees felt weak and her stomach hurt. She wanted to run. She wanted to scream. She wanted to see someone tear Diego's heart out of his sweat-soaked t-shirt.

"For God's sake! Please stay away, Diego," Christi pleaded.

"*Quién, Dios?* For God's sake. For God's sake I will take you before another man does. I will be gentle. I will be good. I will kiss you a little and not cut you if you say the yes and do not struggle too much. *Por favor,* struggle a little." Diego chortled as he reached out and grabbed the front of Christi's shirt. With one sweeping pull he ripped it to her navel, exposing her breasts.

The beauty of her firm, naked breasts hypnotized Diego for a moment. In that moment, Christi hit him hard upside his head with the iron skillet.

Diego reeled to the side for a moment, but did not go down.

"Aieee! I know I must have you now!" he mumbled as he swung the meat cleaver at her arm holding the skillet.

The meat cleaver hit her arm a glancing blow and forced her to drop the skillet.

Diego reached down and picked it up. He held the meat cleaver in one hand and the skillet in the other. "Now! No more this waiting! You take off the pants and lay down for me. Now!"

"Go to hell!"

"Hell? Oh, no! First you look inside my pants and see the surprise I have made for you! Do this now or I cut you until you are wishing for death to come. *Rápidamente!* Do it, or I make love to you now and I do it seven times after I kill you!"

Diego snarled as shoved his face so close she felt his foul spit with every word.

Christi jammed herself hard into the corner. She shook with fear and anger but more with defiance.

Diego took a vicious swing with the meat cleaver. It cracked into the wall only inches from Christi's head. "Now, *señorita!* I will have you dead or alive!" Diego shoved his sweaty, rotund body against hers.

Diego's closeness was so oppressive she wanted to vomit. Taking short breaths of the stale, lifeless air, she gathered her strength and pulled the meat cleaver out of the wall. She could only take a short stroke, but she brought it down on the side of Diego's neck. She saw the blade go in, but there was no blood.

She knew she would soon be dead.

Diego reached up and pulled the cleaver from his neck. For a moment he tried to laugh. His mouth was open, his larynx moved, his tongue flickered, yet he only gurgled.

The blood came first in a trickle, then a small spurt, then a flood. It poured so fast from Diego's neck it soaked Christi before she could move away. Diego fell to the floor without uttering a sound.

Christi recoiled in horror. She stood in the heavy steam of the small galley and took long breaths of what now seemed refreshing air.

Slowly, she walked over to the old gas stove. A large open can of jalapeño peppers sat by the boiling caldron of weak soup.

Christi dumped the whole can into the soup and turned up the burner beneath it. Then she spit into the pot before she turned and made her way back to her cabin.

Christi was shivering as she entered her cabin. She did not expect to find Cosmo sitting there reading the *London Times.*

Her torn shirt was open for a moment and Cosmo's eyes fell upon her blood-soaked breasts. His instinctive modesty was impressive.

Christi was too traumatized to find that endearing.

"My God, Christi, what the hell happened?" Cosmo threw the paper away and ran to her side.

She fell into his arms and he slowly closed them around her as she cried softly.

"I killed Diego. He tried to . . . to. . . .."

"It's okay. Hush now, it's okay," Cosmo soothed.

They held each other quietly for a long moment.

Christi wanted to stay in his arms forever. She felt cold when he finally broke the embrace.

Cosmo picked up a blanket and placed it gently about her shoulders. He stood back and looked at her. His generous Irish eyes told Christi he was both sympathetic and very scared.

"They will kill me, won't they, Cosmo?" Christi said evenly.

He nodded his head slowly. "Only the good Lord knows what they will do. Is he . . . is Diego in the galley?"

"Yes, he tried to attack . . . .."

"It's okay, Christi. Jesus! What am I saying?"

"It's my fault, you aren't involved."

"Bullshit! I knew it! I damn well knew it! Jesus! Women on ships! It always ends the same way!"

"I told you this doesn't involve you!"

"Oh, no? Well, that's not exactly the way it is, is it?"

"What are you talking about? I was almost raped and killed. I killed Diego. You weren't even there!"

Cosmo took her by the shoulders and looked deep into her eyes. "Haven't you wondered why I am still your roommate?"

Christi thought it over and shrugged.

"Hornecker knew this would happen. He knew there was bad blood between me and Diego. Now he can collect his bounty! Jesus!"

"I don't understand?"

"Well, that's just dandy! You don't understand. You don't understand that it doesn't matter who killed Diego. I will be blamed. You, princess, have some value in Cuba. Unfortunately, I do not."

"Hornecker can't do that! I won't let him."

"That's nice. I know I'm saved now."

"Damn you! Damn you! Damn you, Cosmo Collins! How dare you think of yourself when I've been through hell!"

Cosmo was caught off guard. He studied the intensity in her eyes and had to smile in admiration. "I suppose this will teach me I can't run away."

"What are you running away from, Cosmo?"

"Trouble. This kind of trouble." Cosmo sounded irritated.

"You don't have to help. I did it. I'll . . ."

"You'll what?" Cosmo interrupted.

"I'll take care of it!"

"Oh, Christi! You belong in the routine world of church on Sunday, work on Monday, a car breakdown on Tuesday, with a houseful of kids that have small fevers and throw baseballs through windows. You should have the small sins a person confesses red-faced every other week. Now you tell me, how are you going to explain a murder to a motley crew like Hornecker's?"

Christi pulled the blanket close about her. She shivered and tried to think. Her mind was a busy mixture of doubt, fear, and anxiety. She had no answer for Cosmo. She only knew she wanted him close and she did not know how to tell him that. She looked at him with all the softness she could bring to her tear-filled eyes.

Cosmo looked down at her. She hoped the sparkle in his eye was meant as forgiveness.

"We don't have any choices. Come on, we have to go clean up the galley and go see Hornecker before the crew descends on the galley for their meal. They might forgive you for killing Diego, but they'll never understand not being fed on time," Cosmo said seriously.

"I can't go back in there. I can't, Cosmo," she pleaded.

Cosmo took her firmly by the shoulders. "It's time to grow up, Christi. As of a few moments ago, your adolescence ended. I can't clean it up by myself. Now come on, we haven't much time."

Cosmo released his grip and moved quickly to the door.

He looked up and down the hallway and motioned for Christi to follow as he moved toward the galley.

Cosmo entered the galley first. He sighed audibly. He turned and motioned for Christi to wait outside the door. As she waited she could hear him grunting and groaning.

After many anxious moments, he came and motioned her inside.

"I've hidden him in the freezer for the time being. Now, while I begin the cleanup, you begin dinner," Cosmo said with a surreal calmness.

Christi nodded as she reluctantly entered the kitchen. She almost gagged when she saw the blood on the walls.

"Now, Christi! Now! If these baboons aren't fed, we'll really be in trouble," he insisted.

Christi nodded as she moved toward the ship's stove. She took several deep breaths and acted like she knew how to prepare a meal while Cosmo cleaned all around her.

Christi doubted she had the strength to stir the pot. Everything had happened so fast. Too much had happened too soon. She did not want Cosmo to see her like this, but she could not help the dizzy feeling that kept coming over her.

As the ship moved slightly beneath her feet, she fell against the galley stove. She broke her fall by placing her hands on the stove's hottest part. She winced in pain and bit her lip. Tears welled in the corner of her eyes, but she would not let herself cry out from the pain. Her knees were about to give way when Cosmo's strong arms eased around her waist and lifted her up.

"God, have I been an ass! Forgive me, Christi. I was selfish. I didn't stop to think about how much all this must be affecting you," Cosmo said sincerely as he wiped her head with a cool, clean, damp cloth. The coolness of the cloth felt good against her forehead. His arm around her felt much better.

Christi could resist no longer.

She grabbed his face and pulled it to hers, kissing him fiercely on the lips. The kiss was hurried and clumsy, but it was the best kiss Christi had ever enjoyed. As quickly as she had started the kiss, Christi ended it. She drew back, blushing with embarrassment.

Cosmo smiled. "Damn greasiest kiss I ever had!" he chuckled as he wiped grease smudges from his cheek.

They both laughed for a long, pleasant moment.

"I'm sorry . . . I'm just grateful."

"That's all, just grateful?"

Christi heaved a sigh.

Cosmo smirked, knowingly. "Well, I'm sorry I don't have time for any more grateful kisses. I will bank on maybe a few later. Then, maybe I might want to see just how grateful you are," he said mischievously.

Christi turned away from him. As the first real pleasant thoughts she had enjoyed in a long time danced in her head, she began to stir the pot with a new vigor. "I'm not that grateful," she laughed.

Cosmo gave her a playful pat on her ass.

Christi dropped the spoon and turned to protest.

"Wasn't me, miss. Maybe there's pirate ghosts about this place," he said ominously.

Christi took a deep breath and blew it out hard. For a few precious moments she forgot her troubles and delighted in Cosmo's company. She loved this man with all her heart and she hoped she would have the opportunity and courage to tell him that very soon.

She was lost in those thoughts when they were both interrupted by a pungent smell, quickly followed by a mean-looking Captain Hornecker and the vulture-like Pinkus.

"Goddamn it, Cosmo! What the hell is going on here? Pinkus said he saw . . . where is Diego?" Captain Hornecker demanded.

Cosmo slowly dabbed away the last small blood stain. He took a moment to rinse out the cloth. "Christi and I need to speak with you in private," Cosmo said to Hornecker as he stared at Pinkus.

"You done killed him. I seen the body and the blood. Now you done fed him to the sharks." Pinkus shuffled nervously.

"Shut up, Pinkus!" Hornecker snapped.

Cosmo shrugged as he motioned for them to look around the room.

Captain Hornecker angrily motioned for Pinkus to leave.

Pinkus objected for a moment before Hornecker's glare sent him running.

"It smells of death in here, Cosmo," Hornecker said moments after Pinkus was gone.

"That's because he died hard. I had to kill him. It was him or me. You know what a temper he had," Cosmo said.

"Cut the crap, Cosmo. It was the girl. *Cherchez la femme.* Yes, you might have killed him but I think maybe she killed him more." Hornecker was pleased with himself.

"He tried to rape me. He tried to kill me and rape me! Yes! I killed him and I'm glad!" Christi insisted.

Cosmo stepped between the Captain and Christi. "You keep cooking, Christi. You know how mean the crew gets when they aren't fed." Cosmo looked into Hornecker's lifeless, orange eye.

"Ain't no woman cooking our meals. The men are too superstitious, you know that, Cosmo," Hornecker insisted.

"He tried to rape her, Hornecker. Now you know you don't need to make this official. You should never have put her in the galley with that animal."

"Diego? He was an old man who never took shore leave. He wouldn't know what to do with a woman. I think maybe she's just a common murderer who should be locked in my brig!" Hornecker flinched slightly with his one good eye.

"Look, Hornecker, you signed her on under your protection. Sammy Moore's men will be expecting her in Cuba, right?"

Hornecker studied them both. "Mr. Collins, I am many things. Some say bad, some say good, but I do not want to lose a license. I do not condone rape. If it was rape," he paused to eye Christi with contempt. "Perhaps it is a moot point until we reach Kingston. Where do you have him?"

"He's wrapped very neatly in the large freezer."

"Ah! Then I must tell you I have two problems. Two very big problems. I know my problems do not concern you, but they are very important to me." Hornecker paused dramatically.

Cosmo looked at him with disdain. He drew close until they were eyes to an eye. "Hornecker, drop the phony pretense. I know you're one incident away from losing that license. Now, it's obvious you put her in with me to get me implicated. Whether I like it or not, I'm implicated. You could care less about Diego so don't give me that crap. Now, let's make a deal!" Cosmo insisted.

Hornecker chewed his cud until brown saliva formed at the corners of his mouth. "Miss Jones, does Mr. Collins speak for you?" Hornecker asked cynically.

"I killed a rapist in self-defense. Nobody has done anything wrong except Diego!"

"You say this but who knows?"

"Get off of it, Hornecker. What do you want out of this?"

"Me? I want what you want, a safe trip to Cuba. Not a knife in my back from Diego's friends."

"He has no friends except Pinkus and Pinkus won't make a move without your say-so!"

Hornecker thought it over and shrugged. "You say this but who knows?"

"How much?" Cosmo reeked with cynicism.

"We will settle the amount at another time. For now the problem is to get the men fed. How do we do this, Mr. Collins?"

Cosmo looked pensive then shrugged.

Christi thought it over, shuddering as she remembered Diego.

Captain Hornecker grumped to himself for a moment before he spoke. "Diego, he has this prison record but the company makes me hire him because he works cheap. I would like to be on the *Queen Mary*, but we are on the *Calamaria Princess*. It is not a great ship, but it is my ship. It is all I have. You kill a cook who keeps the men happy. I cannot give them much but good food. Now you ask me to forgive that you have killed my cook. You are crazy. Kill my helmsman, but don't kill my cook! Even I cannot keep them happy unless their bellies are full. Go ahead, Mr. Collins. Tell this young lady that after three bells men's bellies must be filled. Can she cook?" Hornecker glared at Christi.

"I hope so, because I sure as hell can't," Cosmo said as he turned and looked at Christi.

"You? Can you cook, young lady?" Hornecker smirked.

Christi thought it over. Sarah had never allowed her near a stove and she despised the heat of the kitchen. She started to say "no" but the deadly look on Hornecker's face made her tell a lie. "Yes, but mostly *haute cuisine*."

"*Haute* what?"

"She's talking gourmet stuff. But you do the basic stuff also. Right, Christi?" Cosmo gritted his teeth.

"Sure. Of course." Christi bluffed.

"You say this but is it true? Ah, we will all know soon enough. You cook spicy or not at all. Understand?"

"Hell! These guys would eat cardboard with enough hot salsa on it," Cosmo joked.

Hornecker was not amused. "So when they ask for Diego what do we tell them, Mr. Collins?" Hornecker asked coldly.

Cosmo thought it over as he studied Christi's grease-stained face with its mysterious kind of beauty. "Tell them dinner is ready."

Hornecker looked skeptical. "Yes. Perhaps. I leave it to you to keep their stomachs so happy they do not think of Diego. That is my deal.

Feed them well or God help us all," Hornecker said with an ominous sounding authority.

"I will try, Captain," Christi said sincerely.

"No, you will do it and you will do it well! Understand?" Hornecker glared.

Cosmo stepped in between him and Christi. "I suppose she had better get started."

"Remember, Miss Jones. This crew wants a lot and they want it spicy. You do that, miss, and maybe we make it to Kingston without a mutiny." Hornecker wiped his sweaty brow.

Christi nodded understanding as she stirred the soup in the huge pot. "Diego let me make this," she said as she offered Captain Hornecker a ladle.

Captain Hornecker walked over and stared down at the pot. He took the ladle and tasted the soup. He almost spit them out before he swallowed.

Christi stepped back nervously.

"Not bad," Captain Hornecker picked up a big shaker of chili powder and one of paprika. He shook them out on the beans until the shakers were empty. "A lot and hot!" Hornecker insisted.

"Yes, sir," Christi agreed.

Hornecker mumbled under his breath as he quickly left them alone in the kitchen.

Cosmo stared at her for a long moment before he cracked a smile. "You've never cooked in your life have you?"

Christi shook her head.

"Jesus! Have you ever seen forty hungry men howling at you while poking empty plates in your face?"

"It can't be that hard." Christi said as she took the ladle and started to stir the beans.

"Christi! God help us," Cosmo said as he took the ladle from her and motioned her away. "Just go to the cabinet and get some more hot sauce."

"You? You can cook, Cosmo?"

Cosmo looked offended for a moment. "Maybe enough to save our asses. Now get the hot stuff, okay?"

Christi broke into a relieved smile. She gave him a grease-stained kiss on the cheek and ran to the cabinet.

Cosmo watched her go with thinly masked delight in his eyes.

Chapter Nine

CHRISTI WATCHED EACH CREWMAN INTENTLY AS SHE LADLED OUT Cosmo's hastily prepared meal. Hornecker had been right. While they ate they were relatively docile. They were, on the whole, a most motley looking bunch and their disdain for bathing was evident by the heavy smell of burnt oil that preceded them when they entered the galley. There were three dozen of them, including Pinkus and Hornecker. He and Pinkus ate first and Christi watched nervously as Hornecker, with stern glares, made sure Pinkus kept his mouth shut. Christi did not know how good the food was. She only knew Cosmo had made enough of it to fill them up completely. As the men ate, they grumbled some but seemed to be generally content. Also, they were too busy washing down the hot food with huge glasses of water to say much.

Cosmo entered some time after the crew was seated. He had always made a habit of eating last because he hated standing in lines. He and Christi wanted his habits to remain as they had been before the Diego incident in order to draw as little attention as possible.

The crew murmured loudly and looked in their direction as Christi served Cosmo. She did not like the jealous looks in their eyes so she forced herself not to look at Cosmo's face. As a result, she ladled hot beans all over his hands.

Cosmo was holding a metal tray which he almost dropped.

The men jeered as Cosmo lay the tray aside, picked up a wet cloth and cleaned himself. He turned and looked at them coldly. Some seemed intimidated. Others flipped him off as Cosmo put down the messy tray and picked up a clean one.

Christi served him carefully and quietly. When the tray was full Cosmo moved over and sat at a table close to Hornecker, but removed from the other men.

Christi busied herself cleaning up the kitchen, stealing occasional glances at Cosmo and the crew. There was obvious hostility between them and Cosmo. Cosmo was such a mysterious man in so many ways. Christi wondered what all he had kept from her and why he, a polished man of substance, was here on board this tramp steamer, as much a misfit as herself.

The crewmen finished and left in small groups without thanking her. Captain Hornecker, Pinkus, and Cosmo sat alone and ate slowly.

Christi could not tell from Hornecker's expression what he thought about the meal. They made eye contact for a brief moment and Hornecker shrugged. Christi took that as a compliment as Hornecker shoved Pinkus along in front of him and left without comment.

For a long time after Hornecker had gone, Christi worked hard at cleaning up the dishes and the kitchen while Cosmo sat and ate in silence. By the time she was through cleaning up, the hard work and steam from the cooking and washing had her in total disarray. Her hair felt limp and the old seaman's outfit she was wearing was caked with grease and food stains.

She looked around once more to make sure everything was clean and in place, and then her eyes fell on Cosmo.

Cosmo had just finished eating. He looked across the small distance between them and half smiled. Finally, Cosmo flipped his fork onto the tray. It bounced off with a twanging sound and hit against the iron wall with a ping. Cosmo shrugged, got up from the table and approached her. He looked at her critically before he slowly smiled with affection. "You had one helluva day, but I give you credit. You came through."

"Thanks, Cosmo. I think they liked the food."

"That was absolutely the worst food I have ever eaten, but by God it was hot and there was plenty of it. To these grunts it was *haute cuisine,*" Cosmo said as he leaned over the short kitchen counter and looked into Christi's tired eyes.

"You did good, Cosmo. I would give you a big hug, but I don't think I'm looking very huggable right now," Christi sighed.

Cosmo sniffed playfully at the air. He moved away in feigned horror. "God forbid I would ever tell a lady she is ripe . . . but if ever I did. Phew!"

"I knew it! The hell with this ugly stuff!" Christi wiped at the grease on her face with the grease on her apron.

Cosmo had to laugh.

"It's not funny, Cosmo! I need a long hot shower and plenty of sweet-smelling soap!"

Cosmo had to agree.

"Will you escort me to the shower and guard me, please?" Christi pleaded.

"I don't know, miss. I'm not much for guarding ladies' showers, but I'm an expert at rubbing their backsides," he said mischievously.

"Cosmo, just give me fifteen minutes beneath some hot water with a bar of soap and we'll discuss terms," Christi said, then reached out and tickled his ribs.

"Tickle a little lower and I'll follow you anywhere," Cosmo teased.

"Cosmo, please. I need that shower," Christi repeated as she picked up a bar of the brown kitchen soap.

"You intend to use that stuff?"

"Yes. It's all there is."

"That stuff will peel enamel off teeth. It's not fit for a lady's soft skin. Let's go to the cabin and I'll see what I can find," Cosmo said as he motioned her to follow him.

Christi happily followed him to their cabin. Once they reached the cabin, she hurriedly opened her old cardboard suitcase. She shuffled her hands around inside until they fell on the smooth cloth of her yellow cotton dress. Quickly she removed it from the suitcase and put it on a bent wire hanger she took from the cabin's small closet.

Meanwhile, Cosmo was feeling under his mattress. He finally smiled with success as he removed a small piece of tinfoil. Slowly, he unwrapped it and held it out for Christi to smell.

"It smells like . . . like rose blossoms," Christi said.

"Wild Irish Rose Soap. Hand made by a virgin spinster who uses only newborn roses not over three days old." Cosmo smiled.

Christi looked doubtful.

"Okay, so I got it at a five and dime in Miami."

Joyfully, Christi sniffed it as they made their way to the shower. Once at the shower door, Cosmo stopped and pulled at the heavy iron door. It creaked open. The shower was lit only by the dim light coming through a small porthole and a small light bulb high in the ceiling that flickered in rhythm with the ship's movements.

"This is one really primitive device." Cosmo shook his head in disgust. "Do you really want to do this?"

"Yes! Yes, I do! Hold this please," Christi said as she handed Cosmo the hanger holding the yellow cotton dress. "I'll be finished in a short while." She smiled inscrutably as she stepped into the dim light of the small shower room.

"You intend to wear this? I don't think that is very smart." Cosmo protested just before she closed the shower door.

Christi had a hard time seeing in the dim light from the small bulb that lit the primitive shower. She fought hard with the rusted control knobs until, at last, a small trickle of cool water fell on her face. She let the water run while she slipped out of the tattered, filthy old seaman's clothes. Finally, a heavier stream of hot water hit her in the face. It was so refreshing she almost lost her breath. With slow, deliberate motions she soaped her young body. The soap was a cleansing agent that made her feel as if nothing wrong had ever happened in the world.

Then she got soap in her eye and became disoriented. Without realizing it, she backed into the door and pushed it open. She fumbled for a towel and got lost in the steam. When her eyes cleared and the steam dissipated she saw a tall figure, outlined by the dim hallway light. At first, she was frightened, then, as the figure moved closer she relaxed.

It was Cosmo standing before her holding the yellow cotton dress on the hanger and trying not to stare. For a long moment, they looked at each other before Cosmo's embarrassment caused him to turn away and her modesty caused her to find the door handle. For some reason, she did not shut the door right away. Cosmo's timidity still fascinated her and disarmed her natural fear of exposing herself to men's leering eyes.

Cosmo's eyes never showed lust and that was almost insulting.

"It's okay, Cosmo. I'll be finished soon." Christi tugged at the door but could not get it to close.

Cosmo heard the creaking and thought the door was closed. He turned back around to see her still naked before him. Naked with delightful rivulets of soapy water cascading their way over her lovely skin. Rivulets that formed irresistible waterfalls of suds as they parted at her generous cleavage, spilled over her rigid nipples, and fell past the inviting cove between her thighs.

"Woman! Do not tempt me more than I can bear!" Cosmo tried to shove the door shut with one hand. It did not move. He placed the hanger holding the yellow cotton dress on a hook and started to close the door with both hands.

Christi held her arms out and stopped it. "You could use a shower also," she said coolly.

"God, Christi. You are but a girl!"

"I am almost eighteen," she paused. "And I need a back rub."

Cosmo pushed hard at the door before he stopped and heaved a sigh of frustration. "Goddammit! What are you doing?"

Christi looked at him with love beyond measure. "I want the first man to know me to be someone I love."

"You don't know what you're talking about."

"You don't have to love me, Cosmo. It's okay."

"God, woman! You are amazing." Cosmo said as he turned and disappeared into the darkness.

Christi hung her head in sadness but there was no regret in her heart. No man would ever have her by force but it was a wonderful feeling to want to yield to a man she loved.

With a light heart, she tried to close the door once more.

A strong hand grabbed it and stopped her. Moments later, Cosmo stepped out of the darkness naked. Christi stepped back a little then smiled a welcome.

Without saying a word, Cosmo reached for the soap, took it and stepped under the shower.

Christi watched the muscles on his arms ripple as he enjoyed the shower. He had the cutest ass she had ever seen and she wanted to reach out and squeeze it. Instead she moved close and eased her arms around his waist. She let her head rest against the firmness of his back and enjoyed the feel of his strength and warmth.

For the longest time he seemed to pretend she wasn't there.

Finally, he turned and eased his arms around her waist. "I'm not saying I love you, Christi."

"I'm not asking that."

"God, you're a girl so beyond your years."

"It's okay to call me a woman now."

"I see. I've thought that since I saw you with Diego's blood all over your face."

"Oh, Cosmo! Just let me stay here with you and hold me for awhile."

Cosmo stroked the soap from her hair and kissed it as he pulled her close.

Christi let the cool water run over them both. She relaxed as his touch made her forget, for a moment, all the discipline Sarah and Mrs. White had drilled into her.

Cosmo kissed her softly on her cool sweet-smelling hair.

"So tell me, young lady. Who the hell are you and what are you doing in my shower?" Cosmo kidded.

"Whose shower?"

Cosmo chuckled as he took her face in his hands and turned it toward him. "You are hard to place. Your hair is long and silky like that of Polynesian maidens. Your eyes are large and round like the Irish. Your skin is fair like the girls of Wales. Your eyes are the smoldering sienna of a Castilian princess. Now, are you Orange or Green or the Black Irish?" Cosmo joked.

Christi pulled away for a moment. "Does it matter?

"No! Just curious."

Christi did not like his probing question. It reminded her of things she wanted to forget. Particularly, at this moment.

Cosmo eased her concern by pulling her close once more. This time there was a firmness in his hold and it was now more scary than reassuring.

Christi was now a little frightened.

He saw the fear in her eyes and eased away. "What about that back rub?" he asked as he let her go and turned around.

Christi watched the water droplets sequin his huge muscles then form a small river that ran the length of his back. She smiled as she watched the water fall over the twin cheeks of his cute ass. She could not resist the urge to squeeze it. She placed one hand on each cheek and with a tender yet firm grip gave them a squeeze. His cheeks were so firm her squeeze barely made a dimple.

"Oh, my! A Swedish masseuse I see?" Cosmo chuckled.

Christi sighed hard.

Cosmo's skin was warm and she felt the urge to stroke his body with the small bar of soap she held in her hand. He seemed to tremble with pleasure as she quietly began to massage his body, first with soap then with open hands. Her hands moved skillfully and she wondered how she, a virgin who had never had a boyfriend, instinctively knew just where to touch to make him tremble with delight.

Christi knew at that moment there were more things human beings knew than they were taught. Some of her fingernails were broken, but Christi sensed that Cosmo would like to be stroked on his back by them.

She poised her fingernails to claw and dug them deep into his muscular flesh stopping only a micrometer shy of drawing blood.

"Ouch!"

"You want me to stop?"

"No! It was a good ouch."

Christi smiled as she stroked his back with her sharp fingernails between pauses to kiss the place she had scratched.

He clearly enjoyed the hint of pain and the relief of pleasure that her actions brought him. She delighted in the ability to control his feelings. She did not realize that she was digging her fingernails deeper and holding her kisses longer until she tasted blood on her tongue. She looked up to see she had made a deep scratch by his shoulder blade and he had not even cried out.

"Oh! I'm so sorry!"

"What?"

"Nothing." Christi kissed the scratch until it stopped bleeding. Then she softened her caresses. "Are you okay, my darling?" Christi whispered.

His reply was a stiffening of his muscles.

"I'm sorry. I didn't mean to call you that."

His muscles relaxed a little as he made a Tai Chi stretch.

"Now I know how Humphrey Bogart felt," Cosmo laughed.

"Oh?"

"Of all the ships in all the seas you had to stumble aboard this one," Cosmo sighed.

"It was gin mills but what the heck!" Christi laughed.

Cosmo turned and took her into his strong arms. They were both soapy and the soap made the touching electric.

Christi turned her face toward him poised for a kiss.

Cosmo let her go.

"What? What is it?" Christi wondered.

Cosmo did not reply for a long moment.

"You're trembling. I'm sorry, Christi."

"No! No, it's not what you think!" Christi reached out and grabbed his hand. She pulled him back and took his face in her hands. She pulled her face up to his and kissed him softly on the lips. He started to turn away, but paused. He put his strong hands underneath her arms and drew her close. He kissed her hot and hard.

Christi lost herself in that kiss. Cosmo broke the kiss, but she felt it long after he had pulled away.

"What? What now?" Christi almost growled.

"You sure about this?"

Christi studied his electric eyes and the underlying tenderness of his strong face. Christi wanted his hand touching her, yet she didn't want it. She was confused in her mind, but her heart took his hand and let it touch her where Sarah had told her to never let anyone touch her. It made her tingle all over. Christi could see Sarah's face and hear her scolding, even as she tingled with pleasure she had never known.

Sarah had made Christi swear on a Bible and before God in heaven that no one would touch her there until after a proper wedding in a church. She believed in keeping that promise until Cosmo had touched her.

Cosmo blew his warm breath against her ear and his hot lips brushed her neck gently.

Christi was too weak with pleasure to respond. She shuddered with pleasure as he lifted her in his arms and eased her gently against the coolness of the shower wall. He pressed his warm body close against hers. The cool water sprayed on their heads, then trickled slowly the length of their embrace. Christi did not realize she had her legs frozen together until Cosmo stroked her thigh and tried to run his hand between them.

Something inside would not let her part her legs, even though most of her being cried out for her to allow his hand to move freely.

Cosmo paused. He looked at the fear in her eyes. Slowly, he released her and stepped back. "My God! You are a virgin. Christi, my darling, sweet innocent Christi. I'm so sorry. I feel like such an ass," Cosmo said sincerely.

"Why? No, Cosmo! It's not you, it's me. Just give me some time." Christi bent her head against his chest.

He stroked her back gently and kissed her softly on her hair. "Ah! That's better. Instead of the fragrance of burnt oil now you smell of Spring, young lady," Cosmo said with a strain in his voice that echoed the tension in his body.

Christi knew he was hurt and that she may never get a chance to hold him again. "We can do it, Cosmo. Let's try!"

Cosmo hushed her with his index finger placed softly on her lips.

"I stink, Cosmo! You saved my life and I can't even give you what you want."

Cosmo covered her with a tender kiss.

"Yes, you can. But just not here. Not just now. I'm sorry."

"Oh, Cosmo. You don't have to be sorry. You don't! It's so crazy. I feel so ashamed," Christi said as the small shower of water turned to a trickle, then stopped completely.

"I should have warned you. You have to shower fast. It's a small tank," Cosmo said as he took a tattered towel from the towel rack and held it out to Christi.

Suddenly, Christi felt very embarrassed. She took the towel from Cosmo and wrapped it around her body. She shoved open the heavy door. Her yellow cotton dress was hanging from the old wire hanger on a rusty nail in a decaying plank on the wall. Christi dried herself quickly and stepped into the dress.

Without speaking, she ran down the hallway to the cabin. She did not stop to look back. If she had, she would have seen the four men emerge from out of the darkness of the passageway, pull Cosmo from the shower and beat him into unconsciousness.

Christi felt very lonely in the cabin by herself.

She still had a slight chill from the shower. She wished she had his arms around her again. She wished she had made love to him in the shower. She cursed herself for being so young and stupid. "He must think I'm a real creep," Christi mumbled. She waited in the darkness for hours. At first, she was not worried. She knew Cosmo was staying away because he was mad at her. As she waited, Christi touched herself where he had touched her.

It made her feel dirty. There was no tingle. She considered going to him. She could not make herself do that. She went to her suitcase and fumbled among the few possessions she had in the world. She found a small bottle of Evening in Paris perfume. It was the most expensive dime store brand her family could afford. Christi hated the smell, but she felt the urge to perfume her body and to make it attractive. She wanted to be ready to give him anything he wanted when he came through the door.

Christi was about to go to sleep when she heard a noise outside the door. Against her better judgment, she had left it open hoping Cosmo would come in. Now she feared it might be someone else.

"Cosmo, Cosmo? Is that you?" Christi peered through the dim yellow light of the room's single lamp into the hallway and the even dimmer light from the single naked light bulb.

A shadow of a man was cast against the far wall of the hallway. Christi fumbled around the cabin frantically for a weapon of some kind. Underneath Cosmo's mattress she found a Bowie knife. Quickly, she withdrew it and poised it to strike the intruder.

The dark man shuffled slowly down the hallway.

His shadow loomed larger and larger.

Christi gripped the knife tighter. She swallowed hard as she heard the man moan. She raised the knife higher over her head as he filled the doorway with his presence. She was about to strike when Cosmo stumbled in and fell at her feet.

Christi dropped the knife to the floor. It hit on its point and skidded against the wall. Christi grabbed Cosmo's head as he fell toward her.

Gently, she took his head down into her arms and cradled him. She could hardly bear to look at him. One of his eyes was swollen shut. He had bleeding abrasions on both cheeks.

Christi started to cry. She thought he was dying.

Slowly, Cosmo opened his unswollen eye and looked at her. He took a breath and blew it out hard. "I didn't get one good hit in, Christi. Damn! I hate a fight when I don't get one good lick in," he said weakly.

"Oh, Cosmo! I'm so sorry. I brought this on you. I'm so sorry!" Christi leaned over and kissed him softly on the forehead.

Cosmo had his arm around her waist. He pulled her close and tried to return the kiss. He was too weak. "I told you, I'm nobody's hero. I'm a real shit. If I had of had my mind on my ass and not your ass, they never would have got me."

"I'm sorry, Cosmo. I really am!" Christi stroked his fevered brow.

"Christi, no matter what, you have to get off at Kingston," Cosmo insisted weakly.

"I can't, Cosmo. I have to meet my Aunt Gladys in Cuba. I don't know anybody in Jamaica. Maybe I could go back home." Christi was suddenly excited.

The cool look in Cosmo's eyes dimmed that excitement.

Cosmo took several deep breaths. He seemed to gather strength. "Christi, you don't have any idea about what is going on in Cuba, do you?" Cosmo sat up a little as he addressed her.

"No. My aunt does though. My mother knows a lot. I don't care about Cuba, I care about you!"

"You can't go there!" Cosmo insisted.

"Why? Is something the matter over there?" Christi asked innocently.

Cosmo coughed hard. "There has always been something going on over there. *Latifundia* land ownership, foreign landlords, parasitic infections on nine out of ten infants. A single money crop and ten people living in one *bohio*. Disease, poverty and physical and emotional rape. Other than that, it is a very pleasant place to live." Cosmo smiled sarcastically.

"It sounds a little like the shanty town I came from," Christi offered.

"I suppose that, times ten," he insisted, coughing harder.

"Cosmo, let's not talk about this now. You're hurt. How can I help? Let me get you some medicine. What can I do?" Christi felt totally frustrated.

Cosmo reached out and touched her face with his huge, strong hand.

"Are you really as innocent as you seem? Is anyone that innocent in this ugly world?" He wondered aloud.

Christi took his hand, held it gently between her small hands, kissing it softly. "Cosmo? Who did this? What's going on? What can I do for you?"

"You don't really know a lot about anything of the outside world, do you?" Cosmo sat up more.

Christi looked a little irritated. "Yes I do. I read a lot," she insisted.

"Do you know what I am? What I really am?"

Christi gripped his hand tightly. She studied his ruddy complexion, his dancing Irish eyes. "No, and I don't want to know. I just want us both off of this ship at the first opportunity," she insisted.

"No, Christi. What happened today only makes it more important that I arrange for you to get off in Jamaica. I have to go on to Cuba."

"No! Not unless you do!"

"I can't. I'm under contract! Okay?"

"Contract?"

"A soldier's contract. Okay?"

"You? You're a mercenary. So? I don't care what you do for a living." Christi seemed unconcerned.

"You are something else, lady. I hope I know you in another life."

"I don't care about another life. I care about us now."

Cosmo smiled then looked serious. "I'm sorry. There is no 'now,' Christi."

"Why do you talk like that. Of course there is. So you have to do a little fighting. I'll wait."

"Oh, Christi. I wish it were that simple."

"It is if we want it to be. Besides there are a lot of ways to make money."

"It's not just money I need these days," he convinced himself.

"I don't understand? Who is fighting in Cuba?"

"The good guys and the bad guys."

"Who hired you?"

"Both sides."

"Oh? For which one will you fight?"

Cosmo was silent for a moment. "The one that needs me the most. Or the one with the most good whiskey and pretty women . . . or maybe a just cause." Cosmo coughed.

"I could never fight for money," Christi mused.

"Maybe you're right. I'll just fight for the hell of it, after all!" Cosmo concluded.

"I've read about the Irish. Hasn't there been enough fighting already, Cosmo?"

"True enough. A lot of my people have been killed in senseless fights."

"Then you won't go?"

"Yes, I will go. But you won't. You get off in Kingston. That's the last word on it!"

"No! Not unless you do!"

"Jesus! You really don't know about Castro and Batista? You're going into this thing blind. How could she do that to you?"

"You know Mother had to send me away. You said you knew Alex and Lucius James."

"That's true enough, but in Cuba there are a lot more with that on their minds."

"I'm not afraid anymore." Christi looked at him with love.

Cosmo studied her eyes. Looking into her eyes seemed to give him strength. "Christi." Cosmo's voice was serious. His face immovable.

"Yes?"

"Go back home at the first opportunity. Your mother meant well, but she has sent you to the worst possible sanctuary. All hell is going to break loose there soon. I care for you. I want you to live." Cosmo sighed as he tried to reach out for her.

Christi looked at him. He was bruised and beaten, but he was still the most handsome man she had ever known. She knelt down beside him. She reached her arms beneath him and drew him close.

"Cosmo, I promised my mother I would be a virgin on my wedding night. I am supposed to become a lady of elegance for Sarah's sake. I love you, Cosmo. I don't care about being a virgin. I don't want to be a lady of elegance. I just want you. I don't want to hear about politics or ships or seas or sealing wax. Alright?"

"Lewis Carroll. My, you are educated." Cosmo seemed impressed.

"It was forced upon me. I wanted to roller skate."

Cosmo chuckled. "I wanted to be a priest. Can you imagine that?"

"Yes. You would have been a wonderful priest." Christi laid her head on his shoulder.

"We will be in Jamaica in the morning. No matter what happens to me, you get off this ship and go home. Take the first available transportation back to Charleston. Understand?"

Christi held Cosmo tightly. He lay his arms softly on her shoulder. "I'll go, only if you go with me. I would rather be in Cuba with you than in Charleston with everyone else I know," Christi said firmly.

Cosmo held her quietly a moment. "Don't love me, Christi. There is only hurt in loving me. Please, if you do love me, go home. Please?" Cosmo pleaded.

Christi smiled in reply. She gently put her arms under his shoulders and helped lift him to his feet. She strained hard under his weight as she helped him to his bed. She lay him down and sat down close beside him. "The hammock sleeps alone tonight, my love," Christi said as she bent over and kissed him.

Cosmo started to protest. She hushed him with a kiss.

Christi took the towel she had brought from the shower earlier and cleaned him off. He seemed content to lie on his pillow and have her attend him.

She studied his strong face and stroked his hair gently.

"I love you, Cosmo. You are the hero of my life."

Cosmo shook his head weakly.

Christi stood up and moved into the small sliver of moonlight coming through the smoky porthole. She unzipped the yellow cotton dress and let it fall to the floor.

"I'm naked, my love. I'm naked! Naked! Naked! God, Cosmo! I can say naked and I don't feel ashamed."

Cosmo raised his arm, starting to object.

Christi put her hand gently over his mouth. She eased into the small bed beside him. She took his hand and guided it down between her smooth thighs. She pressed her firm, generous breasts against his chest. She kissed his muscular chest and felt each smooth roll of his strong arms.

"I love you, Cosmo," she whispered in his ear.

"I will always love you!"

Cosmo trembled. His eyes opened weakly. He looked at her tenderly. "If you love me, you will go back to Charleston at the first opportunity."

"We'll discuss it later, my love," Christi soothed.

Cosmo tried to lift up and push her away. He was too weak.

"Tomorrow morning we will be in Kingston. Go directly to the Constable and ask for asylum. I am not well enough to help anymore. Cuba will be a very unholy place for many years to come. There will be a lot of evil beginning there soon. Tomorrow, you promise me you will go to the authorities in Kingston. Promise me!" Cosmo insisted.

"Yes. Of course. Now rest awhile."

"No! Listen to me!" Cosmo sat up and coughed insistently.

Christi replied with a long, healing kiss.

Cosmo was too weak to respond as he lay back and closed his eyes in pleasure before wincing in pain.

Christi took his strong hand in hers and held it. She kissed his fingers and pulled his head into the gentle valley between her breasts.

Cosmo snuggled against them. He kissed her long and warm with his remaining strength, then fell into a deep sleep.

Christi stroked him gently as the ship rocked slowly in the waves. Once he was in a deep sleep, Christi got up and put on her yellow cotton dress. She wanted to be wearing it when Cosmo saw her first thing in the morning. She vowed she would never take it off again. She picked up all the hideous sailor's clothes and shoved them through the porthole.

Then she decided to sleep in the hammock so Cosmo would not awaken.

Moments later, she lay in the hammock and slipped into a deep, exhausted sleep and dreamed brave, wonderful dreams of her and Cosmo.

So good were her dreams and deep her sleep, she did not awaken as Cosmo gave her a tender goodbye kiss. She did not see him stand above her and drink in her beauty. She did not hear him leave her sleeping as the ship docked in the glow of a glorious sunrise on Kingston Bay.

Chapter Ten

CHRISTI AWOKE TO THE EXOTIC SOUND OF STEEL DRUMS PLAYING A happy Jamaican reggae rhythm. She stretched and yawned and reached over to embrace Cosmo. Then she remembered he was asleep in the bed. She looked over at the bed and he wasn't there. She figured he was just in the bathroom.

She rubbed her eyes, sat up in the hammock and started to call for him. She decided that was too clinging. She looked at the floor. It was not moving. She stood up and delighted in the sensation of a stationary floor. Still half awake she moved over to the greasy porthole. Through the few clear spots in the glass she could make out lush, green vegetation outlined against a clear, pastel blue sky. Immediately below her line of sight on the dock was a sign reading "Welcome to Kingston." There was an old clock on the facade of a government-looking building. It read nine o'clock.

Christi was hypnotized by the clock for a moment. "Nine o'clock," she repeated. "Nine o'clock and they haven't called me to fix breakfast and where is Cosmo?" she mused aloud as an eerie feeling of dread began to overcome her.

She was on the verge of panic when the soldiers shoved the cabin door open and rushed inside with their guns poised to fire.

Christi jumped back in her bed and pushed herself into a corner against the wall. The soldiers looked around the cabin quickly and thoroughly.

They seemed very angry when they found nothing but Christi's old suitcase. One of them gave it a swift kick as he grinned at Christi with a gap-toothed grin. He was the largest of the five men and appeared to be the commander. With angry shouts in a Jamaican dialect he ordered the other soldiers out of the room. Once they had gone, he approached Christi. He bent over slightly and smiled down at her. This time the smile was more demonic.

"Missy, you wish to tell me where this man Cosmo, he hides all the gold?" he said ominously as his eyes bore down on Christi with deadly seriousness.

"What gold? That's a laugh," Christi replied as coolly as her nerves would allow.

"You think I make the joke?" The soldier took the butt of his rifle and jammed it hard against the wall about a foot from Christi's head. "Goddammit! It is not so good to tell lies for this man. This man has much gold, missy. You tell me where it is." His voice softened. "I will tell no one else."

Christi swallowed hard and looked directly in his eyes. "I don't know what you're talking about. Why don't you ask Hornecker?"

The Commander broke into uncontrollable, raucous laughter. "This man, Mr. Collins, he is some man with the ladies. I do not like this man, but he has the way to make the ladies believe anything he says . .
.

"I have to give him some respect in this one thing. He is a thief of hearts as well as a thief of our money." He said as his laughter faded and his voice took on a matter-of-fact tone.

"He's not like that. He's just a soldier."

The Commander looked at Christi and shook his head in disbelief. "No, Missy. I am just a soldier. Mr. Collins is a liar and a traitor with no allegiance to anyone or anything."

The Commander paused and smirked. "So tell me, how many times did he rape you?"

"He's not a rapist and he's not a liar but this ship is full of them. Why don't you start with Hornecker"

"We will deal with the Captain soon enough. Okay, missy. I will let you live in the ignorance of your lies, if this makes you happy. I don't care. We will take Cosmo with us and soon he will tell us everything we need to know. Good day, missy!" he said and turned abruptly to leave.

Christi was a little stunned by the swiftness of the Commander's actions. He was gone some time before she fully realized the import of what he had said.

"Take him? No! No, you can't take Cosmo anywhere!" she yelled as she ran after them down the hallway.

The Commander was already on deck when a nearly breathless Christi finally reached him. She reached out to grab the Commander's shirtsleeve when she froze as her eyes fell on Cosmo.

Cosmo was handcuffed, shackled, and flanked by two mean-looking policemen.

Captain Hornecker and the rest of the crew stood in the background looking very pleased with themselves.

"Christi, for God's sake, stay out of this! Go back below, now!" Cosmo insisted.

Christi was frozen into inaction.

"Maybe you want to go into the hoosegow with Cosmo, missy?" The Commander threatened.

"No! No, you can't take me and you can't take him. He hasn't done anything. It was all my fault but it was self-defense. Cosmo didn't do anything wrong."

"Christi, shut up. Now!" Cosmo interrupted.

The Commander looked at Cosmo with mock admiration.

"See how this man casts the spell on the women?" He paused and looked at Captain Hornecker. "She would hang for him, Captain. Why do we not know such women?"

"Captain Hornecker, please tell them. You know what happened. Please tell them." Christi pleaded.

Captain Hornecker smirked and shrugged.

"No, missy, I think it is Mr. Collins. The poor, innocent Mr. Collins." He hesitated. "But then, maybe Mr. Collins, he is not so innocent as he looks."

"No! You're wrong. Please believe me. Diego tried to . . ."

Cosmo glared at her and she stopped in mid-sentence.

"Christi, I mean it. Shut up! Let's go, Commander Jackman. I'm tired of this loud-mouthed woman and this garbage scow of a ship," Cosmo growled.

Christi could not believe her ears. She looked at Cosmo in disbelief. His eyes found hers for a moment. They spoke softly to her before turning hard once again.

"See, missy. I tell you, but you do not believe me. This Cosmo, he is the number one criminal in the whole world, or maybe number two, but trying harder." Commander Jackman laughed at what he considered a joke. His men laughed obediently with him.

Christi saw no humor in anything.

Captain Hornecker walked across the deck and stood beside her. He looked at her malevolently.

Christi turned away from him.

"Commander Jackman, you must forgive her. She is young and Cosmo has filled her head with romantic notions. It happened just as Cosmo has confessed." Captain Hornecker smirked.

"He's a damn liar! I killed Diego! He tried to rape me. Cosmo had nothing to do with it!"

Commander Jackman and Captain Hornecker exchanged cynical glances.

Commander Jackman motioned for his men to move Cosmo off the deck.

Christi watched in horrified confusion as they began to move Cosmo down the gangplank. She started to run after him.

Captain Hornecker grabbed her arm and held her back.

"If you say any more, both you and he will hang. A deal has been struck. Keep your mouth shut for the good of us all," Captain Hornecker whispered in her ear angrily.

"No! No deals! Cosmo! Stop Commander! He's innocent! I swear he's innocent!" Christi yelled as she shook off the Captain's grip.

She started to run after him but Pinkus and two other crewmen blocked her way. Christi bared her claws at them before she turned and glared at Hornecker. "I don't know what kind of deal you made but I'll see to it that it never happens. Let me go, Captain. Now!"

"Go? Where?"

"Cosmo is innocent and you know it."

"Innocent? Cosmo? You are a young fool."

"I killed Diego and you know it. You can't let them take Cosmo for that. Please."

"Diego? Diego is still hanging with tomorrow's dinner. This is not about Diego."

Christi backed away and looked doubtful. "You're a liar. I don't know what's going on but you won't get away with it!" She said as she watched the soldiers shove Cosmo into the back of a police van at the foot of the gangplank.

Captain Hornecker drew close and whispered in her ear. "I tried to do my best, but you have done your worst. You embarrass my generous self greatly in front of the Kingston authorities. I could have let you be arrested with Cosmo, but did not." Captain Hornecker snarled.

"Fine! Then do it! I would rather be with Cosmo, wherever he is going, than with you," Christi insisted.

"Oh? So soon you have an affection for this vile mercenary? You are so young and silly, Miss Jones. . ."

". . . to you he is the adventurer. But this is not so. It was he who was behind the Country Club killings in Bermuda." Captain Hornecker challenged.

"I don't believe it."

"Believe what you will. I tell you, it is very true! Mr. Collins and a dozen terrorists, they kill fifteen people who never hurt anyone. These men of Cosmo Collins, they walk in with machine guns and kill these people at lunch. Now tell me is this the brave warrior?" Captain Hornecker scowled.

"Cosmo wouldn't do anything like that. Why do you hate him so?"

Captain Hornecker thought it over a moment. "Hate him? No. We were once comrades in arms and if he does not hang we may be again."

"Please, Captain. You can't let him hang."

Pinkus moved in behind Captain Hornecker and glared at Christi as he whispered in the Captain's ear.

"No more talk on this matter. Now you will be the good sailor or maybe suffer a fall overboard in high seas. There will be many high seas between here and Cuba," Captain Hornecker growled.

Christi did not reply as she watched the police van bearing Cosmo drive off the dock in a small cloud of dust. Suddenly she felt all alone. Once again she knew she had to survive until she found a way to escape. "I'm sorry, Captain. I did not mean to embarrass you. You have been kind to me. I suppose I would be locked in a Kingston jail if you had not stopped me. Thank you. Excuse me, but I'm tired. Now that Cosmo is gone, do I have the cabin to myself?"

Christi almost bit her tongue.

Pinkus put his hand on the captain's shoulder and smiled an uneven-toothed grin at Christi.

Captain Hornecker shook Pinkus's hand off his shoulder before he replied. "The ship is too crowded for the private quarters. I have to assign someone to share it with you."

"Who?" Christi demanded.

"Pinkus will share your cabin."

"The hell he will!"

"The hell he won't!"

Christi gritted her teeth and clenched her fists. "If he does then you fill out that report about me being overboard, because I will be," Christi insisted.

Captain Hornecker looked worried for a moment, then he wiped his brow with his forehand. "I will see what I can do. I do not have many possibilities. You understand it is not like I have the ten staterooms for all the queens that come aboard." Hornecker smirked.

Christi looked up at him and glared. "I am still under the protection of Sammy Moore and you don't want to deal with my mother."

"Sammy Moore can help no one. He is dead. It seems someone from Detroit slit his throat. Now you are to go to your work assignment and do what things you are needed to do." Hornecker insisted.

"God! Is there no lie you won't tell?" Christi scoffed.

Hornecker slapped her and she fell to the deck.

"I will tolerate no more insubordination. You will do as you are told, woman! Always! Always! Always, you forget you are just a woman in a man's world." He paused and coughed. He sounded ill. "That is all. The end! No more talk now," Hornecker snapped as he grabbed Christi by the arm and lifted her to her feet.

Christi rubbed her face as she glared at him. "Don't ever hit me again!"

Captain Hornecker shrugged and walked away.

Pinkus looked at her with lust as he licked his lips.

Christi felt ill but she fought it off as she slowly turned and moved toward the galley. As she went, she plotted how she would get off this ship as soon as possible.

She had never been so scared or so mad. The powerless feeling combined with the sense of barbarous entrapment was overwhelming. It was as if a legion of angry giants had her surrounded and it was only a matter of time before they would pounce and torture her endlessly before killing her. It was a totally helpless feeling and she blamed it all on her gender. For the first time in her life, she hated being a woman. She wanted to be Superman, or just a man. A man who could punch Hornecker out and storm the prison to free Cosmo. Or if she couldn't be a man she wanted the brute power that they had over her. The

Delilah in her wanted to shear all their locks and make them as weak as she felt now. She steeled herself to find a way to never again be in such a vulnerable position. She vowed that somehow, someday she would be a woman of power and she would have all the power such men now had—and much, much more!

In the days that followed, such thoughts buoyed Christi's strength. Christi had feared that once the ship was at sea she would be gang-raped by the entire crew. Yet the ship had been at sea three days, and only fifty miles off the Cuban coast and so far nothing had happened.

Christi had to endure the catcalls and filthy innuendos from some of the crew, but it seemed there was a core of decent men that shielded her somewhat from the out-and-out lechers. Captain Hornecker had not put Pinkus in her cabin, but nevertheless she slept with a kitchen knife under her mattress and a chair against her door.

She delighted in the fact that the little Cosmo had taught her about cooking was enough to fake it with men of such limited tastes. Beans and lots of Tabasco sauce was the way to keep their stomachs full and their minds off of mayhem.

On this eve of the fourth day out, Christi was excited about the prospect of being in Cuba by morning. She was tired from a ten-hour shift in the steamy galley, but happy as she made her way through the tight passageways to her cabin.

Christi yawned as she reached the cabin door and opened it. She stepped inside with a carefree abandon stemming from her preoccupation with thoughts of being in Cuba soon. The cabin lamp's feeble lamplight struggled mightily to scatter the darkness as Christi slowly scanned the small room. She could not see into the deep shadows of the room's corners, but she was too tired to look any closer.

She looked at the bed she had shared with Cosmo. She looked at the yellow cotton dress hanging beside it. She had not worn it since Kingston but for some reason she felt compelled to shed the sailor's rags and put it on.

She undressed slowly in a mock striptease pretending Cosmo was watching and he was begging her to take it off. She would tease him awhile then come to him willing and then they would make mad passionate love until the ship docked in Cuba and maybe for some days afterwards.

As she dressed she wondered where Cosmo might be and how he might be doing. She was deep into fond thoughts of Cosmo when Pinkus's scratchy voice interrupted her thoughts.

His hideous face was almost on hers.

"Now, you know there's two ways to do this. One way is to be nice and polite and not make a fuss. The other way is to yell and scream and claw. I like it either way. Sometimes I like fighting the best," Pinkus intoned grimly as he stepped out of the shadows and stood naked before her.

Pinkus was in every way a duplicate of Diego, except Pinkus was skinny. His protruding bones gave him a cadaverous look that would attract a burial detail did he not have some hint of animation.

Christi hoped for a moment it was just a bad dream.

Pinkus moved ever closer into the dim light. When Christi saw the huge knife he was holding in his hands, she knew it was a very cruel reality.

"I swore a holy oath that I would remain a virgin until I got married. I swore it in the church before the alter, before Mary and Jesus. Aren't you a good Catholic, Pinkus? Do you want to go to hell?" Christi tried.

"Go to hell? I am hell!" he slobbered.

Christi moved back on the bed and felt under her pillow for the knife she had hidden there. "Okay. First let me take off this dress." Christi played for time.

Pinkus looked suspicious. Then he shrugged. He moved away slightly.

Christi slowly got up and started to lift her dress over her head.

Pinkus' eyes looked bigger than Spanish doubloons. Pinkus had not closed the door well and suddenly it swayed opened and slammed against the hatchway. Pinkus turned his head for a moment and Christi darted by him. She was almost out of the door when he grabbed her and pulled her back inside. He closed the door hard. The force of his jerk threw Christi across the cabin, against the bed. Frantically, she felt around for anything to help her out of this terror as Pinkus advanced toward her with heavy footsteps.

"All the bullshit is over, lady! You're going to take it now and take it for a long time. Take it until you tell me you like it. Now! Right now!" Pinkus threatened as Christi desperately felt around beneath the mattress.

Pinkus was inches away from her face. She could feel his hot breath.

Her hand found the handle of the kitchen knife she had hidden beneath the mattress. She thanked God and gripped the handle tightly. Just as her hand closed around the knife, Pinkus's hand grabbed her hair. He pulled it hard. Christi nearly dropped the knife as Pinkus yanked her down to the floor and pulled her head toward his groin.

"Now, bitch! I saw Diego's body. You do this now for me. For him and then for the sharks," Pinkus snarled. He was throbbing rigid and ready to enter her. He tore her hair as he drove her mouth toward his groin.

Christi pretended to part her wet mouth.

Pinkus smiled and shivered in expectation.

Christi stood up and drove the nine-inch blade deep into his chest. Pinkus coughed and looked stunned for a moment. He reached out for her, but crumbled and fell to the floor, gurgling in his blood. He did not release his grip on Christi's hair until he had been dead for many seconds.

Christi pulled the knife from his chest. When she did she saw a few spots of blood on her dress. She cursed Pinkus and stabbed him three times in the groin as she cried heavy hot tears of anger and the joy of deliverance.

She cried quietly for a while before she realized she had to get away, get off the ship as soon as possible, any way she could. She did not wait to pack. Instead she made her way up the stairway to the main deck. There was a strong wind blowing out of the west.

The air was humid and small raindrops spotted her face.

She looked around and was relieved to see there was only one man on watch. He was a hundred feet up the deck and he had his back to her.

It was her plan to cut loose a life boat and hope to be far away before they discovered Pinkus' body and found that she was missing.

Slowly, she eased down the deck to the aft lifeboat. One look at the rusty crank and she shook her head in disappointment. There was no way to crank it quietly by herself. She considered what the crew would do to her when they found Pinkus. She started the crank.

She was surprised at how easily it turned and the surprisingly small amount of noise the crank made as it began to slowly lower the boat into the water. She said a prayer of thanks as the wind rose even higher and made loud whistling sounds in the ship's superstructure. The sounds helped disguise the small amount of noise the crank did make. With renewed confidence, she began to crank harder and faster and the boat was almost down into the water when Captain Hornecker's breath felt hot on her neck.

"Going somewhere, Christi?" he said with a thin smile as she turned to face him.

"Damn! Damn it!" Christi cursed under her breath.

"Where is my first mate, Pinkus? It is not like Pinkus to let the passenger wander the decks alone on such a stormy night," Captain Hornecker smirked.

Christi's answer was a cold stare.

"I hope what I'm thinking is not true. Surely a young woman such as you has not killed two men on a single sea voyage. . . .."

" . . .even Captain Kidd was not that bloodthirsty," Hornecker said with some degree of admiration in his voice.

"I killed him and if I were a man I would kill you too!" Christi snarled.

Captain Hornecker stepped back. He looked at her with some fear in his eyes. As he moved back his hand fell on a cargo hook. Christi had never had anyone afraid of her before. It was a very heady feeling. For a moment, she did not feel powerless and it was like being free for the first time in her life.

"I simply do not understand why you fight so hard. Life is very simple. To make it pleasant you go along with the tide and it is like floating. If you do not go along with the tide it is more like drowning," he posed.

"What horseshit!" Christi chortled.

"You do not even try to go along and I have tried. No one can say I have not. From now on you will be treated like the prisoner. No more special favors until we take you to the gallows with your friend Cosmo." Captain Hornecker reached out his meaty hand and grabbed for her shoulder.

Christi stepped aside and ducked under his grab. Quickly, she looked down at the lifeboat. She despaired it was not in the water. She felt the Captain's hand grab the back of her dress. He began pulling her along the deck.

She heard the dress tear and the sound filled her with rage.

She turned and bit his arm drawing blood.

He screamed in agony and he let her go.

Quickly, she ran to the crank and tried to turn it.

"It hurts me to my soul to lose you, Christi, but perhaps this wound will heal." Captain Hornecker sneered as he raised the cargo hook and came at her with fire in his eyes.

There was no doubt in Christi's mind that he was going to kill her. He raised the hook high over his head and its sharp point gleamed in the moonlight as it descended toward her face.

Christi had no choice.

The sea was high with five- to ten-foot whitecaps and there was a cool breeze blowing. The wind caused her to hesitate only a moment as she took a deep breath and dove over the railing into the sea below.

Captain Hornecker stood on the deck and watched in disbelief as his ship left a white wake that disappeared quickly into the darkness. He ran to the railing and peered out into the night. He could see nothing but the empty white wake and the dark sea beyond.

"Captain, what happened?" Second Mate Solano came running down the deck.

"That crazy bitch jumped overboard. I can't believe it," Captain Hornecker insisted. "That crazy woman killed herself for nothing. I was just having a polite conversation with her, trying to calm her and she just leaped over the rail into the sea. You know how crazy she was, Solano. Everybody can testify to that." Captain Hornecker insisted nervously.

Solano looked at the cargo hook in the Captain's hand and frowned for just an instant.

"Yes, sir. Do you want me to turn the ship?" he wondered.

Captain Hornecker sighed a well-acted sigh of despair. "In this darkness, I'm afraid it will do no good, but we'd better do it for the record," he instructed.

"Yes, sir," Solano obeyed as he ran to the bridge.

Captain Hornecker stood in the darkness and tried to keep from laughing.

Chapter Eleven

K IKI CHEVARRA WAS UNCOMFORTABLE IN THE LARGE OCEAN SWELLS. He loved the ocean, but in a more abstract, poetic way than he did when it was stormy and threw his small boat around like an olive in a blender. If he had his way he would not have gone to sea this night. He had objected when his brother El Grande ordered him to Moncada. Yet he was a good revolutionary soldier so he found himself at sea this stormy night, hoping he would not get ill before he made it to solid land.

He was straining his eyes toward the shore, looking for the light that would signal him in when he felt a bump against the boat's side. He ignored it at first, then the bump came again, this time slightly louder.

Cautiously, he moved around the small gangway toward the side where he heard the noise.

He was relieved to find it wasn't a shark but what looked like a bundle of bright yellow wet rags. He started to ignore it then he saw it move. He looked at it carefully and it moved again.

The cool salt air was blowing in his face and the wind whipped the water across his small boat's bow as he reached down to inspect it closely.

It was then that Christi, almost completely exhausted, lifted her head out of the water and gasped for air.

"Oh, my God! It's a woman!"

Kiki shouted into the wind as he made the sign of the cross before he grabbed her shoulders and tried to pull her aboard.

Christi tried to raised her arms weakly to help but she was too weak to hold them up.

Finally, after three pulls, Kiki managed to lift her out of the water and lay her on the deck.

Christi coughed up some of the sea water she had swallowed, then reached up and hugged Kiki fiercely around the neck.

"Thank you. Thank you. Oh Lord, thank you!" she said weakly.

Kiki was a little embarrassed and he pulled away from her slightly as he lay her head on a pillow of coiled rope. He wiped her brow with an old rag. "*Señorita, qué pasa? Cómo está?*" he wondered. Then he remembered she had spoken English. "Why do you come to the sea here? You are in a ship wreck?"

Christi nodded her head slowly "yes," taking the easy way out for now.

"*Tu tienes mucho suerte*. You are one lucky lady. My boat is the only one for many miles," Kiki said almost prayerfully.

Christi was weak and her vision was blurry, but she could see she had been very lucky indeed.

The man who had pulled her from the sea was as handsome as he seemed to be kind. His features were Castilian and as he stood above her in the early morning moonlight he looked like some young matador who had just received ten ears.

"*Cómo se llama?* Excuse me. What is your name?" Kiki inquired as he found a blanket and lay it on her.

"*Me llamo* Christi Jones. *Yo hablo español un poquito*," she replied weakly.

"*Muy bien*. Very good. *Yo soy Kiki Chevarra. Dónde?* Where are you going?" he quizzed.

"To Cuba. To see my aunt. She was to meet me in Manzanilla." Kiki frowned and shrugged as he sat down beside her and looked deeply into her soft sienna eyes. "You have Spanish eyes, but I do not believe you are Spanish. It is not good to go to Cuba these days, even for the Spanish. You are American?"

"Yes."

"Then it is even more bad for you. Many things are happening in Cuba. Many good things for some, many bad for others."

"That's what Cosmo said." Christi shivered as Kiki covered her with another blanket.

"Cosmo? Cosmo Collins?" Kiki laughed.

"Yes."

"You know Cosmo Collins? Ah, *arriba!* If you know Cosmo Collins, then I have done a great thing by saving you. If you know Cosmo Collins, then it is safe for you to go anywhere." Kiki laughed. "And where is that old *cabrón* these days?" Kiki's eyes smiled.

Christi looked very sad before she replied. "He's in a Kingston jail. I hope he is still alive."

"Yes. That is him alright." Kiki chuckled.

"He shouldn't be there. He's innocent."

"No! He is many things but never innocent. Do not worry. He has been in the jail many times and he has never stayed there very long."

"Oh God! I hope you're right."

Kiki studied her face a long moment. "I think he has captured another heart. How does he do this?" Kiki wondered aloud.

"He's a good man, Kiki. Were you friends?"

Kiki nodded quietly for a moment before he replied. "Yes. He is one fine *amigo*. He saved my life twice. He was to help us here. If what you say is true, this is bad for the revolution," Kiki said.

"What revolution?"

Kiki looked proud. "The youngest revolution. The Cuban revolution."

"I see." Christi sighed weakly.

"Cosmo has not told you of this?" Kiki looked irritated.

"He didn't explain very much just that he was on his way here. Maybe he will still make it." Christi hoped.

Kiki sighed hard as he and made the sign of the cross. "*Sí*. If anyone can do this thing it will be Cosmo."

"I hope so. I really hope so."

"You have much affection for this man?"

Christi replied with a smile.

"I will ask El Grande to give me some men as soon as the revolution is won and I will take these men to free Cosmo, if he is not free by this time," Kiki vowed.

Christi did not hear him as she had fallen into exhausted slumber.

Kiki watched her a long moment before he covered her with a blanket. He turned to the rising sun and whispered a prayer of thanksgiving for the splendid bounty he had received from the sea this day.

Chapter Twelve

THE MORNING BROKE CLEAR AND HOT. THERE WAS A STEADY BREEZE coming off the ocean and Christi's dress dried completely in a half hour. A long night's sleep found her refreshed and very glad to be alive. The warm sun felt good on her face as she watched Kiki pull the small boat ashore and began to cover it with palm leaves. Christi did not wait to be asked but helped him and soon the boat was hidden.

Kiki scanned the Caribbean horizon and was satisfied he had not been followed. Then he turned and looked at Christi with a very serious look on his face. "I will take you to Moncada with me, but you know I cannot promise for your safety there. I do not know of your loyalties, but I feel at least you are not an enemy. You are *pobrecita,* like me. Maybe you will even decide to join the fighting. It is very important that you do not tell anyone you are American. You will pass very well for Cuban. Say very little. Perhaps if we are lucky we will find your aunt soon."

"You can take me to her?"

"I do not know this. There is much confusion and these are very bad times, *señorita.*"

Christi understood. "Kiki. *Muchas gracias.* You saved my life."

"*De nada.* If you do not wear this bright yellow dress I do not think I am such a hero."

"Thanks anyway. Let me know if I can help you. I'm no soldier but maybe there is something I can do. Who are you fighting?"

Kiki looked at her in disbelief for a long moment. "You do not know? Cosmo does not tell you?"

"I think Cosmo just likes to fight."

Kiki laughed. "*Sí,* to listen to a man like Cosmo would confuse even me. We fight Batista." He looked at her to see if she understood.

"I'm sorry, Kiki, I was too busy surviving to follow politics," Christi apologized.

"Batista is a corrupt man. I was on his side once. When we fight Prio Socorrias and Batista promises free elections, I believed. So I am a fool, no? Now I have a machine gun filled with fifty votes and it is election time anytime I say it is." Kiki laughed loudly.

Christi smiled with him. A look of horror came over her face as she saw a huge black man coming running out of the trees onto the beach, heading straight for Kiki.

Kiki saw the look on Christi's face and turned quickly to see the huge Ethiopian man only a few feet away. Kiki lifted his machine gun off his shoulder and pointed it at the big black man. "Rat a tat!" Kiki pretended as the big black man threw his arms in the air and feigned dying.

"Garbo! Garbo! *Qué pasa? Qué pasa, mi amigo?*" Kiki hugged the man affectionately.

"Christi, this is Garbo. Don't be afraid of him. He looks like the wrath of God, but he is *un hombre bueno.*" Kiki offered. "He's my right-hand man. How do you say it? My main man! Garbo, this is Christi." Kiki patted the big man playfully.

Garbo growled a gruff hello.

Kiki took Christi aside. "He is called Garbo because he's so quiet and spends much time alone. Some crazy men, they try to hang him when he was in America. He has not spoken too much since then and only if he likes you very much. Understand?" Kiki almost whispered.

Christi looked at Garbo and saw the traces of a rope burn around his neck. The sight of it made her feel queasy. "My God, Kiki! I'm sorry . . ."

"Hush! Do not speak of this. *Comprende?*" Kiki cautioned.

"Of course," Christi assured him as she looked at the towering muscular frame of Garbo.

"Garbo will take us into Moncada. From here on you will understand that I may have to go away suddenly and leave you on your own," Kiki apologized.

"It's okay. You have already done much," Christi smiled.

Kiki looked at her fondly then, quickly, turned away.

Christi saw his look of affection and turned away. Kiki was handsome and charming but she had decided to wait for Cosmo, no matter how long it took.

Kiki took Garbo aside and they talked as Christi walked the beach. It felt good to be free of the confines of the ship.

She sat on a sand dune and watched the bright blue sea roll in, pondering the events of the past days. She missed Cosmo, but did not believe Cosmo was a terrorist. He was Christi's first love. She would love him forever, no matter what anyone said. She prayed he was safe and well.

"I am sorry, *señorita*. Garbo tells me we must head in through the Zapata Swamp. The soldiers are all about. If you want, you can surrender to them and since you are American, maybe you will be okay."

"Can't I stay with you?"

"I would like this but Garbo and I think it is best you go back home to America *rápidamente!* As I have said, Cuba is not so good a place today." Kiki said as he sat down on the sand dune beside her.

Christi looked at Kiki. He was tall and handsome. His eyes were strong and honest. They told her that whatever he did, he did it with all his might. Christi admired that. She also knew he seemed to genuinely like Cosmo. If he really was Cosmo's friend she felt safer with him than with soldiers.

"When your fight is over will you help me find Cosmo?"

Kiki nodded affirmatively. "*Sí,* we must help Cosmo, *mañana.* Today we head into the Zapata Swamp to avoid the soldiers. You wish to come with us?"

Christi nodded.

Garbo, the huge Ethiopian, moved up beside Kiki. He cast a long shadow over the sun-filled beach.

Christi instinctively moved away from him.

Kiki took her hand and stood her up. "Garbo, she is not the American against us. She is running away from home. She is a friend of Cosmo Collins," Kiki announced as he stood aside.

Garbo smiled at the word "Cosmo." He took Christi's small hand into his huge one. Christi was afraid he would crush it. He shook it gently. Finally he smiled.

"I think he likes you," Kiki announced with relief.

Christi sighed in agreement.

Garbo's smile faded into a disapproving grimace.

Kiki walked away for a moment. He looked up and down the beach. He pulled out binoculars and looked again, then rejoined Christi and Garbo.

"I think it is time." Kiki announced.

Christi looked deep into his eyes. There was so much hurt in them.

Christi had seen that look many times before. "Tell me how I can help. I know swamps. Outside of Charleston there are swamps you can't believe!"

"Oh? This is good. Then you know how to pass by the snakes?" Kiki kidded.

Christi looked worried until he smiled.

Garbo looked doubtful.

Kiki paused just before they left the beach.

"Here is a *guayabera* and I have another pair of khaki pants in my pack. Maybe you wish to save such a pretty dress?" Kiki said as he held up a loose-fitting, multi-colored shirt.

Christi looked at the *guayabera* with its beautiful hues of aqua and green. It seemed most attractive. "Yes, thank you, Kiki." Christi said as she took the large shirt and a pair of khaki pants. She looked around for a clump of bushes, excused herself and moved behind them to change. As Christi slipped into the lovely, clean-smelling oversized shirt, she could see through the parted branches of the bushes that Garbo, with extreme gestures of anger, was protesting her presence.

Kiki seemed to finally calm him before she rejoined them.

"Would you keep my dress in your pack, Kiki?"

Kiki smiled as he took the neatly folded yellow cotton dress and stored it in his backpack.

"Garbo is not happy with me is he?" Christi wondered.

"I believe he is concerned with your safety."

"Maybe it is best I go to the authorities. Maybe they can get me to Aunt Gladys. Maybe that's best for all," Christi offered.

Kiki grimaced.

Garbo seemed happy.

"I think maybe yes, maybe no." Kiki paused and cocked his ear. They all listened to the distant sound of guns being fired. "I think for sure, for now we all go into the Zapata," Kiki insisted quickly.

Garbo nodded as he turned and moved through the sand toward the edge of the palm forest. His huge feet left a wide trail that Kiki and Christi followed until they were swallowed by the lush green darkness.

Chapter Thirteen

THE TROPICAL RAIN ROARED INTO THE SWAMP PRECEDED BY THREE waves of oppressive humidity. Christi was a Carolina girl. She had seen Caro-lina humidity make her breath laborious but she had never felt such oppressive humidity or seen anything like the abruptness of the Cuban rain. She, Kiki, and Garbo were surrounded by what, at one moment, were short, navigable streams and swampy water. In the next instant they were swollen with tropical rain and pouring into large ponds and lakes with destructive force.

One newly formed river almost swept them away. As the tropical thunderstorm poured down, they were faced with crossing a roaring river that moments before had been a small stream. The heavy rush of water knocked Christi down.

Kiki grabbed for her. His hands missed and he fell into the rushing water behind her.

Garbo stood tall and strong before the roaring water. He saw where they were and dove into the foaming torrent behind them.

Christi thought she was drowning until she felt a strong hand pull her out of the water. She thought it was Kiki, but was only slightly less happy to see it was Garbo.

"Thank you, Garbo!" Christi coughed.

Garbo sat her on a river bank without replying.

The awesome power of Garbo's brute strength impressed Christi.

She thought to herself that such power was the only thing men had worth envying.

"Garbo? Where is Kiki?"

Garbo looked at her like she was crazy.

"Here I am. Over here." Kiki gurgled.

Christi looked to her right. Kiki was lying on a high mound beneath a large ebony tree.

"We are safe inside the Ebony Forest. Thanks to our savior Garbo. Here we can relax for awhile. The soldiers won't be able to cross that water until long after the rain goes away. *Gracias,* Garbo. *Gracias!*" Kiki offered.

Garbo almost smiled. His eyes did reveal that he had a great deal of respect for Kiki. Garbo turned and sat down beneath a huge tree which was entwined with enormous vines. He turned his face toward the dark clouds and let the rain pelt his shining black skin.

"My God! He's so strong," Christi mused aloud.

"*Sí.* As a young man he was the best at cutting down the nuts of the palm tree. Then he was best at chopping in the cane fields. There is nothing that requires strength he cannot do." Kiki hesitated as he spied a red-orange flower ring of bougainvillea.

He gathered a small bouquet and offered it to Christi.

Garbo gave Kiki a look of disgust.

For a moment, Kiki thought better of it himself then he held them out once more.

Christi smiled. She took the bouquet and smelled it.

"It's our most beautiful flower. We have jasmine, magnolia, and frangipani, but bougainvillea is more beautiful." Kiki offered.

"Gracias. Thank you, Kiki," Christi replied graciously as she took the flowers. She let the sweet smell tickle her nose as the bright sun found a small crack in the rain clouds.

The sun brought no relief. Instead it seemed to raise the humidity level.

"In not too much time we will be in the Sierra Maestra. We will climb high In the mountains where it will be cool and dry. There will be no choking vines or sudden rivers there. We go now. I must tell you, though our mountains are high, they do not hold the snow. I was in Colorado as a young man. I loved the snow. Except to shovel it."

"Did you like America, Kiki?" Christi wondered aloud.

Kiki looked hurt for a moment. Then he shrugged. "I love America. I wish America loved me more," Kiki said tersely as he moved away from her. "Garbo, are we ready to go?" Kiki sounded very military.

Garbo nodded.

"Now, Christi. Let's move out!" Kiki snapped as he moved off into the Ebony Forest, his rain-soaked boots spilling out as much water as they took in.

Christi waited until Kiki had mounted the hill.

Garbo stood beneath the vine-wrapped ebony tree and waited for Christi to go first.

Christi moved out of Garbo's shadow and up the hill behind Kiki.

Garbo stopped and froze. He perked his ears and scanned the thick forest for movement.

Kiki looked at him.

He looked at Kiki.

Christi heard the gunfire moments later.

"Sweet Jesus!! Still they come. We must go faster, Christi!" Kiki said with command authority.

Christi paused until the gunfire sounded ever closer. She picked up her step and almost broke into a run before she tripped over a vine and fell hard.

Garbo started to help her up but Kiki stepped in and offered his hand.

Christi took it and got to her feet feeling a little embarrassed. "I'm sorry. I won't stumble again."

"Oh?" Kiki gave her a look of admiration. "Yes I believe this to be true." Kiki held onto her hand long after she was on her feet. "I believe it is good to have you as an *amiga*."

Christi nodded politely as she pulled her hand away.

Garbo grimaced. He motioned them both forward with wide, quick movements of his strong arms.

Kiki paused to listen to the distant crackle of gunfire. He looked at Garbo. Garbo and he said much with their eyes that Christi readily understood.

"They kill many *pobrecitos* today. We must hurry, Christi." Garbo gave them both a gentle, but firm shove. They followed Garbo's brisk pace down a small path Garbo had chopped and formed with his bare hands.

Once they were through the forest, they crossed a large rain-soaked plain that led toward the foothills of the Sierra Maestra. Suddenly, Christi felt tired and sick. She had been days without much sleep and the trauma slowed her. She resisted fainting. Christi hated the image of the frail woman fainting in the face of danger. She fought it hard but was so fatigued she fell often. Each time Kiki offered to help her to her feet.

Each time she waved him away. Each time she got up weaker than the time before.

Finally she fell hard. Out cold in an exhaustion coma.

Kiki started to attend to her.

Garbo waved him off and picked her up with his strong arms. Kiki shrugged before he smiled with admiration as Garbo carried Christi gently in his huge arms.

Christi slept until they were deep into the narrow trails and cool weather of the wild and rugged Sierra Maestra.

She awoke only slightly when Kiki stroked her forehead with a cool cloth dipped in a mountain stream.

Kiki felt her forehead with his hand and looked worried.

Christi shivered.

Garbo saw Kiki's concern and eased Christi down. He knelt beside her and also felt her feverish forehead. He looked up and stared deep into Kiki's eyes.

Kiki nodded understanding. "We must get her to Anita. Only Anita has the cure for swamp fever. We must hurry, Garbo. Anita does not like for the fever to get a firm hold. We will have to chance heading for Santiago de Cuba."

Garbo nodded agreement.

"Discipline! Discipline! Discipline!" Christi muttered with the hoarseness of fever.

Kiki and Garbo looked at each other with shared concern.

"Yes. Soon it will be too late. Go to the base camp and get a jeep. I will wait by the old Santiago Road, under the ceiba tree at the hill. Hurry, Garbo," Kiki pleaded.

Garbo was already moving down the mountainside before Kiki had finished speaking.

In the distance a muffled roll of thunder signaled the end of the rain. Moments later, the sun came out bright and hot against a light pastel blue sky.

Kiki lifted Christi in his arms and began walking toward the forest of silk-cotton trees a mile away.

The particular silk-cotton tree he would meet Garbo at was one hundred and sixty feet tall. It had vines so big he and Garbo had used them for slides when they were children. It would be a cool place to rest and wait for Garbo.

Kiki did not have Garbo's strength and he had to rest many times before he was able to carry Christi into the silk-cotton tree forest.

Christi was sweating so profusely her *guayabera* became transparent.

Every lovely, graceful curve of her body was outlined against the wet cotton of the thin shirt. Her young nipples stood out so firmly that Kiki had to say many Hail Marys and take many deep breaths in order to avoid touching them.

They were just inside the forest when Christi reached up around Kiki's neck. She embraced him tightly, kissing him firmly on the lips.

Kiki dropped to his knees and lay her gently on the ground. He kissed her back.

She opened her eyes slightly. "Cosmo? Cosmo, I'm sorry. I didn't mean to get you into so much trouble. I'm glad you got away. It's so good to see you. I really missed you." Christi cried as she hugged Kiki's neck then fell back to sleep.

Kiki held her gently. "*Mi amiga,* Mr. Collins strikes again," Kiki said philosophically. He leaned over and kissed her gently on the forehead. "With all my soul I wish I was Cosmo Collins because I could love you too much, *señorita.*"

Kiki lifted her up gently and proceeded down the small path to the huge silk-cotton tree. Once there he lay Christi slightly against it. When she looked comfortable, he went to a small brook and wet a bandanna. He wrung it out, sat down by Christi and placed it softly on her forehead.

"I will not love you, Cosmo Collins. You are without discipline. Go ahead and let them hang you! Ha!" Christi babbled.

Kiki had to laugh. He knew discipline was the last word in Cosmo Collins's vocabulary. "Ah, *querida mia!* How sad for you and for me that you have ever known such a man."

"He is everything a young woman like you should never know. For all the nights of my youth, I wish for someone like you. You are in my arms but I do not have you." Kiki sighed.

Christi opened her eyes slightly. "Cosmo?" she whispered.

Kiki responded with a half-nod.

"I didn't mean that about hanging you. But you left me in the ocean. The ocean is very dark and deep. I'm so afraid of the ocean. I don't swim very well."

Kiki stroked her head with the wet bandanna and swallowed bitter tears of sadness. All he had ever wanted was so close and yet so far. Kiki was a man who prided himself on being disciplined. No amount of discipline was enough to stop him from stealing a kiss from the woman of his dreams.

Kiki knew that in her fever she was kissing Cosmo but for one brief shining moment, his lips were on hers and he could pretend it was him she loved.

That moment would sustain him through much of the sadness that was to come.

"Cosmo, I'm drowning. Oh my God! I'm drowning. Please save me!" Christi pleaded weakly as she shook with chills.

Kiki lifted her tired arms around his neck and pulled her close as he leaned against the giant tree.

She snuggled up to him and held him tightly, falling into a deep sleep.

Kiki kissed her softly on her hair. He had never been so much in love. All his friends would laugh if they knew of his condition. It was something that happened to them, not to "El Macho."

But Christi Jones was different than any woman he had ever known. Without the slightest touch of makeup, with her hair wet with rain and her face on fire with fever, she was still the loveliest woman he had ever known. He had known the moment he pulled her from the sea he would have to have her.

He knew it even more now.

To hell with Cosmo Collins.

If Cosmo was not already dead Kiki could fix that. Kiki had many friends in the Kingston government. It would be easy to arrange. Christi would endure a period of mourning with him there to comfort her. Then Christi would be his. "Yes! Yes, that's what I'll do!" Kiki daydreamed as he settled back against the old familiar tree and slept soundly with Christi cradled in his arms.

Garbo shook Kiki violently for the tenth time before Kiki responded.

"Huh? Oh, Garbo? Oh, I must have been more sleepy than I thought. Christi? Christi? Where is Christi!?" Kiki panicked.

Garbo motioned toward the jeep. Christi lay under a blanket on a stretcher across the back seat of the jeep.

The motor was idling erratically.

Kiki started to run to her.

Garbo held him back.

Kiki tried to shake loose.

Garbo held him firmly.

"Garbo, *qué pasa?*" Kiki asked angrily.

Garbo shoved a small piece of paper into Kiki's hand.

Kiki shook off Garbo's grip and unfolded it.

He read it half aloud, half to himself. "Moncada Barracks? It begins?" Kiki spoke softly at first. "*Arriba!* Garbo, soon we act!" Kiki finished with exuberance.

Garbo took the piece of paper, crumbled it and swallowed it. Kiki ran to Christi's side and whispered in her ear. "Christi, soon I will have much to offer you. When we are successful I will be a big man. Then I will have your love."

Garbo pulled Kiki away and growled his displeasure.

"Okay? Let's go!" Kiki said.

Garbo pointed at Christi then shook his finger and his head in a vigorous "no!"

"It's none of your business, Garbo. She's my prize and no one is taking her away from me."

"Cuba Libre! No time for a woman!" Garbo growled. He balled his fists to strike Kiki. He thought better of it and leaped angrily into the driver's seat.

"I know my duties to Cuba, Garbo! I will do what I have to do but she will be at my side."

Garbo fumed quietly in reply.

"Now we go to Anita's. We get her well. Hurry, Garbo! Hurry!" Kiki insisted as he gave Christi a quick kiss and jumped in the jeep's passenger seat.

Kiki was barely inside when Garbo roared off down the narrow road. Steam rose from the large puddles in the road as Garbo drove the jeep hard through them.

Kiki held onto Christi gently.

Christi was so feverish now she faded in and out of consciousness with regularity. She felt comfortable with Kiki's touch which she dreamed was Cosmo's. "I love you. I'm sorry but I do," Christi repeated.

Kiki came to believe those words were meant for him.

"Please just rest, *querida mia*. We will have help for you soon. Soon we will be at Anita's. She has a cure that will make you well very quickly," Kiki soothed.

Garbo turned and gave Kiki an angry glare.

"Garbo, please try to understand. It is a matter of the heart. Are we not still *amigos?*"

Garbo drove even harder as his reply.

"Am I not the one who found you hanging from that tree? Did I not cut you down and give you the breath of life? Did I not help you take your revenge on the ten cowards who tried to hang you because you would not let your sisters be whores?" Kiki paused to gauge Garbo's reaction.

There was none.

"You killed seven but I got three, one of which had a gun to your head. Is this not true?" Kiki persisted.

Garbo stopped the jeep and placed his huge hand on Kiki's shoulder. He squeezed it hard and glared at Kiki with censure.

"I know, my friend. The revolution is most important. I swear I will let nothing get in the way of victory. Nothing. Okay?"

Garbo thought it over and his mood mellowed a little. He started the jeep and drove it hard.

Kiki touched Christi's brow.

He removed his hand quickly and shook it as if he had been burned. "*Jesús!* Faster, Garbo. Faster!"

Garbo replied by driving even faster down the treacherous jungle road.

Kiki bounced from side to side but held onto Christi so that she felt very little discomfort. Occasionally she had the strength to open her eyes and smile fondly at him.

Each time she smiled his heart was less and less his and more and more hers.

The Caribbean sun was just beginning to peak over the Sierra Maestra in the distance as Garbo wheeled the jeep through a clucking bunch of chickens in the front yard of a very humble house. He braked to a stop and quickly turned to look at Kiki and Christi.

Kiki looked at Anita's humble house and thanked Garbo with his eyes. Gently Kiki lifted Christi and carried her slowly behind Garbo who opened the door to the house.

A grumpy woman growled at them from inside the house until she recognized Kiki.

"Kiki! You are here!" Anita smiled. She was about to hug Kiki when she saw Christi in his arms.

"Who is this woman?" Anita backed off.

"She is to be my wife. She needs your help now!"

Anita looked at Kiki, then at Garbo in disbelief.

Garbo shook his head in disgust.

Anita stood aside as Kiki carried Christi into the small front room. "So El Macho! He has the time for *amor?*" Anita smirked.

"No time for talk. Please get to work." Kiki instructed.

"Help me, Cosmo! Help me!" Christi muttered.

"'Cosmo'? Ah! Your 'wife' she calls for another man. Such a wife she would make!" Anita cackled.

"That's just fever talk," Kiki insisted.

"In the words of fever is much truth." Anita looked deadly serious. "Cosmo? Does she speak of your *amigo* Señor Collins?"

"Are you going to get to work now?" Kiki chided.

Anita shrugged. She looked at Garbo whose eyes told her to proceed. Anita pointed to a small bed in the corner.

Gently, Kiki lay Christi on the small bed.

"Is Señor Collins soon to join us?" Anita teased.

"He is in a Kingston jail and will be hanged soon. We save her first. Then we ask questions!" Kiki insisted.

Anita smiled wryly as she looked at the lovely Christi. She turned to look at Kiki. "Dead? Cosmo? This I would have to see."

"Just get to work. Now!"

Anita started to walk away.

Garbo stopped her.

Anita was not afraid of Kiki, but she never denied Garbo anything. "Does El Grande know about this?"

"You let me worry about that." Kiki snapped.

Anita and Garbo shared a frown. Kiki ignored them.

Finally, Anita sat down beside the bed on which Christi lay. She lit a small candle, watching the glow of the candle on Christi's lovely face for a long moment. Anita felt Christi's fevered brow. She shook her head slowly.

"How long has she been like this?" Anita demanded.

"Not long. As soon as we knew she was sick we brought her to you."

Anita looked indifferent. "Get out of here. Let me work. She is very sick. You have a council meeting. See to it. Go! Go, now!"

Anita was five foot two inches and weighed two hundred fifty pounds. No one talked back to her too often.

Kiki eased around her. He knelt beside the small rough-hewn wooden bed and kissed Christi's forehead.

Anita glared at Garbo. Garbo pulled Kiki away.

Kiki gave Christi a quick kiss on the lips and backed away. "Your best, Anita. Your best," Kiki instructed.

Anita smiled then looked deadly serious.

"El Grande will not want to know you take time with a woman. You go now and maybe I do not tell him!"

"I will be back tomorrow. Understand?"

"Out!" Anita shouted.

Garbo pulled Kiki toward the door.

Once they were gone, Anita walked over and sat in a chair beside Christi's small bed. She dipped a small spoon into a bowl of liquid. Holding Christi's head up slightly, she forced the warm liquid down Christi's throat.

Christi started to spit it out.

"Swallow!" Anita demanded.

Christi swallowed.

Anita fed her several small spoonfuls more.

Christi obediently swallowed then almost awoke.

Anita picked up a young jalapeño pepper from a nearby table. She took her thumb and slightly parted Christi's mouth.

Christi seemed to be dreaming. "It's okay. You can kiss me, Cosmo."

Anita looked very worried as she picked up a large knife.

She held the point close to Christi's carotid artery. "I do not like this woman. There is much trouble in her."

Christi stirred and opened her eyes.

She looked at Anita with kindness before she closed them once more.

Anita took the knife away from Christi's throat. She grimaced as she cut a jalapeño pepper into five bite-sized pieces.

Then she dropped them into Christi's mouth and forced it shut with her beefy hand.

Christi came up out of the bed shaking and jerking.

Anita held onto Christi's jaw with both hands.

Christi tried to spit the peppers out, but Anita held tight. Christi finally swallowed them and Anita relaxed her grip. Christi lay quiet for a moment.

Anita waited.

Christi twitched and rolled uncomfortably. Anita opened Christi's mouth and shoved another whole pepper down her throat. Christi retched almost vomiting. Her back bowed. Her face convulsed.

Anita held her jaw shut while Christi kicked at the air with her legs. Christi struck out at Anita with her weak fists.

Still Anita held firm.

Christi swallowed hard.

Anita released her grip and felt Christi's forehead. Anita smiled. The hot feeling was fading.

Now Christi's face felt nice and sweaty. Anita liked that feeling. That feeling meant her peppers were doing their work. Anita grew peppers with character. Just smelling one of her peppers would make most people break into a sweat. Consuming one would cure most minor ills. Consuming two would break the worst case of swamp fever—or kill you.

"I can't breathe. I'm so thirsty. Please! Please, some water," Christi pleaded as she suddenly sat up.

Anita drew Christi to her ample bosom, almost smothering her. "When the fever breaks, then we will have much water. Now the peppers must cook without water. The fire must burn alone inside until the peppers cook out the poison," Anita insisted.

Christi broke her grip and ran for the single naked faucet in the room. She turned it on.

It spewed and puked air.

Anita laughed.

There was a bottle of dark rum on a shelf above the faucet. Christi did not know what it was, she only knew it was liquid. She pulled it down and threw off the top. It tasted foul, but it was wet and made her burning throat feel better.

Anita watched quietly as Christi downed another swallow and

looked relieved. She nodded with delight as Christi sat down against the alabaster wall, seemingly content.

Another cure was had.

Anita loved modern medicine.

Chapter Fourteen

CHRISTI DID NOT LIKE ANITA AT FIRST. AS CHRISTI SLOWLY CAME back to semiconsciousness, she saw the unsympathetic, almost mean face of an older woman who kept feeding her spicy hot, and hotter, things. Christi was too weak to object to Anita's treatment that consisted of pepper soup, pepper tamales, *picadillo* ground meat with peppers, *ropa vieja*, and whatever food she could sweep from the kitchen floor with peppers.

Christi knew she was ill and was grateful for help. She had no idea who this woman was or why there was so much hatred in her eyes. Christi did learn respect for Anita's approach to medicine. After five days of peppers, Christi knew the essence of Anita's cure. Anita made you so afraid of ever seeing a pepper again, you cured yourself.

It was a huge jalapeño pepper on the third day of her fever that awoke Christi to the world again. Christi looked at it and shook her head violently.

"Please. For God's sake. No more!" Christi begged.

Anita shrugged.

"Americans. They like the *blanco* food. You get many fevers because you do not eat the peppers," she insisted.

"I have Cajun relatives who would love your idea of food. I don't!" Christi smiled politely.

"Cajun? You are from New Orleans?"

"No! I'm not Cajun." Christi thought it over. "I'm mostly of Cuban ancestry."

Anita shook her head in disbelief. "I do not think this is so, but no matter. I say you are well. Maybe you are ready to go back home?"

"I can't."

"Ah! You do some bad things there. I know this!"

"No I didn't. How could you know anything about me?"

"You do not belong here! I have friends at the port. I can fix it so you go home now!" Anita interrupted with fire in her eyes.

"What have I done to you?" Christi reacted.

"I live for Cuba Libre! It is all for us. For you I believe there is nothing but trouble here. I will help you leave this place."

"No! I am going to meet my aunt. I am staying. Kiki wants me here."

Anita's face flashed rage that she could barely restrain. "Kiki is very important to the revolution. You will not make him crazy. I will see to this."

Christi understood Anita's concern but did not like her pushy ways. "Maybe he'll have something to say about that."

"You are very bad for being here now. You say you are Cuban. If this is so you will leave us to do what must be done."

"Why don't you give me a chance to help?"

"Because I know of women like you. You do not make men stronger. You make them *loco* with *amor.*"

Christi studied Anita's face. She could see beneath the ravages of a hard life a face that was once very lovely. "Is that because you are also such a woman?"

Anita stepped back and almost smiled.

"You are Cosmo's friend. Are you Cosmo's lover?" Anita probed.

Christi looked at the intensity in Anita's eyes. She did not answer.

"You need not answer this. I see the love in your eyes. I can help you go to him in Kingston. Is this what you wish?"

Christi had to admire Anita's persistence. The offer was tempting but she did not trust Anita. "Yes. But not right now."

"Then you will go to him soon?"

"After we win the revolution," Christi said coolly.

Anita was unnerved by Christi's poise. She was filled with envy and distrust of Christi, but she did not want to suffer Kiki's wrath. She would bite her tongue and wait for the right time to rid Cuba of this troublesome woman. "You know Cosmo for a long time?"

"Not really."

"He is a most dangerous man."

"Was he your friend?"

Anita shrugged.

"Was he your lover?"

Anita flinched and Christi had her answer. The thought of Cosmo with Anita made her sorry she had asked the question.

"You are much too savvy for the young woman. If Cosmo is in the Kingston jail this is very bad for him. It is not his way to make a mistake. I think you make him crazy so he makes this mistake. You will not do this to Kiki!"

Christi was feeling better until Anita said that. Christi believed maybe it was her fault that Cosmo was imprisoned. That thought stung.

Anita took delight in Christi's obvious pain.

"Maybe I should go to Kingston," Christi mused aloud.

Anita grinned a Cheshire grin. "Good! This is good! I will begin the arrangements tomorrow."

Christi nodded reluctantly.

"How do you feel?" Anita's mood changed to one of pleasant accommodation.

Christi sat up and stretched. She felt bouncy and full of life. "I feel so good, maybe I'll make peppers my steady diet," Christi laughed.

Anita laughed with her.

Kiki opened the door. For a long moment, he stood in the doorway watching them laugh. "*Jesús,* Anita! You do work miracles."

"You make the problems. I make the solutions." Anita threw her arms up in mock horror.

Kiki moved into the room. He paused and put down the large gun he was carrying. He moved close to Christi and put his strong hands on her shoulders. "Are you well enough to go for a ride?"

"Yes. Please!" Christi replied.

Anita looked uncomfortable. "How long is this ride?"

Kiki shrugged.

"I think she stays with me for a few more days," Anita moved up and wedged in between Kiki and Christi.

"Stay out of this, Anita. You sure you're okay, Christi?"

Christi looked at Kiki. She was well enough to see him clearly. He was an imposing man. Straight was his bearing and his facial features were firm, yet with a hint of boyishness, enhanced by a permanent looking five o'clock shadow. "I feel good," Christi turned to Anita. "Thank you for your help."

Anita grimaced and stepped back.

"You remember all we have said?"

Christi did not like Anita's threatening eyes. She turned her back on Anita without replying.

"Let's go! I have things to show you," Kiki bubbled.

Anita pursed her lips. She picked up a large red pepper and bit into it, chewing it with a vengeance. "She must come back and stay with me a few days more. You understand this, Kiki?"

"Maybe. We shall see." Kiki replied.

Christi gave Anita a curt glance as they parted.

"Keep the pepper soup warm. Maybe I'll be back," Christi chided.

As Christi moved to the door, Kiki stepped aside and let her pass. Once Christi was outside, Anita grabbed Kiki's arm and pulled him to her.

"Kiki, you must not do this! I have a bad vision of many things." Anita said as she held him back while Christi proceeded toward the jeep.

"Back off, woman!" Kiki tried to shake her off.

Anita held tight.

"I see your eyes. They are for her. This is not good. Cosmo was our friend. He is a bad man to make an enemy." Anita paused. She looked Kiki deep in the eyes. She gripped his arm even more tightly. "You will not do this!" Anita snapped.

Kiki broke her grip and looked at her with contempt.

"Go away, woman. What happens between her and me is between her and me. Cosmo would understand that more than anyone.

"And the revolution?"

"You worry too much. The revolution will be won. Now go eat your peppers and be content." Kiki smirked.

Anita spit in disgust as Kiki walked away and got into the driver's seat of the jeep next to Christi.

Christi waved at Anita as they pulled away.

Anita slammed her door shut.

Kiki gunned the engine hard. The tires threw dirt and rocks against the side of Anita's house.

Anita put a small curse on Kiki as the jeep disappeared into the weak December sun.

"Kiki, aren't you driving a little too fast," Christi said weakly.

Kiki looked over at her with jealous eyes. Then his face mellowed and he laughed.

"Maybe I will drive as fast as Cosmo Collins or maybe I can never be as good as Cosmo Collins," Kiki griped.

Christi was still a little weak. She did not like the speed with which

Kiki made the turns in the road. She did not like his attitude and she most of all did not like disparaging words about Cosmo. She thought it best not to reply.

"Am I not as good as Mr. Collins?" Kiki persisted.

"Please. I'm very tired."

"This is an answer?"

"I thought Cosmo was your friend."

"I do not know if he is my friend, and if he is my friend, if he is alive or dead. Not knowing these things make me a little crazy," Kiki said firmly as he wheeled the jeep too fast through a narrow gap in a road lined with pine trees.

Christi held her breath as the jeep narrowly missed collision with a few of the big trees and nearly flipped over.

"Please slow down, Kiki."

Kiki turned his face away from her. He drove even harder down the tiny dirt road, through the narrow stand of pines toward the sea coast.

Finally he slowed, took a deep breath and blew it out hard.

"It is said that he is a traitor. That maybe he tells people about our plans to gain his freedom." Kiki paused. He slowed the jeep even more. He looked quickly but hard at Christi. "You know nothing of these things?" he probed.

Christi shook her head.

Kiki's eyes looked at her with disbelief. He bit his lip. "I wish to believe this, but it is most difficult. There are many people who do not wish good things for you."

Kiki said into the wind as much as to Christi.

Christi shifted uncomfortably in her seat. "Cosmo is a good man, Kiki. Cosmo would never betray anyone. I could never believe that of him. Ever!" Christi said a little irritated.

"You know this man but a little while and you have this strong belief?" Kiki sounded skeptical.

"I trust my feelings."

Kiki gritted his teeth and tried not to look jealous. He failed.

Christi saw the jealously on his face and worried.

"You love this man so much?" Kiki could barely pose the question.

Christi did not dare answer as Kiki turned the jeep down an even narrower road.

"You cannot answer this?" Kiki demanded.

"He was kind to me. Okay? He was like a brother. A very loving brother. There was not time for much else."

"Not much time? Cosmo does not need much time. You were with him many days. I do not believe he needs this much time." Kiki was gruff.

Christi wanted to slap him, but she was afraid he would drive them off the road. She was still a little sick and irritable and not in any mood for Kiki's macho bull. "Kiki! Turn this jeep around and take me back to Anita's. Right now!" Christi growled.

Kiki looked angry for a long moment. He stepped on the accelerator and drove even faster.

Finally he slowed and a thin smile crossed his face.

"I want to believe in you and my friend. But you must understand *la revolución* must come first. I cannot have all these confusions and do my job. You understand this?" He tried to be apologetic.

Christi let him stew for awhile.

"No. I really don't understand. You said Cosmo was your friend. I know him well enough to know he is a man of honor and I don't like anyone suggesting otherwise," Christi replied curtly.

Kiki ground his teeth a moment. "You think I am bad for saying these things?"

"No, Kiki. You have been kind to me. Please, take me back to Anita's," Christi said firmly.

Kiki fell quiet once again.

Christi glanced at his eyes. She could see a lot of pain in them and wondered at its cause.

"I will not speak of this matter anymore. Is this alright for you?"

"Thank you."

"I will first apologize for being discourteous to you. Then I will make it up to you by taking you to Panchos Del Mar. There we will have paella. It has no pepper." Kiki paused to chuckle. "Paella, a cold beer, and a good cigar. I will have the cigar," Kiki announced.

"No pepper. You promise," Christi groaned.

"Anita is one good doctor, no? She has the cure for everything?"

"God! Anita may be a good 'doctor' but my throat still feels like it was scratched by a million cats!"

"Ah, *cerveza, muy frío,* will fix that. The peppers, they are hot but they drive away the fever," Kiki insisted.

"Yes, and I've lost five pounds," Christi said as she pulled at her loose-fitting clothes. "Where is my dress?"

"It is safe. My sister sews the tears and is cleaning it. Do not worry I will have to buy you more dresses. Pretty new ones, not these old rags," Kiki said looking at the old dress Anita had given her.

"You've done enough. I want you to help me get to Havana, to see my Aunt Gladys. I'm tired of being a burden. I need to get my life back."

"I have already asked *mi amigos* to look for your Aunt Gladys. Havana is very difficult these days, as is Kingston. You and I, we do not have control of such things. You cannot go to Havana yet. That is not possible," Kiki said with finality.

Christi looked at the handsome young man who had saved her life twice. When the jealousy was gone from his face he was pleasant-looking. In another time she could have found him irresistible. He was all any woman could ever want. He was young, handsome and appealing.

He was not Cosmo Collins.

Christi knew Kiki knew all there was to know about Cosmo. Things she was dying to find out. Yet, she did not know how to ask Kiki about Cosmo without making him mad. Maybe, if she waited long enough, Kiki would volunteer all she was curious to know. "I am grateful for all you've done, Kiki. Thanks. Please thank Anita. Thank you both and Garbo, too."

Kiki shrugged as he turned the jeep down another road that led into the main road that forked.

One side had a military sign that warned "Guantánamo U.S. Naval Base. Authorized Personnel Only." Christi looked at it fondly. It was good to see something from home.

Kiki seemed to notice the look in her eye as he turned the other way and drove toward the ocean.

"If you go there they might help you get back home. Is that what you want, Christi?" Kiki seemed worried.

The word "home" sounded strange to Christi. She thought of Sarah and became melancholy.

She wondered if she would ever see home again. Except for Sarah, she wasn't sure she wanted to see home again.

"No! Not now. Just help me find Aunt Gladys. I'm not ready to go home just yet," Christi said softly.

Kiki seemed somewhat happy with her reply. "You will like Pancho and his paella. It is the finest in all of Cuba." He looked away. "See, there he is now just coming in with the fresh catch to go into the paella," Kiki said as he waved at a grizzled-looking old man getting out of a small boat by a shaky appearing dockside, a few hundred feet ahead.

The old man squinted as he peered in their direction. Finally he returned a tired wave.

"I hope you like the seafood," Kiki said as an afterthought as he parked the jeep by a small tin shack.

"Yes. I like shrimp a lot."

"Oh, you tell Pancho the kinds you like and that is the only kind he will put in the paella, and no peppers," Kiki grinned.

Kiki had an engaging grin. Christi watched him intently as she got out of the jeep and walked to the dockside with him. Christi was beginning to feel real comfortable and secure with Kiki.

She could see how Cosmo had liked him as a friend.

Christi would also be his friend, for her sake and Cosmo's.

"Pancho, this is *mi amiga, señorita* Christi Jones. Christi, this is my old friend and only father I have ever know, Pancho Pietras." Christi held out her hand.

Pancho looked critical for only a moment. He walked up and gave her a big hug, as if they were old friends. "*Mucha bonita!* Ah, cingowa! Kiki, you have done it this time,"

Pancho bubbled as he released Christi.

Christi nodded politely.

"You come to show off my paella? To eat my paella, drink *cerveza* and watch the ocean waves come in and go while the moon shines above? *Oye!* To be young again," Pancho needled.

Kiki put his arm around the old man's neck as they walked into the tiny shack.

Christi trailed slightly behind. She paused to watch the ocean. It was so peaceful and romantic and so very deadly. For a moment, she thought of Cosmo and wondered where he might be, how he might be. She hated all the confusing thoughts that crowded her mind now. "Discipline! Discipline, Christi!" Mrs. White tried to crowd into

Christi's thoughts. Christi took a deep breath of the refreshing ocean air.

She felt very undisciplined as she went inside the small shack.

Kiki handed her a cold beer just as she entered. Christi took a swallow. She was not much of a drinker, but it was cold and wet and she was thirsty. She drank it faster than she should have. She was surprised how quickly it made her dizzy. She smiled as she sat and watched Pancho and Kiki carry on an animated conversation in Spanish while Pancho cooked the paella.

The paella was excellent and Christi had one more beer.

Christi had never drank two beers so the alcohol went right to her brain. She and Kiki walked for some time before she was sober enough to stop a seizure of giggles that had her laughing uncontrollably.

When her mind cleared, they were in a small grove of pine trees on a small cliff overlooking the ocean. The black-orange setting sun lit a sparkling patch of ocean that seemed to skip just above the gentle waves and stop at their bare feet. Sea gulls dived for elusive meals. Another couple walked arm in arm in the distance.

Kiki sat down with his back to a tall pine tree. He held his hand out for Christi's.

Christi paused. She took his hand and sat down with some distance between them.

"I feel the nervousness in your fingers." Kiki looked concerned.

Christi looked coy.

"Please, Christi. I am not the enemy."

"I know."

Kiki's facial expression looked almost desperate. "These feelings I have for you. They are something I did not want." Gently, Kiki took her chin in his hand and turned her face toward him. "You do not have such feelings for me. I know this. It is too much too fast. I know this also." Kiki looked deep into her eyes. He touched her hair softly. He seemed embarrassed by the equally embarrassed look on her face. "I am sorry. I have said too much so soon! I am very *estúpido!*"

"No. It's okay, Kiki. The beer made me woozy too."

"It is not the beer, *señorita*. Come, I will take you to the U.S. base. That is the best thing for all of us."

"No, Kiki. Not yet."

"Yes, You should go home. That is where you belong," Kiki said firmly as he stood up and reached down for her hand.

Christi took his hand and let him lift her up. They embraced for a moment. He felt good against her. He pulled her into his arms and kissed her tenderly. She resisted for a moment. His arms were strong about her waist and she felt secure with them around her. She parted her lips and let him kiss her harder.

He paused a moment.

"*Mi corazón*. I love you so!" Kiki sighed as he pulled her tightly against his firm body and kissed her fiercely.

Christi had never known such fire in a kiss. Her legs felt weak and she felt more dizzy than she had with the beer. It was a kiss that Sarah had warned her against. It was the devil's kiss. It made her want to take off her clothes and run naked into the sea with Kiki.

It made her want all of his body. "Discipline! Discipline!" Mrs. White repeated.

Kiki kissed her even harder and she was about to become a part of his desire, but the words of Sarah and Mrs. White persisted.

Kiki paused. "I feel you have some desire for me." He smiled.

Christi gasped for breath.

Kiki started to kiss her again. He stopped. His ears perked. Christi heard nothing.

"We have to go. We must hurry!" Kiki cursed as he pulled her along from the beach.

Christi started to question when she heard the loud reports of gunfire echoing through the forest.

Kiki stuffed some money in Pancho's shirt pocket.

Pancho ran into the woods.

Christi and Kiki jumped into the jeep and roared off into the night down a trail so narrow it made Christi duck down in her seat. The pine branches whipped over their heads as Kiki turned off the lights and headed away from the sound of the gunfire. Kiki was cursing under his breath. Christi was trying to remember forgotten prayers. As they drove faster down the dark trail, the night became more and more humid. Lightning crackled in the distance and hot raindrops pelted them in the open jeep.

"I'm sorry. We have no top. It is a stolen jeep!" Kiki apologized quickly.

Christi nodded understanding.

Kiki seemed to drive harder. He pulled into a small ravine in the densest part of the darkness.

He looked at her with more concern than love. "I must take you to the U.S. Navy."

Christi studied the worried look in his eyes. "I'm okay," Christi paused. "I want to stay with you".

Kiki's concern turned to unabashed love light. He would have taken her in his arms but the gunfire was too close.

The tropical rain was falling harder now. It hit the small pine boughs and picked up speed on the rebound as they roared into the night. The floorboard of the jeep held water well. Soon her feet were in three inches of it.

Kiki stopped the jeep and got out of his seat. He fumbled around beneath the back of the jeep and brought out a large tarpaulin. He pulled it over both of their heads. It smelled of old oil and wet clothes. As Kiki held it over their heads the gunfire seemed to fade in the opposite direction.

Kiki listened intently for a moment. He seemed pleased as he put his arm around Christi.

He leaned over to kiss her, but Christi pulled away.

Kiki looked puzzled. "The rain. Ah! The rain has cooled your passion?" Kiki grimaced.

"I do not trust myself with you, Kiki. I am very afraid and confused. I need some time," Christi said nervously.

"Yes. Maybe this is so," Kiki agreed. He took her hand and held it gently in his. "I am most sorry for having moved so quickly. The world moves very quickly for me. I do not understand it moves slowly for others. You are so young, Christi. I hope soon you can understand why I do these things,"

Kiki said as he gave her a quick kiss on the cheek. He reached to start the jeep's engine, but paused as gunfire erupted from the distance once again.

The rain was coming down very hard now. Christi took the big piece of canvas and held it over their heads as Kiki turned toward the gunfire.

She looked deep into the darkness ahead of them.

Kiki was silent as the gunfire became louder. Christi feared for herself and Kiki. The jeep hit a large rut and she bounced from her seat into the night.

"*Madre Dios!*" Kiki screamed as he brought the jeep to a hurried stop. "Christi, Christi!" he called out in the darkness. He turned the jeep around and put the headlights on bright. He sloshed through the swamp that once was a forest and called for her.

Christi was unhurt but shaken as she saw him coming for her. "I'm here, Kiki," Christi shouted. She staggered out of a dense flowering jacaranda bush.

Kiki stood outlined against the bright headlights of the jeep.

He sighed hard with relief as he dropped to his knees and gathered her to his arms. He held her tight.

They did not speak.

Christi hesitated a moment. She put her arms around his neck and held him tight. "I promised my mother before the sacred Eucharist I would be a virgin when I married. Please respect that Kiki. Don't let me be weak!" Christi trembled with confusion.

Kiki started to kiss her, but held her close instead.

"Yes, I have much respect for this. I will personally see that you are a virgin when you are married because it will be me that you marry!" Kiki said sincerely.

The gunfire got louder and closer.

Christi lay her head against his muscular chest. He felt cool against the heat of the rainy night. "Can we go to Havana tonight? I need to find Aunt Gladys. I need to call home."

Christi acted like the young, frightened, wet girl she was.

Kiki stroked her rain-soaked hair.

He picked her up and cuddled her. He sat her gently into the jeep. He kissed her softly on the lips. "Yes, I will see you to Havana. We go into Santiago to see my men first. Then we go to Havana. From now to then, querida mia, I hope to convince you to be my bride," Kiki said evenly.

Christi did not respond until Kiki had driven the jeep some distance. She could see his face as the rain clouds broke letting glimmers of a full moon shine through. He was a handsome man and he radiated love for her.

Maybe she could learn to love him.

"I really like you, Kiki. Maybe I will know the answer to that question in Havana," Christi said honestly.

Kiki glanced at her as a pine bough slapped against the windshield. He steered back onto the trail. He nodded slightly as he pulled the jeep off into a dense grove of plantain trees. The gunfire seemed to come from all around them. Kiki seemed worried.

"We must stay here until the fighting stops. Then we will go to Santiago and I will have my men look for your aunt in Havana." "Please, try to rest for now," Kiki said as he tried to tuck her into the wet tarpaulin.

"It's not a blanket," Christi objected gently.

Kiki felt the stiffness of the canvas. He looked frustrated as he tried to find something softer. "I am sorry that I did not come prepared for this. I am prepared for total war, but not prepared to keep a lady comfortable. This will not happen again. From now on my life is dedicated to keeping you comfortable," he insisted warmly.

Christi smiled. The rain trickled off her forehead and filled the dimples in her cheeks.

As Kiki shined the flashlight at her face, Christi held her hand up to shield the light.

Kiki turned it away so that it lit his upper body. His shirt was open and his smooth skin glistened with silver raindrops. He was so muscular that the raindrops clung to small hills and valleys of his muscles before spilling off his body and falling to the forest floor.

Christi could easily have given into him at that moment. But once again the image of Sarah, Mrs. White, and Cosmo caused her to turn her face away from him and look into the night. She felt his strong hand on her wet hair. He gave her a kiss on the side of her face and dismounted from the jeep. Christi felt suddenly alone as Kiki walked away from the jeep.

"Kiki? Where are you going?" Christi sat up in panic.

She could see the flashlight and a shadow of Kiki standing several feet away.

"I must take a walk and let the rain cool my thoughts. Then I will return and we will go to Santiago," he said just before he turned and walked out of her sight.

Christi started to follow him but thought better of it. Slowly she wrapped herself in the tarpaulin and scrunched down in the small seat. She shivered slightly, even though the rain began to abate. She wanted to call out to Kiki, and yet she was mad at herself for the weakness of her flesh.

The rain had stopped completely before Kiki returned to the jeep. Without speaking, he pulled the back seat out of the jeep and placed it on the ground. He paused only a moment to look in Christi's eyes. "Tomorrow we go to Santiago. Good night, Christi," he said coolly as he flashed the light in her direction.

"Goodnight, Kiki," Christi replied. "Yes, that will be fine. Tomorrow," she repeated.

A large raindrop rolled off the limb of a high pine tree and hit Christi square between the eyes.

Christi laughed.

Kiki laughed with her.

"Thank you, Kiki. Thank you."

"For what?"

"For just being around," Christi smiled.

Kiki made a bed of his field jacket and the seat cushion. He lay down on it before he replied.

"I will be around for a long time. That you can count on, Miss Jones. Get some sleep. We will have the long day tomorrow," Kiki said coolly.

"Goodnight," Christi replied just before Kiki switched off the flashlight, leaving them both to ponder their separate thoughts in the quiet darkness of the deep forest.

Chapter Fifteen

IT WAS LATE IN THE AFTERNOON OF JULY 25, 1951, WHEN CHRISTI AND Kiki arrived on the outskirts of Santiago. Christi was born into poverty and experienced it all her life, but nothing she had ever seen had prepared her for the squalor she saw in the slums of Santiago. Everywhere they drove, Kiki had to stop the jeep quickly for fear of hitting naked children with hungry looks in their eyes that would run in front of the jeep without warning. As she looked at the saltine-cracker houses with their ill-fitting roofs, Christi understood why they preferred the dangerous streets to their homes. Christi had always felt overcrowded in her small three-room shanty, until she saw the *bohios* of Santiago where three families lived in one room, literally packed like canned fish.

They were in the middle of a particularly depressing group of shanties when Kiki pulled to a stop. He motioned toward a small door at the front of one of the tiny *bohios*. Christi followed him inside. As they entered the small room, Christi's nose picked up the smell of burnt wheat flour and old sweat. Once inside, the room appeared to be empty. Then out of the shadows three young men appeared.

The three men had schoolboy faces made old by world-weary eyes. Christi did not like such sadness on such young faces. She stood close beside Kiki.

"Luis! Concha! Roberto." Kiki introduced her as he embraced each in turn. He felt the stiffness of their embraces and knew they were displeased with him.

"Do not be hard with me, *compadres!* I bring you a good woman for she has survived Anita's poison," Kiki offered.

Their disapproving eyes mellowed somewhat as they shook Christi's hand politely and showed some admiration for her surviving Anita's "cure."

The heavy-set man called Luis stood back and eyed her with suspicion. Finally he stepped up and spoke. "This is the friend of Señor Collins?"

Kiki nodded.

Luis was a sweaty-palmed man with a glint of evil in his eye. He had three gold front teeth that needed polishing real bad. When he grinned you knew what he had recently eaten. "You are the one who is the friend of Cosmo Collins? *Está muy malo.* I am sad for you, *señorita,*" Luis intoned with mock sympathy.

Christi looked puzzled.

Kiki stepped up and eyed Luis with contempt. "He was once everyone's friend," Kiki insisted.

Luis stepped back and smirked. "I think he is a friend of the worms now!"

"Shut up, Luis!" Kiki cautioned.

"*Es muerte!* All his friends, we are sad. Kiki has already told you this, no?" Luis ignored Kiki.

Christi knew the horrible meaning of the word *muerte.* She refused to let her mind translate it.

She looked at Luis with disbelief. "I believe they have said that about him many times," Christi offered.

Luis nodded his head and shrugged. "Everyone knows this is true. But this time I think it is much more true."

"Maybe some just wish it was true," Christi challenged.

Luis shrugged as he stepped away from Christi and Kiki. "I only read the papers. They say he is shot trying to escape the Kingston jail. Maybe these newspapers they lie?" Luis shrugged.

Christi tried to ignore him as she turned to Kiki.

Kiki avoided eye contact.

"Maybe you could show me this newspaper?" Christi asked oozing cynicism.

Luis started to make a move.

Kiki held up his hands and stopped him.

Christi gave Kiki a long, cold stare. "There are such papers, Kiki?"

"I have not seen such papers."

"That's not what I asked."

"I know what you ask. I say let it go."

"No! If Luis has them I want to see them."

Kiki thought it over a long moment. He shrugged and motioned for Luis to get the paper.

Moments later, Luis returned with a Spanish language newspaper.

He threw it at Christi's feet. He and Kiki exchanged angry glances as Christi picked it up. Christi's Spanish was rusty but the picture of Cosmo combined with the word "terrorist" and *muerte* was enough to shake her for a moment.

"My mother told me not to believe anything I read in newspapers." Christi quickly regained her composure.

"Your mother has spoken truly," Kiki agreed.

Christi glanced at the paper once more and threw it at Luis's feet. "*Basura!*" Christi insisted in fluent Castilian Spanish.

"Garbage? Maybe this is so. Maybe not. *Quién sabe pero Dios!*" Luis grinned a disgusting dirty gold grin.

Christi felt queasy but she did not want to let down in front of Kiki and his men. She took a deep breath and blew it out hard. She gave Kiki a steady gaze. "Where is my dress?"

Kiki looked puzzled.

"My yellow cotton dress!"

"Oh? This one I have had fixed up nice for you. It hangs in the closet in the next room."

Without replying Christi moved quickly into the adjoining room. Once there, she proceeded directly to the closet and lifted the yellow cotton dress out. She felt better just seeing it. She took it off the hanger and held it close hiding her face and her fears in the softness of its familiar warmth.

"Are you okay, Christi?" Kiki poked his head in the door.

Christi did not look at him as she replied. "Is it true?"

"About Cosmo?"

"Yes."

"It's what the papers say."

"Don't tell me that. What do you believe?"

"You really want to know?"

Christi nodded slow agreement.

"Would you trust my answer?"

Christi thought it over as she looked at the love in his eyes. "You would like for it to be true."

"No, Christi. I know you would never come to me if I wished for this thing."

"God, Kiki! It has to be a big mistake," Christi said weakly as she held the dress even closer.

Kiki studied the look on her face. She looked like a child lost and desperate to find her parents. He wanted to take her in his arms but felt a coldness between them that made him back away.

"You know Cosmo, how he was, how he hated confinement. He tried to escape. I am sorry. There was a time when I loved him too."

Christi looked at him with tears in her eyes. "At least you had the time to love him."

Kiki almost touched her face when she got up and moved away. He was about to follow her when Roberto entered the room and whispered something in his ear. Kiki gave Christi one more look and moved out of the room. As he entered the next room where Luis and his other men waited he stopped and looked serious.

"Moncada. Tomorrow it begins! The day we have hoped for is here!" Luis intoned with pride.

They all shared a hug of victory, broke out a bottle of rum and started sharing it. As they drank, Luis' laughter turned to a mischievous grin.

"You have something to say, Luis?"

"Cosmo's woman. She must not know of this!"

"I will take care of it."

"Ah! After the tears she will be yours, *amigo?* I have helped much, no?" Luis was pleased with himself.

Kiki almost shook Luis's arm off his shoulder. "No! It was wrong. Soon enough, I will tell her the truth."

Luis looked cynical then scornful.

Kiki glared at Luis then turned for the door.

Roberto held him back. "Luis is right, Kiki. Tomorrow is too important. We have decided the woman cannot know of this!" Roberto intoned seriously.

Kiki looked at him in disbelief then respect. He scanned the serious eyes of his men. His men nodded agreement in unison. Kiki sat down on an old crate and sighed.

Sitting quietly in the next room, Christi watched out of the small window at the little children playing in the open sewer. The sun was high and the smell of raw sewage made her eyes water, but did not seem to bother the children. She slid down against an adobe wall and hugged her dress. Mrs. White and Sarah had never let Christi feel sorry for herself. Christi did not now.

She was simply confused. Christi did not understand herself. How could she understand how she felt about others. The romantic ideas she had only dreamed about a few weeks ago had become reality all too fast. Sarah forbade her to date or even talk to men. Her stepfather had been her only close encounter with a man.

She shivered as she remembered that moment. Before Cosmo, she had no experience dealing with romance. Romance was something in a book. It was not real men holding you and making you feel alive and good. It was not the real pain of losing someone you loved.

Kiki had shown her strength and kindness. He was a good man with a generous heart. Yet she feared him more than she cared for him. She sensed his feelings for her, knowing that soon she would have to hurt his feelings by turning him away. In her heart, Christi saw Kiki as a man to be respected like a good father, a kind brother, a friend sought out in time of trouble.

To her he was a wonderful, good person to be loved, like you loved Christmas and teddy bears.

Christi tried to compare Cosmo and Kiki as Sarah and Mrs. White had taught her to compare men. "Choose the man of breeding and means or the man of power. Between the two choose the man of power for he can obtain all else."

Christi considered them to be equal in both those respects. Neither had any means, little apparent breeding and were as powerless as she.

Kiki made her feel comfortable and cared for.

Kiki did not excite every fiber of her being like Cosmo had. Cosmo was so vibrant she would not believe he was dead until she saw his dead body herself. Yet she knew that would be impossible because she could never bear to look at it.

She looked up at the clear blue Caribbean sky through a grove of coconut palms. She tried to cry but the tears would not come. It was a horrible feeling. She was a thousand miles from home, completely dependent on people she barely knew. It was a wearying, numbing, exhausting feeling of powerlessness.

Christi hated that feeling. She despised not being able to take some action when confronted with problems.

She hated the confusion being powerless brought with it and

loathed the thought of anyone having control of her life.

Her young heart was maturing with a bent toward malevolence.

As she began to discover herself she wondered how dumb it was to love someone like Cosmo Collins. After all, Cosmo was understanding, but not basically kind. He had absolutely no sense of family. He was a loner who actively sought out trouble, and he was a major cause of a lot of self-inflicted mischief.

He was an impish Irish leprechaun who did not deserve the attention of someone of her grace and beauty.

She decided he would no longer be in her thoughts until she found herself lost in wave after wave of rolling tears she did not bother to hide.

Christi stopped crying when she saw the tears were staining her yellow cotton dress.

She was angry with herself for letting anything make her do that. She gathered her composure and promised herself never again would she be totally dependent on anyone.

Never again did she want to feel helpless, alone, and powerless.

She sensed the Peter Pan in her young soul was losing out to a mean world of Captain Hooks. She did not want to grow up, but to survive she would do whatever it took.

She rubbed her eyes and started to go join Kiki in the other room. She paused as she saw Garbo standing over her.

Garbo growled displeasure as he stood over Christi, his huge shadow blocking out the sun.

His towering presence was intimidating but Christi did not show fear.

Garbo seemed impressed by her courage. He found a tissue and dabbed a tear from the corner of her eyes.

"Kiki makes such tears?" Garbo asked.

Christi remembered Kiki said Garbo only spoke to people he liked. She felt honored that he would speak to her.

"No! Just a little homesick. Thank you for your concern."

Garbo handed her the tissue and moved into the next room.

Roberto and Luis both stepped aside as Garbo stormed into the room.

"Are we ready? So soon," Kiki said rhetorically as Garbo stepped in front of him and glared.

"*La señorita!* She cries." Garbo growled.

Kiki looked puzzled for a moment. "Christi? I had to tell her the bad news about Cosmo. She read the papers. She will be alright," Kiki soothed.

Garbo frowned in disapproval. "There will be no more tears!" Garbo threatened.

Kiki smiled. "So, you have taken a liking to her also? *Es bueno,* my big friend!"

Garbo looked a little embarrassed.

"Garbo, my special friend, please believe me, the last thing I want to do is hurt her," Kiki trailed off as Christi entered the room, feeling very embarrassed.

All eyes turned toward her. Some of them filled with a quiet loathing.

Garbo stepped between Christi and the condemning eyes. His presence made them turn away.

"Are you okay? How do you feel?" Kiki asked.

"Just very embarrassed. Tell your friends I'm not always so childish."

"I will. But they have to be going. Right, Luis?"

Luis shrugged. He turned to leave and was soon followed by the others.

Garbo watched them leave before he turned to Kiki. He stared at Kiki with eyes that conveyed a quiet understanding. Finally, he seemed satisfied. He took one last look at Christi and left the room.

Suddenly she and Kiki were alone.

Christi was sad and afraid. She was still sad for Cosmo. She was afraid for Kiki's feelings. The small room felt even smaller. The summer morning felt cold.

Kiki approached her slowly, taking her gently into his arms. He held her gingerly until she relaxed. It felt good to have his arms around her but she fought off allowing herself to like it too much.

Kiki took her face in his hands and kissed her softly on the mouth.

Christi felt the same urges she had felt on the beach. She closed her mouth tight.

Kiki broke the kiss and backed away.

"I understand your feelings, *mi corazón.* I loved Cosmo as much as you. But you know how he was."

"He did not linger on such things. He would want you to go on with your life. *Por favor,* forgive me for saying this now, but I hope I can be a part of that life, Christi," Kiki said as he opened his arms to her.

"I don't want to think about such things right now."

Kiki lowered his arms. "I understand. I have a very important meeting to go to this day. We will have a nice dinner when I return. We can talk about things then. I'm sorry, Christi. I wish there was more time to be more civilized. I am not always so quick with the heart. This place will be yours for the day. Only Garbo will remain to watch over you. Please rest," Kiki said with sincere concern.

He let his eyes linger on Christi's lovely face.

Christi looked into his eyes. How they sparkled when he looked at her. It was very disarming. "Thank you for everything, Kiki. You are a wonderful man," Christi said with affection.

Kiki stepped back and looked irritated.

"I am not your father or your brother, Christi. I am a man that loves you. Understand?" Kiki's voice trembled. "I want from you. I want some fire when you hold me . . . or maybe we do not hold each other at all. I must go now!" Kiki snapped.

Before Christi could reply, he picked up his hat, turned and stomped out of the room.

Christi shook her head in amazement at the volatility of the Latin temperament. Moments after Kiki was gone, Garbo poked his head through the torn-curtain doorway. He looked around and seemed satisfied. "There will be no more tears!" He ordered.

Christi nodded.

"Yes, thank you, Garbo. Everything is fine. I think I'll take a little nap. I'm very tired." Christi smiled.

Garbo closed the curtain tightly and left Christi alone in the semi-darkness of the *bohio.*

Christi sat on the side of a shaky bunk. Her thoughts drifted to memories of home. She wondered how Sarah was doing. She hoped Lucius's brother wasn't going to try anything to get even. "No, he was too afraid of Sarah for that." Christi laughed as she thought of the irony of sitting on a rickety straw bed in a shanty in the poorest slum in Cuba. It was the complete opposite of Sarah's and Mrs. White's plans for her.

"A lady of elegance," Christi laughed. "If they could only see me now!" she half-laughed. "Oh God! Please don't let them see me now," Christi prayed quietly as she started to lay back on the bed. She stopped when she heard a noise from the back of the room. She felt uneasy as she heard faint footsteps and saw a spooky shadow on the wall. She got up and started to move outside to get Garbo.

"*Por favor!* Please, *señorita,* don't leave. I can talk with you please?" A kindly looking older lady pleaded as she stepped out of the shadows and addressed Christi.

"I am Consuela. I am Kiki's mother. Please can we talk *un momento?*"

"What?" Christi was caught off guard.

"He did not speak of me to you?"

"No!"

"He speaks to me much about you."

Christi did not feel comfortable with this woman but she was reluctant to offend. "Garbo is outside. Maybe you want to see him?"

"You say this because you fear me?"

"I'm too tired to fear anything right now."

"Then I can have a moment?"

"Sure. Why not?" Christi shrugged.

Consuela nodded politely and sat down.

Christi sat down in a chair beside her.

Consuela looked very tired as she stared into Christi's eyes. Christi had seen the same look in Sarah's eyes when Sarah was world-weary.

Christi could tell that beneath the tired look was a once-beautiful woman. A beauty grown old before her time.

"I must tell you some things and I must trust you. That is why I study your eyes. *Por favor,* I am not to be rude, but I can see if you are to be trusted in your eyes. *Es muy importante!*" Consuela said evenly.

Christi gave Consuela a steady gaze.

Consuela seemed satisfied. "Kiki will go to war tomorrow. He will most probably be killed," Consuela said coolly.

She paused for Christi's reaction.

"He seems to know what he's doing," Christi replied.

"They will go against Batista who has many trained soldiers. They will lose. There will be much bloody revenge. They think I am an old woman with nothing to say. I have already lost two sons to Batista. I do not want to lose Kiki," Consuela heaved sadly.

"Yes. I understand. But these are grown men."

"No! They are boys playing at war. In the morning when they attack they will find the soldiers waiting for them."

"Have you told Kiki this?"

"I tell him this too many times. I have heard from all his friends he thinks of you *con much gusto* . . . he likes you much. He is my last child. They will not make him go if he does not want to. He has the *macho* as all the young *muchachos*. I think maybe you can talk to him. Maybe you can stop him," Consuela paused. She reached out and took Christi's hand in hers.

"I have lit many candles and said many prayers. I now ask you to help. If I lose Kiki, then my life is over also. If you have some caring for him, you will talk to him. You will stop him, no?" Consuela almost prayed to Christi.

For some reason Christi did not trust Consuela. It showed in her eyes.

Consuela looked hurt. "You will not do this!"

"Look, I really don't know how much influence I have over Kiki. If he won't listen to his mother why would he listen to a friend like me?"

"No. It is much more than friends. Kiki, he does not talk about you like the other *señoritas* before. He speaks of you like one speaks of *la esposa*. He speaks of you with respect and reverence. *Es amor!* He loves you. He will listen to you."

"Other *señoritas*? How many?"

Consuela's face became rigid. Her stare was penetrating and unnerving. "This does not matter now. Now there is none other but you and you are my only hope."

"Don't tell me that. I don't want to be anyone's only hope. Besides what would he do about Luis and the others if he did not fight?" Christi wondered aloud.

"You could both hide in the mountains where he knows many places. You have come to Cuba looking for your aunt. I have friends in Havana who know of Gladys Feliciano. I must tell you she is not the respectable woman. She is a friend of Batista . . . and . . . I am sorry."

"I'm sorry. I don't believe that."

"It is true! She is not the godly woman. She is like the Mary Magdalene. It would not be safe for you in Havana. Your only safety is here with Kiki, alive at your side," Consuela insisted.

"My aunt is a prostitute?" Christi scoffed.

Consuela made a hurried sign of the cross and nodded.

"I know you love your son but you won't help him with such lies."

"I do not lie! Think what you will but you must think of this. Unless Kiki lives, there is only the grave for all of us. You would be dead now if not for him. When he is gone who will save you from those who do not wish you well?" Consuela interrupted.

"I think you'd better go now."

"No! Anita says you are some part Cuban. If so, you must be a spiritual disciple of José Martí, one of the children of Fernando Ortiz. I make the big mistake. Kiki was christened José. I named Kiki after José Martí and I make him read all the maddening books."

"I really don't see what this has to do with me."

"Please. I will tell you. Pedro, Kiki's grandfather, died in a battle along with Martí. His father was killed by Machado's men, before the 'Little Sergeant' Batista comes to power. Batista is responsible for Kiki's brothers' deaths. Kiki has much reason to hate the government. I understand this. Because I understand this, I know he will kill or be killed unless someone he loves softens his heart. I have lost too much already. *Por favor,* I do not want to lose him,"

Consuela reached over and lay her hand on top of Christi's hand.

Christi patted Consuela gently on the hand. A child consoling a mother. Christi knew how strong-willed Kiki was. She knew there was nothing she could say that would deter him from something he wanted to do.

She also knew Consuela needed a little hope.

"I will do what I can but I can promise nothing," Christi said sincerely.

Consuela looked at Christi with misty eyes. "And he must not know I have come to you. If you do this thing I wish for you many blessings on you and yours, *señorita.*"

Consuela leaned over and gave Christi a kiss on the forehead.

Christi feigned a smile.

Consuela gave her one last hard look, made the sign of the cross and left the room.

Garbo poked his head into the room moments after Consuela was gone. He looked around and looked puzzled.

"It's just me, thinking out loud," Christi smiled.

Garbo looked skeptical.

"I'm okay, Garbo. No one is here." Christi smiled warmly.

Garbo took one more quick look around the hut. He seemed satisfied and mumbled under his breath and went back outside.

Christi sat back on the creaky bunk and leaned against the damp wall. She was still a little weak from her bout with fever and the sad news of the morning made her very tired.

She fluffed up the one small pillow on the bunk and lay down on it. She was tired of all the Cuban intrigue and talk of war and dying. All she wanted now was for them all to leave her alone with her dreams of her lost love, Cosmo.

No matter what any of them told her, or what she read in the papers, she would never believe Cosmo was dead.

"Cosmo, I love you. I will always love you and I don't believe them. They just want me to help with their stupid war. Well, I won't let them drag me into it. I will find some way to survive and I'll be here whenever you come to me!" Christi tossed feverishly. "I will not betray you for anyone. I will be yours and only yours forever. I'll find you again someday. I will! I will my darling! I promise!" Christi swore to the heavens with all her heart before she slipped into a passionate dream of love.

Standing in the shadows just outside Christi's window, Consuela listened and her heart filled with hatred.

Chapter Sixteen

CHRISTI'S DREAMS OF COSMO WERE INTERRUPTED BY IMAGES OF Kiki lying dead before her and Consuela pointing to her as the cause. "God! Why can't they all just leave me alone?" Christi swore in a half-awake stupor. Christi resented the adult world she had been thrown into so rudely. Everybody wanted something from her. All she had of value was a yellow cotton dress and a lot of doubt about everything. She felt she had so little to give and everyone wanted so much. If they didn't want something, they made you make hard decisions about serious adult things. They had many more years to think about these things. Why didn't they have all the answers?

Christi would be eighteen in a few days. If she lived until then she would finally, legally be an adult. Yet Christi knew deep inside she was still some part a frightened little girl. She had aged rapidly in the last few months without gaining any wisdom.

Christi wished Sarah were around. She wished she knew how to find her way to Havana. She wished Cosmo would come take her in his arms and whisk her away to a remote castle in Ireland.

"Christi, are you sleeping?" Kiki asked softly as he entered the room and took a seat in a chair by her bed.

Christi opened her eyes slightly.

It was good to see Kiki's pleasant face.

He looked clean and polished in a freshly starched and ironed uniform. He took her hand in his and held it firmly. His touch felt nice and comforting. She looked at him fondly.

"I missed you today. I'm sorry, the business, it takes so long. Ah! But it is over now. Now it is time for the dinner. But first, you can take the bath." Kiki smiled as he handed her a bar of soap with a rope on it. "And maybe, if you wish, you could put on this for me?" he concluded with a flourish as he handed her a present wrapped in shiny paper.

Christi took the present and tore off the wrapping as thrilled as a kid on Christmas morning. "Oh, Kiki! Oh! It's lovely. It really is!" Christi giggled as she stood up and held the elegant black dress in front of her. It was strapless and very feminine in all the right places.

It was exactly the type of dress she had always wanted to wear but Sarah had forbidden.

"It is the most elegant dress I could find in this place. Someday I will buy you a very fine one," Kiki insisted.

"Oh, no! This is perfect! What about shoes? I need some black spike heels and some really sheer nylons to go with it!" Christi bubbled as she gave him a quick kiss on the cheek.

"Oh? I see. I will find them for you soon. I promise."

"Okay. I'll take a shower and try it on now."

Kiki laughed. "We have no shower. There is a tub in the other room. I will have Garbo fill it for you."

Christi lay the dress on the bed.

She reached up and put her arms around Kiki's neck like she had done to her favorite Uncle Eli. She gave him a niece's kiss.

She started to pull away.

Kiki lifted her under her arms. He held her at arm's length. Christi delighted in the secure feeling of his strength.

Kiki pulled her to him and kissed her fiercely on the lips. He lay her across the bed and pressed his weight on top of her and she became absorbed in the hypnotic warmth of his kisses, until she remembered the dress.

"Oh no! Not the dress. You'll wrinkle it! Get up, Kiki. Get up!" Christi demanded.

Reluctantly, Kiki backed off. He stood up and looked down at her, frowning.

Christi picked up the dress and examined it. "Oh, it's okay. Oh, good," she sighed.

Kiki started to reach for her but the spell was broken. He lowered his arms and shrugged. He pondered her girlish ways and pined for the woman behind them. "I'm going to start the preparations for dinner. Garbo will fill the bath. You take a bath, get dressed and join me in the kitchen. We have the *bohio* to ourselves so maybe we will have a nice dinner, no?" Kiki winked.

Christi was too busy with a mock fitting of the dress to respond. "Also a string of pearls."

"What?"

"Silly man! Basic black requires a string of pearls. Okay?"

"Okay!"

Kiki shook his head in dismay as he made his way outside to look for Garbo.

Christi took her time soaking in the bath. It was the most relaxed she had been in a long time and without realizing it she dropped off to sleep. It seemed as if she had slept only minutes when she felt a gentle hand on her bare shoulder, shaking her awake.

She looked up to find Kiki looking a little embarrassed.

"I was worried. You have been in here for two hours. Are you alright?" he asked as his eyes fell on her naked breasts.

Christi jumped up, grabbed a towel and wrapped around her naked body. "Out! Out, Kiki! Out!" Christi shouted.

Kiki paused for a moment, looking at her.

Christi could see the love and lust in his eyes. She turned her back on him.

"Okay! But hurry. I'm hungry and the dinner is overcooking." He paused. "As am I."

"Out! I mean it!"

Kiki gave her a long look then turned and left her in the room alone.

Christi dried herself nervously. She was mad at Kiki, at first. Her ire cooled as she put on the new dress. It fit her perfectly and the way it framed her curves made her feel like a grown woman. Even without the stockings, the shoes and the pearls she felt she was ready for any cotillion. There was a cracked mirror in the room. She abandoned herself to vanity and took measure of herself from all angles.

She could hear Mrs. White's voice warning her against excessive vanity, but then where the hell was Mrs. White when she was needed on the *Calamaria Princess!*

Kiki was sitting on the rough-hewn kitchen table playing a tune on a guitar when Christi made her grand entrance. He stopped in mid-strum and looked at her, his mouth widely agape.

"*Está muy, muy bonita, mi corazón!*" He paused and sniffed the air. "And you smell nice, also," he smiled as he put down the guitar and got up to greet her with a hug.

"No! Don't mess me up. I'm not as altogether as I wanted to be, but I had limited working material," Christi pulled back coyly.

"Okay, my little *mariposa.* Your way for a little longer . . . but not much longer," Kiki said ominously before he cracked a slight smile. "Now, I will fix you Kiki's famous frijoles and carne. But first we will share this bottle of Madeira I have saved for a little while." He bubbled as he uncorked a bottle of wine and poured Christi a glass.

Christi wasn't much of a wine drinker but it was hard to refuse Kiki after receiving such a gift. She wondered if the wine would make her unable to resist him when she had to, or if she would want to.

"You understand I do not let everyone see me do this woman's work. It is not good for the men to see me doing these things, but I like to mix with the foods," he laughed as he tossed things in pans and gulped wine, stopping to sit beside her for brief moments.

Christi has some sense of the extent to which this was a humble, non-macho act and she was a little overwhelmed by Kiki's gesture. "This is very good wine. I haven't drank a lot of wine but this is good," Christi offered as Kiki served her a plate of food.

Kiki smiled, then looked deeply into Christi's eyes as he put his arm gently around her shoulders. "You are truly *la señorita bonita.* I thought this when I pulled you from the ocean. I also think this is lucky for you that I am there. But it is I who was very lucky," he bubbled as he drew his mouth close to her.

Christi was less nervous now. The part of her that had wanted to run was numb while the part that wanted to stay beside Kiki was mellow. "Thank you, Kiki. The food is very good. You are a good cook."

"You will not say this in front of the men?"

"No! Your secret is safe with me."

They laughed together.

Kiki stopped laughing and looked serious.

"Do you like me, *señorita?*" he asked as he drew even closer.

"Yes. Of course, Kiki. I like you very much," Christi replied.

"Then why are you so nervous?"

"Maybe it's the wine."

"I do not think so. It is thoughts of another. I know this." Kiki kissed her gently on the cheek and smiled. "I would like to make love to you, but I do not believe you want me." He withdrew.

Christi nervously swallowed some wine before replying. "It's not you, Kiki. I told you, I swore I would be married. You are Catholic. You respect that. Don't you?" Christi looked coy.

Kiki looked at her in disbelief for a moment, then shook his head in admiration. "Then this thing you tell me is true. You have not been with a man? Not even . . . Cosmo?" he almost whispered.

"No! I have not."

"Then you are truly the most wonderful lady. I love you. Will you marry me?" Kiki blurted.

Christi stared at him in disbelief.

"I am sorry. I would not do this but the wine sometimes makes me *loco*. I say the *estúpido* things," Kiki apologized.

Christi's head was buzzing with a mixture of wine-soaked thoughts that left her too dizzy to reply for a moment.

"*Jesús Cristo,* I have embarrassed you too much. I am very much embarrassed also." Kiki blushed.

Christi studied Kiki's boyish blush. "You don't have to be embarrassed. I think it was flattering." She looked deep into his eyes.

"Maybe it is just the wine. Maybe I am just too afraid of tomorrow. It is very crazy, but this is the strangeness you have over me." Kiki looked very sad.

"Oh? Then you didn't mean it?"

Kiki looked to see if she was mocking him. He seemed satisfied she was not.

"I do not make a joke when I speak of marriage."

Christi looked at his serious eyes. "Is this because of what will happen tomorrow?"

"What has that to do with anything?" Kiki looked at her suspiciously.

"You plan to attack this Batista guy, don't you?" Christi replied.

"Who tells you this?"

Christi thought better of replying.

"Ah! Consuela." Kiki uttered under his breath in anger. "*Mi madre.* My mother, has she been here today? She has talked to you."

Christi looked him straight in the eye. "No, I heard some of your men talking."

"Please do not lie. My mother she does these things. She is a little *loco* with the old age."

"I don't think so. She's just very worried."

"So! She did come to you."

"I'm not blind, Kiki. Those weren't good guys chasing us through the jungle a few days ago. We always seem to be running, so they must have us outnumbered. I like you. I don't want you to get hurt," Christi lied with such ease she amazed herself.

Cosmo would have been proud of her.

Kiki grunted in displeasure. "We might be outnumbered, but we believe the soldiers do not wish to defend an unjust cause."

"What if they do?"

"No matter. The people will join us and make the revolution unstoppable. But maybe it is a little bit possible that we are wrong," Kiki almost whispered.

Christi nodded understanding.

"I helped nurse my grandfather through a shotgun wound. It was ugly. I don't want that for you."

"I move too fast. I am known as the 'bullet dodger.'" Kiki tried to feign laughter.

Christi gave him a cold stare. "I will go to Havana if you go to war."

Kiki touched her hair gently. His eyes were impressed by her concern. "You cannot go to Havana and I must go to war."

"So I just stay here and wait for the bad news?"

"Why do you not have some faith in me and our cause?"

"I'm from the South, Kiki. I know all about lost causes."

Kiki was stunned for a moment. Then he nodded and sighed hard. "If I die I know exactly what it's for. If I do not fight I would be killed anyway or suffer many years in prison. You would want this for me?"

Christi shook her head and studied the intensity on his face. Suddenly Christi realized if Kiki died she would be all alone in a very strange and hostile land. She shuddered when she thought about what Luis or one of the others would do to her without Kiki's protection. It was hard to dismiss nice romantic notions and concentrate on such mean things but her fears told her she had to be practical. She did not like being practical.

Sarah and Mrs. White were practical. That's what old people were like.

Yet she knew to survive she would have to imitate them.

Christi felt the urge to grab Kiki and hold onto him.

She knew somewhere in her confused heart she wanted him for the wrong reasons. She didn't care. She needed to have him make her feel safe and secure. She remembered Consuela's words, "Without him alive, it is the grave for all of us."

She looked at his handsome features and the love in his eyes and decided it was best to keep him around awhile.

"Kiki, did you mean it when you said you wanted to marry me?"

Kiki looked happy, then confused. "You wish to make fun of me?"

"I'm very serious."

Kiki studied her face. "You know this is something I wish with all my heart. I ask you not to toy with me."

"If I married you would you forget about tomorrow? Could we go up to the mountains and stay out of this war? I will marry you if you forget about tomorrow," Christi insisted.

Kiki started to agree. His hands writhed with indecision. His face told Christi he could never forget about tomorrow. He turned away, then turned back and looked at her. "Would you marry me for love?" he asked firmly.

"What kind of question is that?"

Kiki looked disappointed for a moment. He stared at her with a look of censure.

"I know I love you, Christi. I will wait for you to say this to me. I do not know about tomorrow. If that is what you most sincerely desire . . . perhaps it is possible. I would give up much to get much. You make me mad with crazy thoughts. I would have you more than I would have life . . . but tomorrow is also my life."

"I would not want to have you just for one night, Kiki."

Kiki opened his mouth to lie to her. He hesitated.

She looked almost indifferent.

He kissed her hair gently. "I do not know, *mi corazón*. Maybe tomorrow is not to ever be . . . maybe . . . if I could just fight this one battle, then no more. Will you marry me if I fight this one last battle and then no more?"

Christi touched him gently on his soft, warm lips. "If you really want me, you want to live. If you really want me you will marry me tonight and we will go away to safety tomorrow," Christi said as she kissed him gently on the neck and stroked his back.

Kiki trembled beneath her touch. He seemed lost in another world. He slipped his strong arms around her waist and kissed her almost politely on her cheek and forehead. His eyes gleamed with love. "I wish I had a thousand years to do this in the proper way, but I do not, so I hurry everything up. I will do as you desire. Oh, *querida mia!* In my heart there is a consuming passion for you. How could I kill anyone with so much love in my heart? If you will marry me I will love you for always." Kiki seemed very nervous and looked away for a moment.

Christi pulled his lips down on hers and kissed him hard until his lips relaxed and there was no tension in his body.

"I would be very proud to be your wife," she whispered as their lips parted an instant.

Kiki looked at her with love in his eyes as he returned her kisses and held her in a tight embrace. "You have made me a very happy man. I will go now and make the arrangements with the priest. Garbo will take you to my sister Maria's where you can get ready for the wedding. *Está bien?*" Kiki looked at Christi anxiously.

"Can it be done so fast? Is it legal?" she wondered aloud.

"It is the revolution. The priest understands these things. Everyone understands these things!" Kiki said as he drew Christi up in his arms and kissed her with a passion they almost became lost in before Christi somehow found the strength to gently push him away.

"After the wedding, Kiki. You will have me after the wedding," she whispered in his ear.

"*Sí!* Yes, after the wedding."

He shuddered as they held each other quietly.

Chapter Seventeen

THE WEDDING PARTY GATHERED AT 10 P.M., JULY 25, 1951, IN A FRESHLY scrubbed *bohio* in the poorest part of the slums of Santiago de Cuba. Christi had watched in amazement as Maria, Kiki's lovely sister, had put the affair together on such short notice. Everything was done under the watchful eye of Consuela who kept giving Christi strokes of approval to her face while she fumed with hatred behind Christi's back. Christi was not comfortable with all that had passed between her and Consuela, but it seemed too late to turn back now.

On the practical side, Christi knew deep down she was saving her life and Kiki's as well. On the romantic side, she had reservations but convinced herself she would work them out tomorrow. There was no time to get a formal wedding dress so Christi wore her yellow cotton dress with a white mantilla to cover her head and a pair of Maria's off-yellow low heels for shoes. She had wanted to save her favorite dress to wear at her wedding to Cosmo. The fact that she might be married when she found Cosmo was a minor detail to be worked out later. She felt strangely at ease as she placed the white lace mantilla on her head.

She liked the look of innocence it gave her. Christi approached her wedding more like a high school field day than serious business. Everyone around her was nervous and excited. She was mostly bored.

"Are you married, Maria?" Christi asked as Maria adjusted Christi's dress before a full-length mirror.

Maria looked at Christi in the mirror. Their eyes met. Maria's eyes looked sad as she shook her head.

"I'm sorry. I didn't mean to pry."

"It's okay. All my sisters they have many children so I can stay the *señorita* forever."

Christi smiled with sympathy. She wondered what Maria really thought of her. Christi desperately wanted a girlfriend and hoped Maria would be one. "Do you approve of this marriage, Maria?"

Maria looked angry for a brief moment before she shrugged.

"Why don't you tell me what's bothering you? I would like to be your friend."

Maria gave her a few finishing touches before she replied. "I am hoping you love him."

Christi had no immediate reply. She did not have to. Maria saw her answer in Christi's hesitation and the downcast look in her eyes.

"He is a good man, Maria. I will try to make him happy."

"I do not want to see him hurt."

"I won't hurt him. I promise."

"I believe he loves you too much."

"I have strong feelings for him, Maria. I am open to the love you hope for."

Maria looked doubtful before she smiled. "You will not tell him we speak of these things?"

"Oh, no!"

"*Gracias!*"

"Can we be friends?"

Maria hesitated.

"When you come to tell me you truly love my brother I would be glad to be your friend."

Christi did not reply as Maria led her to the door leading into the makeshift wedding chamber. Maria looked her up and down once more, nodded approval, then opened the door.

"It is time," Maria announced.

Christi took Maria's hand. "Thank you. Will you give the bride away?"

Maria looked stunned for a moment. She pulled her hand from Christi's and shook her head. "This is not for me."

Christi felt hurt by Maria's rejection but hoped in time to make her a friend.

They perked their ears as they heard the sound of a guitar coming from the other room.

"You must go now!" Maria insisted as she stepped back into the shadows.

Christi took a deep breath and blew it out hard as she moved into the makeshift wedding chamber.

Luis strummed a semblance of a wedding march on an old wooden guitar as Christi entered the room. There was a smattering of applause from the small group.

Christi nodded a polite greeting. Anxiously she looked for Kiki. For a moment she could not find him in the candlelit room. Finally, her eyes found his.

He looked very handsome in the candlelight. "Maybe it isn't a mistake," she thought to herself.

A tired-looking, kind-faced young priest stood before a makeshift altar and seemed somewhat uncomfortable as he instructed an assistant to give Christi some papers to sign.

Christi signed them quickly, then reached over and took Kiki's extended hand.

Christi had always dreamed of a big church wedding and she knew that was what her mother would have wanted. As she stood in the flickering candlelight of the small room and held Kiki's hand, it didn't seem to matter.

She prayed silently that her mother would understand.

"Welcome all," the priest intoned as Christi stood beside Kiki in the soft candlelight of the small orange-crate alter and held his hand fiercely.

As the priest continued the words were beautiful, though she only faintly heard them. They seemed to pass her ears as a pleasant rhythm without meaning. Then there was a strange quiet and everyone was staring at her.

"*Señorita?* Please, you must answer," the priest looked frustrated.

"Oh!"

"*Sí* or No."

"Oh? Yes. I will!"

Kiki sighed in relief.

"Kiki?" The priest turned to Kiki.

"*Sí!* I do."

"You are now man and wife. *Vaya con Dios.*" The Priest gave them his blessing as Christi fell deep into Kiki's arms and enjoyed a long, wonderful wedding kiss that helped dismiss all her fears.

When they broke the kiss Christi's eyes found Maria's. Christi held her breath until Maria smiled approval.

Suddenly a hundred arms were around them both and Christi was being kissed by men she had never seen before. She didn't care and was soon so caught up in the spirit of things she was kissing them back. Kiki tried to act as if the touching and kissing of his bride didn't bother him until the kisses became much too familiar. Pretending to dance a tango he lifted her up and whirled her towards a far corner. Then he pulled her along through a narrow hallway that led outside to the small house he had rented. Kiki started to lead her through the door, but Christi balked.

"Lift me up, silly man!"

Kiki looked confused.

"Carry me through the door. The threshold," she needled.

"Oh! Yes. I'm sorry. Here, my lovely bride. We must respect each other's customs, of course." He laughed as carried her into the small house.

Once inside he put her down in a large chair.

Christi took three deep breaths.

Kiki looked at her lovingly as he lit a kerosene lamp. "I apologize for going too quickly, *mi corazón*. But I do not think it takes long to know when you have found the right one. I knew it moments after you are on the deck of my boat. It is a matter of the heart and does not mean anything to the mind. . .

"I want to keep this special moment forever in my heart," Kiki said as he held out his hands and pulled her gently toward his arms.

"That's nice, Kiki."

"I do not have much to give you, but I give you this because it was my mother's and her mother's and has much more value than money can buy," Kiki said as he took a crucifix from his pocket and hooked the clasp around her neck.

"But I have nothing to give you," she said sadly.

"Do not say this." Gently he took her face in his hands and kissed her lovingly. He picked her up and carried her into a small bedroom. Carefully he lay her on the bed and lay down beside her before he replied.

"You have agreed to be my wife forever. You are most beautiful and I am the most lucky man to have this honor. You have given me the greatest gift of all. You make me proud to be a man," he said sincerely.

Christi got up from the bed and slowly and carefully placed the lace mantilla on a chair. She smiled at her husband as she slowly slipped out of the her dress.

She was surprised she felt no shame. She thought about Sarah and

Mrs. White. She felt good in the knowledge she had not betrayed them. She had kept her promise and been lawfully married by a priest in a religious ceremony. It was strange so simple a ceremony had seemed to relieve her of much of her maidenly modesty. She suddenly felt a sense of sexual freedom. Now it would be alright to enjoy being a woman. She thought even Sarah and Mrs. White would approve of her being married by a priest.

She did not let herself think about the other part of her promise—to marry a man of means. For now Christi did not care about anyone's approval. She was mellow with wine and the thoughts of having sex without guilt.

Gracefully she turned and walked toward the bed where her husband waited. He stood up and kissed her. He broke the kiss and stepped aside to undress himself. He turned away from her as he did. Christi watched with admiration as he exposed his muscular body, seemingly more ashamed of nudity than she.

When he was undressed, they sat on the edge of the bed a moment. He looked at her lovingly before he slowly took her in his arms and laid her gently down on the bed. This time his movements were quicker and he was silent as he kissed her with an ever-increasing fever.

Christi welcomed his firm, warm body against hers and sighed as his hands caressed her thighs and breasts.

"*Querida mia!*" Kiki whispered as he kissed her neck and let his hot wet tongue track its way until it stopped just short of her erect nipples.

He held his tongue inches from her nipples and looked up at her with a mischievous grin.

Christi grabbed his hair and pulled his hot mouth down on her nipples.

His tongue teased her until his mouth closed around her breasts and he suckled her.

It was the most intense pleasure Christi had ever felt.

"Oh God, Kiki! Do it now!" Christi pleaded as he let his hand run the length of her smooth thighs before she parted her legs slightly. She could feel the pressure from his erection against her leg and was a little afraid. "Kiki, please go slow," Christi whispered.

"I will," Kiki swore as he rolled his firm body on top of hers.

She felt a sharp pain as he tried to enter her. "Oh God, Kiki. It hurts!"

She shuddered.

"I am sorry, *querida mia.* I will wait." Kiki started to pull back.

"No! Go ahead. It's better now."

"Christi. You are a virgin. *Jesús!* You are my virgin bride." He looked contrite and started to back away.

"Where do you think you're going, husband?" Christi grabbed his shoulders and pulled him back.

"I did not want to hurt you."

"Then just do it!"

Kiki sighed agreement. He shuddered with anticipation as he eased back down.

She forced herself to relax and as she did the pain began to ease and she felt her body blend with his. As his thrusts went from long and slow to faster and harder she began to feel nothing but intense pleasure. Once they were in complete rhythm she invited him in deeper and deeper.

"*Jesús! Madre de Dios!*" He shivered with passion as he gathered her body in his strong arms. "Christi, I love you so much," he whispered in between kisses.

"And I love you, Kiki. I can say it! I love you!" Christi murmured weakly as Kiki's thrusts took her mind away from any thoughts except reaching the top of this passionate cliff side—a cliff side she leaped off with a screaming orgasm that was heard the length of the village.

Chapter Eighteen

COSMO'S FACE WAS VIVID BEFORE HER. HE WAS IN PAIN AND REACH-ing out for her across a vast watery distance. She had a life pre-server in her hand and was trying to throw it to him, but someone or something kept holding her arm back. Slowly Cosmo sank beneath the waves as she tried and tried to throw him the preserver, but the force that held her back was too strong. She watched in horror as Cosmo sank out of sight.

She awoke screaming.

As she shook off the dream and faced reality, she realized Kiki was holding her close to his chest and rocking her like Sarah used to when she was a baby.

"Kiki! Oh, Kiki! It was such a horrible dream!" Christi shuddered.

Kiki pulled her closer and kissed her softly on her hair.

"You called for Cosmo. You called his name not mine. Do you dream this dream many times?" Kiki asked stiffly.

"No . . . I don't know. I don't like such dreams. He was dying, Kiki. I saw him dying!" Christi broke Kiki's embrace.

Kiki looked at her in the glow of the early morning moonlight. He did not try to hide his hurt.

There was a sadness about his face Christi had never seen before.

"You wish him to be alive?" Kiki asked matter-of-factly.

Christi sat back on the bed and looked through the small bedroom window toward the bright tropical moon high in the Caribbean sky. Finally she turned and looked at Kiki. "You are my husband, Kiki. It was just a dream."

Kiki gritted his teeth. He stifled his anger. "I give you some little time to forget this man." Kiki turned his back on her. He was quiet for a long moment.

Christi reached out and touched his back. He recoiled and moved further away. Christi moved close and tried to touch him again.

He turned on her and grabbed her arms in his firm hands. Christi had never felt such a powerful grip.

"Dammit, woman! You are married to me! There will be no dreams of anyone else. *Comprendo?* You understand?" Kiki hurt her wrists, he held her so hard.

Christi jerked her arms out of his grip and slapped him hard. Kiki formed a fist with both hands. His eyes were full of anger. It was a frightening dark side she did not like at all and Christi feared for her life.

Kiki mumbled curses under his breath for a long time before he relaxed and hung his head in shame.

Christi took a deep breath and blew it out hard. She sat on the floor and watched him carefully.

He got up from the bed and moved over to the bedroom window. He stared out at the clear sky sparkling with stars and a bright moon. "I do not like jealousy. I have never known it before this night. It is the women who are jealous before this night, not I who weep for them."

"There is no need to be jealous, Kiki."

"I have never understood it, but always the women like Cosmo more than me. To me he is moody, unkempt, and unstable. Am I not more handsome than he?"

Christi was frozen by the question.

"Ha! That is good. I do not want an answer to this question."

"I think . . ."

"No! Forget it. I am sorry if I hurt you." Kiki grimaced.

Christi got up slowly. She walked over to the window and stood a few feet behind Kiki. She marveled at the beauty of his muscular body glistening in the moonlight.

"I married you, Kiki. I told you, it was just a dream," Christi offered.

Kiki turned slowly toward her. He reached out and took her hands in his. He looked at her wrists as he massaged them. "Are you hurt?"

"No. Just a little shook up," Christi sighed.

Kiki pulled her gently into his arms. "*Querida mia!* I love you too much. You make me crazy with such love. Maybe this much love is too crazy," Kiki said sadly.

Christi returned his embrace.

She held him tightly and he seemed to relax. "Kiki, could we go to the ocean?"

"Yes. Someday when it is safe."

"No. Now. This morning. I want to see the sunrise over the ocean. Please?"

Kiki broke their embrace, looking away nervously. "No, this morning is bad. Later we will go for many days."

Christi did not like the tone of finality in Kiki's voice. "I need it this morning."

"Why? There will be many other days."

"Are you sure?"

Kiki could not answer.

"I used to go down to the Oceanside in Charleston when I was little to get well from trouble. Whenever I was upset I used to go down there and sit in a magnolia tree and watch the ocean and the big houses and dream wonderful dreams. The ocean makes me well. Please, let's go there . . . and maybe make love on the beach?"

Kiki was very nervous now. He cracked his knuckles. He held his face in his hands. He took a deep breath and blew it out hard. Finally he walked over to the bed stand, picked up his watch and brought it over to the window. He looked at it and seemed almost satisfied. "Maybe for one hour only we can do this."

"Thank you, my love." Christi gave him a small, affectionate kiss and moved to the small bathroom to freshen up. As she washed her face and put on her makeup, Kiki dressed and left quietly.

He was gone for some time before Christi heard the jeep's motor running outside the front window. For a moment she wondered where he had been, but concentrated on getting ready and thought little else of it.

When she was ready she moved toward the front room. As she walked past the front window her eyes caught Kiki's face in a deeply pensive mood. Christi felt guilty for having such a dream, and then she felt stupid for feeling guilty about it.

Christi watched the displeasure on Kiki's face and knew he was jealous of her feelings for Cosmo. Christi also knew she could not help those feelings and, as she moved toward the door, she knew they would surface again. As she watched Kiki and pondered these thoughts, she wondered if she had made a bad marriage. Cautiously she got into the passenger side of the jeep.

Before she was fully in her seat, Kiki sped off toward the ocean. They said little as the jeep roared through the early morning mists. They were almost there when Kiki broke the silence with a nervous laugh. "We will stay at the beach for one hour before I go to the command post. There we will make love in the surf, but we have to be *mucho* careful in the sand." Kiki tried hard to be funny.

"Command post. Did you say command post?" Christi wondered aloud.

"Yes. I must report in two hours," he answered easily.

"But you are no longer a soldier."

"No, *querida mia,* I am always a soldier."

"What are you talking about?"

"I have to earn money the way I know how."

"You're going to fight that Batista guy, aren't you?"

Kiki chuckled. "Batista? No! I just have to report in and talk a little on the radio to the other men."

Christi let the cool morning air wash her face and hair.

She did not want to pursue the matter any further. She was only slightly worried. She was secure in the knowledge that he loved her enough not to go to war. "It's my honeymoon and we'll talk about happy things. Where we will live. How many children we will have. Those happy things," Christi insisted.

Kiki smiled. "*Niños?* Oh yes. We will have many children."

"Five is my absolute limit!"

"Five? This is not enough. My mother had twelve. We must do better!"

"Oh Lord, it hurts to think about it," Christi held her stomach in mock pain.

Kiki laughed as he turned down a small road that ran between the two rows of palms. He drove out onto a lovely beach that was sparkling with the bright silver light of the Caribbean moon. "Ah, we have made it in time. We will be at our place before the sun is fully on the horizon," Kiki said as he accelerated a little faster.

Christi was mesmerized by the beauty of the dark ocean falling on the sparkling white sand. She felt very much at home now and would not entertain any ugly thoughts. She was going to enjoy every moment with Kiki and dismiss any competing thoughts from her mind.

Kiki pulled the jeep up in a grove of tall pines that stood on a large sand dune which offered a spectacular view of the sea. Kiki extended his hand and led her from the jeep to the highest point.

Once there, he put down a large brown bag by a grove of bright orange flamboyane trees and opened it.

"Now for the big surprise. While you were dressing, I go to the *cantina* and wake up the cook. Since we did not have a wedding dinner, he has made us a wonderful wedding breakfast of my favorite food—*el hamburger grande!*" Kiki announced.

"Hamburgers, in Cuba?" Christi quizzed.

"Ah, yes. I like the capitalistic system for three things. *El hamburger grande* and Coca-Cola and, of course, the beautiful women it produces. Today I have all three," Kiki concluded as he pulled two bottles of Coke from the bag and offered one to Christi.

"Coca-Cola in the morning. Hamburgers in Cuba. What have I gotten myself into?" she kidded as she sat down by the tree.

Kiki knelt down beside her.

"Ah! Not just Coca-Cola," he pulled a bottle of rum from the sack. "But Cuba Libres! And for our love for always and always!"

He handed her a drink.

Christi sipped the rum-laced Coke and almost spit it out. After the first swallow it got easier and she even liked it a little. "Tell me, is it possible to stay right here in this wonderful place forever?" Christi bubbled.

Kiki's face clouded for a moment. "Not now, but soon. When the *colonos* have been chased away, when every *pobrecito* has much land."

"That might never happen."

Kiki looked hurt for a moment. "Yes! This will happen soon. Soon every man will have a job and all the *muchachos* will have food enough to eat. Then we will come here and stay for as long as we want."

"Swear to me now that you are not thinking of going off to that stupid war."

He looked irritated for a moment, then tossed her hair playfully. "You are still too much *americana*. You cannot understand and maybe that is good for us. Maybe I understand too much. I am sorry. For the rest of our time I will not talk of the revolution. I will only talk of happy things." He downed his rum and Coke and poured another.

Christi decided it was best to let him cool down. She drew up beside him and placed her arm around his big shoulders. They stared at the sunrise quietly.

"Tell me, have you ever made love in the surf? In that cool water?"

"Me?" he feigned ignorance. "But I am the virgin also. Last night was my first time."

"Yeah and I'm the queen of England. Come on! Right down there in the waves, before God and the world."

Christi stood up and unzipped the back of her dress.

"But, Christi, the sun will be up soon and the sunbathers will fill the beach." Kiki shook his head.

Christi unbuttoned his shirt and scratched his hairy chest with her long fingernails. "Just tell them it's our honeymoon, they'll understand." She kissed his chest and neck, then turned and ran down into the surf. As she ran, Christi slipped out of her dress and let it fall casually to the sand. The instant her bare feet hit the ocean spray she felt like a little girl again and all bad thoughts left her mind.

Here in the sand and sea she was at peace with the world. Joyfully, Christi threw herself into the crashing surf. The water was delightfully cool and it made her feel clean and unashamed. For a few lovely moments she was home and everything was just right.

Kiki looked somewhat embarrassed as he undressed. Finally he ran into the ocean and joined her. His body felt warm and she grabbed hold of it, pulling his firm muscles against her wet but hot body.

"Don't you just love it!" Christi exclaimed with glee.

Kiki looked doubtful until she pressed closer, then his face lit up and he nodded enthusiastically.

There was love and desire in his generous Spanish eyes as he held her face up with his hands. The ocean crashed around them as Kiki kissed her gently and moved his hands to her waist. Slowly, he lifted her in his arms and lowered them both into the midst of the foamy surf. As the waves hit he placed his back to them so he absorbed the shock.

Christi lay before him in a small eddy of relative calm.

"Oh God! She makes me crazy again!" Kiki whispered to the wind as he slowly bent over Christi and kissed her softly on the navel.

Christi shivered beneath his kiss as a wave knocked him over on top of her. As he fell she broke his fall with her hands, then let them slip around his body until she held him in a firm embrace with her legs locked around his waist. The salt water poured over them, but Christi was oblivious to it as Kiki's passion mounted and his kisses took her breath away.

The next wave rolled them over in a giggling ball of delight as they grabbed for each other and missed several times before they rolled up on the beach in the soft wash of the tide line.

Christi rolled on her back and laughed as she had not laughed for some time.

Kiki rolled over beside her and kissed her slowly and gently the entire length of her body. A cool breeze came off the sea and made his kisses feel even warmer. Christi had not felt all her senses the first time she made love as she did this glorious morning. Kiki's every touch awoke sensations she did not know she had. His fingers gently stroking the nipples of her breasts caused her to almost faint. His kisses made her blood run hot. She had to strain to get her breath.

With wild, unbridled passion she reached out and grabbed Kiki by his long, dark hair. With savage force she pulled him down on top of her and nibbled, almost to biting, on his neck.

Kiki pulled away for a moment and let out a primordial scream. He was about to scream again when Christi dug her nails in his back and pulled him down once again.

As he slowly entered her she was gathered up by the moment and let out a primordial scream that exceeded his.

Kiki paused for a moment. He smiled down at her, then pressed the full weight of his body on hers.

Christi shifted beneath him until she was comfortable, then swallowed his lips with hers.

He made love to her with deep, wonderful thrusts that were pain intermingled with pleasure.

She did not know which one she liked more for they soon became part of a seductive rhythm she never wanted to end.

In white hot heat they were bound together, locked in a rolling ball of sexual fury. They tore at each other like mating lions roaring louder than the surf until they shared a final scream of ecstasy that caused the rising sun to blush.

Chapter Nineteen

THEY BARELY HAD THEIR CLOTHES ON WHEN THE SOLDIERS CAME. Christi and Kiki were holding hands as the grim-faced soldiers approached and Christi could feel the tension in Kiki's hand. As they came closer she felt sick inside. There was no doubt in her mind what the soldiers were coming for. They were coming for Kiki and they were going to take him to war. Christi was still glowing from her lovemaking with Kiki, but the glow quickly faded as the soldiers stopped and motioned for Kiki to join them.

Once again Christi saw a major change coming in her life and she felt helpless to stop it. Once again she was filled with an empty feeling of helplessness she hated with all her heart. "Kiki, let's go home now. Please?" she said as she tried to pull him away.

"No. I must talk with them. Wait here," Kiki commanded as he broke her grip.

Before she could reply, he hurried over and met the soldiers a hundred feet from where Christi waited.

Christi watched with a sad heart as Kiki and the men talked in loud tones and made wild gestures with their arms. Christi turned and walked toward the ocean and gazed at the new light of morning just breaking on the distant horizon. She picked up a few sea shells and absent-mindedly tossed them into the surf.

"I am sorry. I have to go!" Kiki apologized as he lay his strong hand on her shoulder.

Christi was more numb than surprised. She turned slowly toward him and looked him in the eye. "You have to? They can't do it without you? No! You tell them no!" she insisted.

"I do not want this, but I have no choice. I would like your support in this thing."

"What about your wedding night promise? Doesn't that mean anything to you?"

"Of course . . . it means everything . . . please try to understand . . ."

"No! I'm not losing anything else! No! You go and you go to hell!" Christi said angrily and turned her back on him.

Kiki took her by the shoulders and turned her back around. "Do not send me away with these angry words."

Christi shoved him away. "Stay away from me!" She snarled as she backed into the surf.

Kiki started to move toward her.

Christi backed even further into the surf.

Moments later a huge wave knocked her down and she went under. As she struggled to the surface another larger wave hit her and she disappeared. Kiki saw her distress and dove in after her. "Christi! No!" Kiki said in desperation when he came out of the water without her. Frantically he looked around but she was not to be seen. "Christi! I will stay! I will stay! Please! I will stay!" Kiki shouted to the wind.

He was almost in tears when he felt a bump against his leg. He dove in and his hand fell on her body. Quickly he wrapped both arms around her and lifted her out of the water. Gently he lay her on the beach and placed the palms of his hands on her chest.

With measured strokes he pushed water from her lungs until she began to cough, then take short labored breaths.

When she was breathing easier, Kiki held her close. "I'm so sorry, *querida mia!* I do not want to lose you!"

Christi placed her arms around his neck and started to hug him. Instead she pushed away.

"Are you okay?" he asked.

"You will stay?" she said between coughs.

Kiki answered with his silence.

Christi got to her feet and wobbled a little before she regained her balance. "You still intend to leave me?"

"What can I do?"

"What can you do? It's very simple. You tell those soldiers to go away."

Kiki sighed hard.

"Damn you! I married you. I kept my part of the bargain!"

Kiki gave her a hard look and turned away for a long moment. "You did not do this thing for love?"

"What are you talking about?"

Kiki's face contorted with hurt. "Maria has told me of this. I love you but I am no fool. Am I not more the big brother protecting his little sister than your husband?"

"What about last night. Was that brotherly love?"

"Ah, no, *querida mia!* Perhaps for this short time you do love me. When I return we will have much time to decide this."

"If you go with them I will get an annulment!"

"Not in Cuba. My uncle is the bishop."

"God! You've thought of everything haven't you?"

"These things were not planned. They are happenings beyond our seeing."

"So! That's it?"

"I hope in time you will see none of this could be avoided."

"Great! You expect me just to sit around and pine away for my man? Should I take up sewing?"

"It would be a great happiness for me to believe you would wait. But I do not expect you to be here when I return."

"You've got that right!" Christi shook with anger and chills.

Kiki moved toward one of the soldiers and took his coat. He brought it over and placed it around Christi's shoulders. "Maybe you need one of Anita's peppers."

"Oh God! Not that!"

They looked at each other and could not resist laughing. Without realizing it they found each others arms.

Christi held onto him fiercely.

"We will not lose each other, *querida mia!* I will see to it. I will be so careful. I will not bruise my toe. I promise," Kiki said as he kissed her tenderly.

"Oh, Kiki. I did not want to love you . . . but I think I do!" Christi sighed.

"I wish to believe this with all my heart."

"Then stay and I will show you it is true every day."

Kiki started to reply but was interrupted by a chorus of loud shouts from the soldiers urging him to hurry.

"You're going, aren't you?"

"I will be back soon. You will wait?" he asked nervously.

Christi broke their embrace and turned away. She turned back when a huge shadow fell over her. She looked up to see Garbo.

"Garbo will stay close by your side. Soon it will be dangerous everywhere. You are to go nowhere without him." Kiki said firmly.

Christi smiled at Garbo.

Garbo nodded then walked a few feet away.

The soldiers gestured wildly and yelled at Kiki.

"It is time." Kiki grimaced.

"Then go!" Christi shrugged.

Kiki reached for her and put his arms around her waist. He tried to pull her close.

Reluctantly, Christi moved into his embrace.

Kiki stroked her hair, kissing it softly. "It is not good to leave with a lie between us. Since this is not good, I must tell you that Cosmo is not . . . Cosmo, he might still be alive," Kiki sighed.

Christi pulled away from him. "I knew it! Yes! I knew it!"

Her joy at the news visibly hurt Kiki. He released her and stepped back.

"Where is he? Is he coming here? Is he okay?"

Christi persisted, her face bright with anticipation.

Kiki was too hurt to respond.

Christi saw the hurt in Kiki's eyes.

For a brief moment she enjoyed his misery.

"He was shot escaping but no body was found. No one knows where he is." Kiki paused and sighed hard. "If you are fortunate you will see him soon. Goodbye, Christi." Kiki turned to leave.

Christi grabbed his shirt and held him back. "I am your wife, Kiki."

"It's okay, Christi. I have confessed all. I go to do this thing with an easy mind."

"I will be here when you return."

"I will not depend on it."

"You did not think I would love you if I knew he was alive?"

"I loved you too much to take that chance."

"I take wedding vows seriously, Kiki."

"No annulment?"

"I believe it was well-consummated."

Kiki smiled and his eyes danced with fond memories.

Luis moved out of the group of soldiers and shouted for Kiki to hurry.

Garbo glared at Luis.

Luis backed off.

Kiki took Christi by the shoulders, turned her face to his, then kissed her gently. "I loved you from the first moment you are on my boat. For you I will win today. Then I will fight no more."

Kiki looked like a frightened child. Christi could not hold her anger. She reached out and put her arms around his neck. She lay her head tenderly on his chest.

"I do not know what will happen, *querida mia*. Before I fell in love with you, all the answers come easy. I do know I can not do this thing without your love. You do not have to say it. Just pretend with me for a moment." Kiki insisted.

As he held her in a fierce embrace, Christi toyed with her crucifix. She pulled it too hard and the necklace broke and the cross dropped into the sand.

Quickly Kiki reached down and picked up the cross with reverence. He was relieved to see the clasp was only slightly bent. He fixed it and replaced the necklace around Christi's neck. He sighed in relief as he kissed the silver figure of Jesus and made a slow sign of the cross with his hands. Then he kissed Christi on the forehead. "Never, never let this necklace from around your neck. Please promise me, *por favor*. Never, never my love!"

Christi had never seen such fear in Kiki's eyes. "My! You are superstitious. Yes, I promise. It's my favorite wedding gift. Actually it is my only wedding gift," she kidded.

"No! My heart was also given. It will always be with you."

Kiki kissed her with lips hungry for a loving response.

Christi felt like biting his lip but relented and gave him as much a kiss of love as she could fake.

They broke the kiss and he seemed satisfied.

"With your love and the people behind me I have nothing to fear. The people will join us as soon as the Moncada barracks are in our hands. You will know it is over when the streets fill with people cheering for us. Then I will return and we will enter Havana in triumph." Kiki looked happy once more.

Christi looked doubtful for a moment then forced a smile.

"Do not worry, *querida mia*. The soldiers will surrender when they see the anger of the people. History is on our side. How can we lose?"

"Just keep your head down."

"Do not worry. I am bulletproof," he chuckled

Christi did not chuckle with him.

"I will see you when I return?" Kiki looked deadly serious.

Christi half-nodded.

Kiki grimaced. "I must hurry now. They are waiting for me," he said as he kissed her with a long kiss of desperation. His lips searched hers in vain for the hope of love.

Her lips left him cold.

Kiki broke the kiss, turned and walked quickly toward the soldiers.

Christi wiped the kiss from her lips before her husband had disappeared into the mists of the new Cuban morning.

Chapter Twenty

GARBO SAT IN A DIMLY LIT CORNER AND WATCHED CHRISTI intently. His gaze was mellow, but she did not feel comfortable being watched over. She avoided looking at him directly. She tried to busy herself around the small *bohío* that was planned to serve as a dispensary.

It was now past ten o'clock and the small staff was very nervous. The attack should have been over by now and the victorious troops should be bringing in the wounded.

Christi walked over to the window and looked out across the town toward a dark cloud of smoke in the distance. She prayed everything was going well.

If she could have seen thirty miles away, she would have known all was not well.

She would have seen the ground strewn with the bodies of the *pobrecitos* and student activists who believed the Batistas would surrender easily, only to meet stiff opposition.

She would have seen that there was no uprising of the so-called 'oppressed people.'"

She would have seen an overwhelming hail of bullets and a legion of determined soldiers that did not lay down their arms and run as predicted.

She would have seen Kiki, blood dripping from an open wound, being led shackled into a prison cell jammed with a hundred of his defeated brothers.

Christi could not see these events, but inside she knew something was very wrong. Her nerves were so jittery she dropped the plate she was washing.

Garbo looked at her with concern.

She smiled that everything was okay, but Garbo's expression showed he was not so sure.

Moments later Luis stumbled through the door. There was blood pouring from a wound on his head. He staggered just inside the doorway and fell to the floor.

Garbo rushed to his side.

Christi and one of the "nurses" joined him.

"You must all get out. Now! They will be coming. Kiki says for Garbo to get Christi on the next boat to Caracas," Luis mumbled as his wounds were being dressed.

Garbo looked doubtful.

Christi waited until the "nurse" had bound Luis's wounds before she questioned him. "Kiki . . . is he . . . where is he Luis?" she asked as she knelt close beside him.

Luis raised his head slightly. "They have taken him away. He is alive, but they have taken him away." Luis grimaced in pain. "His instructions are for you to go to Caracas. You must obey!" Luis coughed blood.

"Well, forget that. I'm not going to Caracas or anywhere else until I know he is safe."

"You do not care for him enough to do this?" Luis spit.

"Tell me where he is and I will go to him!"

"Ha! There is no time for your stubbornness, woman!" Luis coughed and retched. "Garbo, he said that you would know these are his orders if I told you 'the sons of José Martí are dead.' You understand this?"

Garbo nodded. He moved to Christi's room to pack her bags.

Christi and Luis shared a look of disdain.

"Where have they taken him, Luis?" Christi demanded

Luis smirked.

"Where, Luis? I won't go anywhere until you tell me where Kiki is," Christi insisted.

"Oh? You love him so much you wish to be with him?" Luis spewed contempt along with blood.

"Just tell me where he is."

"Oh! Look at the love light in her eyes. She will run to her husband with her arms wide open," Luis mocked her with hatred in his eyes. "You whore! I do not know why he cares for such as you."

"Where, Luis?" Christi demanded.

Luis started to spit at her. He died before he could purse his lips.

"He's in jail with all the others." Maria stepped out of the shadows. "It is his wish that you are taken to safety in Caracas and that is where you will go."

Christi slowly got to her feet and thought it over as she looked at the deadly serious look in Maria's eyes. "I want to see him first, Maria."

The small staff in the makeshift dispensary looked at her as if she was crazy.

Maria looked disgusted. "If you are not gone before Roberto and the others get here you will be dead. Understand?"

"Why? What have I done to anybody?"

"You are American."

"I thought we were friends."

Maria looked at her with contempt. "My brother found something to admire in you. I do not!"

"But I just can't go and leave him like that! I am Cuban also, Maria!"

"You will not say this ever again! You are American and many of my people are dead because your government sides with a tyrant. Now go!"

Christi backed away shaking her head. "I don't have anything to do with the government. Let me stay and help. I can make bandages. I can . . ." Christi stopped when she felt a strong hand grip her arm. She turned and looked into Garbo's stern face.

"We go!" he said firmly and decisively.

"Garbo, give me a minute . . ."

"We go now!" Garbo ordered.

Christi started to protest but Garbo's bulk made such a protest futile.

As people scurried around evacuating the small dispensary, Christi moved sadly to the jeep. In the distance she could now see the smoke from a dozen fires. Once again, she felt heartsick and betrayed.

Once again, her world was being turned upside down and she was powerless to stop it. But this time she was a little stronger and she was not going to give anyone the satisfaction of seeing any regret.

"Let's go, Garbo. I can't wait to see Venezuela." Christi returned Maria's glare as she moved to the jeep. Once she was seated in the front seat of the jeep Christi ran the crucifix through her fingers. "You want me to pray, Kiki? Then I pray for power. I pray for the power to stop people from jerking me around. I pray for the power to make people do what I say and the power not to have to listen to them ever again. I pray for the power to get home and get away from these crazy people," Christi swore to herself as she pressed the crucifix hard against her breast.

Garbo slammed the two small suitcases into the back of the jeep. He leaped inside and started the engine with one motion. As he pulled the jeep down a narrow alley and drove away from Santiago toward the ocean, gunfire could be heard closing in on them.

"Are you taking me to a ship, Garbo?"

Garbo nodded.

"I have to tell you, I hate ships. I don't want to leave the island. Let's go hide out in the hills until things settle down. I really hate ships, Garbo!" Christi repeated, remembering her first voyage.

"You cannot stay. I make the promise to keep you safe. I do not break promises," Garbo said with pride.

"The one ship I have known was not very safe. This island, no matter what is happening, is safer. Believe me!"

"The wife of Kiki Chevarra is not safe within a thousand miles of Cuba after this night. We go to Kiki's friends in Caracas, and that is that," he snapped.

Christi knew any further pleading was futile. As Garbo drove into the bright midday sun, Christi looked back at the fires burning all over Santiago. She wondered where her husband was and how he was doing.

If Christi had the power to see through the dark smoke of the fires into Kiki's cell, she would have seen him jammed against a wall by the press of his former comrades who ignored the pain of his wounds. She would have seen him push his way through the crowd until he was by the window, looking out on the sea. She would have seen the tears of sadness in his eyes for the lost revolution.

She would have seen the tears of happiness he cried, secure in the knowledge his faithful friend Garbo had his beloved bride safely on her way to Caracas.

"Do you believe Kiki will survive, Garbo?" Christi asked as he drove the jeep down a small dirt road that led to a small, remote inlet.

Garbo thought it over a long moment. He heaved a sigh.

"When do we return?"

"I do not know this."

"I will come back soon, I'll tell you that," Christi assured herself.

Garbo frowned.

"Why do Maria and the others hate me so?"

He looked away.

"I did love Kiki. I really did."

Garbo grimaced.

"Why Caracas? Please just tell me that?" Christi asked as Garbo turned down a small dirt road that led to a remote inlet. He thought it over a long moment. "It is very far from this place. This is good. This is enough," he said with his usual tone of finality.

"Just tell me when you think we can come back?"

Garbo shrugged.

"I will come back soon!" Christi assured herself.

He smiled a faint smile of admiration. "You are the most strange woman of all Kiki's women."

"Oh?" Christi paused. "How many women are we talking about?"

Garbo looked embarrassed. He shrugged.

"That many?" Christi laughed.

"I say too much sometimes." Garbo fumbled.

As they came over a hill Christi could see a ship in the distance. The sight of a ship's outline gave Christi the creeps. She watched with increasing anxiety as Garbo drove the jeep toward a longboat where three grubby-looking men waited for them.

Garbo had her bags unloaded almost before the jeep came to a stop. He motioned for her to get out. What she saw coming towards her made her freeze with revulsion. At first, Christi thought she was in a bad dream. She sat in the jeep and watched the man approach her, but would not let herself believe what she saw.

"We must go now!" Garbo shook her arm.

Christi still did not move.

"NOW!" he insisted.

"No, we don't. I don't go anywhere with this man, ever!" Christi screamed as she jumped into the driver's side and tried to start the jeep.

Garbo reached over and grabbed her hands off the steering wheel. He lifted her out of the jeep and deposited her on the sand. "You must not act crazy now. We have no time. We go!"

"No, Garbo! No!" Christi growled as she stepped away.

Garbo looked at her quizzically, then he saw the grin on Captain Hornecker's face.

"You know this man?" Garbo paused.

"Yes! I go nowhere with this man! I will take my chances in Santiago. I mean it, Garbo. I really mean it!" Christi insisted as she got back in the jeep.

Garbo looked puzzled for a long moment. "Kiki has used this ship many times for many things. This captain has not failed Kiki. He will not fail Kiki now."

"That's right, Garbo. I've always delivered the goods. I can be trusted for sure," Captain Hornecker grinned.

Christi was sick to her stomach. "Well, you deliver somebody else's goods. You'll never get me aboard that garbage scow again in this life," Christi snarled. She turned to run. Her way was blocked by ten armed men and Garbo.

There was the sharp crack of gunfire very near as Hornecker spoke.

"You do what you want, but there was an army patrol by here only a few minutes ago. They'll be back soon, Garbo. I have to push off if we are to get to the ship and sail with the tide," Hornecker said calmly.

"God, I hate you!" Christi spat at him. "He and his men are rapists and murders, Garbo!"

Garbo shrugged and looked amused.

"Oh? I see. And is that alright with Kiki?"

Garbo had to think that over.

"I do not know why. Anyone can look at you and see you came to no harm on my ship. Is she not a fine healthy young woman, Garbo? Do you see any marks on her?"

Garbo looked at them both skeptically. The gunfire was coming closer. "We go now!" He scowled as he lifted Christi out of the jeep and carried her, kicking and screaming, to the longboat.

Captain Hornecker smiled as he picked up the suitcases and followed after.

Christi fought him all the way, but Garbo managed to get her aboard ship and locked in a cabin.

As she pounded on the door, Garbo folded his arms and stood silently on guard.

Christi sat on the bed of the same cabin she and Cosmo had shared what seemed like so long ago.

She didn't know whether to laugh or cry. It was all too incredible to believe. She looked over the familiar but hated surroundings and shivered a little. As she cooled down, she regretted having taken her anger out on Garbo.

Slowly, she got up from the bed and walked over to the door. She tapped on it timidly and quietly called Garbo's name.

There was no answer for a long moment.

She swallowed hard in fear that she was alone. "Garbo? Are you still there? Please don't punish me. Say something?"

She was relieved when the door opened and she knew he was standing guard. "I'm sorry, Garbo. If you only knew the bad time I had here before. Hornecker is truly an evil man. He will most probably have us both killed ten minutes out to sea, but it's not your fault. I'm sorry. Come on in and sit down . . . if you can find a place to sit," Christi apologized.

Garbo moved through the door behind her and sat on the floor in a far corner.

Christi sat down on the bed. "This was Cosmo's bed," she said wondering why right after she had said it.

Garbo gave her his withering look of disapproval.

"Nothing happened. Kiki knows I was pure on our wedding night."

Garbo looked doubtful, then indifferent.

"Did you know Cosmo well?" Christi mused aloud.

Garbo rubbed his shiny, shaved head vigorously with his big right hand before replying. "No one knows this man. He is like the wind that blows hard with much evil then is gone," he replied.

"He protected me. I would not have survived to be Kiki's wife if he had not."

Every time she mentioned Kiki, Garbo's eyes brightened.

It was not lost on Christi that Garbo's love of Kiki was now the key to her survival. "Hornecker is the one responsible for Cosmo being captured. I'll bet he betrayed Kiki also."

Garbo thought that over for a long moment. "Cosmo is the betrayer," he posed.

"No! I don't believe that. I would never believe that."

"I protect you for Kiki's sake and for our people. You must know I kill Cosmo if I see him," Garbo said evenly.

The terrible finality in Garbo's voice made her hope that he and Cosmo would never meet again.

Christi felt her hair was undone, her makeup askew, her dress in tatters. She felt she looked a mess. When she felt that way she felt powerless, although the most attractive of women did not seem to move Garbo. The old feeling of creeping despair pressed in on her and she despised that feeling. She did not know when or how, but someday, some way she would take every opportunity to grab all the power she could and never be helpless again.

"I killed Hornecker's first mate. He will be coming for me."

Garbo looked disturbed for a moment. "Pinkus? One less cockroach. This was a good thing."

"You knew Pinkus? Then you know Hornecker is a pirate and a cut-throat that would put Blackbeard to shame," Christi insisted.

"The passage money has been paid. He is not such a fool as to harm the wife of El Grande's brother and favorite commander," Garbo said without much certainty.

"This El Grande, where is he?"

"He waits in the mountains."

"While Kiki rots in jail?"

"There will be another day."

"You big, sweet, lovable ox. Can't you see they have no power over Hornecker now? I'm sorry, Garbo, but we've got to get off this ship. Please believe me, we really have to." Christi walked over and looked deep into Garbo's eyes as she pleaded with her hands.

"Hornecker is a devil but he is not stupid." Garbo looked into her eyes and shared some of her concern. He pointed to the floor. "I will sleep here and you will not leave my side for anything!"

Garbo spoke with such force that Christi knew further argument was useless. She smiled and gave him a quick hug.

He quickly broke away from the hug and looked embarrassed.

Christi marveled at his shyness. "Oh, Garbo, it was just a friendly hug. I'm sorry, I didn't mean to embarrass you."

Christi was interrupted as Captain Hornecker opened the door and stepped inside with the usual sheepish grin on his face.

"I just came by to ask if you two would join me for dinner. I would also like to tell Miss Jones that any unpleasantness she might have experienced on her earlier voyage is regrettable. You can expect no more problems. In the future you will be treated like the very important passenger you are. I will personally see to it," he grinned.

"I'll bet you will," Christi said under her breath.

Garbo stood between Christi and Hornecker.

"Garbo, you know I don't want to tangle with you." Captain Hornecker backed off.

"Don't come in here with that grin like nothing ever happened and all is forgiven. You don't fool anybody, Hornecker," Christi said.

"Please, Mrs. Chevarra. Your circumstances have changed and so have mine. As Garbo can tell you, Kiki is my biggest customer. Kiki is one important person. When the revolution is successful he will be a most powerful man." Hornecker paused to cackle. "If the revolution is not a success, then that changes everything, now doesn't it?"

Christi was not the vulnerable, frightened little girl Hornecker had known only a few months ago. Christi was no longer a virgin in the physical or in the mental sense.

She now possessed a maturity born of necessity. Where she was naive, Christi was beginning to acquire wisdom.

Where she had lacked foresight, she was beginning to see clearly. Where she had lacked courage, she was beginning to be brave.

She still hated Hornecker, but she no longer feared him.

"We'll have dinner with you if you cater it to our cabin," Christi said.

"Oh, Miss Jones, you have an exquisite sense of humor," he paused and looked at her cynically. "Why don't you wash up and join me in my cabin at six bells. Unless, of course, you would rather eat in the galley with the men," he replied sardonically.

Garbo moved into Hornecker's hideous face. His towering presence caused Hornecker to take a step backward.

"I was just kidding, Garbo." Hornecker swallowed hard.

Garbo jabbed a huge finger in Hornecker's chest. "If Mrs. Chevarra is missing a single hair I break all your bones. I will take a long time to do this."

"Yes. I understand. Okay. I will have all meals served in my cabin. There will be little or no contact with any of the rest of the crew. I don't need any trouble," Hornecker pleaded as he backed away.

"Then we understand each other?" Christi felt bold with Garbo at her side.

"Yes. Yes, we do," Hornecker said assuringly as he left the cabin quickly.

Christi laughed nervously after he was gone. "Thank you, Garbo."

Garbo acknowledged the thanks with a nod.

"Maybe this won't be so bad after all." Christi looked deep into Garbo's troubled eyes.

He looked out of the porthole at Cuba.

"You're worried about Kiki, aren't you? Is he going to be alright?"

Garbo sighed as he shrugged his huge shoulders and looked very sad. "No one knows this, except God," he almost whispered.

Christi nodded agreement as she looked at the crucifix still clutched in her hand. "Whoever and whatever God is," Christi muttered cynically.

Christi moved to the small greasy porthole and looked out of a clear spot toward the coastline and the smoke from the fires still raging in the city beyond. She gripped the crucifix and prayed. "Please, God. Watch over Kiki. And keep us all from harm's way."

"Amen," Garbo intoned reverently as the ship lurched beneath their feet, signaling the beginning of their journey.

Chapter Twenty-one

CHRISTI WAS PROUD OF HERSELF. SHE WAS NOT THE LEAST BIT nervous as she and Garbo entered the Captain's cabin promptly at six o'clock. She did not even recoil at Hornecker's toothy grin, or feel ill when he took her hand and led her to the small table.

Hornecker sat her in the chair to his right and Garbo down the table from them. Garbo almost fell out of the small chair as Christi shifted her chair closer to him and away from Hornecker.

"Ah! There is still no trust in me. So be it. I have had a rare treat prepared for us tonight. In honor of Miss Jones . . . Mrs. Chevarra, we will have New York steak fed in the Iowa pens with corn for goodness. It says this on the box. How can this be? A New York steak from Iowa?" Captain Hornecker laughed.

Christi shifted nervously in her seat.

Garbo's hunger showed in his eyes.

"And I also have some good red wine to wash it down. The finest red available in Port-au-Prince," Hornecker continued as he poured Christi a glass of wine. He started to pour one for Garbo. Garbo turned the glass over, cracking it with the force of his movements.

Captain Hornecker shrugged. He put the bottle down across from Garbo and walked back to take his seat at the head of the table.

Garbo's eyes followed him all the way.

"I want to say that we have had our differences, but that is all over. I support the revolution and have all due respect for Kiki. His wife will be treated with respect aboard this vessel. I have ordered it." Captain Hornecker lifted his glass to toast Christi.

Christi reluctantly lifted her wine glass and shook her head as she proposed her toast. "To the truth," she smiled.

The wine was unusually good. Christi drank only half a glass. She did not want to fall over in a drugged stupor. She wondered if her wine was poisoned.

The steak was delicious, but Christi thought of condemned men and their last meal as she ate it. Captain Hornecker tried to be so charming she began to wonder if he was lying, or had undergone brain surgery since she last saw him. She decided that no surgeon in the world could rearrange Hornecker's brain to make it normal. It was only a matter of time until he made some kind of move.

Christi placed her small hand on top of Garbo's long muscular fingers. She wondered where her husband might be.

"You do not like me, *señora*. You do not like me because of the things that happened before now. You must understand, I do not have Cuban citizenship, but I have a Cuban soul. I support the revolution. Kiki was my teacher. I sell him the guns, I give him some guns. Please relax. Kiki is my *amigo*. Why else would he entrust his wife's safety to my hands?"

Christi could not resolve the fact that Kiki even knew a man like Hornecker much less had dealings with him. She concluded that wars make for very strange bedfellows. "He did not entrust me to you. He entrusted me to Garbo and his other friends."

Christi looked Hornecker in his good eye.

"Oh? Who knows? If the revolution is not successful, maybe Kiki has no friends," Hornecker said grimly.

Garbo growled audibly.

Christi stared at this ugly caricature of a man. What Captain Hornecker was suggesting might be true. She felt a sickening awareness of déjà vu as the ship rose and sank with each battle with the open sea. "If you believe in the revolution, why weren't you with Kiki?"

"Ah! But bringing the supplies is also very important. Right, Garbo?"

Garbo nodded halfhearted agreement.

"Thank you for the meal, Captain. I'm very tired. If you will excuse me I will retire to the cabin."

"The cabin you shared with Cosmo Collins?"

Christi stopped and glared at Captain Hornecker. She looked at Garbo.

Garbo looked stoic.

"Garbo knows nothing happened. Nice try, Hornecker. Goodnight!" Christi responded, genuinely tired.

"Of course. Tell me, Mrs. Chevarra, do they tell you Cosmo is dead?"

Christi tried to ignore him.

"He lives, you know. Many have seen him. Maybe he comes for you?" Captain Hornecker baited as he watched for Garbo's reaction.

Garbo revealed no emotion.

Hornecker seemed irritated by that.

Christi smirked and left the cabin.

Garbo also smirked, threw a soiled napkin at Captain Hornecker and followed after her.

Captain Hornecker fumed.

As she and Garbo made their way back to the cabin, Christi mused aloud. "He's a sly one . . . Garbo . . . what if the revolution does fail?"

Garbo shrugged his big shoulders and looked blank for a moment. "This will not be."

"I'm sorry. I'm not so sure, Garbo. Tell me the truth. Is there anyway, any hope of ever seeing Kiki again?"

Garbo gave Christi a happy smile. "Those who stayed behind are even now at work."

"Is that a yes or a no?"

"It is the answer."

"You should have been a politician." Christi shook her head.

Garbo grimaced and looked ill.

They were almost back to their cabin, when the first shot sounded on the deck and reverberated down the passageway.

Garbo pulled Christi along quickly into the cabin before the last echo died.

He pointed to the far corner of the room and told Christi to go there with his eyes.

Three more shots rang out as Christi moved to the dark corner.

Garbo frowned as he reached into his loose shirt and pulled out a seven-inch knife and a small pistol. He took one more affectionate look at Christi and moved into the passageway, slamming and locking the door behind him.

Standing in the corner near the porthole, Christi could hear that some of the shots were coming from a few yards off the side of the boat. "Oh Lord, let it be Kiki! Let it be Cosmo!" Christi prayed as she fought off the thought it could be anybody else.

She was pacing the room nervously when she saw the handle on the door turn, stop, then turn once more.

"Garbo? Garbo, is that you?" she almost screamed.

There was no answer as the handle turned all the way and the door slowly opened. The passageway was empty for a long, agonizing moment. There was a low groan, then a huge shadow. Christi thought she saw the bent figure of a big man.

"Garbo? Who is there? Garbo?" Christi stopped as she saw Garbo's hurting eyes and heard his cry of pain.

Garbo staggered into the room with blood pouring from an open wound above his eye. Quickly he grabbed Christi's hand and led her out into the passageway and up the stairs toward the ship's stern.

"Garbo, you're hurt. Let me help you!"

Garbo's answer was to quicken the pace.

The shots now came in sporadic scattered volleys and they seemed to be behind them as Garbo cautiously led Christi out onto the moonlit deck.

"Garbo, please tell me something before I have a nervous breakdown," Christi demanded.

Garbo picked up an old rag and wiped off his forehead. The rag was dripping with his blood as he replied. "It is Franz. He comes for the guns and he does not take prisoners," Garbo snapped. "Here, you hide in here and we do not speak again until he is gone," Garbo insisted as he pulled her into a small utility room. Christi obediently followed Garbo inside the small room. She shivered from the cold as she sat down beside him to wait.

For several long moments they were inside the closet in complete silence.

The silence was followed by quick starts and stops of voices and footsteps going off in all directions. The heaviest footsteps seemed to be coming their way.

Garbo held the rag to his head until the footsteps were only a few feet away.

Garbo looked to see if Christi was okay. He took the rag away and broke open his gun revealing the last remaining bullet. Finally, he stood up beside the door frame and held his knife in the ready position.

The footsteps passed the door at first, and Christi sighed in relief.

She broke her sigh as the footsteps turned and stopped directly in front of the door.

Cautiously, a hand turned the knob. Several times it toyed with the knob before it angrily shook it. Then it was quiet again.

Christi began to hope once more when a shot exploded into the closet, blowing away the doorknob and opening the door partway.

Garbo was out of the door and on top of the man in an instant. His knife blade gleamed in the moonlight as he raised it over his head to drive it into the man's chest. His arm was on the downward flight when a volley of bullets ripped into his huge body, causing him to fall over on his side and jerk violently before he lay still.

Three men approached his body cautiously. They were only a few steps away when Garbo jumped up and tore into them. His knife took the closest one out. The final bullet from his pistol took another. The last man emptied a full magazine at Garbo's chest, knocking him down on the deck where he lay motionless.

Christi was out of the closet in a rage. "Oh Lord! No! Not him too! I'll kill you! I'll kill you all!"

Christi yelled as she made a grab for a gun lying on the deck.

She picked it up. It was a heavy .45 caliber automatic. Her small hand barely fit around the handle. It was cold in her hand and felt clumsy and useless. She had never understood why men loved guns so much. She understood it less as she tried to grip the awkward weapon.

Her hands struggled to find the power of the gun. She reached the furthest length of her finger's grasp. Her hand now was on the handle and the trigger. She pulled the trigger and the gun exploded, the recoil knocking her on her back. The bullet went into the distant reaches of nowhere.

Christi had missed with the first shot she ever fired from a gun, but she did not miss the lesson of power the gun taught her. She had seen the fear in men's eyes when she pulled the trigger. She did not have to be accurate to have power, she simply had to hold the gun. It was a strange new feeling.

Scary but exhilarating.

Someone kicked the gun from her hand.

Christi looked up with tears of rage in her eyes to see a man's face. The tall man had long, blond hair and classical Nordic features which were accented by the moonlight falling on his face.

"I wonder. Could this spitfire belong to Kiki?" He smiled sardonically.

Christi jumped up and went after him with her claws. She managed to barely scratch his face when two burly men pulled her off and held her securely.

"Yes! I am Kiki Chevarra's wife. He is a General in the new Cuban army. If you touch me, he'll get you. I swear!"

"Kiki took a wife?" The blond man chuckled as he studied Christi's face and nodded understanding. "Ah, yes! You are Kiki's bride. Kiki would not marry unless he could have such a woman as you. But then he doesn't have you anymore, does he?"

The man smiled coldly.

Christi spit in his face. "You bastard, you've killed a man worth a million times more than any of you. So you'd better kill me or so help me, I'll kill you," Christi snarled.

The blond-haired man looked down at Garbo's body. "You mean that big nigger?" he chortled.

"Damn you! I mean that beautiful black man. He was twice the man you'll ever be!" Christi kicked at him.

"I thought you Spanish hated niggers?" He looked puzzled.

"No! I'm a nigger, just like him!" Christi growled.

The blond man looked genuinely stunned. He drew closer to Christi and again studied her face in the moonlight. "I don't know. You are very different. It would be hard to classify you racially. Fascinating, very fascinating. There was nothing like you at Buchenwald or Treblinka. I thought I had seen all types, but nothing like you," he mused aloud.

Christi shivered quietly as she wondered how to react to such a curious stare. "Kiki will get you. He will get all of you. He and Cosmo will be coming after me anytime now, and they'll get all of you," Christi almost cried.

"Cosmo? Kiki? Oh, I hope so. My employers would pay me well for either of those hides." The blond man laughed, then fell strangely quiet.

Christi gritted her teeth. "I don't know who you are but you will pay for this. I swear!"

"Who am I? I am Franz Kurtz, Señora Chevarra!"

He probed, obviously hoping she had heard of him.

Christi shrugged angrily and looked away.

"Perhaps Kiki didn't have time to tell you of me. That's okay, we have plenty of time to discuss such things before we reach Brazil," he snapped as he directed his men to take Christi overboard to a huge shining white ship tied alongside.

"I have nothing to say to you ever again. You hear that! Nothing! Ever!" Christi fumed as they drug her away, kicking and screaming.

Franz watched her go and looked pleased.

"A fascinating woman. Utterly fascinating. You did well, Kiki. Thank you, my old friend," Franz Kurtz whispered to the wind as he followed along behind.

❋ ❋ ❋

Franz's converted PT boat was fifty miles away, headed due south at forty knots when Cosmo and his men reached the burning, listing *Calamaria Princess*. Hurriedly, Cosmo boarded the ship. The smell of burning flesh made him sick. He had smelled it many times before, but had never taken it personally until tonight.

"Damn!" Cosmo cursed his tardiness as he looked at the deck full of dead bodies. "Search it. Search every inch! We can't go back without her. Understand?" Cosmo stopped as he noticed the great hulk of Garbo lying only a few feet down the deck. Quickly he ran to Garbo's side and knelt down. "God! Not you, big fellow. Not you!" Cosmo fumbled for a pulse. For a long agonizing moment he felt nothing, then his fingertips picked up a faint heartbeat.

"I knew you were too tough to die! Johnny! Mac! Get on the radio and get a PBY in here now. I want this man in Georgetown yesterday," Cosmo ordered.

"What about the woman?" Mac hesitated.

"You can stop looking and set a course for Rio. That goddamn Nazi son-of-a-bitch has done it again!" Cosmo clinched his fist and shook it at the dark, empty horizon.

Chapter Twenty-two

CHRISTI AWOKE TO THE FEEL OF SATIN SHEETS AND A VELVET COMforter. THE cabin she occupied was decorated with polished furniture and lovely raised-print wallpaper. She hated Franz with all her heart, but she had to admit he knew how to furnish a ship's cabin. She was tempted to awake slowly and enjoy the luxury of the moment, but then remembered how she had gotten here. She shot up in bed, frantically looking for some weapon with which to kill Franz.

There was nothing but lavish luxury meant to comfort not kill.

She was pleasantly surprised and yet a little curious she had not been raped the previous evening. She shuddered as she remembered the way Franz had looked at her on the ship. She felt it was only a matter of time until he grew tired of looking. She prayed she would have some weapon whenever he made his move.

The only weapon she found before Franz entered the room was an oversized hairbrush. She raised it over her head for a moment, then lowered it, almost laughing at the futility.

"I have a saber wound on this cheek." Franz pointed to his right cheek. "A bullet wound in my left side, and another just below the knee. A hairbrush wound I do not have. That would be unique. Yes, I think so." Franz stood above her and looked down at her with an angelic smile on his face.

His posture was impeccable and he had the "prettiest" face Christi had ever seen. It was boyish and had the look of innocence. Looking upon the countenance of his doll-like face it was hard to believe he was evil.

Christi only had to remember Garbo's body lying on the burning deck to remember how evil he was. "Please, leave me alone," Christi begged sincerely.

Franz looked at the hairbrush.

Christi tossed it aside.

"Mrs. Chevarra, it's wartime. Not like World War II, but just as real. Please be a good soldier and accept the fortunes of war. It is a long way to Rio. Why not make the trip as pleasant as possible," Franz pleaded.

Christi pulled the velvet covers up around her naked shoulders.

Franz drank in her every movement.

"You must be crazy. Do you know how much I loved Garbo? Do you know how much I love my husband?" she snapped pulling the covers even closer.

"You say nothing of Mr. Collins?"

Christi was caught off-guard.

"He will come when he hears of this. Both of them will come."

"You think they are better men than I?"

"Oh, yes! Oh, yes!"

"Then why have they abandoned you?"

The word "abandoned" hit Christi's psyche hard.

She had no quick answer.

"This thought disturbs you?"

"It isn't over yet."

"I see. If I was really the evil man you take me for, would I not take you at my leisure or maybe give you to my men?" Franz demanded.

Christi was frightened but refused to show it. "You touch me and I'll kill you!" Christi reached for the brush.

Franz gestured wildly. "Oh my goodness, a real live virtuous woman. Why, I thought all you little American bitches were cracked as soon as you bled." Franz feigned falsetto.

"You're disgusting. Leave me alone! I feel sick." Christi grimaced.

Franz's doll face took on an ugly appearance. The evil within him was clearly visible now. "It's amazing how Americans defy authority with impunity. It's fascinating to watch how your minds work. You are completely powerless, completely in my power, totally subject to my will. A good German would recognize the situation for what it was and make the best practical use of it. You Americans fight it. Why? To what end? When will you learn to defer to power? Deep inside you know I am in command of this situation. Sooner or later I will take anything I want," Franz insisted.

His look made Christi shudder with an unclean feeling. "You have no power over me. You can kill me, but you'll never have me, never!" Christi's voice shook with fear.

Franz grinned contemptuously. "No power? Suppose I give you to my men. They have been at sea for almost four months. After they are finished they will throw you in the hold with the rats.

"Or suppose I offer a fine dinner, fine wine and good company. Is that not power?"

"You want to dine with a corpse?"

Franz sat down on the bed beside her and grabbed her wrist. The covers dropped and Christi's partially clad body was exposed. Franz's eyes fell on the lovely graceful curves that formed the cleavage between her two generous breasts. He smiled and reached toward her. As she recoiled, he pulled the comforter up around her shoulders.

Christi looked puzzled.

"I am a civilized man, Madame. As you recall you chose this skimpy outfit from a closet full of clothes last evening."

"I was tired and confused."

"And it is very pretty. . . . as are you." Franz leaned close to her and reached to stroke her hair.

Christi picked up the hairbrush and hit him.

He didn't flinch.

Christi had never seen such cold defiance in any man's eyes. A small trickle of blood from a tiny cut above his eyes rolled down his cheek. As it passed the corner of his mouth he reached out with his tongue and licked it. He obviously enjoyed the taste.

Christi turned her head away. She crossed her legs and held them together tightly.

Franz reached down and stroked her smooth thigh.

He leaned over and gave her a gentle kiss in the graceful valley between her breasts.

Christi pulled away.

Franz let her go. He stood up and looked at her imperiously. "Anytime I want. Anyway I want. That was the smallest display of the power I have. I will give you a little time to appreciate your position and decide to come to me voluntarily. We will try it the civilized way. When I have tired of trying it that way, if you have not decided to cooperate, I will do it whatever way pleases me."

Christi rubbed the bruise he had caused on her wrist and pulled the covers tight around her. "I'd rather take my chances with your men," Christi bluffed.

Franz looked puzzled. He scowled, then broke into open laughter. "Are you Jewish?"

"What?"

"I knew some Jews like you. They would spit at the muzzle of a gun just before I put it in their mouth and blew their heads off. They didn't understand power either. Of course, you know what happened to them."

"You were one of those Nazis? You killed women and children? I think I would rather die than have you touch me ever again."

"No, you are much too lovely for that alternative. Was I one of them? No, I was THE one. They didn't recognize it but I was. I started the euthanasia program in Grafeneck when all the rest of the high command were still timidly asking the goddamn Jews to simply register. Can you imagine ASKING a Jew to do anything?"

Franz huffed as he drew even closer to her.

"Yes, I was a Nazi. An SS in the Einstatz. The elite of the elite. The finest group of men ever assembled. The most misunderstood men that ever lived.

"Yes, until August of 1944 I was proud to be SS. Until then I was commandant of hundreds of thousands of people's lives. I could have taken any woman I wanted from a hundred thousand virgins. Power over life and death. You cannot imagine such power. I was more than a king, I was a god. It was the happiest time of my life," Franz almost cried.

Christi slipped deeper into the satin covers as she eyed Franz contemptuously.

"Oh, don't be so coy. You will learn to like me for I will see you are protected as I protected the *Kinderliebens* so long ago. I only killed the infected ones. The Jews and Gypsies and all the worthless people of the earth."

Christi pointed toward the mirror. "No! Not all the worthless. You missed one." Christi looked him directly in the eye. She hated him so much she was no longer afraid.

Franz rankled a moment at her insult, then smiled wryly. "Because you are a victim of propaganda like all Americans, I will overlook your insults . . . for a time. The ship is not a proper place for my plans for you, so perhaps I will wait until we reach my villa in Brazil."

"Never!"

"I understand your position. Most of my men held the same views. Once I educated them they became loyal followers."

"You are insane!"

"Insane? For ridding the world of rubbish. Once you understand the truth you will agree we did the right thing," Franz said with convincing sincerity.

Christi was appalled at how casually he viewed such a horror. "The right thing? You call killing women and children the right thing?" Christi shuddered. "How could you hate any race so much you could kill women and children?" Christi was more angry than curious.

Franz looked as if he had just been shot. "Oh, what a great ignorance you have. You are a great beauty and a fascinating study, but you are appallingly ignorant to ask such a question."

"You had them killed, didn't you? In those ovens. Innocent little children. How could you?"

"Oh, you recall your biased school lessons. You remember what was written in books published by Jews. The same thing happened in Germany. I do not blame you." Franz paused. "We could not read anything but Jewish filth because they owned all the publishing companies and all the book stores, not to mention all the other stores. It's happening in your country. Why do you think your country would hire me if it wasn't happening there?" Franz boasted.

"My country, the United States of America would never hire you!" she gasped.

"Ha! You're not so damn condescending now. Do you think Germany has some monopoly on racism? Do you want to see a copy of my contract with your government? Do you think I can attack a ship such as Hornecker's and go my way without your government's protection?" Franz laughed.

"I don't believe it. I would never believe it!" Christi shook her head in disbelief.

"Oh, you naive little girl. I will tell you this about the American government . . .

"A free-lance warrior like myself can always make a buck with your country if he calls himself an anticommunist no matter whether he is or not. Hell, I like Kiki, but your government is irrational toward commies. You have more reason to hate your government than you do to hate me," Franz argued.

Christi looked at him with stern eyes. "Kiki is not a communist. I don't care what anyone says, I will never hate my country. I've seen all kinds of bad things, but they don't have ovens for little children."

"No, they hang them from trees. Tell me, can blacks vote? Can they sit down and eat at public places with whites? Are they taught how to read and write?" Franz smirked.

"No, not yet, but it's coming. The government has started some things." Christi looked doubtful.

"Oh, that stupid faith. Well, Christi, I am going to start the Fourth Reich and if you want to join we won't ask them for anything. We'll tell them exactly what to do." Franz stood at attention.

Christi shook her head sadly.

"Don't look at me like that." Franz smarted. "You have the audacity to look at me like I was inferior. I am of pure blood. I have a respected identity."

Christi smirked.

Franz started to strike her but held back. "You dare mock me? You who have a hundred different looks in a hundred different lights. You belong to nobody. Your blood is so polluted it doesn't know what color it is," Franz huffed.

Christi was hurt by his words. "Whatever my blood is, I'm glad it isn't yours. There must be a special place in hell for murderers like you."

Once more Franz started to hit her but stopped and smiled.

"You must forgive me. Sometimes I get carried away. My scientific instincts don't always prevail. Please indulge me. Do you know of your racial pattern?" he probed.

"My what?"

"Your ancestors, were they all Africans, Spanish, Cuban? Afro-Cuban? The children of Ortiz? Your father was he . . ."

"I don't care about such things, okay? My parents are as good as anybody. Now, can we talk about something else?"

Franz knew he had struck a nerve. He savored it a moment.

"Yes, yes we can! Just answer me this question and I'll be satisfied. Was your father Aryan?"

Christi turned away and had no answer.

"I didn't mean to be insulting. It is merely a scientific curiosity."

Christi turned and looked him in the eye. "You're asking me about my race, aren't you?"

"Yes, race is important. Don't you agree?"

Christi thought about all the men Sarah had known. She had doubts about her racial category. She would never let Franz know that. "You've heard of peaches and cream. Well, I'm chocolate and cream with a dash of chili pepper. I'm high yellow and brass ankles. Irish and African and Spanish. Every bit as common as an Eurasian, but not quite so celebrated," Christi said evenly.

Franz seemed impressed.

"I was once mistaken for German." Christi paused for effect. "Another time I was mistaken for being Jewish." Christi delighted in pointing a needle at Franz's inflated ego balloon. "I found that flattering."

Franz smirked.

"You are not of pure blood, but you are lovely so there must be some Aryan blood. You are also a liar. No one would ever see you as Jewish."

"Oh, no? Do they all look the same? . . . I've known Jews that look just like you!"

Franz's face contorted with rage. Then he broke into a crooked smile. "My, what a quick wit for such a young mind." He paused and looked impish. "So did you tell Kiki how many times Cosmo took you?"

"Cosmo didn't . . ." Christi stopped and thought it over. "All I remember is he said he would kill any other man who touched me."

"Oh! I am so scared."

"Just let me go. Please! If you do I promise neither Kiki nor Cosmo will come after you."

Franz chuckled. "But, my dear, that would mess up the whole scenario."

Christi thought it over. "My God! You are using me as bait. Then you are crazy. Why? What have they ever done to you?"

"Not a thing. I like them both. However your CIA doesn't share my warm feelings."

"I don't believe that. You are such a liar! Americans defeated your kind. We don't make deals with crooks like you."

"You are the most beautiful woman I have ever seen, but you are as ignorant as all Americans. Sometimes it is hard to endure such ignorance. Someday, someone will have the guts to write the truth. Then people would look upon my kind as saviors. Then you will regret your ill feelings toward me," Franz said with complete faith.

Christi decided quietly that he was insane. She sensed any rational argument would just make him madder. She knew she was all alone in his power in the middle of the ocean so she decided to humor him so long as he did not try anything physical. Maybe once they were on land she could figure a way to escape. "I'll admit I never read a book sympathetic to your cause," Christi offered politely.

Franz's face relaxed, but he look puzzled, then angry. "Don't be condescending to me. I believe what I say. My cause was just. Damn you! My cause was just!" Franz pounded his fist.

"If you have some books explaining your side, I would like to read them," Christi tried to sound sincere.

Franz studied her face while pacing the room. He stopped and assumed a military posture of attention. "You are a cunning little witch, but we shall see. It will be a fun contest. Maybe you will let me win?" he wondered aloud.

"I don't know, Franz. You must remember, I am a bride of only a few days. I still have strong feelings for my husband. I need some time." Christi looked at him sincerely.

He studied her face a moment then relaxed his stiff posture.

"The man who truly wins your heart has conquered a great thing," Franz said sincerely.

"I like lots of romance before anything serious, Franz."

Franz studied her face and seemed satisfied she was sincere. "I never had time for romance. I always thought I wanted to be romantic. I never knew what people saw in it. Those little trashy paperbacks! *True Confessions, Confidential,* and all the pulpy magazines. Or is it Beethoven and good wine? A fireplace?" Franz paused. "I am truly sorry about Kiki. I liked him very much and I understand your feelings. It is only natural. However, you realize Batista has executed many people. Others are buried in a jail forever." Franz sat down beside her, reached out and touched her hair.

"Please, please don't. Not now. Slow, remember?" she pleaded while her skin crawled.

Franz sighed. He looked sincerely sad.

"You are the only woman I have met in my life I could be romantic with. Of course you need time. I am a German officer and also a gentleman. You will have your time."

Christi tried to hide her contempt. She smiled sadly.

Franz leaned over, his voice becoming a whisper. "Christi, if you'll just keep an open mind. You must remember you are from a place that has very few Jews. It is hard for you to understand our problem. I realize that. I will find you some books. If I do, do you sincerely promise to read them with an open mind?" Franz chided.

Christi nodded slowly.

"Good. It's a simple matter of education. I'll bet you have never seen a real live Jew," Franz mused aloud.

Christi thought it over a moment. "Mrs. White," Christi thought aloud.

"Mrs. White? White is not a Jewish name," Franz said sternly.

"Oh, no! Her name was Goldman. She changed it. She said it made things easier for her." Christi stopped herself, realizing she had volunteered too much.

"See! See how sly they are. They changed their names in Germany, but I found them anyway." Franz was angry once again.

Christi had never seen such violent mood changes. She knew she was dealing with a dangerous, mentally ill man and it would take all her cunning to survive. "Now that I think about it maybe you are right."

"God! I wish I could believe you believed that."

"I just never thought about it that way."

"Perhaps. In any case, as I said, it is only a matter of time and education. Already your mind is considering the fact this Mrs. White did not use her real name. Think about her. Think about all she did. The more you do, the more you will see her as the sly Jew she is," Franz insisted.

Christi could not hold her tongue. "Mrs. White is the nicest lady I ever knew. She is a concert pianist. She speaks seven languages fluently and is an award-winning poet. She was very pretty. Please don't insult her anymore," Christi said defensively.

The look on Franz's face made her wish she had remained silent.

"What was this Jew to you?" he demanded.

Christi held her mouth shut tightly.

Franz laughed contemptuously.

"She was my tutor. She taught me everything I know. She taught me how to be polite, to consider other people. She taught me how to be a lady of elegance. You have no right to laugh like that!" Christi's better judgement lost to her anger.

"Oh? And did she teach you to stay out of trouble? Did she teach you how to survive in the real world? No! You are as helpless as her people were. She taught you all she knew, but she did not know the basic lesson of life."

"At least she is no murderer!"

Franz slapped Christi hard.

It took all of Christi's strength but she did not flinch.

"How sad. How sad for you, Christi. I must go see to my crew. You will have some time alone, but we will talk again. You WILL read the books I order you to read. I will fill in the areas Mrs. White missed. You will be the mistress of my villa in Brazil. You will think like me in time." He bowed politely before resuming his mocking laughter.

Christi was boiling with resentment, but she knew any words would be lost to this madman.

Franz moved to the door and turned the knob slowly. He looked back at Christi and his laughter ebbed. "When we get to Brazil you will be brought a book every three days. I expect them to be finished and you to be ready for questions at the end of the third day after you have received the book."

"I hope they aren't very thick books."

"They are thick with wisdom. You are a literate woman. In a very short time you will understand all the things you have not been taught. When you are fully educated you will understand Mrs. White was wrong to waste time trying to teach elegance, how to wear nice dresses, how to walk and be polite, how to act with graceful restraint." Franz paused. "Elegance, like grace and dignity, cannot be taught. They are inborn. If she had served you well, Mrs. White should have taught you to be a woman of power." Franz paused, savoring the assumed profundity of his words. "Power is the essence of everything." he agreed with himself as he opened the door and walked briskly out of the room.

Christi heaved a sigh of relief when he was finally gone.

She slipped down in the satin sheets and pulled the oversized satin pillow over her face. She hated to admit it but Franz was right about power. Power was all she thought about lately. With enough power she could have all that she wanted. With enough power she could go home and make sure Sarah was protected. With all the power in the world she could do away with all the evil people and she would have the men she loved back in her arms.

She closed her eyes tightly, pushed her face hard into the pillow and thought of the ocean at Santiago. She thought of how good it would be to have Kiki beside her. Then her thoughts turned to her shower with Cosmo and she savored that memory. For a moment she despaired of ever seeing either of them again. Then she laughed to herself at the thought of how Sarah had sent her away to keep her from trouble.

"Oh God, Mother! If you only knew," she sighed into the pillow.

Her fingers reached up and felt the coolness of the crucifix still around her neck. It was comforting to hold. She remembered some prayers Sarah had taught her and repeated them, time after time, until she fell into troubled sleep.

Chapter Twenty-three

IN OCTOBER 1951 RIO DE JANEIRO WAS STILL THE CAPITAL OF BRAZIL. It was still the city of nonstop carnival with a batucadas, samba orchestra, for every citizen insuring that the melancholy Rio spirit always danced to a rhythmic beat. It was still the most beautiful harbor in the world and Pao de Acucar, Sugarloaf Mountain, still guarded the entrance to Guanabara Bay. The lush green hills full of the *favelas* that housed the poor still overlooked the glitter and gleam of Flamengo, Copacabana, and Ipanema beaches, filled with slender women, among the most beautiful in the world.

Christi sat between two burly men in the back of a long black car with heavily tinted windows. She could not see out well, but well enough to wonder that the *favelas* of Brazil were even worse than the *bohios* of Cuba. She would have loved to have had time to take in the more scenic sights, instead she was hustled ashore on a drizzly October morning. Two huge men ushered her into a ominous-looking limousine with darkened windows. The last thing she saw before she was thrown into the back seat between two bigger men was the name of a street on a street sign. It read "Aléia Rio Branca." She remembered from her geography lessons that Aléia Rio Branca was a long, wide avenue with a promenade of splendid buildings and the graceful beauty of the Central Carioca Fountain.

She could see nothing out of her dark windows and the glare of the men guarding her discouraged her from trying to look.

Had she been able to see out she would have seen them drive her past the famous Candelaria Cathedral, past the stately palms of Avenida Beira Mar, up a mountainous road past the grotesque images of the strangely formed Organ Mountains. Once they were in the remote region of these mountains the men relaxed, lit cigarettes, and rolled down the windows.

Christi resisted engaging them in conversation. Partly because she was too angry and partly because they spoke a Portuguese dialect she had never studied. Instead she looked out of the open window as they drove through a hundred small villages. Dusty little hamlets with legions of small children wandering around with dark skins, hungry eyes, and extended hands. Half-naked children stood by open sewers boiling with every foul thing man can discard. Beside the gaunt children were the crumbling *favelas* of the starving beggars. They sat semiconscious in the dim morning light, frozen in mute prayer before a hundred religious artifacts.

They were now past Bauma, past Preto, past outposts of humanity not on any civilized map. They drove for hours down terrible roads that always threatened to dead-end. Christi's hope of rescue faded as the car went deeper and deeper into the foreboding darkness of the thick jungles of southeastern Brazil.

When Christi was finally allowed out of the car, it was late afternoon. The setting sun reflected off the high gloss white paint of a huge mansion.

For miles in every direction Christi could see nothing but impenetrable jungle. Jungle everywhere, except directly in front of her. There stood a magnificent white antebellum plantation home with huge Doric columns.

Franz, dressed for riding, stood by one of the columns and smiled a self-indulgent smile.

Christi was very impressed by his mansion, but did not want to show it for an instant.

"I apologize for rushing you up here but I'm afraid if you had seen Rio you would have wanted to stay."

"You are a sick animal. You'd better lock me up because I'll go there the first chance I get!"

"There will be no restraints put on you here. As you can see, there is nowhere to go except the jungle. The jungle is no place for elegant ladies." Franz still mocked her.

"Whatever sick thing you have planned do it now because I've had it with all this king of the pirates crap!"

Franz shook his head and sighed hard. "Wouldn't you like to rest up? You look too tired to do a good job of clawing my eyes out."

"Don't worry we'll get to that!"

"I hope so." Franz looked almost orgasmic.

It was such an evil look it chilled Christi's anger and she played for time. "May I have enough privacy to take a shower and change clothes?"

"Of course. The Wolf's Lair is nothing if not genteel and gracious in this hostile world that surrounds us."

"Wolf's Lair was an apt name," Christi thought to herself.

"Where is my suitcase?" she asked wearily.

"You won't need it. Shades, my manservant, will provide you with some new garments. I think you will find we live very comfortably here. You will learn to like it. Come, I will show you around," Franz offered.

"No! You find my suitcase! It has my dress in it!"

For a moment, Franz was impressed by the fire in her eyes. "There is a closet upstairs with a hundred dresses in it."

"None of them are mine!"

Franz thought it over. He walked over to one of his men and gave him some instructions. He turned and looked at her.

"And what would this dress look like?"

"It's yellow. Bright yellow."

"And?"

"That's all. Okay?"

Franz scoffed until he saw the look in her eyes. He turned and gave his men some hurried instructions then moved back toward Christi. "My men will look for it," he paused and looked curious.

"This dress has some meaning?"

Christi nodded.

"I see. Now we will go inside." Franz extended his hand.

Christi declined to accept it. She reluctantly followed him up the walkway and steps that led inside the huge house.

As much as she disliked being here, Christi was relieved to be off of ships. She vowed she would never again set foot on one as long as she lived. She wondered how long that would be.

The inside of the house was the most lavishly furnished place Christi had ever seen. As she entered the ornate archway, just inside the front door, she noticed a tall, thin black man standing at the foot of a long, gracefully curving stairway.

He was dressed in a black suit and black shirt and wore large, coal-black sunglasses.

"This is Shades. He will be your personal bodyguard and attendant while you are with us. Shades, this is Señora Chevarra," Franz introduced.

Shades nodded slightly.

Christi gave him a polite return nod.

"Shades will take you to your room, and after you have cleaned up and rested you will join me for dinner," Franz ordered.

"I'm not hungry. Just tired and icky."

"Oh, maybe not now. But sooner or later you will be hungry. Dinner is always promptly at seven. You will be on time," Franz intoned icily.

Christi did not reply, but walked quickly up the stairs ahead of Shades who responded to Franz's stern gaze and bounded up behind her.

"This is you room, madam," Shades said as he moved ahead of her and opened the door.

Some of Christi's anger left her as she viewed the beautifully appointed bedroom. The theme was blue. Every color of blue in the spectrum was used in one place or another. There were blue satin comforters on the raised pedestal bed. Above the bed was a gossamer pastel blue canopy.

Blue orchids were placed in expensive vases on matching blue occasional tables. The carpet was a dark blue, peppered with a half-dozen patterned throw rugs. The lamp shades were white with small blue specks and the ceiling was mirrored from wall to wall.

Christi walked slowly over to the bed and stood beside it. A long-stemmed bluish-red rose lay across it. Around the stem of the rose was a gold ring with a large, glimmering sapphire stone.

Christi tried to hide her amazement.

Shades saw her wonder and smiled thinly.

Christi looked at Shades. She knew he was as captive as she. She held no ill feelings for him. "Thank you," she said politely as she picked up the rose and toyed with the ring. "I suppose he was expecting someone," she said as she put the ring on her finger.

It fit perfectly.

She begrudgingly admired Franz's precision.

"We have heard of your coming for sometime," Shades said with a West Indies accent.

"Jamaica? Are you Jamaican?" Christi smiled.

Shades was obviously surprised and pleased. "Yes. You know these things?" he asked.

"A little," Christi paused to remember.

"I only heard Jamaican spoken one sad morning, but I'll always remember it."

Shades saw the sadness in her eyes. He seemed nervous.

"I have to leave you now. I will knock at ten minutes to seven. You must not be late. I will be blamed."

Christi nodded understanding.

She removed the beautiful sapphire ring. As she did, her eye caught sight of a book lying on one of her pillows.

"*Mien Kampf,* an English translation of Adolf Hitler's autobiographical work," she read. "Do I have to finish this before dinner?" she smirked.

"By the evening of the third day," Shades intoned seriously. Christi could not see his eyes because of the dark glasses.

"I'm sorry. I don't want to be hard on you. Did his majesty tell you what I am to wear for dinner?" Christi walked over to a wall-length closet stuffed tightly with lovely, elegant clothes.

"There are nine closets full of various sizes of women's clothes. If you do not find a fitting, tell me and I will see that you have it within the day."

"Thank you," Christi replied as she let her eyes look up and down the length of the closets. "Shades, tell me something," Christi posed as she ran her hands down the long rack of lovely clothing hanging in the closet. "Whose are they?" she wondered.

"Why, they are yours, *señora.*"

"Okay! Whose were they?"

"They were everyone's and no one's," Shades smiled.

"Well, was everyone pretty and where is she now?"

Christi paused on one lace-embroidered black velvet gown.

"Some were very pretty, but no one as pretty as you," Shades oozed.

"Old doll face has really got you well trained," Christi laughed.

"No, *señora.* Please do not ever call him that."

"But you have to admit, he's got a doll face."

"Many have said so, but ONLY once," Shades insisted grimly.

Christi nodded understanding. "Okay, I won't call him that if you will tell me about the last lady who was here," Christi said as she moved from one lovely gown to another.

"*Señora,* she was just a lady. Nothing special. The commandant gets lonely like everyone."

"And when he gets lonely he just plucks an apple off anyone's tree?" Christi relaxed and let her mind wander. She delighted in the comforting feel of the marvelous clothes.

"I must leave you alone to rest. I will be close if you need anything. Please lie down and rest. I will be back at ten minutes of seven to escort you to dinner."

Christi pulled a black velvet dress from the rack. She held it in front of her and admired it in a full-length mirror.

"Suppose I don't go to dinner."

Shades stood silent for a long moment. She could not see his eyes, but she could feel the urgency emanating from behind the glasses.

"There is no 'no' in this house. The commandant has not heard that word in many years. When I come for you, you will have to go. I am sorry, *señora,*" Shades said sternly.

Christi shrugged reluctant agreement. "Maybe it is time he heard 'no'!"

Shades stepped away from her. His body language showed fear.

"Please do not think these things. It would be bad for everyone."

"I'm sorry, Shades. I suppose you are in the same situation I'm in. Let's be friends." Christi offered her hand.

Shades shook her off. "It is forbidden to touch a mistress. I must go. I will be back at ten of seven. Please be ready."

Shades snapped to attention, turned and left the room, closing and locking the heavy wood door before she could reply.

Christi walked over to the large dressing table and sat down on the overstuffed bench. She looked into the large spotless mirror. She was displeased at the dark circles under her eyes, but was glad to see her face was otherwise alright. Slowly, she opened each dresser drawer and investigated the contents. There was no hint anyone had ever used the room before. Each drawer was neatly filled with some feminine condiment, but all were fresh and new.

Mrs. White and Sarah had frowned on the overuse of makeup so Christi had no idea what most of the things were for. She was somewhat overwhelmed by the presence of so many beauty aids. Christi had taken pride in her natural beauty.

Sarah had always said that Christi's face glowed naturally.

Christi didn't feel very glowing tonight. She was only months beyond her eighteenth birthday and she felt eighty. As she studied herself in the spotless mirror she wondered what to do. If she dressed to kill it would only make Franz more predatory. If she didn't, it might make him even crazier. Christi eyed the lovely black velvet dress she had placed across the bed. She turned back to the mirror and rubbed her temples with her forefingers. "Now, Christi, if you are ever in a position where your life depends upon a man's benevolence, you must bend a little for awhile.

"You must wait for your moment, look for his weakness. Wait for your moment and use that weakness against him. It sounds cold and vicious, but it is simply the way things are." Christi remembered Mrs. White's words.

She laughed quietly as she thought that Franz believed Mrs. White taught her nothing of power. Mrs. White had taught Christi that grace and beauty were subtle powers that could be used to achieve one's goals. Mrs. White had also taught Christi that beauty, charm, and wit were sometimes the only weapons a woman had to use.

But Mrs. White was talking about a civilized society. Not a hellhole where she was hopelessly trapped by a graceless madman.

She chuckled as she considered using Cosmo's "ugly" defense and smear herself with hideous cosmetics. She decided against that not knowing how crazy Franz would react.

Christi sighed hard. She held the crucifix in her hand and kissed it. "Kiki forgive me!" She heaved a sigh as she looked into the mirror with a face of innocence now masking a hardening heart.

Chapter Twenty-four

CHRISTI LOST HERSELF IN THE LUXURIOUS FEELING OF THE HOT bubble bath in the elegant marbled pool that filled half of the enormous bathroom. If Christi did not hate Franz so much she could easily have been seduced by the elegant surroundings. Had he been an honorable man, she might have admired his attempt to bring civilization to this remote corner of the Brazilian jungle.

Instead the mere thought of him made her feel dirty and she scrubbed herself hard with the sweet-smelling soap.

It felt good to be clean, to smell of perfumed soap and have a lavish bedroom to lounge about. It was funny. The bedroom was larger than the *bohio* where she had married Kiki. She looked at the closet full of fancy clothes. She would love to try them all on. She looked at the dirty dress she had thrown aside. She was embarrassed by it. She picked it up and stuffed it in the laundry hamper. She opened the drawers of the large dresser and found a stack of pretty blue lace panties. She pulled out a pair and stepped into them. She was only a little surprised to find they were exactly her size. Beside the panties were a dozen strapless bras. Christi picked one up and tried it on. She felt good to find it was too small. She tried the others.

The last one fit perfectly.

It was almost six-thirty as she stepped into the black velvet dress, zipped it up and stood before the full-length mirror.

Sarah and Mrs. White had taught Christi not to be arrogant about her great beauty. As a result, Christi was more shy than aggressive when it came to tooting her own horn. Tonight she knew she looked beautiful. She hoped she looked good enough to win the favor of a crazy man and yet keep him at arm's length. It would be a dangerous game but she had to play it to buy some time. Her mind protested but her heart made her believe Cosmo would rescue her soon.

She paused as she found a flaw in her appearance.

The slightly bent crucifix did not go well with the dress. She reached up to take it off. Her hands fumbled with the clasp. It wouldn't work its way loose.

She decided that maybe it went well after all.

Shades came for her promptly at ten minutes to seven. He sighed in relief that she was ready. Only a thin smile gave away his approval of how she looked.

Once she was at the top of the huge staircase, Shades disappeared. She looked down to see Franz, dressed in formal wear, waiting on her.

Franz's eyes were on her from the moment she stood on the staircase until she entered the huge dining room.

Christi felt she was naked as a Vargas painting as she sat down at the long table in the chair farthest away from where Franz was sitting.

"You are simply enchanting this evening. I tell you freely you are the loveliest woman to ever enter this house. The loveliest in Brazil and no doubt the loveliest in the world." Franz spoke as formally as he looked in his white military dress uniform. His posture was perfect and his manners impeccable. In the romantic candlelight he was a captivating presence.

Christi almost forgot she was looking upon pure evil.

"Thank you for the clothes. When can I go home?" Christi said as she looked away from him.

Franz chuckled into his white-gloved hand. "My, you are a spirited lady. I give you the highest praise and I get back slings and arrows. Please have a pleasant dinner with me. Just this once. For a few moments forget the past and enjoy the present." Franz smiled. His doll face looked as innocent as a newborn. It was hard for Christi to look at that face and imagine what monstrous atrocities he had committed.

Christi lifted the crystal glass full of white wine and sipped it. It was the smoothest wine she had ever tasted.

"St. Jacque '37 Chardonnay." Franz was delighted with himself.

Christi held the glass up to the candlelight and eyed it critically.

"A crisp, subtle understated white, wouldn't you say?" Franz smiled.

Christi was no wine drinker but Mrs. White had made Christi memorize vintage years of the finest wines.

She knew 1937 was not a vintage year.

"1935 was better and even 1941. 1943 was the best for this vintage," Christi said softly.

Franz looked surprised only a moment. He pushed his glass aside and called Shades in. They talked a moment. Shades returned with a bottle of St. Jacque '43. Shades poured them both half a glass in fresh crystal glasses. He left the room and Franz deferred to Christi for the first taste.

Christi lifted her glass. She studied the clarity and sniffed the bouquet, then tossed a small amount on the back of her tongue. It was excellent. She could not hide her enjoyment.

Franz could not hide his delight in her beauty and grace. "You are very much a lady of elegance to know this wine. To look as lovely as you do in such a short time, and to have picked the one dress out of a closet of hundreds that I admire the most. You are perfect, except for one small detail." Franz hesitated.

Christi sipped her wine quietly.

"The cross about your neck does not go well with the contours of your graceful neck." Franz peered at her. His eyes fell more on her cleavage than her cross.

"It's a lucky piece."

"Oh? And has it brought you much good fortune?" He smirked.

Christi was stung by the question. She hated the look of satisfaction on Franz's face. "There is still time."

"I do not believe in luck. But I do have such a cross. An iron cross given to me by the Fuhrer himself. It is in my room. Will you come to my room to see it? Will you come voluntarily tonight?"

Christi glared at him as a reply.

"I apologize. That was crude of me," Franz looked somewhat embarrassed.

"You promised me a little time. I take you to be a German officer and a gentleman."

Franz looked uncomfortable. "Yes. You are quite right. Now we will have dinner."

"Good, I am hungry. What are we having?"

"Se pait de la cordon bleu. Jean, the chef's specialty."

"That is very tasty," Christi said politely.

"You have had it many times before?" Franz looked cynical.

"Yes, of course, but only when we were out of pheasant."

Christi smiled thinly as she picked up a solid silver fork.

She toyed with it, drawing imaginary circles in the heavy white linen tablecloth.

Franz looked deadly serious. "You found the book?"

Christi looked across the three candelabrums glowing with five candles each. Franz's eyes seemed to dance with devilish images.

"You said I had three days to read it."

"That is true. For such a great work I will give you an extra day. You will enjoy it. It is easy reading."

Christi remembered Mrs. White telling her that *Mein Kampf* was an evil book written by a monster, but one should never fear a book or they would be as bad as the book burners.

"I am looking forward to reading it," she said.

"This is nice to hear. They say many things about the Fuhrer but they can not say he did not tell them what he was going to do!"

Christi smiled politely. "Shades tells me he is Jamaican. Do you know much about Jamaica? Do you have friends there?" Christi probed.

Franz played with his salad, ignoring Christi for a long moment. "I have told you I would give you some time. But I do not think so now. All you would do with time is dream of Cosmo Collins or Kiki. You will not think of me. There will be no more mention of them or Jamaica. Those names have been mentioned for the last time in this house. Shades sometimes forgets I pulled him out of a Kingston jail one day before he would have died. You forget I took you off a ship a few days before Hornecker would have found some way to sell you out. Have I not been kind? In the weeks aboard my ship, did I approach you? Have I not been patient? I am a German officer, yet I am still a man."

Franz was mad with jealousy as he got up out of his chair and approached Christi.

Christi pushed away from the table and stood up.

"So, the Jew lady wanted you to be a lady of elegance. Well, look around you. Have you ever seen such elegance? And in the middle of the darkest jungle in Brazil." Franz grabbed Christi by the waist and pulled her close. He kissed her hard and clumsily on the mouth.

Christi pushed him away.

"You half-breed bitch! Don't you dare shove me away!"

Franz slapped her hard.

Christi fell against a chair. It hurt her ribs. Slowly, she got back to her feet. She stood erect and defiant. "Don't you ever touch me again!"

Franz looked a little ashamed but quickly regained his erect bearing.

"What I will do and when I will do it is no longer your decision!"

"I mean it! Come near me and I will kill you!" Christi picked up a silver table knife and snarled at him.

"My! You are remarkable." Franz soothed. "I have much to teach you but perhaps there is much I could learn from you."

"I don't want to know anything you have to tell me except how a depraved person like you got so much power over people!"

"By being strong as you are now. My God! The anger enhances your beauty!"

"Just keep away from me!"

"Why do you deny your true self, Christi?"

"What?"

"You have the same hunger for power as I. I can see it in your eyes. We are much the same."

"No! I could never be like you!"

"Do you not wish for the power to kill me, perhaps? Power is like muscle, it is meant to be used only by the strong. If you don't use it, it withers and is useless to everyone. Yes! There is no doubt you would kill me if you had the chance, Christi. How does that make you different from me?"

Christi lay the table knife down and backed away. "Mrs. White was a German citizen, just like you. She was only twelve years old when she was raped and her family taken away and killed. That's not power. That's madness."

Franz looked hurt. He raised his glove to strike her.

"Don't you ever compare me to a Jewess. They are not Germans and never were! Do you understand?"

"Her relatives fought in all your wars."

"Zionist lies!" Franz let his anger abate. "I will let that pass because you are still young and have much to learn. Alas! I believe it will take much longer than I had hoped to teach you."

"No!"

"No?"

"Either let me go or kill me!" Christi fumed.

Franz's face turned lavender. It looked almost comical against the white of his uniform. He struggled for words. He shook with rage. He took her face and held it firmly in his hands. "I'm tired of debate. Only weak people debate. The waiting has ended. You will go to your room. You will look in the third dresser drawer on the right side. There you will find a light blue nightgown. You will put it on. You will pull back the covers on the bed and wait for me. I will come to you soon. You WILL be ready when I come to you!" Franz ordered.

"The hell I will!" Christi shook with fear and rage.

Franz rang a small bell.

Moments later Shades walked in.

"See to it!" Franz ordered as he gave Christi a stern look and goose-steeped from the room.

Shades looked at Christi and shook his head in sadness.

Christi looked at him for sympathy but the sunglasses hid his thoughts. She pushed open the French doors that led out onto an expansive tiled veranda.

There was a full moon illuminating the pampas grass. It looked so peaceful.

Christi's eyes scanned the distant horizon. There was thick, impenetrable jungle all around. She turned and looked at Shades. "I will die first, Shades. I will kill myself first."

Shades turned away a moment, then turned back and walked toward her. "Please, *señora,* when he is happy it is so much easier for the rest of us. I would not wish this for you, but many will go hungry and many will be hurt much and he will have what he wants anyway." Shades seemed apologetic.

"The hell he will! Isn't there a gun or a knife or anything?" Christi fumed as she picked up a solid silver knife from the table. "This is silver. It will even kill werewolves. It ought to kill that Nazi bastard!" Christi held it tightly.

Shades took her hand. Firmly but carefully, he unwrapped her fingers from the handle. "There may be a time, but it is not now. Now you must go to your room. I am truly sorry, *señora,*" Shades insisted as he took the knife away.

Christi looked at her reflection in Shades' sunglasses. She looked back at the open door and the darkness of the jungle beyond the veranda.

Slowly, she moved past Shades, up the stairs to her room. Once inside, she slowly closed the door and leaned her back against it.

She scanned the room for a weapon. She ran across the room and picked up an oversized hair brush, then threw it down, disgusted at her stupidity.

She opened the drawer of beauty aids and started to throw them away. As she gripped them her anger turned to mischievous delight.

She giggled at the idea.

Quickly, she slipped out of the black velvet dress, searching the closet for just the right outfit.

She found it and was almost laughing by the time she had dressed and fixed her makeup. Then she sat in an overstuffed chair and waited for Franz to arrive.

Franz did not knock. He rattled the doorknob and kicked at the door. Finally, he used a key and shoved the door open. He marched inside and closed it behind him with a loud thump. He almost dropped the bottle of wine and glasses he was carrying when he saw Christi standing before him.

Christi wore a pair of bunny pajamas with out-sized spots of garish colors against a green background. She had used bobby pins to fasten huge pink hair curlers, along with every pair of tasteless earrings she could find all over it. Her hair was frizzled as if she had just removed her finger from a light socket. She had so much mascara around her eyes only the whites were visible. She had used every shade of lipstick to make errant designs all over her face.

In one nostril she had stuffed a ball of cotton and an oblong earring was hanging from the other. Her teeth were blacked with eyeliner and pancake makeup gave her mouth a black face outline.

Altogether she looked like a Christmas tree assembled by the Marx Brothers.

Anyone but Franz would have thought it funny.

Slowly, he walked over to the dressing table and set down the wine. He turned his back to her as he spoke. "In order to be strong one must remember their basic principles. When the strong forget their basic principles, they are treated just as foolishly as the weak. This is a good lesson you teach me. You will not let me be friendly and I should not have tried to be friendly. For a short time I was the fool. Now you have dressed the fool to remind me. I thank you for this reminder." Franz gripped the edges of the table and shivered visibly.

Christi had hoped to cool his passion.

She feared she had made him too angry.

Franz turned and glared at her. "A lady of elegance? Ha! Hell, you don't know the first thing about it. A true lady understands a difficult situation and accepts it with grace. You are a clown, and a stupid one at that. Never again in your miserable life will you have a chance to have such elegance. You could have had all this and more. But now I will take you then commend you to the slums of Rio where you will find little to laugh at again!" Franz screamed as he ran amuck ripping the clothes from the closets, throwing them wildly about.

Christi recoiled in fear.

Franz picked up the dressing table bench and threw it into a full-length mirror. He turned and glared at Christi. "Okay, you Jew-loving bitch! I should have known better than to try to be a gentleman with you. You don't understand the first thing about gentility." Franz popped open the buttons of his spotless coat.

"So, enough! Now I will treat you like the low-bred bitch you really are!" he hissed as he unbuckled his heavy belt and pulled it from the loops.

Franz drew back and struck Christi hard across the shoulders with the leather belt. It stung but she did not let herself flinch.

Suddenly he stopped and grabbed her by the hair. He jerked her along behind him toward the bathroom. He gripped her by the throat with his strong left hand as he turned on the hot water with his right hand.

"I am going to bathe you. Then I am going to fuck you! Then I am going to kill you," Franz said with delight as he opened the cold water tap above the huge marble pool bath.

His grip was so hard about her throat that Christi could only gurgle in response.

The marble pool was only half full when Franz released his grip on her throat.

Christi lay on her back and took in deep breaths of air. Franz towered over her. He dropped to one knee. Using both of his large hands he ripped her pajamas opened. As her lovely young breasts were exposed he became less ferocious.

When she was completely naked before him, his eyes mellowed and he weakened.

Christi took the opportunity to dig her claws into his eyes. "Bitch! Goddamn bitch!" Franz screamed as Christi's fingernails broke the skin of his eyelids. He took a full swing and hit her with a closed fist against her jaw.

Christi felt her teeth loosen.

She bit her tongue and felt the hot taste of blood in her mouth. "Bastard! You goddamn bastard!" she cursed, spitting blood as she hit him in the balls and dug her teeth into his throat.

Franz screamed in pain. He lifted her up and slipped on the wet tile. They both tumbled into the small pool. Franz came up gasping for breath.

The water was only three feet deep, but Franz seemed to have a fear of drowning.

"Oh God, I can't breathe. I must breathe!" he gasped as he struggled to find the edge of the pool.

Christi sensed his weakness. She grabbed him around the neck and pulled him back down into the water.

Franz flayed about like a dying fish. He swung wildly, hitting Christi full in the chest. She had to let go.

"I will kill you!" Franz coughed. "I will kill you!" Franz panicked as he spit water mixed with blood. Franz struggled out of the pool. Twice he slipped on the wet tile. He turned and looked back at Christi.

Never had she seen such evil on anyone's face.

The "doll-face" was now a twisted ugly visage.

Then she saw how he looked at the water with fear. It was then Christi knew what to do.

"Franz, come on, let's take a swim. Come on! I want you. I want you to take me. I want you to do it in here. Now! Here I am. Freely yours. Come on in." Christi stood up and washed herself clean of the makeup as Franz watched, spitting soapy water from his mouth.

Christi was only in three feet of water but that was enough to make Franz wary.

"Accursed bitch!" Franz eased to the water's edge.

Christi enjoyed the confusion in his eyes. He wanted her, but he was afraid of the water. She had to admit he was right about one thing, power felt good. Now he was the victim. He looked like a helpless little boy.

She knew better.

Christi was now clean, her body sparkled golden. She smiled a mischievous smile and looked coy. Slowly, she drew an erotic soap circle around her erect nipples.

Franz shook with desire. He eased a foot into the water.

"Come on, lover! My specialty is making love in the bath. I want your body, Franz. I want you to take me and take me again. Let's do kinky things and do them all tonight!" Christi cooed.

Suddenly Franz lost his fear of the water. He jumped in and grabbed her. He was about to devour her breast with a vicious bite when he slipped.

Christi went down with him, shoving his face under the water.

Franz was going under for the second time when Shades broke into the room.

Shades looked at Christi, then at the drowning Franz. He looked both happy and fearful. "Please leave him to me and get dressed. They will be here in a short time." Shades insisted.

Christi let Franz go and wrapped her arms around her breasts, now a little ashamed. "They? I don't understand," she wondered as she stepped out of the pool and wrapped herself in a bathrobe.

Franz blew frantic bubbles, pleading for his life. He reached out for Shades.

Shades shook with confusion. "You go! This man who is coming. Mister Franz said you knew this man."

"What man?"

"He is called Señor Collins?"

Christi was too stunned to reply.

"He has already engaged the outer guard. He and his men will be here soon. Please get dressed and go." Shades insisted nervously as Franz struggled toward him.

"Will you be okay?"

"Just go now!" Shades insisted.

The news was so startling Christi could not move for a moment.

"Go!" Shades insisted as he turned to Franz.

Franz was spewing water and gasping for breath as Christi moved to get dressed. Franz swung at Shades' jaw.

Shades grabbed Franz by the throat and threw him down into the water again. Shades held him under until Franz seemed to struggle no more.

Christi was dressed when Shades moved slowly into the bedroom. Somehow his glasses were still on though he was soaked from head to toe.

"Please hurry. They will come for you at the airstrip."

"Are you, okay?"

"Yes. Many of the guards have fled. You have done a great service to many people. Go quickly!" Shades insisted.

Christi shook her head. "I'm not going anywhere without you," she insisted.

Shades inadvertently knocked off his glasses.

Christi stepped back in horror. One of his eyes was completely closed with scar tissue, the other half-closed.

Shades dropped to his knees and fumbled for his glasses. Christi picked them up and put them back over his nearly sightless eyes.

"Shades, I'm sorry. I had no idea."

He smiled proudly. "I fool everyone. I see much from my good eye. I know my way around so good they do not know I have the one bad eye."

Christi took his hand and kissed it.

He smiled then looked deadly serious.

"Now you must go. The master has left orders in such an attack that no one lives unless he does. You really must hurry!"

"Then he is dead?"

"He lives to do evil no more. Go now. I will take care of other matters." Shades paused in horror. "No! I felt something in my soul. Oh God! Did I fail at this thing?" Shades turned toward the bathroom door.

Christi's eyes followed. She saw what Shades intuition had told him.

Franz stood before them very much alive. "I would shoot you both now if I did not need you. Get my evacuation gear together, Shades. The bitch will go as she is. We leave in two minutes." Franz coughed water as he pointed an ugly Luger at them.

Chapter Twenty-five

COSMO TOOK THE HIGH MOUNTAIN ROAD TO FRANZ'S HIDEAWAY. He and Franz had once fought side by side in postwar China and done more than twenty contract jobs together. No matter how long he had known Franz, Cosmo had never liked him. The thought of Christi anywhere near Franz made Cosmo furious. He knew there was a price on Franz's head but Cosmo had taken this job for free.

Cosmo did it for love, though he would deny that in loud terms if asked.

Cosmo checked the load in his machine gun and motioned his driver to turn the jeep off the main road onto a trail that looked like it led nowhere. "About three miles up this road, Sanchez," Cosmo instructed as the three other jeeps turned in behind.

"Ah, Señor Cosmo, this is not a road." Sanchez shook his head.

"You got that right, but you can bet old Franz has twenty men on each side of that main road. This way maybe we can surprise him just a little," Cosmo responded as he looked back at the three jeeps of Kiki's men following him.

Three miles away in the main house, Franz held the gun on Christi as he burned some papers. He set a detonator timer in motion and used the barrel of the gun to push her out of the front door.

"Why don't you give it up, Franz? Maybe if you cooperate I'll ask Cosmo not to kill you," Christi baited.

Franz shoved the gun hard into her sore ribs. "Just move!"

He motioned her into a jeep.

Christi was surprised to see Shades behind the wheel.

Shades bowed his head in shame and looked away from her. "Miss Christi, his men hold my family. I am sorry. Please understand," Shades apologized as he started the jeep.

Christi nodded.

"You don't owe this bitch anything, Shades. You owe me everything. Now just get me to the airplane," Franz snarled.

Reluctantly, Shades started the jeep's engine and drove toward the airstrip.

Cosmo stopped his men when they were half a mile from the clearing where Franz's house sat. With prearranged hand signals he ordered the men to disperse into the jungle in teams of two. Cosmo and Sanchez took the point. Cosmo loved the delicious feeling he got right before he was to confront his enemy. He smiled as he made his way quickly through the heavy foliage. It was hot and humid. Cosmo didn't sweat as he made his way to the edge of the clearing, then paused to survey the situation.

Only a few yards away, Christi and Shades dismounted the jeep.

Franz glared at her then put the Luger in Shades's hands.

"Oh God! Now, Shades! Shoot! Shoot!" Christi demanded.

Shades raised the gun to fire at Franz.

He shook with confusion as he slowly lowered it.

Franz grinned. "He has been reminded that each of his children and his brother's children are in jeopardy. He will be a good nigger. Now, get aboard!" Franz ordered as he opened the door to the twin engine four-seater.

Christi thought about turning and running.

Shades leveled the gun at her head. "Please, Miss Christi. I'm sorry."

She admired his loyalty to his family and wondered if he really would shoot. She turned and glared at Franz. "I should have drowned you myself. He doesn't know how much water it takes to drown a rat. I do!"

Franz shrugged. "In Peru there will be another drowning pool. You and I will have another chance at love." Franz coughed a slight amount of water as he sat down hard in the pilot's seat and tried to start the engines.

The sound of the engine starting reached Cosmo's ears just as he approached the large house. "The house is empty, Sanchez. Quickly, we have to go to the airstrip. *Ándale!* Follow me, hurry!" Cosmo ordered as he broke across the huge jungle clearing at a dead run.

Franz started the plane's engines after they failed to respond five times. He cursed them in German, but the tone was universal. The small engines sputtered and smoked before they roared into life. Franz relaxed. "A German plane would have started immediately," he announced as an afterthought.

Christi shook her head and Shades looked out the window as if he could see his home a hundred miles south.

Just ahead of them, Cosmo was going full speed which was not as fast as he would have liked. It was hard to run with the heavy gun and ammunition. Quickly he threw off two ammo belts and wriggled out of his small explosives pack.

The overweight Sanchez labored behind him.

"Hurry! I hear the engines. Damn! Why didn't I remember the plane?" Cosmo muttered through hard, fast breaths of air.

"Peru?" Christi mused aloud as Franz began to taxi the plane.

"What does it matter. You won't have any time for touring!" Franz smiled as he taxied the plane out onto the grassy runway that ended in a dense growth of jungle.

Cosmo broke out of the jungle onto the runway at the opposite end from where Franz revved the engine in preparation for takeoff. Automatically, he checked his machine gun. He saw the rising sun on Franz's face. He saw two other figures in the plane and figured one was Christi. He ran toward the oncoming aircraft as if he could stop it with his naked will.

Franz pulled the throttle all the way back. He was at takeoff speed when he recognized the figure running toward them.

"Ah! Señor Collins! Here is your savior. As always too little too late!" Franz chortled.

Christi almost jumped out of her seat, but Shades shook his head and restrained her.

"Keep her still and quiet, Shades." Franz ordered.

Shades looked doubtful.

"Don't defy me! Hell if you're a good little darkie maybe I'll let you have a go at her too!"

Shades reacted with barely concealed anger. He, reluctantly, grabbed Christi by the arms and held her down.

"Shades! Don't help this creep any more. He's going to kill everybody anyway!" Christi looked into the expressionless sunglasses.

Shades was frozen with indecision. Then he lowered the gun and let her arm go.

Franz decided Shades could no longer be trusted. He grabbed the Lugar from Shades hand and stuck its cold muzzle into Christi's face as he held the steering gear with the other hand. "Shut up or I'll blow your face off! Understand?" Franz spewed.

Christi turned her face away angrily.

Cosmo stopped fifty yards away from the airplane and leveled his machine gun. He was about to pull the trigger when he caught a glimpse of Christi. At the last moment, he pulled the gun up and fired a dozen rounds at the empty sky.

Franz smiled as he pulled back on the stick and gently lifted the airplane into the air, passing the landing gear only inches over Cosmo's frustrated head.

Christi started to wave at Cosmo but held back, more angry with his tardiness than she was glad to see him. As the plane leveled off at fifteen-thousand feet she could not bring herself to look back at the tiny figure of Cosmo slowly disappearing from view altogether.

"Your friend is a most resourceful person but as you say in America, 'he is always a day late and a dollar short.'"

"It's not over, Franz!"

"Oh? I think it is. He was an adequate compatriot but never my equal," Franz mused aloud.

"Well, you better believe he'll find me and if he doesn't, Kiki or one of his men will. Your best bet is to turn this thing around and let me go," Christi snapped and rubbed her wrists as Franz banked the plane slightly to the right. For a moment she hoped Franz was going to set her free and she felt wonderfully relieved. Her feelings of hope suddenly vanished when Franz turned the plane once again due east.

"You Americans. You always worship the wrong heroes. Now, I would have rescued you. Mr. Collins was never very good at planning anything. If I know him, he stopped in a bar in Rio for a little refreshment and a dancing girl or two."

"I know him better than that!" Christi insisted.

"Oh? He had me outmanned and you see who is escaping. No one can save you, *señora*. You are mine. What happened before is nothing to what will happen soon. I owe you a lot of pain, and I pay my debts. You are American. You Americans like the installment plan? I will give you a lot of pain on the installment plan," Franz concluded, very pleased with himself as he banked the plane left and began a victory roll.

"No! No! This can not be!"

Shades grabbed Franz's gun hand.

"What are you doing, nigger! You want your family to die?"

Shades shook his head and gritted his teeth. "I do not wish them to live in a world such as yours!" Shades almost yanked the gun free.

"Arrraggghh!" Franz grunted as he let go of the steering gear, causing the plane to dive sharply and throw Shades and Christi into the front seat.

"You crazy nigger!" Franz snarled as he fumbled for his gun.

His fingers found it and unwittingly jerked the trigger. The gun popped twice sending one bullet into the instrument panel and one through the windshield.

Everyone froze as the instrument panel sputtered into an electrical fire that filled the cabin with acrid smoke. The plane began to dive in uncontrollable spins.

Franz fought desperately to control the dive. He thought he had the plane almost level when it clipped the tops of the tall acacia trees and plunged onto the jungle floor.

A hundred miles away, Cosmo stood in the quiet of a jungle clearing. He raised his machine gun toward the empty sky. Overwhelmed with frustration, he fired a full clip into the face of the morning sun. The sun shook off the effects of the bullets and continued to rise.

Book Two

A Woman of Power

"I recall the yellow cotton dress flowing like a wave on the ground around your knees . . . and after all the loves of my life . . . after all the loves of my life I'll be thinking of you . . . and wondering why . . ."

—Jimmy Webb

Chapter Twenty-six

CHRISTI LAY MOTIONLESS, HALF-BURIED IN THE THICK JUNGLE MUD for three hours before she could make the smallest move. She achieved consciousness only long enough to barely perceive she was being picked up and placed on a crude stretcher. At first she thought she was paralyzed. When she was finally able to move, her first real sensations were the stiffness in her back, caused by the hardness of her bed. She was sore all over her body and it hurt to breathe. When she was finally able to open her eyes, she saw the broken tile roof of a small *bohio* and the face of a very tired old woman looking down at her.

"Where am I?" Christi mumbled feverishly.

"*No comprende, señora. Uno momento.*" The woman leapt up from her chair and ran from the room. Moments later, she returned, dragging Shades by the arm.

"Oh, good! Thank God," Christi rejoiced.

"Yes indeed! Thank God! It is so good to see you alive, *señora*," Shades said as he fumbled for her hand.

Christi did not understand his awkwardness. Then she saw he had been led to her bedside by the old woman and his every movement was that of a blind man.

"Shades, are you okay?"

"Oh, yes. Maybe a little not so okay."

"I'm sorry."

"We walk away so it is a good landing, no? Except I lose my good eye. It is not funny? I wear my glasses to protect my good eye. I break my glasses in the crash and they cut me. They take away the little I can see. Now I have no eyes. I have to see only with my heart," Shades said philosophically, smiling. "And I see you are well. This makes my heart happy."

Christi offered him her hand. "You saved my life. Thank you, Shades," she whispered hoarsely.

"No, Miss Christi. Not I. The good people of this village."

"Franz? What about Franz?"

Shades gave a slit-throat sign.

Christi smiled. "Are you sure?"

"The airplane burned to ashes. Only you and I escaped. You need not fear him any longer."

Christi breathed a sigh of relief. She hurt all over, but news of Franz's death made her feel much better.

"The soft mud of the jungle floor is very kind. We are both not hurt too bad. To be alive is the best thing," Shades offered no hint of self pity.

"Yes, it is." Christi paused.

"Does anyone else know we went down? Where are we? Where is this?" She tried to get up but was still too weak.

"This village does not have the telephone here, but there is one in San Pablo. I would go there for you, but Mr. Franz, he has many friends there who will not like to see us too much." Shades apologized.

"Surely someone has a radio or something," Christi muttered.

"No, *señora*. This is a very poor village. You are American, it is hard for you to understand these things but the money they have buys the day's food, no more."

"I'm sorry. If I could just get a message to Cosmo or Kiki they would come help us." Christi sat up excitedly for a moment then lay back in pain.

"Even if we knew where they were we could not take a chance on sending a message out. We have to be careful. I cannot bring harm to this village. The *policía* and the government, they are friends of Mr. Franz. Dead or alive, he is still very powerful. His body has not been found."

The thought of Franz's missing body gave Christi a chill. "Why would the police and government be friends of a Nazi?" Christi stopped as the answer was obvious. "Money?"

Shades shrugged.

"The police and Franz are very much alike. They would hurt my people very much if they think we kill the man who gives them much money. For many of us it is not who is right or wrong but who has the most dollars." Shades shrugged.

Christi knew of the powerless feeling of poverty and nodded her head sympathetically. "How hurt am I?" she asked.

"I am sorry. We cannot afford the doctor. Father Maldonado can do some things, but he does not know *mucho*," Shades apologized.

Christi took a deep breath and forced herself to get up. The sharp burning pain in her chest told her, her ribs were broken and she immediately lay back down.

"I think it will be awhile before I can do that!" she coughed.

"We will do what we can, *señora*." Shades offered as he touched her hand with tenderness.

Christi looked up at Shades and the cracked sunglasses he insisted on wearing, even though he was blind. "Shades, would it be better for your people if you turned me in?"

Shades looked visibly hurt. "No, Miss Christi. No!"

"But you've done enough. I don't want you hurt because of me."

"No! You are too important to us all. You must live."

"I'm not any more important than you and your family."

Shades shook his head in vigorous disagreement.

"For you there is some great destiny to help many people. I feel this. For you, Kiki will come and liberate us all. We endure much to fulfill this hope," Shades insisted.

"I hope you're right. But I wonder if I'll ever see my husband again outside of prison. Do you think he was with Cosmo?" Christi asked as the figure of a priest clad in the brown habit of a Benedictine came into the room. She watched with interest as the priest moved into the dim candlelight.

"Hello, I'm Father Maldonado. How are you feeling?"

Father Maldonado's face was young, yet very tired looking.

He had the same look of world weariness Christi had seen on her mother's face so many times.

"Better, thank you, Father," Christi returned his smile.

"You have several cracked ribs. You have a compound fracture of the tibia and a broken wrist. I don't have x-ray equipment, but I don't think you have any serious internal bleeding. If we are careful you should be back to normal in three to six months."

"Three to six months! No! I can't stay here that long. No!"

"Please don't get excited, it just delays the healing. I am working on some things and maybe you won't have to stay in this village that long. I cannot turn you over to the Contradistas so we must be very careful," he chided.

"Father, can you get word through the church to Kiki Chevarra for me? Can't you ask a bishop or somebody to pass the word to a priest in Havana?" Christi brightened.

Father Maldonado shook his head sadly. "No. The church is not of one mind on this issue and there is betrayal even among us."

"Oh Lord, *padre!* Can you just get me home?" Christi pleaded.

The priest looked her over with clinical eyes devoid of lust. "It is not a good time to go anywhere. I promise, as soon as it is safe and you are able I will try to get you out," he said as he began to exam her wounds.

Christi took his hand and touched it to her lips. Her lips were dry but she kissed his hand gently. "Bless me, Father."

"Yes. Bless you, my child. Please rest now. Alas, it is the only medicine we have," Father Maldonado apologized.

Christi reached up and felt the cross about her neck. She took comfort in the feel of it.

Father Maldonado watched her eyes.

She watched his.

It was nice to see kind eyes on a man. It was comforting to know he did not care for her as a woman.

"It is an interesting crucifix. Would you like a newer one? The Indians make beautiful ones of ebony and acacia," he offered.

Christi gripped her bent cross tightly. She shook her head. Her neck was still sore and each shake hurt.

Father Maldonado lay his gentle hand on her forehead. "Just relax, Señora Chevarra. *Por favor.* You are among friends now. Somehow, some way we will get a message out to your friends."

"She is the strongest of women. She will heal soon."

"Perhaps if Shades's will was medicine you would be well today. However, now is a time to rest and heal. Please excuse us, Shades. I must change the bandages. Please call Señora Gomez."

Moments later, Señora Gomez entered with hot water and bandages. Father Maldonado walked away and stood in the corner of the room. He bowed in prayer before he returned to assist Señora Gomez in dressing Christi's wounds.

Christi's ribs were so sore she could not breath deeply.

Father Maldonado lifted her gently as Señora Gomez peeled off the old bandages. Christi watched the *padre's* eyes as the last bandages were peeled away and her young breasts were exposed to his eyes. His eyes reflected honest concern for her health. There was no hungry look at her nakedness. His hands were gentle and warm. They did not transmit the slightest sensation of desire and they made her feel comforted, clean and wholesome.

Once the new bandages were applied and Christi was fully covered, Señora Gomez moved back into the shadows of the room.

"I'm sorry to invade your modesty but Señora Gomez does not know how to wrap broken ribs. I learned in your army as a combat medic. I hope you understand I am the only 'doctor' or poor imitation there is in this remote part of the world."

"Soon Señora Gomez can take care of your needs alone. Everyone's modesty will be better served at that point." Father Maldonado blushed.

Christi delighted in the serenity his presence inspired. He was the one man she had ever known whom she trusted immediately. He radiated such peace that she did not want him to leave her side. In a fever-induced flight of fancy, she believed she was in love.

"You won't leave me, will you, Father? Not like the others. Please! You won't go off to war?"

"Oh, no! Those days are behind me."

"You are a beautiful man, Father!" Christi blurted.

Father Maldonado smiled knowingly. "I am a surrogate healer and a priest. Some people find that an irresistible combination.

Then I tell them I have jungle rot between my toes. . ."

". . . I only have a few of my real teeth left. I don't bathe often and I am totally committed to God," he said easily.

Christi reached up and touched his face politely with her fingertips. "Thank you, Father. Thank you for everything. Ow!" Christi grimaced in pain as she tried to get up.

"As you can see, I'm a lousy doctor. Ribs are not my specialty. Broken hearts? Perhaps. But broken bones?" he kidded.

"Father?" Christi whispered.

"Yes," he replied firmly.

"Father, please just hold my hand. I'm very tired. I just want to rest. Just don't leave like the others. Please?" Christi reached out for his hand.

He started to deny her, then reluctantly let her take his hand.

Christi held his hand tight and enjoyed its comforting warmth. It was like a magic sleeping pill. She immediately felt relief as all the bad memories eased.

She took a shallow breath and it didn't seem to hurt as much. "Father," she whispered.

"Yes, my child," Father Maldonado assumed a priestly posture. "I love you, *padre!*" Christi said sincerely as she drifted into an untroubled sleep for the first time in many months.

Father Maldonado dropped to his knees and began a rosary.

Chapter Twenty-seven

FATHER MALDONADO WAS THE BEST THING THAT HAD HAPPENED TO Christi since Kiki. The gracious *padre* had a manner and presence that made Christi feel good, and in a little over three months not only was she walking without crutches but the pain in her ribs was completely gone. Christi said many prayers of thanksgiving that Shades had brought her to Father Maldonado. She knew she would not have been alive without this good priest's help.

It was now late spring of 1952 and as they walked together in a lovely meadow just outside of the small village Christi was feeling very good about the future.

"You have not given me any news of Cuba in many weeks. Don't you think I'm well enough to hear it now?" Christi probed.

Father Maldonado smiled a boyish smile that made his tired face look happy. "I hope so soon. But why would you want to leave this lovely country?" he kidded.

"*Padre,* you're a real joker. Look, I can walk without any pain," Christi said, as she wobbled a little.

Father Maldonado chuckled, then looked concerned. "I'm sorry you did not have better care. I believe you will always have some pain because of my crude medicine. Please forgive me."

Christi paused a moment then threw her arms around his neck and hugged him dearly.

Father Maldonado blushed and pushed her away politely.

Over the months she had taken to heal, he had pushed her away politely many times. Christi had never fully understood her power over men, but men had led her to believe she had such power. She was still too young to realize that all men were not alike and they would reach to her in different ways. This beautiful priest was the first man she had ever known that had not acted in a predictable manner. She had no power over him.

That fascinated and tempted her.

"I love you, you wonderful man. You saved my life. I owe you so much. If you want I will marry you," Christi stopped herself. "Oh, I'm sorry. I forget that you're a priest and you don't like women," she teased.

"Oh? I love women very much and I would not take a bride who is already married."

His words brought Christi back to reality. For an instant she thought of Kiki. Just as quickly she dismissed thoughts of him from her mind. It was Father Maldonado she wanted to take to her bed. It was an exciting thought. What a conquest that would be.

She became moist thinking about it. It was funny. This hunger she had for him was what men felt for her. What a terrible hunger it was. What a mad world where one experienced such hunger pains and could not just reach out and eat one's fill.

Why should there be any forbidden fruit? After all, she was Christi Jones, all men wanted her. She found that thought satisfying. She decided it was just a matter of time before he would be hers. Her eyes revealed her lust and Father Maldonado's eyes revealed understanding and disappointment.

"Please do not vex yourself so, my child."

"Please don't call me a child, *padre*. You're not much older than me."

"Perhaps this is so. I wish for you that your thoughts belong properly with your husband."

"I don't love him anymore."

"Christi, you must not say these things."

"Can't I love who I want?"

"I take it you were married as a Sacrament?"

"There was a priest but it wasn't in a church."

"It was sanctified nevertheless. You must honor your vows as I honor mine."

"You don't like me, do you?"

"I have a lot of affection for you, Christi."

"Like you care for a puppy dog?"

"I must tell you that it is rumored that Kiki has escaped."

"I don't care."

"Please do not talk like this."

"I am not a little girl or a puppy dog, *padre*. I am a grown woman and I know how to make a man happy."

Father Maldonado's eyes flashed anger as he gave her a steady gaze.

"If you say any more you will endanger our friendship. I do not wish this."

"I love you. Doesn't that mean anything?"

"No!"

"No?"

"Go to the chapel and say a novena now!"

Christi drew close to him and let him inhale her scent. She smiled when he did not back away. "I will if you swear before God you do not want me."

For a long moment Father Maldonado did not reply.

Christi was encouraged by the smallest glint of desire in his eyes.

"I give myself freely to you." Christi invited a kiss.

Father Maldonado backed away and shook his head in disgust. "I will forgive this talk because I understand your youthful passions. Please go to the altar now."

Christi tried to force her mouth on his.

He pushed her away and she tripped and fell. She got to her feet and looked humiliated and hurt.

"I'm sorry, Christi. Are you alright?" He reached out to help dust her off.

"Leave me alone!"

Christi reacted feeling the sting of rejection. "Just leave me alone!"

Father Maldonado nodded his head and turned to leave.

Christi cooled off and felt ashamed. "I'm sorry, *padre*. Maybe I'm still sick."

Father Maldonado turned and looked at her with understanding.

"To say this is to be well."

"I didn't mean to embarrass you. You've been so good to me. I'm sorry."

"I am also sorry if I gave you any wrong impressions. Perhaps I was too attentive."

"No. You did nothing." Christi thought it over a long moment. "Why did you give me so much attention?"

Father Maldonado looked like a kid with his hand caught in a cookie jar. "I must confess that what I did, I did with hope that you will some-day help the people of Camp Preco."

"Help? Me? But how? My mother, Mrs. White, Garbo, and Shades all say this. Why? I'm can't even help myself."

"Ah, but you are destined for great things."

"Why does everyone believe that except me?"

"God has given you much. Much will be asked."

"I don't understand it but I do know if I do ever have a chance to help anybody I promise I won't forget you. I could never forget you." Christi looked at him with love. "Not ever!"

"And the people of the village. They helped much."

Christi shrugged. She heaved a sigh of disappointment.

"I hope that you find what it is that your heart aches for. You were not meant for a man married to God. You were meant to be a grand lady. A grand lady who helps others by her position."

"Please. I don't want to hear that anymore. I have no idea of how to save the world, even if I thought it was worth saving. Which I don't."

"It's not a very nice world where all the men a woman wants are either married to God or lost somewhere to some stupid war. I would rather have a man married to God than a man married to war. Does that make me bad?" Christi said.

Father Maldonado looked at her sternly. "There is no time in this land for frolic. Each *favela* is full of misery. I have human fingers, but I also have strong eyes that see things my fingertips can't touch. In another life I might have loved you also, Christi. You are a very desirable woman. In this God has given you the power to do much evil or much good. If it is for good, I wish that you come back to help the *pobrecitos* of Camp Preco. The small ones overlooked by everyone. There are no more poorer people on earth. I have prayed for you to survive and go from this place." He paused and looked at her, sadly.

"You could love me?"

"Not in this time, Christi."

"Then when? I'll wait for you?"

"I was speaking about the man that I was before I became a priest. That man no longer exists."

"Then why would you give me hope?"

Father Maldonado looked sad. "Perhaps I misspoke."

"No, you didn't. I won't ever let you take that back! I'll wait for you no matter how long it takes."

"No! Stop it! No!" Father Maldonado's hands trembled with confusion before he regained his composure. "You will control your emotions as I control mine. If you persist in this bewitching behavior you will lose me as a friend. Understand?"

"I understand you said you could love me."

"I did not mean it that way!"

"I think you did."

"Do you want me to never speak to you again? Is that what you want?"

"No. I just want you to give our love a fair chance."

"Good God, woman! Is there no end to your beguiling?"

Christi's heart leaped as she saw love light in his eyes. She looked at the warm spring sun and smelled the heady fragrance of the wildflowers. She felt alive and hot with desire. She threw her arms around his neck and offered a kiss.

This time he did not push her away.

Christi felt giddy as their lips met for an instant before he pushed her away. "What? Why? Why?" She stepped back looking bewildered and embarrassed.

She tripped and fell down in the damp clover. She stared at him in disbelief.

"Take care to guard your immortal soul, Christi Jones!"

"I don't believe in that anymore."

"Say no more!"

"You are a liar, *padre*. I know you want me. I know how a man's body feels when he is aroused. It's a big lie to deny that."

Father Maldonado nodded. His face was consumed with doubt before he regained his composure. He reached out with his strong hand and helped her to her feet. "For these thoughts I will pray many novenas."

Christi saw the love light disappear from his eyes and she felt empty.

The awkward silence that followed embarrassed them both. Christi barely found the courage to break the silence. "Can you get me to Cuba?"

"I think it is time."

Christi sighed hard.

"Please be of good cheer, Christi. Much good awaits you beyond the small confines of Camp Preco. Once again I ask that you not forget this humble little village."

"I would rather stay in Camp Preco and be your assistant, like Señora Gomez," Christi hoped.

Father Maldonado walked up the clover covered hill. He looked down at a winding river, barely visible in the dense foliage below. Then he turned his face toward an array of golden shafts of sunlight beating back ominous storm clouds. He seemed at peace as he stared at the heavens.

Christi watched as his cassock blew in the soft breeze and wondered how cruel God was. The only man she really wanted she knew she would never have. Every man she had known had failed her except Father Maldonado. She decided at that moment that in this life or the world hereafter she would have him, or she would have no one.

A rainstorm was gathering as Father Maldonado returned to her. He smiled his peaceful smile.

Christi wanted to hold him but she knew she would just embarrass him. Slowly, she turned her head to the sky and took several delicious breaths of the clear spring air. "Can I ask you something very personal?" Christi finally posed.

"Sure! As long as it isn't about my sex life." He laughed.

"Well, it is, sort of. I just wondered why a great-looking guy like you would become a priest,"

Father Maldonado thought it over for a long moment. He turned and gave her a steady gaze. "It is no great mystery. I wanted to be a priest since I was eight. I love my people. I love my God. I have hope that evil will pass away only if enough of us pray hard enough while we're working our tails off. And finally, somebody has to do it." He picked up a long blade of grass and let it go free on the wind.

"I wish it wasn't you," Christi said.

"Many times I wish this also."

"I won't bother you again, *padre*."

"It is for the best. You will not think ill of me and you will remember the people?"

Christi nodded as she turned her face to his. "Father Maldonado, would you do me a very big favor?" she asked hesitantly.

"Almost anything, Christi."

"Can I kiss you just once? Nothing more, just one chaste kiss?"

Christi looked deep into his eyes.

"Christi! Please!"

"I am asking for a memory no one can take from me."

Father Maldonado started to turn away, then blew out his breath hard. He kissed her quickly on the cheek.

"No, *padre*," Christi took his face in her hands and pulled his lips down on hers. For one long glorious moment he let their lips blend together.

Christi inhaled the kiss. It was all she had every dreamed a man's kiss could be.

Their mouths met not as strangers but as lost loves finding each other after ten thousand years of searching. The force of this kiss was not in its passion but in a deep spirituality that lifted the soul more than it excited the senses.

Here was true love found and lost in an instant.

After he broke the kiss, she felt more alone than she had ever felt in her life.

She opened her eyes to see a glimpse of love light in his eyes that he quickly made disappear. "I will always believe that you love me. You can't lie about what we just felt."

Father Maldonado walked away a few steps then turned and looked at her with misty eyes. "No, I cannot lie about my feelings. I am a man who will always love you but a priest who never will." He looked away from her and towards the heavens for help.

"That's crazy. God meant for us to be together or none of this would be real!"

"No! No! Get behind me, Satan!" Father Maldonado shook with the rage of confusion as he turned and shoved her away.

Christi fell backwards in disbelief mixed with the hope of love that his actions portended.

"Oh, yes! See! I know it. You want to love me . . . so just do it!"

Father Maldonado steadied himself and regained his composure. He looked contrite and embarrassed. "I am sorry I pushed you. Such anger is best directed at my sick soul. I have to go now, Christi. I implore you not to test our friendship or further endanger our souls." Father Maldonado turned to leave.

"All I know is that you are the love of my life and no one—not even

God—can take that away from me!" Christi insisted.

Father Maldonado stopped and looked at her with kindness. Then he looked stern and unforgiving as he turned his back on her and walked away.

With a heavy heart, Christi followed him down the small road lined with thick jungle foliage without speaking. They were only a few yards from the village when Christi saw Cosmo standing on the road in front of her.

"Cosmo? Cosmo! Thank God!" she cried as she ran into his waiting arms.

Father Maldonado folded his hands in prayer and looked to the heavens with thanksgiving.

Chapter Twenty-eight

THE C-47 THAT FLEW COSMO AND CHRISTI TO MEXICO CITY WAS filled with a mix of Cuban and American soldiers celebrating their recent release from prison. In the spring of 1952 Batista had declared a general amnesty and emptied his jails. Kiki was released and sent to Mexico City with a promise that he and his men never return to Cuba.

Cosmo had explained the politics to Christi, but she didn't care about politics. She was glad to be alive, and it would have been the happiest time of her life, except she was full of mixed emotions. Her heart was still full of romantic notions about Father Maldonado, and she liked the feeling of having Cosmo at her side. She felt guilty about not being more excited about seeing her husband. But it had been almost a year since she last saw him and she had lost much of her feelings for him in that time. As she sat close to Cosmo, her heart quickened and she knew that true love for her lay somewhere between him and Father Maldonado.

She would have to wait and see about Kiki.

Christi wondered how Cosmo felt about her after all this time. She knew he felt strongly enough to pursue Franz across half of South America. She was flattered by that fact. Yet he insisted on returning her to Kiki. If he loved her why would he do this?

Cosmo, as was his way, did not explain.

Gently, she lay her hand on top of his strong hand and looked into his dancing eyes. Christi loved and hated Irish eyes. They were pretty, but they sparkled all the time and she could never tell when they were sincere. "Cosmo, how is Kiki? What does he look like? Will I be able to recognize him?" Christi was more curious than worried.

Cosmo looked at her affectionately. He seemed to understand her mixed emotions. "I only know what I heard. They roughed him up quite a bit. I know from personal experience prison makes you old quick." Cosmo seemed irritated.

"Do you like him, Cosmo?" Christi probed.

"What kind of question is that?"

"He believes that you betrayed them."

"That needs to be cleared up."

"That's all?"

"Yes, that's all. I was supposed to be with him. Except for an unscheduled stop in Kingston I would have been," Cosmo needled.

"Well, I'm glad you weren't in Santiago," Christi said sincerely.

Cosmo grimaced, obviously uncomfortable with the line of talk. "You're a married woman, married to a friend and comrade in arms. I am taking you to him and that is all there is. I'm a louse, Christi, but I have never made moves on the wives or lovers of my friends."

Christi sighed as she looked out of the small window of the plane at the unremarkable land below. "Cosmo, don't make me bare my feelings, I have some pride. Marrying Kiki was a mistake. I did it to stay alive. You can't hold that against me. I didn't know if you were alive or dead."

"Ancient history."

"No! I have to know Cosmo. Before we land, I have to know how you feel," Christi demanded. Cosmo squirmed in the cramped airplane seat.

"Christi, you know I don't like this kind of talk."

"You can't always avoid facing things, Cosmo. I can tell you I do not feel the same toward Kiki as I did a year ago. I don't even know for sure if I even liked him. It was a bad time. I was very scared and he was protective. I was concerned for my life!"

Cosmo thought that over for a moment. "It doesn't matter. The facts are what they are."

"What does that mean?"

"It means you are a *señora* not a *señorita*."

"In name only. You weren't there. How could you know what it was like being alone and afraid in a strange country. How can you judge me?"

"You had reasons for what you did. Okay. That changes nothing."

"It changes everything!"

"There is a lot you don't know."

"What? What don't I know?" she demanded.

"For one thing, you don't know Kiki saved my life and I his more than once in this deadly circus of Latin American politics. He and I go back before all the clowns that are now on the scene. Whatever feelings I have for you are not proper at this time."

"Just like that? You turn it on and off just like that?"

"Look, dammit! Kiki is hurt badly. They messed him up in the Moncada prison. Christi, you should never have been involved, but you are. You are married in the church's eyes. For all my indiscretions, I am still baptized a Catholic. A priest I respect married you. Kiki is my friend," Cosmo said, his eyes once again revealing nothing.

Christi looked at Cosmo with unbridled anger. "God, I hate the Catholic church!"

"I don't want to hear stuff like that."

"Oh? What would you like to hear?"

"How about some concern for your husband's welfare?"

"Kiki?"

"Yes. God! You are cold!" Cosmo looked at her in disbelief.

"I will have my marriage annulled."

"Not in his world you won't."

"Then I'll find a world where I can."

Cosmo looked at her and felt some sadness for the hurt he now saw in her bewitching sienna eyes. She was still a breathtaking beauty but there was now a sadness about her countenance.

"I want you to treat Kiki with respect."

"Why? I told you it's over."

"Why? Because they broke his legs so badly he limps. And because he loves you more than he loves life! Okay?" Cosmo looked at her with pain in his eyes.

Christi looked worried. "He limps?"

"Yes! But you will pretend not to notice. Right?"

"I am past being tired of guilt trips, Cosmo."

"Look! Luis told me Kiki did not want to see you. He wanted me to take you to Charleston so you would never see him as a cripple. This is my idea. I know how such a man feels. It will be most painful for him to see you when he feels he is less than a man. I respect his courage in agreeing to see you. I cannot dishonor a man under these circumstances. No matter what is between us, we do not dishonor Kiki! Understand?" Cosmo said, more forcefully than anything Christi had ever heard him say.

Christi reflected silently for a moment.

She looked at Cosmo with mixed emotions. "What is between us, Cosmo?"

Cosmo was obviously stuck for a reply.

"I am sorry for Kiki. But I don't love him anymore," Christi offered sincerely.

Cosmo gritted his teeth. For a moment he looked at her with love in his eyes. Then he turned quickly away. "You will not display any pity. Understand?"

"What are you talking about?"

"I know what went on in that prison. Many cut their own throats rather than face the torture he endured. He's a man's man. Don't put him between you and me. I'm an asshole, but I'm an honorable asshole," Cosmo insisted.

Christi frowned. She had never felt so rejected. She decided that she would purge herself of any feeling for Cosmo.

Cosmo reached into his coat pocket and brought out a packet of letters and handed them to her.

Christi jerked them from his hand and glared at him.

Cosmo looked out of the window as he spoke. "They are from your mother to your Aunt Gladys. Your aunt was killed in Havana. She was a double agent. It was good that you never made it to see her. Meeting and marrying Kiki saved your life. Whatever we feel, we must not feel. He has paid a terrible price for his life and yours. When he comes to you on his broken legs, if you do not honor him, I will hate you, Christi, and you will lose both of us," Cosmo said slowly and firmly. The plane touched down, bouncing slightly. It jarred the letters in Christi's hands. She did not answer Cosmo as she tucked the letters into her handbag. They both said nothing else as the plane taxied to the debarkation gate and waited until all the other passengers had disembarked.

Cosmo stood up and gave her a stern look then turned and walked quickly out of the plane.

Christi took her compact from her purse and fixed her makeup slightly. She got up and walked purposely down the walkway to the waiting area. As she broke out of the walkway into the open area, she saw Kiki.

She almost recoiled in horror, but caught herself and smiled. Kiki was leaning on a crutch and looked a hundred years old. He hobbled on one leg toward her as Christi looked across the way toward a far corner.

Cosmo stood in the shadows watching.

Christi tossed her head at him before she reluctantly opened her arms and greeted her husband.

Kiki fell into her arms, off balance. She had to steady him. He hugged her fiercely and kissed her hotly.

He did not speak as he cried unashamedly and openly. "*Mi amor, te amo, querida mia!* I love you more than life, my darling bride. God has been good. The crucifix has preserved us. I never thought I would see life again. Now I not only see life, I see my bride. God brought Cosmo to me and Cosmo brought me my bride. I love you! I love you!" Kiki repeated as he hugged her tightly.

Christi held Kiki up as he hugged her. Kiki's tears wet her shoulder as she glanced out of her eye at Cosmo.

Cosmo looked displeased.

Christi looked more displeased.

Kiki broke the embrace. "Cosmo? Cosmo, come here! Share this moment with us. You have brought it about. *Por favor.* Please come!" Kiki turned and motioned Cosmo to join them.

Cosmo walked slowly over and joined them.

Kiki hugged Cosmo. "Cosmo, *mi amigo.* You found my bride. Many thanks, my friend," Kiki bubbled.

Cosmo shook his hand.

"I didn't do anything. She did it all. She's quite a survivor." Cosmo gestured with admiration.

"It is good to have my favorite people together. In the cell in Havana I think I will never see the sunrise again. But we are free now and we will get much money and better guns and next time we will win."

"What?" Christi stepped back.

"This time we win, *querida mia!*"

"Then you win without me." Christi turned to walk away.

Cosmo held her back.

Kiki looked at her in disbelief.

"The revolution is everything. You know this. There is nothing else."

"You men are crazy. All of you." Christi glared at Cosmo.

"I want to go back to Brazil."

Kiki looked dumfounded.

"She still has a touch of jungle fever. Hey, tell you what. I'll buy you guys a Cuba Libre at Harry's Cantina," Cosmo interjected.

"Brazil? This was a joke, *querida mia?*" Kiki stared at Christi holding his breath for her reply.

Christi was too tired to argue. She shrugged.

Kiki smiled and put one arm around Christi and another around Cosmo as they walked into the airport terminal. "No, I will buy the first Cuba Libre. Then you can buy one and I can buy one and we will get stinko and laugh and cry, but we will not cry too much!" Kiki bubbled. He paused and coughed hard, coughing up a pink substance he tried to hide.

Cosmo stood between him and Christi as Kiki cleaned himself with a handkerchief.

Cosmo stared hard into Christi's eyes.

"I just do not handle this high mountain place too well. I am the swamp child. Mexico City is MUCH too high," Kiki apologized.

"A Cuba Libre will cure your cold. It cures everything eventually. As the wise old man said, the more you drink the quicker the cure." Cosmo laughed as he held his friend up.

Kiki looked at Christi with sad eyes.

Christi found it hard to look at him with affection. He looked so much older and so full of pain.

His forlorn look melted her heart enough that she decided not to add to his pain. "Just remember, I am not strong enough to carry either one of you home so maybe I'll get drunk and you both can carry me home," Christi kidded.

They both looked at her and smiled.

She smiled back and they shared a group hug.

Once in the bar, Christi watched with some emotional detachment as the two men she cared about drank themselves into blissful forgetfulness. She was somewhat fascinated by the deep bond of friendship that Kiki and Cosmo seemed to share. She didn't fully understand it but she was satisfied that Cosmo would be there when he got over this "honor" thing. She decided that this night she did not care. This night she felt young and alive and vibrant. This night she let herself enjoy their attention. She steeled herself not to get angry when they turned away from her and talked of war. It occurred to her that after a hard time with so many enemies, she delighted in having such good friends. The drinks and music made her numb to anything but enjoying life and they frolicked into the late hours.

In her cups, Christi wanted to take them both home and cradle them to her breast, to hold them as friends and keep them as lovers.

Reality came in the brutal starkness of the early morning sun streaming through the *cantina* window. The owner shooed them out with loud gestures and Christi reluctantly led her two favorite people to their small cottage as best she could.

"Hey, Cosmo! We are alive and well. We have the most beautiful woman in the world. We have a bottle of rum and a bottle of the Coca-Cola. We make many more Cuba Libres! Are we not the lucky men?"

Kiki paused and kissed Christi softly on the cheek. "Is she not the most beautiful woman in the world?" Kiki coughed.

Christi and Cosmo paused as Kiki coughed hard.

"No! It is okay!" Kiki shrugged off help. "I do not need the mother hens!" Kiki laughed. He coughed hard again.

"Yes, Kiki. She is the most beautiful woman in the world. There is no question about that." Cosmo smiled at Christi then looked serious. "Now I must leave you here. I have the meeting we discussed. You will be okay in this cottage the committee has arranged." Cosmo paused and handed Christi the bottle of Coca-Cola. "You and your bride enjoy the Cuba Libres, but don't forget you must meet with Eduardo tomorrow."

"*Sí!* Tomorrow?" Kiki wobbled.

Cosmo looked deadly serious as he looked at Christi. "He must be at Eduardo's tomorrow!"

Christi would never understand how Cosmo could drink so much and think so clearly. Christi could not think at all when she was drinking. Cosmo seemed to think better. Christi wished she was going home with Cosmo as she looked at him then at her drunken husband.

Kiki leaned on Christi as he waved his crutch at Cosmo.

"Eduardo?" Christi mused aloud.

"Eduardo! He is one fine man and one fine doctor!" Kiki whispered.

"Yes. Now get some rest, Kiki. Goodnight," Cosmo looked at Kiki and not at Christi.

Kiki leaned more heavily upon her. "The doctor? Eduardo? Yes! He gives us the money and position to fight the revolution."

"Then I will see that he is NOT there!" Christi fumed.

"Ah, but Christi. He is also a good bone man. Maybe he can make my legs better. They broke them but forget to fix them. Maybe Eduardo can fix them good." Kiki tried to laugh.

"Maybe so, my friend. Goodnight." Cosmo said before he turned and walked slowly away into the night.

"Wait, Cosmo! I need you help to get Kiki inside!" Christi called after him.

Cosmo disappeared without replying.

Christi was suddenly alone with her drunk and crippled husband. "I hate you, Cosmo Collins! I hate you!"

"No! No! You must not say this thing!" Kiki almost fell.

Kiki was a pitiful sight. There was little of the man she had once felt love for. She fought off revulsion by thinking of him as a lost puppy dog she must take in and care for. She hoped that would be enough to keep her from running away at the first opportunity.

Until then she would stand beside him as long as her heart would allow her to endure it.

Chapter Twenty-nine

June 4, 1952
Dear Momma,
So much has been happening I don't know where to begin. I hope you haven't been too worried. I couldn't write sooner. I'm not with Aunt Gladys. I am married and living with my husband in Mexico. You would like him, he is a good man who is very rich. He is under the care of a doctor for a temporary illness so I will not be able to come home for awhile. I hope you are well. Please don't worry, I am safe. I love you. I will write again. Take care.
Love,
Your daughter,
Christi

Christi had written the letter in haste after reading the packet of letters Cosmo had given her. She knew Sarah was worried. She also knew Mrs. White would be criticizing her grammar so she made it brief. She was more worried about Kiki and his appointment with the "doctor."

Once they were in the bedroom, Kiki had fallen on the bed and passed out. Christi was relieved he had not tried to make love to her. If he had, she would have submitted out of duty, but her heart would not have been in it.

She hated herself for having these mixed emotions.

She was still his wife and her religious upbringing and sense of honor would not let her forget that—even though he was now a stranger to her.

This morning they both awoke slowly to the bright light streaming through the thin curtain windows. Kiki opened his eyes and groaned, pulling a pillow over his face to block out the light.

For an hour he tossed and turned, mumbling crazy things. Christi could not sleep and got up to make an early breakfast. As she began preparing to cook, she heard Kiki moaning in the other room. She eased her head around the kitchen door and watched as Kiki tried to get up and dress himself. It was painful to watch him grimace with each movement. Even from the distance between them, Christi could see scars all over his once-beautiful body. Finally she went to help him. Once at his side she tried to assist him into his shirt, but he shoved her aside.

"I am no invalid. You go back to the kitchen. I will do this alone," he insisted weakly.

"Are you sure?"

"Yes. Please! Just leave me alone," he insisted.

Christi slowly walked back to the kitchen. With one ear listening for Kiki she resumed cooking. She had just finished when he limped into the kitchen and leaned against the doorway.

Kiki stared at her without saying a word. His once-fiery eyes had dulled and his once statuesque posture was bent with pain.

"I will have something ready in a minute. Have a seat at the table, Kiki."

"Where do you learn this cooking?"

"It was part of my therapy in Brazil."

"Cosmo did not teach you this?"

"No! It was . . ." Christi paused to enjoy a warm thought about Father Maldonado. "It was a priest."

"You spend a long time with this priest?"

"He saved my life, Kiki."

"I have saved your life also."

"Yes! Now sit down and eat," Christi replied as she put the huevos rancheros on the table.

"You have much love for this priest?"

"What are you talking about?"

"You wish it was Cosmo sharing this food with you?"

"I don't like this kind of talk, Kiki. I married you, didn't I?"

"You married me, but you do not love me."

"What?"

"You heard me. I am a broken man but I am no fool!" he chortled.

Christi turned and stared. "Why are you talking like this?"

"Then you love me with all your heart?" Kiki smirked.

Christi's answer was in her silence.

Kiki was visibly hurt by her silence. He wobbled to the table and sat down. "You do not need to do these things for me. Anita will come soon."

"That's not necessary."

"For God's sake, Christi! Leave me a little dignity! Do not look at me with those pitiful eyes. You understand this?"

"I wasn't . . ."

"Yes, you were! I cannot stand to look upon myself. I do not expect it of others. I cannot bear it coming from you."

"It just takes some getting used to. Okay?"

Kiki's eyes showed he wanted to believe that.

"I never lied to myself, *querida mia.* I never expected to have you forever. If you go now, perhaps you can remember me as I was before."

Christi walked over and stood beside him. "You are my husband, Kiki. In the time we were apart I never forgot that and I honor it now. I will always honor it."

Kiki wanted desperately to believe her. He knew he could not. "I do not want honor. I want love. Or I want nothing." He shivered in pain.

Christi knew her feelings were those of pity and little else. As she looked at him in pain she knew it would break her heart to add to his suffering. She steeled herself not to reveal any hint of rejection. "Just give me some time to get used to us being together again," Christi said sincerely.

Kiki studied her eyes. His hunger to believe her overcame his doubts. "Yes. Maybe you will love me again when the revolution is successful. Today we go to see the doctor. He will try to help heal my bones, but he will also help us get much money for the revolution. With so much money we will win this time and I will be whole again. Perhaps, then you will love me again." Kiki sounded satisfied with himself.

Christi stepped back in disbelief.

"The revolution? More guns? My God, Kiki! What does it take to get to you? How many times do you want to be put through hell? I know I don't want to ever experience what we've been through ever again!"

Kiki looked at her critically for a long moment. "I expect to lose you, Christi. The revolution is all I know that I have forever," he said sadly.

Christi had to think it over.

"I never said you were going to lose me, Kiki. But if you persist in this revolution talk I can't say what will happen." Kiki poured a cup of coffee from the server Christi had placed on the table. He savored the aftertaste for awhile. "I want you to be a dutiful wife for a time. Help me return to Cuba in triumph and I will set you free to be with Cosmo," Kiki offered coolly.

"What are you talking about, Kiki?"

Kiki got up. He hesitated a moment then turned the kitchen table upside down and threw it across the room. It narrowly missed Christi as it crashed into a wall. "You know damn well what I am talking about!"

Christi moved into a corner some distance from him.

Kiki looked a little ashamed.

"I am talking about practicalities. I have had nothing but painful time to understand how to face reality. The reality is that you love Cosmo. . . . and don't say anything because it will be a lie!"

Christi was lost for a reply.

Her silence hurt Kiki more than anything she might have said.

"My God! You cannot deny this!"

" . . . yes I can . . ."

"Liar! I see it in your eyes. I also see your revulsion for me and my broken body. I do not blame you. A young woman has many needs and I'm afraid I will no longer be able to satisfy any of them. Say it. Let's not live a lie!"

Christi wiped her face with her apron and struggled for some words that might soothe him but he was right—they would all be lies.

"Kiki, don't talk like this. I don't like it."

"Ah! But we must talk like this. You must help with the doctor. We must separate him from his money. While you are my wife I will expect this assistance," Kiki said coldly.

"What? . . . are you suggesting what I think . . ."

"Yes! You are a whore. Be a whore for a just cause!"

Christi ran across the room and slapped him hard.

Kiki smiled. "Good! At last one honest thing has passed between us." He took a deep breath and sighed hard. "The coffee is good. What's for breakfast?"

Christi turned away from him. She gathered herself and turned back with a wry smile on her face. "Do you intend to eat on the floor?"

Kiki shrugged and picked up the table. He plopped down in a chair beside it.

There was a long painful silence that was broken by the frying pan overheating on the stove. Christi grabbed the pan and threw it down. "Do you like them well done?"

They both forced a smile before they broke into laughter.

"Perhaps just a *cerveza?*"

"For breakfast?"

Kiki shrugged.

Christi thought it over. She moved to the refrigerator and brought out two beers.

She opened them and sat down at the table beside him. She paused a moment then lifted her beer to her lips and pulled down a quick swallow.

Kiki smiled and did likewise

Two beers later, they laughed together, and for a time shared a memory of happier moments. Then they fell into a painful silence that haunted them as they quietly prepared to visit the doctor.

Chapter Thirty

THE DOCTOR'S HACIENDA WAS A LOVELY COLONIAL STYLE HOME IN the picturesque old Tlalpan section of Mexico City. It sat high on the slopes of Ajusco, a supposedly extinct volcano that still rumbled nervously on occasion. Christi and Kiki entered an ornate wrought iron gate and passed through a lovely garden before they arrived at a heavy carved oaken door.

"You look exceptionally beautiful today, *querida mia*. That is good. Doctor Eduardo De La Cruz is most important to our cause. If we do well here there will be much money for us. Please help me on this one thing," Kiki instructed as they paused before the great door.

"You know how I feel about your stupid revolution. My promise was to be civil and that's all I will be," Christi chided.

Kiki tweaked her cheek playfully, but looked desperate. "This is just a little plaything. Just go along with me on this a little and you will be rid of me all the sooner."

"Kiki, you promised to stop that kind of talk!" Christi snapped.

"Ah! Your anger only adds to your beauty. The doctor will like to see you very much." Kiki rang the bell.

Christi felt like a piece of bait, but was curious to see what this doctor looked like.

The entry way was decorated with lovely blue and white on yellow mosaic tiles and the large archways were solid mahogany. Christi was very impressed as a prim butler led them into the library to wait for Eduardo.

Kiki shifted nervously on the velvet couch and Christi wished he weren't so nervous. It made him seem even weaker. She yawned. Her yawn turned to a slight gasp as the handsome doctor, Don Eduardo Ricardo De La Cruz, entered the room.

Eduardo looked like the painted image Christi had seen on posters advertising bull fights. He was more than handsome, he was beautiful. His eyes met hers for a moment and he smiled wryly just before Christi turned away.

"*Como está*, Kiki?" he said warmly, extending his hand to Kiki who rose and tried to come to attention.

"Don De La Cruz, *con much gusto,* I would like to introduce *mi esposa,* Christi," Kiki offered, motioning Christi to stand.

Eduardo took her hand and kissed it, holding it for a brief moment. It made Christi feel uncomfortable.

"She is very lovely, Kiki. You will have to guard her closely," Eduardo kidded.

"She has been wanting to meet you ever since I told her of your exploits in Caracas," Kiki lied.

"Ah! A beautiful lady with an adventurous soul. But alas, she is already married." Eduardo feigned a sigh.

Christi looked unimpressed.

"How about a glass of Madeira?" Eduardo offered as he picked up a crystal decanter and poured the golden wine into three silver goblets.

"Thank you, doctor." Kiki took one and gave one to Christi.

As they drank, Eduardo stared at Christi over his goblet and she felt like she was stark naked.

Kiki noticed Eduardo's attraction and moved to make the most of it. "I was hoping while I am in Tampico you could watch over Christi for me. I will be there maybe two weeks and Cosmo is in Merida."

Christi glared at him. It was the first she had heard of such an arrangement.

"Of course. If this arrangement pleases the lady."

The desperation in Kiki's eyes caused Christi to almost suppress her anger. "I will be fine, Kiki. I have no need for guardianship."

Eduardo looked at her with genuine admiration before he replied. "Yes. I have heard of your survival skills. Perhaps you will watch over me?"

Christi was disarmed by the sincerity of the compliment. "It was mostly a lot of luck and the help of some good people."

"You are very modest, madame. Tell me. Have you seen much of our city?" Eduardo asked.

"No. Not too much," she replied

"It is a lovely city. If you will allow me, I will show you everything from Chapultepec Park to the pyramid at Cuicuilco, with Kiki's permission, of course," Eduardo nodded toward Kiki.

"I would be honored, doctor. I know I leave her with a gentleman,"

Kiki replied politely.

"Stop speaking about me like I was some orphan waif!" Christi glared at Kiki.

Kiki looked past her to see Eduardo's reaction. He seemed relieved when Eduardo smiled.

"And now I suppose you want to discuss that very nasty subject of *dinero*." Eduardo sat down in a red velvet chair and his look became stern.

"If you please, doctor. I wish it were not so, but you know of the problems." Kiki sat down opposite Eduardo.

Christi could not help but notice the striking contrast between her crippled husband and the statuesque doctor. Kiki wore the starched OD clothes of his pickup army. The doctor wore the garnet velour and lace of the Castilians. Kiki almost groveled at Eduardo's feet. Eduardo seemed above it all.

"As I told El Grande, I am not sure of another armed approach so soon. Moncada proved the people are not mad enough yet," Eduardo probed.

"But that was nearly a year ago. And we will not make an all-out assault this time," Kiki chortled.

"Oh?" Eduardo seemed more interested in stealing glances at Christi than listening to Kiki.

"Yes. We will go into the Sierra Maestra and attack the police stations and army patrols. We will not move this time until we have built up the sentiment among the people," Kiki pleaded.

Eduardo looked at Kiki skeptically, then glanced warmly at Christi. "I do not have unlimited resources. I must think about this. I will talk to Prio and some others. Give me until you return from Tampico. Bring me good news of support from our friends in Tampico and perhaps I will tell you of my decision at that time," Eduardo said.

"*Gracias,* doctor. *Gracias!*" Kiki almost bowed, to Christi's embarrassment.

Christi got up and moved toward the door.

"Will you stay and have dinner with me?" Eduardo invited.

Kiki started to say yes, but Christi interrupted him. "No, thank you. I have already prepared ours and we cannot afford to waste anything." She smiled.

"Of course, *señora*. It has been a pleasure meeting you. I look forward to showing you Mexico City." Eduardo kissed her hand once more.

"Thank you for the kind offer but I will await my husband at home." Christi moved toward the door.

Eduardo nodded graciously. "Perhaps another time."

Christi left without replying.

Kiki waited a moment to make sure Eduardo was smiling. He turned and hobbled quickly after his wife.

Once they were alone in the garden courtyard Kiki grabbed her by the arm and spun her around. "I am very ashamed. You were very cold to the doctor. I think maybe you have lost us the revolution!"

Christi had never seen such a look on Kiki's face and could not reply for a moment.

"Kiki! He was looking at me like I was naked. I am your wife!" she said finally.

"I tell you this is just a plaything for a little while. I ask nothing but that you smile and treat him as a great and good friend. You must be more friendly until we have the money," Kiki insisted angrily.

"Well, why don't I just go back in there and jump into bed with him?" Christi pulled away from her husband's grip.

Kiki appeared unconcerned by her remark.

"My God! You don't care, do you? All you care about is your damn revolution. I'm just a disposable part to be used and thrown away. Is that it?" She walked away.

Kiki gritted his teeth and looked at her coldly for a minute, then mellowed. He leaned heavily on his crutch.

"I am sorry, Christi. Sometimes I forget the heart of a woman. I wish the revolution was as important to you as to me. But I can see it is not. I only wanted this small thing. A smile, a wink, no more." Kiki tried to approach her.

Christi moved further away.

"That's not all HE wants," she quipped.

"Christi, I promise. I do not ask you to do a bad thing. Do you not believe I care for you and would not do this to my wife. The doctor and his friends in your country might give us many, many millions of dollars. I cannot let that pass easily. I owe too much to my people." Kiki slammed his fist on a wrought iron railing, almost losing his balance.

Christi shook her head sadly, helping him steady himself.

"I will not stay here and deal with this doctor. I will go with you and help you raise money in Tampico. That's all, Kiki. I mean it."

Kiki looked frustrated. He took in a deep breath and blew it out hard. "There is still a war going on. A war you cannot see, but a very deadly war. There is no protection for us in Tampico. There is little here except for Eduardo. You do not think it hurts me to see his looks? But he is a man of honor. He was once the best matador. I can trust only this man."

"Suppose I let him take me on this tour and he makes a move on me?" she challenged.

"He will just show you off, no more. I will be back in three, maybe four weeks and then it will all be over. I promise. I promise." Kiki's tired eyes evoked sympathy.

"I have seen the sad eyes in the *bohios* too, Kiki. I know what's happening and I promised a very lovely priest I would help, but if that strutting peacock so much as touches me I'll scratch his eyes out," Christi insisted.

Kiki looked at his wife lovingly then pulled her to himself in a close embrace. His crutch fell away.

Christi broke the embrace and picked up his crutch. She placed it under his shoulder.

Kiki steadied himself, posturing as if looking into a camera. "Tell me, do I make a good poster boy?"

"What?"

"I am told I will be photographed and placed on many posters. I will win many hearts to our cause, while others will use it for target practice." Kiki laughed at himself.

Christi looked into his eyes. They seemed so tired except when he spoke of the revolution. When he spoke of the revolution he was young again. She had sympathies for the poor of the *bohios* but she did not share his passion for the revolution. She did realize how much it meant to him and promised herself to make a determined effort, if not to help, not to stand in his way.

"As long as it isn't a wanted poster." Christi smiled.

Kiki laughed and let his crutch fall to the ground. He leaned against a wall and looked at her with love in his eyes. "I do not wish to ask these things of you. I wish the world was not so bad for us. I know this doctor cannot give me back my body free of pain. But maybe I can stop them from giving this pain to others." Kiki reached out for Christi.

Christi let him take her in his arms.

Kiki held her so tight it almost cut off her breathing. "I do love you more than the revolution!"

Christi patted him gently, stroking his back.

He shook slightly and she felt the heat of tears on her shoulder. In the closeness of that embrace, Christi's heart went out to Kiki and she knew she would care for him always as one cares for a father or a kind brother. There was no passion in her being for him, but a deep sense of caring and loyalty one feels for a dear friend.

She prayed friendship would be enough for him.

Kiki broke the embrace and stepped back. "I am sorry I acted like the little boy. I have such self-pity sometimes," he said as he dried his eyes quickly with his stiffly starched sleeves.

"It's okay. Are you alright?"

"Yes," he paused and for an instant there was the old brightness in his eyes. "I will always love you, *querida mia!*"

She started to reply. He put a strong finger on her lips and silenced her. He studied her eyes and seemed satisfied. He looked relieved and put his arm around her shoulder after he picked up the crutch with his other hand. He leaned on her as they slowly and quietly walked out of Don Eduardo Ricardo De La Cruz's courtyard into the teeming streets of Mexico City.

Chapter Thirty-one

K IKI WAS IN TAMPICO ONLY A FEW HOURS WHEN EDUARDO SENT
his car for Christi. Instead of taking her to his house as she
expected, the driver dropped her off at a lovely park where
Eduardo waited to meet her. As he walked toward her, Christi was taken
by his statuesque bearing. He walked tall without swaggering and there
was a matador's grace in his every movement.

He greeted her graciously and directed her toward the great
pyramid of Cuicuilco. The huge pyramid stood against the lavender
afternoon sun, casting the same shadow on the fertile green plain that it
had for fifteen hundred years.

Christi stood in that shadow and wondered what sort of people built
these imposing edifices so long ago.

Eduardo read her thoughts.

"There were still active volcanoes in those days. They cooked on open
fires between volcanic hearth stones. The maize dough was flattened by
hand into *tlaxcalli,* or pancakes as you call them." Eduardo began his
lecture as they walked down the broad avenue once strolled by Aztec
kings. "There were great palaces built for the kings and *bohios* of
sun-dried brick, mud, and wattle for the *pobrecitos.* The floors of
the huts were beaten dirt and they were rather bland-looking except
where the imaginative ones painted frescoes. Ah! but the palaces, they
were splendid."

Eduardo paused and looked a little embarrassed. "Am I boring you?"

"No. Not at all. Tell me about the palaces."

"Of course. The palaces were built of the finest stone with roof tim-
bers of sweet-smelling cedar. They were flanked by exquisite gardens
with an endless variety of lovely flowers, canals, and fountains. Many of
the kings had very representative, private zoos with well-stocked aviar-
ies."

"I feel a great deal of kinship for the Aztecs. Cortez did to them what
the slave traders did to my ancestors."

"Cortez? Yes." Eduardo looked a little uncomfortable. "Cortez once
described Teculitli's palace as more beautiful than those of Spain. It had

marble belvederes with hand-carved jasper floors. There were three hundred servants just to feed the birds." Eduardo stopped in mid-sentence and looked very embarrassed. "I think we Mexicans get our love of gardens from our Aztec heritage. I'm sorry. Perhaps I speak with too much pride of these things."

"No. I find it very interesting. I have read the book *Many Mexicos.* You have a fascinating history," Christi offered.

Eduardo looked impressed.

"You are surprised that I am well-read?"

"I must say I have not met many such women who also have your beauty."

"Men! They always see the body never the mind."

"Señora Chevarra, I want you to feel comfortable with me. I enjoy the company of a lovely lady such as yourself and I would like to assure you I am a gentleman," he insisted as they stopped before the steps leading up to the top of the pyramid.

"I'm sorry. Maybe I have been cold toward you, but you have quite a naughty reputation." Christi smiled.

"But, *señora.* Look behind us and you will see Grandmother is never more than thirty steps away." Eduardo shrugged.

Christi looked over her shoulder to see a dignified older lady rambling along, eyeing her suspiciously.

Christi felt spied on, but more relaxed. "Your grandmother is a handsome woman."

"I would introduce you, but she is not so handsome to talk to," Eduardo apologized.

"I sense the Aztecs were a lovely people," Christi changed the subject as she looked up at the pyramid.

Eduardo stood behind her and nodded. "Yes, but we would consider the blood sacrifices barbaric. They named themselves after nature, like your Indians. Names like Garland of Flowers, Eagle Wings, Necklace of Stars. Much prettier than Eduardo, yes?" He noticed Christi glancing at his grandmother. "My grandmother is the big boss since my wife died. She does not object to you because you are married and cannot be after me to marry me for my money," Eduardo joked.

Christi looked back at the old lady once again. Their glares met and Christi turned away. "Surely she knows you're a big boy now."

Eduardo smiled. "Ah yes! But what would she have to do if not to worry about me? Your mother, is she still living?"

The question stung Christi and she had to stop and think it over. She had given little thought to Sarah for some time now.

"Yes. I hope so. I haven't seen her in over a year." Christi sighed.

"You care for her very much?"

Once again Christi had to pause and think it over. For some reason her love for her mother was no longer something she felt easily. "She was a good mother. When Kiki returns maybe I will go home for awhile."

"I think when Kiki returns he will want to go to Cuba. That is, if they have sufficient money and arms." Eduardo paused before a stone wall and gestured for Christi to sit beside him.

"God! I knew it. Sooner or later men have to talk of fighting." Christi turned away angrily.

"I'm sorry. I will not speak of it again."

"They break your bodies and destroy your lives but you still go back for more. What does a cripple like Kiki think he can do against an army of able-bodied men?"

Eduardo gave her a look of disdain as his reply.

"I'm sorry. That wasn't nice. He is still my husband. But you have to admit this war stuff is crazy!"

"No, *señora*. I must risk your anger and say I support the revolution also."

"Why? You aren't a *pobrecito*."

"It is not a cause of the pocket book but a cause of the heart."

"I think it's just macho bull. Anyway, hasn't Kiki already done enough?"

"Yes. Perhaps this is true."

"Maybe he will listen to you. Please don't give him any money to get arms. I don't want to have him put back in prison. They'll never let him out the next time. It's crazy. You know that little band of dreamers can't win against all those soldiers," Christi pleaded.

Eduardo stepped back and smiled. "I do not believe what I'm hearing. I expected you to flirt with me and then ask me for many dollars. But the heart has its own will, no? You would agree with me that the revolution means nothing if we lose *amor*." Eduardo smiled.

"I think all wars are stupid. They're just excuses for men to leave home."

Eduardo chuckled. "But, you see, I believe in the revolution as much as Kiki so I am afraid I can not help you in this."

Christi sat beside Eduardo and looked at him warmly. "Why? They aren't your kind. They want to eliminate your kind."

Eduardo looked at her with admiration. "You are very insightful."

"For a woman?"

"No. I do not think that. My ancestors made much money from slaves and human misery. If I can use it to free some people from misery, perhaps something is made even. I have seen the *bohios* and I know the revolution must come. Maybe they will forgive me if I help them," Eduardo philosophized.

"Help them all die?"

"These are the risks I'm afraid."

"Men! I think you would fight even if there was nothing to fight over. All those suffering people, where were they at Moncada?"

"They were supposed to rise up as one and help at Moncada, but my husband and his men never received that help."

"This is true. But I believe it to be more a matter of timing than the political will of the people."

"Kiki has already paid too much for this dream, Eduardo. I might be betraying him to ask you not to help, but that is what I'm asking."

Eduardo could not hide the genuine respect he felt for her honesty. He started to reach out and touch her sympathetically but thought better of it and withdrew his hand.

Christi stepped back, slightly.

"I promise I will think about all these things and will reconsider my plans. But please, for awhile let us talk of other things. Look, I have brought the wine and cheese and bread. We will sit on the steps of the pyramid and have a feast," Eduardo soothed.

Christi's frown turned into a smile as she nodded and followed Eduardo up the steps of the pyramid with the glare of his grandmother following her every step.

When they reached the top of the pyramid, Eduardo smiled as he looked at his grandmother, looking very small and far away at the bottom of the pyramid. "Now we can enjoy the wine and cheese in peace."

He sounded pleased with himself as he found a small shelf for them to sit on and opened the wine. He produced two crystal glasses from a small velvet pouch and a silver cheese slicer. He lay the cheese on a blue velvet napkin and sliced it quietly. Then he poured the wine.

Christi thanked him and drank it quietly as she enjoyed the dark green beauty of the Mexican plain. "Up here the world seems so peaceful. I don't think I want to go back down there," Christi mused aloud.

"Then we won't. We have enough provisions to last at least an hour or so," Eduardo announced jovially.

Christi laughed. It was an easy, purgative laugh that relaxed her more than she had been in a long time.

It was scary how comfortable she felt with this stranger. She told herself to be careful with the laughter and the joy of his company.

"On Kiki's wishes I have had my mother's old room prepared for you. I think it is appropriate because I believe she would have liked you," Eduardo said, his eyes laughing.

Christi was caught off guard. "What?"

"This is the promise I made Kiki. There are some enemies of his and mine about. It is not safe where you are now. It will be quite proper. My grandmother will be in the room next to yours."

"Kiki wanted me to stay at your house?"

"Yes. Properly chaperoned of course."

Christi looked down the steps at the slight figure of his grandmother, who was straining to see them. She looked back at Eduardo and sighed hard. "No!"

"Oh? May I ask why not?"

"Eduardo! Aren't Kiki's motives plain enough?"

"Of course. But my decision was made many months ago and it had nothing to do with your charms."

"Then you are going to help him?"

"I am sorry, *señora*. It has already begun."

They fell silent for a long moment as Christi sipped her wine and studied the small figure of Eduardo's grandmother at the bottom of the pyramid. As she did, her survival instincts overcame her distaste for this mess of Kiki's making. "Your grandmother has agreed to this arrangement?" Christi wondered aloud.

"Yes. After I threatened to hide her false teeth," he laughed.

Christi laughed with him once again and was surprised at how easy the laughter came. "That will be nice. Thank you, Eduardo. But what about the cottage?"

"Please forgive my presumptuousness, but I have already taken care of that."

"Oh?"

"My home is yours and Kiki's, for the remainder of your stay in Mexico. Or if you leave Mexico, whenever you return. You know our saying, *mi casa es su casa.*"

"We have one in America. My room is off limits to everyone. Okay?"

"I have told you I am a gentleman, *señora*. Is this not enough?"

"I'm sorry. That was rude. Thank you for your kind offer."

"You are most welcome." Eduardo said, his eyes still shining. "You will have a key to a strong lock and if you wish I will have her sit outside your door."

"No, thank you. A lock will be enough."

Eduardo nodded and smiled. "Then it is settled?"

"Yes," Christi paused and looked at his perpetually dancing eyes. "This all comes so easy for you, doesn't it, Eduardo?"

Eduardo's eyes dimmed, but only for a moment. "I do not believe anything worthwhile comes easy. As a young man I found it hard to go in the bullring but I know I must do it. I was much bolder then. But never as bold as Kiki or Thomas or, God help us, Cosmo Collins."

"Cosmo Collins. Another war-loving idiot!" Christi sighed wearily.

"Cosmo is no idiot. He is the best soldier in the world. But I am sure Kiki has told you this."

Christi feigned distaste. "He was—no, is—the most asinine individual I ever met. I mean, what a liar! What a low individual."

"You must like him very much," Eduardo smirked.

Christi tried to be angry. She failed. "Okay, he did help me out of a few messes but he's still a cad."

"He has that effect on us all. He is one remarkable man. Too bad he is on the wrong side this time," Eduardo said evenly.

Christi looked puzzled.

"We have reason to believe he is CIA-contracted. I hoped it wasn't true, but it seems to be so. There is still some checking to do, but he has been on so many sides. I do not know." Eduardo seemed sincerely saddened.

"Cosmo? He's no angel but I don't believe that," Christi insisted.

Eduardo looked deeply into her eyes.

He seemed satisfied and looked away into the distance. "I hope you are right. I like him as much as anyone. Let us hope that my information is wrong. More wine, Christi?" Eduardo offered.

Christi held out her glass, but did not watch him as he filled it. Her thoughts were far away with Cosmo, wherever he was. Christi hated Cosmo's rude behavior but she felt sharp pains of fear whenever there was a threat against him. Whatever he was up to she believed it was the right thing to do. Besides if he was doing wrong and needed strangling she would be the one to do it.

How she loved him. How she hated him.

Suddenly, Christi felt a little ill and just wanted to be alone.

Eduardo had just finished filling her glass when Christi pulled it away, stood up and looked down at him.

"I would like to go now, please," Christi insisted.

Eduardo shook his head knowingly. "Yes, I understand. Of course. You must be tired. Please forgive me. We will leave at once," he said crisply.

Christi could not stay angry with Eduardo. He was the most refined man she had ever known and his grace and charm were instantly disarming. At last, she decided to relax and trust him. After all, the grandmother was close by and it would be good to enjoy luxurious living for a time.

It was a strange but exciting feeling, and she took his hand to walk back down the steps of the pyramid. His hand was strong but supple and, most of all, reassuring. She dismissed her doubts and fears and decided she would live this new adventure to the fullest.

She was not entirely sure where she was going or why, she only knew she was not reluctant to go there.

Chapter Thirty-two

AT FIRST HER MOTHER STOOD ALONE ON THE HIGH WINDY HILL ABOVE her. The wind was cold and her mother wore a yellow cotton dress with a frayed hem. She was calling to Christi, but Christi couldn't move. Suddenly her mother was joined by her sister Etta May and her little brother Eddie. They were crying and holding their hands out to Christi. Still she could not move.

Their faces were so vivid Christi wondered how she had been able to get home so quickly. Then she saw Father Maldonado join her family and smile beatifically. She felt hot and sweaty, but still immobile. Now Kiki and the ragged people of the *bohio* joined the group. They all began walking toward Christi and their faces were tired-looking and there was a look of hunger, pleading and tears in their eyes.

Christi woke up screaming.

As Christi sat up in her bed and thanked God it was just a dream, Eduardo came running into her room and knelt beside her bed.

"Christi, are you alright? What was it?" He looked worried as he picked up her hand and held it gently in his.

"I'm sorry. It was just a bad dream. I don't usually have dreams like that. It scared me. I'm okay now." She took her hand away as his grandmother entered the room with a look of disdain.

"We were just having breakfast. Can I get you some coffee or juice?" Eduardo sounded very concerned.

"Maybe a cup of coffee would be nice. Give me a few minutes and I will come downstairs." Christi looked past the old lady's stare.

"Are you sure you're alright?" Eduardo looked at her with deep concern in his eyes.

"Yes! I'm fine now," she half-smiled.

Eduardo got up and moved out of the door.

His grandmother waited another moment to give Christi one more scowl, then turned and huffed out of the room.

Christi took several deep breaths, got up and turned on the water in the bathtub. When it was full, she eased her body into the soothing embrace of the hot water. She lay there for twenty minutes before she was interrupted by a knock on the door.

"It's Eduardo. Are you okay?"

Christi shook her head in dismay, yet was somewhat flattered by his concern. "I will be down in a few minutes!" Christi yelled out of the bathroom.

"I'm sorry. I did not mean to disturb you." Eduardo sounded a little displeased with himself.

"I'm fine. Just give me a few minutes."

"Of course." Eduardo said before his footsteps moved away.

Christi eased out of the bath and toweled off her firm young body as she looked at herself in the mirror. With quick pinches of her thumb and forefinger, she examined her waist line and was relieved to see there was no loose flesh. Eduardo had been feeding her the finest food in the world for three months now and she felt fat.

She was glad she didn't look it. Slowly, she opened the large closet in her room and stood back to admire the racks of clothes, in her exact measurements, Eduardo had given her.

Franz's closet was a bargain basement compared to the fancy clothes Eduardo had purchased over his grandmother's objections.

Christi had been reluctant to wear his clothes at first, but they were so lovely she had finally given in. She felt guilty about her love of fine clothes, so once in awhile she would dig out her old yellow cotton dress to remind her of her roots.

She had not looked at it for some time now.

It was funny about her dress. She had said nothing to Eduardo and had believed it lost in the jungles of Brazil. She had almost forgotten about it when she found it cleaned and pressed on a hanger in the darkest corner of the closet. She was curious about how he had managed to find it but decided he would tell her when he was ready.

Casually, she selected a full-length red velvet dress with a fluffy collar. She liked the feel of velvet and felt she looked best in red. She brushed just a hint of color on her face then slowly walked down the long hallway to the ornate stairway.

She moved down and across the huge dining room into the small but elegant breakfast veranda.

"You look exquisite," Eduardo greeted her.

His grandmother gagged on her food. She snorted something unintelligible, got up from the table and left hurriedly.

"Thank you, Eduardo. You have good taste in clothes."

"It is kind of you to say that." He smiled as he poured her a cup of coffee from the crystal urn.

"But I must confess I have a personal buyer, *señora*."

"Oh? Well whoever she is she knows her stuff. And for the last time call me Christi. Please?"

"Yes. Of course. Christi, if it is okay with you, today we will go to Tepozotlan. I would like for you to meet my friend Tomas, the curator of the Colonial Art Museum."

Christi shook her head and looked worried. "Not today, Eduardo. I'd better stay around here and wait to hear from Kiki."

Eduardo looked sad for a moment before he replied, "I must be honest with you. I do not think you will hear from Kiki until he returns in person."

"Why not?"

"Kiki cannot write and he is too proud to admit it. He will not call so as not to break security. Did he not tell you these things?" Eduardo wondered.

"I suppose he might have said something. If he doesn't contact me, maybe Cosmo will." Christi's spirits brightened.

"Cosmo is out of the country. He will not return this year."

Christi looked at Eduardo and caught the sparkle of smugness in his eye.

"You've got it all figured out, haven't you?" Christi tapped her fork on her china plate.

"I don't understand?"

"I'm sorry. That was uncalled for."

"Christi, I do not like it but, at times, I must tell you things which are unpleasant. I understand you do not want to hear them but please do not shoot the messenger."

"I'm sorry. I just feel so captive sometimes."

"I understand this. However, I treat you with respect and kindness and you look at me as if I am a jailer. Are not the doors always open? You may leave anytime you wish?"

Christi nodded. "Kiki said three weeks and it's been three months."

"There have been many complications."

"Maybe it is time I went home."

"Cuba?"

"No, Charleston."

"But you have told me many times this is not a good thing."

Christi did not reply as she thought of going home without the "rich" husband she had been writing of to Sarah. She looked at Eduardo's elegant bearing and considered his enormous wealth. She had been denying it to herself, but it was Eduardo she was writing of all the time.

The decision came so easy this time. Eduardo would be her next husband. It was a delicious thought. Not only the thought of going back to Charleston a rich woman but the anticipation of the hunt. The subtle but relentless pursuit of Eduardo using her whole arsenal of charm. She would make him beg to marry her and then only give in when he had made Kiki and Cosmo apologize for ignoring her. To do it all in the face of his hated Grandmother would make it even more exciting.

It was official. She had become a predatory woman.

"I see you need to be alone with your thoughts," Eduardo lay his napkin on the table and walked into the next room.

Christi got up from the wrought iron chair and put on her most seductive glow. She found Eduardo sitting on a large leather couch in his library flipping rapidly through some oversized book.

"I'm very sorry. I have been a lousy guest. Please forgive me. I am confused and have been for some time. Have you been away from everyone you love for a long time? Have you been alone in a strange land, Eduardo?" Christi sighed.

Eduardo looked up at her with fiery Spanish eyes.

Christi met his fire with her own.

He was so dazzled he looked away first.

"I think you do not understand the revolution is everything to Kiki. He has fought against Batista since his father was killed by him when he was only seven."

"I know. I just forget sometimes."

"His mother folded cigars for pennies a day that sold in your country for three dollars each. One of his sisters was a prostitute at the Hotel Americana in Havana. The big question is why did he marry you in the first place. You are American. Kiki hates everything American. He must have loved you very much." Eduardo smiled thinly.

Christi did not reply.

"Please forgive my asking, but did you love him?"

Christi gave Eduardo a steady gaze trying to look coy and seductive at the same time. "I was very frightened, Eduardo."

"And are you frightened now?"

Christi drew close to Eduardo. She took his hand and kissed it tenderly. "No. I owe you for that."

Christi felt his hand tremble as she released it.

She knew she had him.

"Will you help me go home to Charleston. Today?" Christi pleaded.

Eduardo walked over to his well-stocked bar. He poured three fingers of tequila and drank it in one gulp. He turned and looked at her with some fear in his eyes. "I must tell you truly, I do not want you to go home. I feel for you like a sister. No! This is a lie. I feel for you like I've never felt for any other woman" Eduardo seemed embarrassed. He poured another drink quickly.

Christi knew what was coming. It was almost too easy. She walked away from him as if she was bored. "I feel for you like a good brother. Please don't make me make any more difficult decisions. Just help me go home," Christi said as she stepped into the shadows.

"The shadows will not hide your beauty, Christi. They will not hide the lie that is your marriage. You give me the word and I will have it annulled today."

Eduardo's power was more exciting than his presence. Christi could hardly wait to make that power hers.

"Maybe Cosmo could help me get home?"

"Cosmo? Cosmo is a bastardly rogue who helps no one!"

"I would not be alive without him."

"This man, Cosmo Collins, hires out to the first contract that offers the most money. You will not see him for some time. If ever."

"Is he in South America?"

"No! With your American CIA in some stupid hamlet called Vietnam."

Christi had never heard of Vietnam and figured Eduardo was making it up. It didn't really matter. His anger showed his jealousy and his jealousy meant he was hers.

"I am glad he's gone. I always had a difficult time choosing between Kiki and Cosmo."

Eduardo stepped closer to her and threw down another shot of tequila. "Cosmo will not return because he fears you. Kiki will not return because he cannot live with the pain of your rejection. Neither man is worthy of you. I think you know this."

"And who is worthy of me, Eduardo?"

"You can run to Charleston, but these men will haunt your memories. I offer myself as a path to forgetfulness." Eduardo posed gallantly.

Coyly Christi adjusted the neckline of her red velvet dress. Eduardo's eyes watched her fingers move down the lace toward her generous cleavage.

"I am a married woman, *señor*."

"That is easily remedied."

Christi tried to look unimpressed. She stepped back into the bright morning sunlight and stood closer to Eduardo.

Eduardo smiled. He touched her hair playfully. "I know there will always be shadows on your heart. Kiki is a pure *revolucionario*. When this one is over he will find another. He does not know, as I do, the Indians made it possible for Cortez to win. He does not know that El Grande is just another Cortez. I will not repeat the mistakes the Aztecs made. I don't raise my own gallows."

"But you give them money?"

"I ease my guilt over having money by giving it to them. My problem is over when they have the money. Theirs, I'm afraid, just begins." Eduardo poured another drink.

A cold rush of conscience overcame Christi as she thought about Kiki back in prison being tortured. "I'm sorry. I can't stay another day in this house. Thanks for your help but I must see Kiki!"

Eduardo raised the tequila to the morning light and let the sun reflect through the cut crystal and dance on the velvet wallpaper before he replied, "This is not possible, Christi!"

"Oh? Why not?"

"Even now El Grande and a hundred men are loading an old yacht of mine that will take them back to Cuba."

"What?"

"I have already given them ten million pesos and, with what they have gathered in other places, they believe they have enough to start a successful revolution. My yacht was designed to hold ten people. Does that tell you anything of their chances?" Eduardo drank deeply from the glass. "Perhaps they all drown and all our problems are finished."

"My God! Are you that cold, Eduardo?"

"I believe we share the same freezing point." Eduardo looked at her with contempt.

"What?"

"You take me for a fool, Christi? You try a game that I have perfected many years ago. It was fun to watch but I think you must beg a little before I decide to let you come to me."

Christi was caught totally off guard. His words stung her to the core of her being, yet she was not without admiration for his cunning. "Come to you? What an ego! I will never ask you for anything! Ever!"

"Ego? Yes. I have a grand one. But in my case it is well-earned. When you have as much to lose as I, you must guard it well." He paused and drew close to her. His steely eyes melted a little. "You tempt me to risk it all."

"You are such a liar!"

"Yes. And you are such a schemer. We are a good match, no?"

"No!"

"Then I was wrong to believe you wanted my money and my power?"

Christi hated being found out. Any fondness she had for Eduardo he had just destroyed. She swore to herself he would live to regret ever having made her stare the truth in the face.

"That's not what attracted me, at first," Christi almost kidded.

She smiled inside knowing she had hit him squarely between his ego and his pride.

"Oh, Christi. You do try so gamely."

"Oh? You don't think of yourself as handsome?"

Eduardo tried to shrug but it was insincere.

"I have been told this as have all men with wealth and position."

"The rich men I knew in Charleston were all bald and fat."

Eduardo thought it over and chuckled. ·

Christi chuckled with him.

Before their laughter ended they found themselves in each others arms.

Eduardo's kisses were fierce and hot. He probed her mouth with his tongue before she made him welcome. His hands abandoned gallantry and rushed to ravish. She let him become fevered before she broke the kiss and pushed away.

Eduardo was embarrassed by his barbaric demeanor but he was now too enamored of her to apologize. "Name your price, Christi."

"My price?"

"Anything you want short of marriage."

"You wish me to be a high-priced whore?"

"I will make of you a lady of means and elegance."

"No! If you want me you will make me a wife."

"You are a married woman!"

"You said you could fix that today."

Eduardo had to think it over. "*Madre Dios!* Who has known such a woman?"

"Then you'll do it?"

"Marry you?"

"I was thinking of the annulment."

Eduardo studied her eyes.

"You would marry a man you do not love?"

"I do it all the time."

Eduardo shook his head in admiration. "I could not trust such a woman as you to be a good wife."

"Just as good a wife as you would be a husband."

"Yes. We are what we are."

"Whatever that means."

Eduardo tried to take her in his arms again.

Christi turned away and started to walk from the room.

"You are not married to Kiki." Eduardo snapped, causing Christi to freeze in her tracks.

"What?" she turned.

"The priest who married you was defrocked for revolutionary activity. Your marriage is annulled. The paperwork is on my desk." Eduardo said coolly.

Christi tried to study his eyes for a glint of weakness, but he had the smug look of truth on his face. "Why are you telling me this now?"

Eduardo started to pull down another drink but thought better of it as he put the drink down on the bar. "Kiki is leaving tonight. I want you to go see him. After you have seen him if you return to me then we will talk of us."

"What if I don't want to see him?'

"I insist. I will not have long shadows of guilt across our future."

"Our future?"

"Yes!"

"Oh? Then why waste time on goodbyes?"

"Because I wish it."

"No."

"Yes."

"I do not want to see him. Force me and I will go home to Charleston first thing in the morning."

Eduardo smirked. "Really?"

"Really!"

"No, you won't."

"Oh? And why not?"

"Because you have not yet married the rich man you speak of in your letters to Momma."

"You bastard! You read my letters. How . . ."

"Don't insult me. I am a gentleman. It seems you do not guard your writings when the maids are about. They thought this information would win my favor. They have been dismissed."

Christi was too embarrassed to speak.

"Don't fret. You may still get your wish." He paused and grinned sardonically. "Then perhaps you will not. I expect you downstairs and ready to go within the hour," Eduardo ordered as he left the room.

Christi picked up a letter opener and started to run after him. She swore at him under her breath. She paced back and forth in anger.

She sighed hard and moved upstairs to dress.

Chapter Thirty-three

THE SECLUDED GULF COAST HARBOR REMINDED CHRISTI OF Cuba. She was hoping Eduardo was lying until she saw the eighty-odd men dressed in khaki loading a small yacht with crates.

Her eyes searched frantically until they fell upon a bearded and now plump Kiki, leaning on one crutch, having an animated conversation with a group of five men.

Christi looked into Eduardo's eyes. They demanded that she go to Kiki. She returned a look of displeasure before she reluctantly got out of the open car and walked across the deep sand of the beach toward her husband.

Kiki did not see her at first. Then his eyes turned toward hers and laughed for a moment before they looked old and sad.

Kiki was almost unrecognizable as anyone she had ever known, much less loved. Christi almost stopped and turned back but Kiki's painful look compelled her to continue. She stopped within inches of his arms.

Kiki clumsily reached out with one arm and held her. It was not the warm embraces she had known in Cuba, or in the early days of Mexico City, but a friendly hug.

"*Querida mia!* I did not think you would come here tonight." Kiki dismissed the other men with hurried gestures.

"Kiki, you never wrote or called or anything. You are leaving without me. Just like that?"

"I believe this to be the best thing. Please forgive me. I wish for you much happiness."

Christi still had a great deal of puppy-dog fondness for Kiki. She was glad he looked happier than she had ever seen him look. "Will you be alright?"

"Yes! Eduardo has made it so that we cannot fail!"

"I see."

"You do not think I leave you with a heavy heart?" Kiki fought off tears.

Christi gave him an affectionate kiss on the cheek. "I wish you well, my husband."

Kiki looked a little embarrassed. "Eduardo has not told you?"

"Told me what?"

"In the church's eyes we were never married. Please forgive me." Kiki braced himself on his crutch and looked into her eyes. "Eduardo is a man that can be trusted. You know what I have to do. Please remember I have left you with a man who can take very good care of you. All of this he has provided," Kiki apologized.

The sea breeze blew unusually cold on Christi's skin as she now felt indifferent. It blew back the serape she was wearing to expose her black velvet dress.

Kiki looked surprised and a little hurt before he spoke.

"This is our wedding dress? You wear this to honor me?"

Christi did not have the heart to tell him it was a dress Eduardo had bought for her. She had burned the dress Kiki had given her.

Kiki took her face in his hands and kissed her gently on the forehead. "*Querida mia.* To come here like this is to do me great honor."

Christi looked indifferent.

"We must be in Cabo Cruz by December. When it is over I will send you a message. I wish only one thing—that you will march into Havana with us after our glorious victory!" Kiki exclaimed.

Christi smiled and tried to look interested.

Kiki pulled her up to his face as the strangely cool Caribbean sea wind made their closeness welcome.

"*Querida mia,* I have loved you dearly. They have taken much away from me but this love I keep forever. You will forget many things. Please do not forget I have loved you."

For some reason, Christi was tempted to tell him, "To hell with your revolution! I'll give this rich man what he wants tonight. What do you think of that?" Instead she smiled some encouragement.

Kiki started to gather her in his arms, but finally let them drop to his side and turned toward the yacht where El Grande was yelling for him. "I must go with my comrades. I will always love you." Kiki sighed hard. He turned and hobbled away, then stopped and looked back for Christi. The mixture of sadness and bittersweet joy on his face was almost too much for her to look at.

Christi looked toward the dark ocean then back at Kiki. Suddenly the thought of another man leaving her was too much to bear.

She ran at him and jumped on his back. They tumbled to the ground. They came up spitting sand.

"Christi? What are you doing?"

"You love these men more than me!"

"*Querida mia!* What is this you are doing?"

"Nobody leaves me anymore! Understand?"

Kiki took a deep breath and blew it out hard. "Do not do this in front of the men. Please! I do not understand."

"I want the whole damn world to see! I'm a million miles from home and don't know if my mother is alive or dead and you tell me I don't understand. Well, I'll tell you something. I DON'T understand. I don't understand why my mother put me on a ship with a bunch of gangsters. I don't understand why Cosmo thinks he can get away with turning his back on me! And you have been away for three months leaving me with a stranger. Most of all, I don't understand why you want to go to Cuba to get killed. Look at that small boat. You will most probably die at sea, from drowning. Okay. Go ahead! Eduardo wants me! This is our wedding dress and I'll marry him in it!"

Christi swung a fist at Kiki's head. He ducked. Her arms missed and she fell to the sand. She waited for him to help her up but he turned away.

"It is not a small boat when you are with the men who have suffered the great hurt with you. I had wished you might understand this dream. I am sorry you do not."

Kiki paused as he watched El Grande wave him to the boat. "I only wish you do this one thing. You do not marry in this special dress."

The hurt in his pleading eyes made Christi's anger abate. She felt a little foolish as she shrugged. "Maybe I will, maybe I won't, but I do know I'll marry Eduardo and with his money and I'll stop crazy things like this! Once I'm rich no one will ever leave me again!"

Kiki gave her a fatherly smile. "Maybe it is you who should fight Batista. We surely do not lose then." Kiki paused and smiled. "I wish we had time for a few *cervezas.*"

Christi had to laugh. "I'm sorry, Kiki. I'm just a little confused. Please be careful and take care of yourself."

Kiki reached out and touched her hair with a goodbye touch. "I think you will be a fine Aztec queen."

Christi shook her head sadly. "There were no Aztec queens."

Kiki let his crutch fall to the sand. He saluted Christi. "God has been good. I prayed you would come and beg me not to go. You do not know the strength this gives me. I am the most fortunate of men. In another time you are the woman I die for or with God's grace live for!" Kiki stopped as he heard angry shouts from the men hanging out of the boat. "I have to go. It takes longer for me to walk a step than most men. *Adios, querida mia.*" Kiki gave her another salute and turned away again.

As she watched Kiki hobble toward the leaky, overcrowded boat without his crutch, for a moment, she still wanted to follow him.

She looked up toward the hill at Eduardo. The lights on his car gave an eerie glow that penetrated the deep tropical darkness.

He looked statuesque and elegant with the bright light behind him.

Kiki paused and turned a final time. He gave her a look of undying love that would have melted her heart had she not now hardened it to all but cunning and survival.

Two big, heavily armed men lifted him up and carried him to the boat before Christi could move.

She stood and watched him board the small boat. It looked very silly overflowing with men and challenging the waterline as it putted slowly away toward Cuba in the heavy sea swells.

Christi was reluctant to look up the hill toward Eduardo, so she walked toward the ocean and kicked off her shoes. The struggling boat with Kiki aboard was slowly fading behind a distant jetty as she waded into the surf.

She could hear them singing rousing choruses of liberation songs and wondered if Kiki was looking in her direction. She felt very sorry for herself. All the men she had ever known told her how beautiful she was. They all vowed undying love and they all went away. She turned and looked back at the tall silhouette of Eduardo on the hillside.

"Fuck elegance! Fuck beauty! I want power! On my life, I want power!" Christi swore just before a large wave hit her, knocking her down into the fierce grip of an undertow that drug her out to sea.

The salty water burned its way into her nose and throat.

She gagged and coughed before she lost consciousness.

She did not see Eduardo, a man deathly afraid of water, run into the surf and gather her up into his arms. She did not feel his frantic kisses of concern, or hear his expressions of undying love as he lay beside her, exhausted and praising God on the warm safety of the beach.

Chapter Thirty-four

CHRISTI AWOKE SLOWLY. SHE SHIVERED SLIGHTLY AND COUGHED residual seawater from her lungs. For a moment she wondered if it had all been a dream. Then she saw Eduardo sitting in a small chair by her bed, peering down at her. She instinctively moved to pull the covers around her neck. As she did, she realized she was naked. She looked at Eduardo suspiciously.

He smiled wryly.

"I'm sorry, grandmother was asleep, the maids are gone and I had to get you out of those wet clothes."

Christi glared at him a moment, but found it hard to be mad at him. "Did you take a nice, long look?"

"No. After all, I am a gentleman as well as a physician."

"Oh, I see, doctor. Did I pass the physical?"

"Yes, you did. You passed on every point. Superbly."

Christi let the covers drop slightly. "Would you like to take a long look?"

Eduardo's stern demeanor melted and his eyes danced with his answer.

"You know the price of admission to this peep show?" Christi teased.

Eduardo regained his composure and nodded

"Until then, would you mind leaving the room so that I can dress?"

Eduardo grinned. "Putting clothes on you Christi is like covering the Sistine Chapel with a tarpaulin. Here, please look this over when you have a chance," Eduardo said as he lay a wax-sealed envelope on a silver tray by her bed.

Christi looked at it quizzically.

"It is the annulment papers, translated into English. You slept almost twenty-four hours. I have been busy."

"I see you have." Christi started to reach for the envelope and absentmindedly let the covers slip. She felt no sense of nakedness as her breasts lay bare before Eduardo's hungry eyes. She was fascinated by the way her body caused him to lose his composure. He was the most solid man of breeding she had ever known yet he seemed weak before her beauty. With a slow teasing motion she grabbed the covers and pulled them back around her.

Eduardo stood up and looked down at her from his full six foot three inch height. He trembled slightly as he addressed her slowly and evenly. "I have been most patient. I have understood your feelings and have respected them for a long while. For all this time you have had the hospitality of this house without incident. That is no longer good enough," he said, reaching down and pulling away the sheet, exposing Christi's nude body.

Christi angrily grabbed the sheet back, tearing it as she pulled it from his hands.

Eduardo grabbed her by the shoulder and yanked her out of bed. Before she was completely on her feet, he pulled her into his strong arms and held her against his masculine chest. He ignored her kicks and screams as he reached down and grabbed her face in his huge right hand. He looked deadly serious as he pulled her mouth hard up to his.

Christi tried to turn away but his lips were on hers and she found herself giving in.

Eduardo's kisses were more pleasant than she wanted them to be and she let herself enjoy them for a few moments before her old fears caused her to turn away. "Let me go, dammit! Eduardo, let me go now!"

"Now that wasn't so terrible," Eduardo said as he let her sit down on the bed.

"Yes it was! I don't like it, Eduardo. Don't ever grab me again. No one manhandles me. That's it! I'm leaving. I've stayed too long. I owe you for your hospitality. I'll send you a check!"

"Oh? And where will you go? Do you really think you can go live among the *pobrecitos* now? You have lived in the center of the most luxury money can buy. Go ahead, I dare you to try and leave it. What will you take? The few clothes you brought are gone. Everything here is mine." He waved his arm around the room.

"Wrong! There is one yellow cotton dress that belongs to me." Christi ran to the closet and searched for it. "Where is it? Where?"

Eduardo left the room a moment. He returned with her dress on a hanger and looked puzzled. "It looked out of place among the others. God! It is but one dress, Christi A simple dress at that. I have seen you change clothes five times in one day. I have seen your face light up when you put on the velvet dresses I provided. I have also watched you enjoy being served. You run my servants ragged. You intend on going into the world outside with one yellow cotton dress? And what will you do?"

"I'll find something. I'm not a cripple. Give me my dress!" Christi reached out for her dress.

Eduardo held it back. "Christi, this is foolish. I love you and want you to be my wife. Am I so hideous you cannot consider it?"

"That's why you attacked me?"

"I am sorry. That was frustration."

"It's what you stupid men do! I'm past being tired of it! I have to leave and think things over. I have to!" Christi shook with rage.

Eduardo shrugged. "You are a most willful lady. I will not try to stop you. I have offered all I can, so go. Go! Go find out how cold it can be in Mexico City without friends and money." Eduardo stood aside and motioned for her to pass.

"Do you mind if I get dressed first?"

Eduardo shrugged, threw the dress at her, then turned and stomped out of the room.

Christi picked up the yellow cotton dress off the floor and stroked the warmth of its comforting material. She looked at the closet full of velvet dresses. She thought about ringing for a handmaid to attend her. A butler to run an errand. She fought back tears of self-pity.

As she wiped the moisture from her eyes and looked at herself in the mirror, she wondered if she wasn't being very stupid. Eduardo had everything she could want. She walked over and looked out the window, across the city, and suddenly felt very cold.

As her anger vanished, her practical side made her sit down and think about things.

There was something basically wrong with the thoughts she allowed herself to have. Designing thoughts without a trace of guilt. This man was hers for the taking and now she felt no qualms about taking him. She picked up a gold and pearl inlaid brush and brushed her hair as she sat before the oversized mirror.

"It is time," she acknowledged quietly. She did not like the new coldness in her eyes. It was not inborn, but acquired. Christi would not wait the widow's year, or even a widow's month, if indeed she was a widow. In her mind, Kiki was dead and her new and better life was about to begin.

Christi drove the cold shadows from her eyes with a sly grin. "No more poverty!" She held the crucifix tightly. "God forgive me, I want it all!" She sighed hard then broke into girlish laughter. "What the heck! I can learn to love him," she said as she checked her hairdo one more time.

She hung her yellow cotton dress in the darkest corner of the closet, purposefully placing it out of sight so she would not see it when retrieving one of the more expensive dresses. It was funny. She felt it didn't fit her anymore. She felt only a small pang of remorse as she hid it away to take the silk dressing robe with its expensive gold embroidery.

She was barefoot and naked beneath the silk dressing robe as she walked out of the room. The thick Persian carpets felt good on her feet as she made her way downstairs to Eduardo's library.

She hoped he would be there alone.

She took two deep breaths then slowly opened the huge polished oak door.

Eduardo stood with his back to her, holding an open book in his hand. He turned to look at her as the door clicked shut. He smiled and closed the book as Christi walked toward him, placing it on the nearest table and holding his arms out to her.

Christi walked into his embrace and let him lift her face with his hand until his lips fell upon hers. His kiss was warm.

"Eduardo, is that annulment paper real? I have lost so much I can't afford God's hatred." Christi sighed.

Eduardo nodded. "You were not married in the eyes of God, Christi. A defrocked priest has no ecclesiastical powers. It is as if it never happened." Eduardo toyed with the knotted string holding the robe together.

"If you still want me, I will marry you, but it must be a real priest, in a real church and I want a real wedding dress!"

Eduardo feigned a sigh. He seemed disappointed for a moment. "You hold me to this great price?"

Christi put her arms around his neck. He kissed her fiercely and hungrily. "Great price?" Christi broke the embrace.

"So many are against it. It will cause much trouble in my family."

"I'm sorry. It's your decision."

"Yes. Yes it is," he nodded sad agreement.

"Eduardo, please stop my mail from Charleston. You have influence. Please tell them all back there I am dead. I want to be dead to that world and to Kiki's world."

"I really want to marry you, Eduardo, but in fairness to us both, I want to start a new life. Do you have enough power to bury my past?" Christi pulled his mouth down toward her cleavage.

Eduardo trembled with nervousness as his mouth gently kissed the part of her breasts exposed by the low-cut robe.

"All of it?" Eduardo paused.

"Yes," Christi whispered.

"I do not know if this is possible."

"What?"

"You wish to forget even your mother, Christi? *Su Madre?!*"

Christi reached back and loosened the rope holding the robe, letting it fall below to her nipple line. "Especially my mother!"

Eduardo saw the lovely pink outline of the areola around her firm nipples and asked no more questions.

Christi let him bury his face in wild, passionate kisses between her breasts. Trembling with passion he tried to pull off the robe.

She kissed him coolly on the forehead and pushed him away.

"After the wedding, *mi amor.* After the wedding," she cooed.

Eduardo started to ignore her and pull her to him.

Christi's look of defiance made him stand back and stare at her in frustration.

"Soon, love, soon!" Christi looked coy.

"You American bitch!" he spewed.

"You Latin bastard!" she retaliated.

He looked menacing.

She growled playfully.

Eduardo removed his clothes, revealing a manhood that defied further argument. He walked over and stood above her. She touched his throbbing manhood with a soft hand.

"Oh, Christi. Oh God! Christi." He shook with desire.

Christi stroked his throbbing manhood, touching his thighs with the tips of her fingernails and drawing them back in a teasing, racking motion. "After the wedding, darling. After the wedding."

Eduardo was bent by frustration. He was one more tease from a rape. His eyes showed a mixture of disbelief, hurt, and anger.

"Please understand, technically I'm still a virgin. I will keep that for your wedding night." Christi closed her robe and backed away.

Eduardo would not be soothed. He grabbed her hair and pulled her to the floor.

Christi hit her head hard on the floor. She came to her feet spewing blood and defiance.

Eduardo started to grab her again. He cooled when he saw the blood. His face revealed overwhelming guilt. "God! Please forgive me. Please understand you provoked me beyond madness. Leave me! Go now, witch! Go before I am as mad as you!"

Christi wiped the trickle of blood on her sleeve.

She pulled the robe back over her exposed breasts. "I wouldn't marry you now if you were the last man on earth!"

Eduardo nodded half-agreement. "Oh! I think you will. You want all this even if to have it is to live a lie."

"You're a liar too!"

"Perhaps. To have what we desire, at times, I must lie and you must lie."

"Two liars may not make a good marriage but we will be married and on our honeymoon night you must be prepared for many thrusts of love," Eduardo fumed as he walked to the doorway. Once there he stopped and turned. As his passion ebbed, he spoke in a stern, commanding tone. "Or maybe I do not come to you at all!"

Chapter Thirty-five

THE WEDDING WAS HELD IN THE BASILICA OF GUADALUPE, ONLY A few yards from where the Blessed Virgin is supposed to have appeared to an Indian boy, Juan Diego, and imprinted her portrait on his cloak. The cloak, set in gold, is protected by a thirty-ton railing of silver and is the most venerated shrine in South America. Every twelfth of December, forty thousand people gather at the shrine to commemorate the appearance of the Virgin. It is a feast that rivals the Mardi Gras in Rio for the intensity of the revelry.

Eduardo had loved the feast day since he was a child. He had the wedding scheduled for the early morning hours, hoping to have it over before the streets filled.

Christi, against Eduardo's grandmother's objections, wore an exquisite full-length white gown of Irish lace with a matching mantilla. Grandmother De La Cruz didn't care that the Pope himself had signed the annulment. In her mind Christi was a divorcee, a designing gold-digger, and too vile to be dressed in white.

Christi knew the dress was not Granny's problem. Christi was mature to the world's ways now. She knew Granny resented more the loss of power over Eduardo. As the priest blessed them, Christi respected the ceremony.

She had decided in her heart and soul that Kiki was dead, Cosmo was working on being dead, and as she looked at her handsome bridegroom she said "yes" willingly.

This time the ceremony was performed by an archbishop in the splendid old Basilica, crowded with the most fashionable people in Mexico City.

Eduardo was very handsome in his dark blue traditional suit trimmed in white lace. The church was literally lined with flowers of all kinds. Ring bearers and flower girls were dressed in the finest tailored clothes and the air was thick with the smell of old money.

In her anger at her mother for what Christi now thought of as a gross betrayal she had not invited her. Now, Christi wished she could have waited until she could arrange for Sarah to be with them.

She was still unsure how she would explain it all to her.

"*In patris dominus sancti.*" The bishop began the mass that followed the ceremony as Christi and Eduardo knelt on red velvet pillows before the shining altar besplendored in Aztec gold.

Christi closed her eyes and thought of happier times. As the words of the priest slowly faded from her consciousness, she was awakened from her trance by Eduardo lifting her off the floor and giving her a long, excited kiss.

"I give you my beloved bride, Señora De La Cruz!" Eduardo smiled to the crowd's applause. Moments later, he led her along behind him, to the waiting car.

Flowers and rice rained down on them as they got into the car. The driver drove slowly through the crowds that were gathering for the feast of Guadalupe.

Eduardo waved to the adoring crowd as he pulled Christi over by his side and looked at her lovingly as he held her face in his hands. "I will be the best husband ever. I will make you very happy. Very, very happy, *querida mia!*" Eduardo insisted.

"*Querida mia?*" Christi repeated. She had to fight off a laugh as she wondered if all men used the same words of endearment—and if they really meant them.

"What?"

"Nothing." Christi smiled and looked at Eduardo with affection. "I will try to be a good wife, Eduardo. Please be patient with me." She lay her head on his strong shoulder.

The driver smiled into the rear view mirror as he turned the car up the hill toward Eduardo's house.

"Today you will meet some of the most important people in Latin America. I hope you will be proud to be a De La Cruz. They are important and powerful people, but they do not have such a lovely wife as I," Eduardo sighed proudly.

"Let's skip the reception." Christi tickled his chest with her fingernails.

"You would rather go straight to Rio? Or perhaps your home in Charleston?"

"Charleston? You know how I feel about that!"

"Yes. You speak of it often in your dreams."

"I do?"

"Yes. In time we will go there and exorcize the demons."

"No. We have to talk about that, Eduardo. There is something I haven't told you. If I do go home, I think it's best if I go alone." Christi swallowed hard.

"I know how you feel about your mother's apparent betrayal. I would like to see this resolved." Eduardo frowned.

"No. I don't want you to go there. I'll go alone."

"My wife does not travel alone."

"You don't understand."

"Then you will tell me how to understand."

Christi shook her head in frustration. "God, Eduardo! I'm a *campesino*. All my people are dirt poor. You'd die if you had to spend ten minutes in the shanty town I'm from. I just can't let you see it. I would die of embarrassment," Christi insisted.

"You do not think I know about such things?"

"No, I don't!"

"Why do I spend millions to support the revolution if such things are foreign to me? No! You will not return home alone." He looked stern as the driver pulled the car into the landscaped driveway and drove them to the front door.

Ramon, the butler, opened the door of the car before Christi could reply. "Congratulations, Señora Guevara," he offered as he helped her from the car.

The other servants gathered behind Ramon and applauded.

Grandmother De La Cruz stopped at the stoop of the steps and frowned.

The receiving line was made up of Eduardo's relatives and near relatives, all of whom had the relaxed look of the longtime rich. Christi felt out of place as the bejeweled people passed through the line smiling warmly at Eduardo.

They gave her a cool greeting, at most. She admired Eduardo for having the courage to marry her. It was obvious it was not a popular move among his kind. She hoped she could remain pleasant and calm, but her hatred of snobbery ran deep and she knew it would take only one carefully placed insult to set her off.

"I am Eduardo's first cousin from Caracas. My name is Consuela

Carmella Rosita Gomez Montoya de Guiterrez. You must come to visit our villa in Caracas sometime. Perhaps you could come this winter after we return from our summer home in Switzerland," she grinned.

Christi stayed quiet and smiled thinly. "It's very nice to meet you."

A short but stiff-backed gnome of a man approached her. "I'm Pierre. I'm the French branch of the family. I'm a direct descendent of Maximillian. You will have to come riding with us sometime. Do you ride?" he quizzed.

"Yes I do. Nice meeting you," Christi lied.

"You are an American? I do hope I can make it there one day. They say you are from the South. I understand that is where all the Negro slaves were. It would be interesting to visit that area," a snotty looking old dame chuckled.

The condescending way she said "Negro" made Christi want to reply, but she held her temper.

"Eduardo, please excuse me. I have to leave the line for a moment." Christi moved away, to the astonishment of many of the stiff-necked guests.

"Please excuse us!"

Eduardo apologized as he followed Christi out of the room onto the veranda where she stood taking deep breaths and blowing them out hard. "Christi, what is it?"

"Eduardo, it's not my place. I just don't fit in with these people. They know it and I know it. Can't you see they can barely keep from laughing. Can't you see that?" Christi almost cried.

Eduardo took her shoulders in his strong hands and held her firmly. "Christi, you stop this! You see devils everywhere and there are none. It is enough. If they slight you, it is jealousy. They have not your beauty and there are many that would have given everything to have been my wife," Eduardo explained.

"Eduardo, please promise me something. I will go back inside if you will promise me one thing."

"Of course, whatever I can do."

"Starting tomorrow I want you to get me tutors. I want courses in Castilian and advanced French. I want to learn to ride horses like those overdressed bitches in there. I want to relearn all the grand things Mrs. White and my mother taught me. I want to know all and more than those damned snobs. Will you promise me that, Eduardo?"

Eduardo stroked her hair softly and nodded. "You are Señora De La Cruz You can have anything you wish. These things you will do tomorrow. Today we must do our social duty." He kissed her then took her hand and led her back into the house.

"Duty," a word Christi understood but hated. "Yes. Of course." She put her head up high and walked gracefully across the room to her place in the receiving line.

Eduardo's words, "You are Señora De La Cruz. You can have anything you wish!" gave her a heady feeling of power. It was the feeling she had waited on for so long.

She was feeling wonderfully happy from champagne and power as the last guest left.

Eduardo gathered her in his arms and bounded up the stairs into the bedroom.

"So many nights I slept here alone, wondering if I would ever have you," he said as he lay her down on the bed.

Christi reached up and pulled his lips down on hers. "I had so many things to work out. I'm glad now you waited for me. I will really try hard to be a good wife, Eduardo," she promised sincerely.

Eduardo kissed her almost politely at first. His kisses became more fierce as he kissed her about her shoulders and between her firm breasts.

Christi let herself yield to his desires. She would now be his and think of no one else. She would give him the finest honeymoon any man ever had. "Just a moment, darling." She eased away from him and stood up.

Eduardo watched with fascination as she unzipped the bridal gown and stepped out of it and stood before him in her lace panties and bra.

A bright moon lit the dark velvet and gold of the room and made Christi's smooth bronze skin glisten golden. She watched his face as Eduardo studied her flawless figure for a moment.

He seemed to be dreaming as she stepped out of the lace panties.

Eduardo got up and began to undress himself as she unhooked her bra and let her lovely breasts spill into his hands. "Yes, my love. This night I am the most fortunate man on earth." Eduardo kissed her between her breasts and pulled her warm body to his. "*Mi corazón*," Eduardo murmured as he lifted her up and lay her across the velvet bedspread then stood above her and admired her beauty.

"Come to me, my husband!" Christi said as she reached out and embraced his body.

Eduardo kissed her firm thighs. He ran his hands the length of her legs and kissed her gently on her naval.

Christi shivered with pleasure.

He kissed his way down between her thighs.

She writhed in ecstasy.

"Eduardo, *mi amor*. I am dead to the old world. I will be a grand wife. You will have no more lonely nights!" Christi insisted as she dug her fingernails into his thick dark hair and pulled his hot mouth deeper into her flesh.

Eduardo mumbled something.

He continued his hot kisses and she slowly parted her legs. As he entered her, Christi's thoughts were of pleasure and pain. She held his firm, muscular body close to hers and enjoyed his strokes of love.

The fire with which he took her was so intense she almost lost control. She resisted that urge. She would enjoy it but not let him be the master of it. Many times, she halted his passionate thrusts by pushing him, ever so gently away. She would wait for him to shiver with anticipation then allow him to continue.

He was mad with long-restrained emotion when he exploded in a primeval yell of victory and fell over exhausted.

Christi held him in her arms and stroked him as Sarah had always stroked her.

She could not stop her mind from wandering to old loves lost. Old loves she knew she now had the power to regain. Never again would a man leave her unless she wanted him to leave her. She had access to the biggest, most powerful fortune in South America. It would take some time, but she would learn how this power worked.

Then it would be time to settle old scores.

"I am Mrs. Eduardo Ricardo De La Cruz, a woman of great power. Watch out world, here I come!" she whispered quietly to herself.

Chapter Thirty-six

Mrs. White poured Sarah a tall glass of iced tea. She looked at Sarah's eyes. The once-strong eyes looked tired and worried. Mrs. White was also worried. She had loved Christi like the daughter she had never had. "You had no way of knowing what was going to happen in Cuba. No one can ever blame you for sending her as far away as possible from Lucius's brother and the bad elements of this community."

Sarah gave Mrs. White a look of disagreement.

Neither of them saw Etta May watching them from the shadows of her room. Etta May missed Christi sometimes, but sometimes she was glad Christi was gone. Christi always seemed to get the best of everything. At least now she didn't have to listen to how perfect Christi was, and now she had a room to herself. But Etta still got mad when she considered God had given Christi so much and she and Eddie so little.

Little Eddie didn't get involved in family politics, or any politics for that matter. He was just a happy-go-lucky kid who dismissed Etta May's pouts as jealousy.

Etta May took extra care to groom herself to imitate Christi. She hated the sting of the harsh chemicals she had to use to try to achieve Christi's look. Etta believed she was naturally more beautiful than Christi and never understood men who chose Christi over herself.

"You listening again to something that ain't none o' your business? I swear, Etta May! Your ears are going to fall off," Little Eddie interrupted Etta's thoughts.

"Get your tight ass out of here! This is my room now that Christi is gone! Don't you be spying on me, you fool," Etta snapped.

Little Eddie stepped back a little. He was dressed in an ill-fitting Air Force uniform.

"Etta, I'm big enough now to fit into Daddy's uniform. I'm going to be a jet pilot," Little Eddie insisted.

Etta May turned and looked at him with contempt. "You dumb fool. Nobody knows who our real daddy is, much less the white folks is not going to let you in the jet pilot school. Hush up and go away, fool!"

Etta chided.

Little Eddie looked hurt. He flipped her off when she turned away.

Etta put her ear to the small crack in the door.

Little Eddie backed away into the shadows and listened as Sarah spoke.

"I'm just going to have to find some way to go down there to Mexico and straighten this thing out, that's all there is to it!" Sarah insisted.

Mrs. White sipped her hot tea, politely agreeing.

"God knows what all happened in that heathen den of communists in Cuba. God knows what they did to my precious girl. My God! Mrs. White, it goes against everything we ever tried to teach her. But I don't blame her none," Sarah waxed melancholy.

"She's sometimes more like someone else than she is the Joneses," Sarah nodded in agreement with herself.

Mrs. White smiled thinly.

"I think she's exactly like you, inside, Sarah. She's all that you were and were denied, all that you hoped for and lost, all you thought but never had the opportunity to act upon," Mrs. White offered.

Sarah looked at her hard before she smiled. "You are just an old school teacher. I'm just a kitchen helper. What do we know about Cuba and revolutions and Mexico, and where my Christi is and what she's doing now?"

"Christi was my challenge and my love. I worry for her also. I have some small savings and I've always wanted to see Mexico. Write her and tell her we're coming. I think we deserve it!" Mrs. White bubbled.

Sarah looked doubtful. "She don't write back no more."

"We have her last address. I'll assume that is where she is," Mrs. White insisted.

"I don't know. Lord! I just don't know." Sarah looked at her rough hands made almost manly by hard labor. "Christi has such long, feminine fingers," Sarah said wistfully.

Mrs. White agreed. "Those hands have earned you the right to take a vacation. I will arrange it. You write Christi and tell her we are on our way. We'll go whether she answers or not." Mrs. White stood up and acted firm.

Sarah pondered the thought and reluctantly nodded agreement.

"Oh God! They's going to go to Mexico," Etta exclaimed as she burst from the room.

"Etta May?" Sarah looked puzzled.

"Momma, I'm sorry. I didn't mean to be listening but you just said you and Mrs. White are going to Mexico. Momma, I want to go too!" Etta May pleaded.

Etta May was holding Sarah tightly around the waist as Little Eddie entered the room.

"I suppose you want to go also?" Sarah asked.

Little Eddie shrugged until Etta May gave him a dirty look then he nodded.

Sarah looked at Mrs. White and sighed. "I can't leave this family to go off God knows where."

Mrs. White thought it over a moment. "I'm an old school teacher who was taught to save for a rainy day. Perhaps today it is raining. Sarah, Etta May, Little Eddie, you are my family. My whole family goes or no one goes!" Mrs. White beamed.

"No! No, it just don't seem right. If that chile had wanted me to come she would of done sent me some word. If she has this here rich husband and all the things she talked about she would of sent us some kind of invite. No! There's something that just ain't right and until I figure it out we won't be going nowhere." Sarah released her hold on Etta May and looked at Mrs. White soberly. "But I thank you for your generous offer anyway." Sarah said her eyes brimming with tears of sadness.

Mrs. White started to reply and thought better of it.

Etta May ran back into her room.

Little Eddie followed a moment later.

Etta May motioned for him to close the door. Once it was closed Etta May did a dance of celebration. "Maybe Christi is dead! Yes! Maybe that stuck up bitch is dead!" Etta May reached out for Eddie to join the dance.

Little Eddie looked at her like she was crazy.

Chapter Thirty-seven

I T WAS ALL BEYOND CHRISTI'S WILDEST DREAMS. THE FIRST YEARS OF HER marriage TO Eduardo were the happiest of her life. Nothing she wanted was denied her and she was introduced to many delights she never knew existed. At first she was anxious about being surrounded by luxury. Sarah had taught her that most rich people got their money through evil deeds. Christi did not know how Eduardo came by his money, and after a while it did not matter. She was totally seduced by the world of money and the power that came with it. To ease her conscience she thought about Sarah and her past life less and less every day.

Christi was being schooled in all the social graces by the finest tutors in the world, and the more she learned the more she sought to learn.

She still had problems with turned heads and snide tittering at fancy social gatherings. It had hurt at first, then Christi, to their complete shock, would tell them off in their own language. Grudging respect would follow sometime later.

The guilty pleasure she enjoyed most of all, was walking into the finest restaurants in Rio and feeling all eyes on her. It was almost embarrassing to see the hush fall over a room she entered.

The unspoken envy of other beautiful women was so thick you could cut it with a plastic surgeon's scalpel.

It might have been a little too much adoration were it not for the way it made Eduardo swell with pride and put him in a mood to lavish her with even more wonderful things.

At one gala in Brasila she was stunned to hear that Miss Brazil envied her beauty. Of course Eduardo had said that but she delighted in it nevertheless.

Grandmother De La Cruz's reservations had begrudgingly given way to respect. Grannie's eyes lit up brightly when Christi addressed her in Castilian Spanish, mixed with French idioms and peppered with anecdotes told in Gaelic.

Most of all, she admired the way Eduardo and his friends rode their horses.

Christi was a little afraid of horses, but her social training would not be complete until she could ride well. With some reluctance she asked Eduardo to make her into a horsewoman.

In deference to Christi, Eduardo selected an old mare without spirit from his stables.

Christi was no expert on horses, but she knew there was something wrong with her mount. Poco was hard to goad into moving, and when she moved it was at an invalid's pace. One bright September morning in 1961, close to a newly opened resort called Acapulco, Christi halted Poco and looked over at Eduardo.

Eduardo was riding his magnificent white Arabian stallion named J.C. Eduardo wanted to name the horse Christo, which is a Spanish derivative of Christ.

His grandmother would not permit it. His grandmother did not know how much more sacrilegious a horse named J.C. was.

"Damn it, Eduardo! This horse is lame. Let me ride J.C."

Eduardo vigorously shook his head.

"Will you please stop overprotecting me. Please let me ride your stallion." Christi reached out for the reins but Eduardo waved her off.

"J.C. does not let strangers sit well. You have had only two months of lessons." Eduardo stopped as J.C. reared and bucked, snorting violently. "As you can see you aren't ready for this horse yet," Eduardo insisted.

Christi grabbed at the reins.

J.C. bucked a moment before he snorted into submission.

Christi looked Eduardo in the eye. "See. I have a way with men." Christi gave Eduardo a quick kiss.

Eduardo looked doubtful.

"No, Christi, J.C. will hurt you. He is a one-man horse. It took me two years to get him used to my boot."

"I won't give him the boot and tonight you will have that new kama sutra position you read about." Christi stroked Eduardo's soft dark hair.

Eduardo tried to be firm but her magic touch still worked. "God! You are such a witch. You can have anything you want but I love you too much to let you on this horse!" he said with a tone of finality.

"Okay," Christi shrugged as she dismounted Poco.

Eduardo dismounted J.C. and was adjusting his cap when Christi leaped into his arms.

Eduardo fell over, holding her as he fell on his back in the tall hillside grass.

The horses bumped and snorted as they played.

Christi took Eduardo's head in her hands and kissed him gently. "I love you, Eduardo. You have given me everything I've ever wanted but you have never given me your trust."

"What are you talking about?"

"You don't believe in me. I can ride that oversized jackass." Christi paused as she watched J.C. walk between her and the sunlight. J.C. was a magnificent stud. He had won four million pesos in purses and gained Eduardo thirty-five million pesos in syndication fees. Christi associated such a horse with real power. Every day that passed and she had not tamed it to do as she wished, she felt was an insult to her position.

There would be no mustangs on the Christi range.

Christi was really a little afraid of the prancing temperamental stallion. J.C. had thrown one trainer who was still in the hospital with a broken neck. J.C. defied anyone but Eduardo to touch him. Christi watched with admiration as the magnificent horse stood outlined against the sun. He was a proud animal that exuded a kind of erotic power that made Christi both uneasy and aroused.

"Make love to me here. Now!" Christi demanded.

"Here? But the other riders will be along soon." Eduardo raised his head to look around.

Christi pulled his head down between her breasts. She lay back on the wildflowers, a small moss-covered boulder provided her pillow as Eduardo began to gently undress her.

Christi helped him with the buttons. She had not worn a bra.

Eduardo lowered his mouth slowly onto her bare breasts and helped her out of her silk panties. He kissed them before he threw them away.

Christi parted her legs and let him enter. She enjoyed his caresses and kisses as, out of one eye, she watched J.C. prance freely in the open meadow.

J.C. would not be so easily conquered. J.C. would be a new challenge. The thought of taming such a magnificent animal caused her to shudder with passion. She had the most fantastic orgasm she had ever experienced.

Eduardo was extremely pleased with himself.

Chapter Thirty-eight

IT WAS NOW PAST NINE O'CLOCK. SARAH JONES WASN'T HOME AND ETTA May was very worried. Sarah was always on time. Etta May was the oldest in the family now that Christi was gone, and she was supposed to be in charge when Sarah was out. Etta May hated responsibility.

Etta May liked loud rock and roll music, thinking about whether to give herself to her lover, Morris Winfield, or to keep herself for marriage. Etta May had made the same promise that Christi made. Etta May felt some resentment that Christi was so far away and could do anything and Sarah would never know. Etta May bet Christi was not a virgin when she was married. If she was really married.

Etta May loved Morris. She loved the feel of his touch. It was hard not to let him have his way with her. Etta May looked into the mirror and sighed. Only nine more months and she would be eighteen. On her birthday night she promised herself she would let Morris have anything he wanted whether they were married or not.

A few blocks away Firman James III, a scion of Charleston society and grandson of its favorite United States Senator, was drinking with his buddies. He, his cousin Macon Myers, and a friend Byron Hoskins had been drinking since noon. They were celebrating Firman's football scholarship and anything else that came to mind.

The bar they began their celebration in was just off Ocean Drive Beach and the warm sea breezes made the booze even more potent. There was a single go-go dancer who stood above them and wriggled her meager assets while they swilled thirty-cent beer and howled at the good time they were having.

It was five hours later, in the early evening twilight, when they began to feel the frustrations of voyeurism without relief and seriously began searching out a woman. The three drunken buddies staggered down the street insulting everyone. They did not realize they were being insulting. They were so drunk they believed everyone loved them. No one had the courage to tell them differently.

It was almost 11 P.M. when they staggered out of the south side bar holding onto each other as they loudly discussed the merits of old whiskey and young women.

The three buddies stopped at a take-out store and picked up two quarts of malt liquor. Once outside, they cracked the caps and began to drink out of the bottles. They sang old songs and verbally accosted every female, eight to eighty, along their path.

It was unusually hot outside and Etta May walked around the house naked except for a sheer slip that pressed at her firm young body at the most revealing places. Etta May waltzed into her bedroom, happy that Christi was gone and she had the room and radio all to herself. She switched the radio on to her favorite station and began to dance to the rhythm and blues as she admired her voluptuous body before the bureau mirror. Christi might have more "looks," but even Christi might admire Etta May's body.

Etta May did not notice the tattered old curtains of the broken bedroom window revealed her to the people passing on the street.

"Hot damn, Firman! Would you look at that!" Macon exclaimed as he pulled down a long swallow of malt liquor and admired the lovely figure of Etta May Jones only a few yards away.

"Goddamn! That girl ain't got nothing on. Look at those tits!" Firman chortled as he pulled a Swiss Army pocketknife from his pants pocket and opened it. "Hot damn! Let's go in there and fuck the shit out of her!" he grunted.

"Hell no! I ain't raping nobody. That's real sick, Firman." Hoskins waved him away.

"Well, goddamn, Hoskins! That ain't anybody anyways. That's just some nigger gal. She's had so many long cocks in her, yours and mine ain't going to make any difference!" Firman insisted.

Hoskins frowned, then took a swig of the malt liquor and looked at the lovely young body in the window one more time. "We don't hurt her none. We just go . . . and . . . and do it and then leave. That's all!" Hoskins insisted through his drunken stupor.

"Yeah, man. That's all," Firman cautioned as they moved across the yard full of junk to the side of the shanty and stopped beneath the window where Etta May danced, singing along with Jerry Lee Lewis.

"Whole lot of shaking going on! Whole lot of shaking going on!" she sang as she danced before the mirror massaging her hips playfully.

"Damn it, man! I can't take it anymore," Firman James said as he lifted himself up to the window sill and flipped over into the room.

Etta May heard the noise before she saw the man. When she saw him she reached for her hairbrush, ran over and hit him on the head.

The plastic brush broke.

Firman looked up at her and smiled. "Hey, girl. I just want a little of that black pussy. Now you just act friendly and I won't even hurt you. Hell! I'm just a short-peckered white boy. I ain't got nothing like any of those black boys you been dicking." Firman giggled as Macon crawled through the window and joined them while Hoskins waited outside.

"You honkie bastard! Get out of here! My Momma's got a shotgun and I'm going to get it and blow your ass away!" Etta May challenged as she started toward the door.

Firman tackled her just before she reached it. As he lay on top of her he put the knife to her throat. "Now, you just open those legs, nigger and I'll fuck you a little then let you go! If you give me any trouble I'll cut you bad," Firman spewed.

Etta May spit in his face and tried to move from beneath his heavy body. "I told you get off me. Now!" Etta May challenged again as Firman pulled at her slip and ripped it until it exposed her breasts.

He started to reach down and slobber on them when Little Eddie Jones filled the doorway, holding a shotgun almost as big as he was. "Oh shit!" Firman almost wet his pants.

Hoskins looked through the window for an instant then he broke and ran.

Macon was frozen with fear.

Firman poked the knife closer to Etta May's throat.

"You want to see this nigger die or you want to go away?"

Little Eddie Jones smiled and backed out of the doorway into the shadows.

"Now see. There ain't anyone to help you anymore," Firman grunted as he started to jam his hand between her legs.

He never touched them as the twin barrels of the shotgun took his head off at the shoulders.

✳ ✳ ✳

There were a dozen police cars around the small wood frame house when Sarah and Mrs. White returned from the travel office.

Little Eddie was in handcuffs and crying.

Etta May was in handcuffs and cursing everyone.

"The motherfucker tried to rape me! Don't that mean something?" Etta May yelled at the arresting officers.

Sarah ran to Etta May's side. She looked at Officer McDaniels. "Officer McDaniels you know my Etta May. You know she's a good girl. I swear by almighty God. My Eddie, he wants to be an Air Force pilot. He has a good record at school. You got the wrong folks here," Sarah cried.

Sheriff McDaniels eased over beside Sarah, smiling knowingly. "Mammy Jones, we mostly believe Etta May and Little Eddie, but goddammit, they killed Firman James, the Senator's grandson. Now we have to take them in. I've known you for twenty years and you know the way things are, Mammy Jones."

"My name is Sarah Jones!"

"Sarah? Okay, Sarah Jones."

"They shot a white boy?"

"No, Sarah. Not just a white boy. They shot Senator Firman James's grandson. When I got here Etta May and Eddie was talking about how they got revenge for what went on between you and Firman Jr. I don't want to hear anything else tonight. I'm taking them into protective custody. I don't want no riots here, Sarah."

Sarah looked pensive. "God's justice comes full circle," Sarah mumbled.

"What?" Sheriff McDaniels asked nervously.

"I need to talk with her," Sarah pleaded quietly.

Sheriff McDaniels started to agree. He saw the headlights of a procession of cars off in the distance. He quickly shook his head. "No! I'm arresting you too, Mammy Jones. Now come along," the sheriff said as he grabbed her arm firmly.

"You ain't gonna do no such thing!" Sarah slapped his face.

"Goddammit, nigger! Can't you see those cars! I'm trying to save your life. Now get your black ass into that car," Sheriff McDaniels snarled.

Sarah paused and looked him in the eye. "I done told you I'm SARAH Jones, Tommy McDaniels," Sarah said defiantly.

Mrs. White moved out of the shadows and stood within Sheriff

McDaniels's line of vision.

"Mrs. White, you best get home to your part of town."

Mrs. White looked at Sarah who nodded agreement.

"I'll have a good lawyer there as soon as I can, Sarah. You hear that, sheriff?" Mrs. White said firmly.

"Dammit all, Mrs. White! You and Sarah see what's going on. That's a lynch mob coming down that road!"

Mrs. White had to nod agreement. "Where will you take them?"

"They're all going to the Sumter County Jail until this clears up. Now no more talk." He paused and waved his men to their cars.

Little Eddie and Etta May looked at Sarah with soulful eyes. They were crying as the officers stuffed them into patrol cars and roared away sirens screaming.

"He's just doing the best he knows how. Go home, Mrs. White. I'll do some praying on this tonight and tomorrow God will make it more clear to all of us. Tonight the devil rides a high horse."

Sheriff McDaniels led Sarah to his car with a firm hand, put her in the back seat and slammed the door. He cursed under his breath as he watched the procession of cars roaring down the old highway to shantytown.

Sarah's eyes followed his.

Mrs. White looked at them, then turned to Sarah with stark fear in her eyes.

"You better come along." Sarah insisted.

Sheriff McDaniels started the car. "Jews and niggers," he swore quietly to himself. "If you're coming, woman, move your ass!" he shouted.

"Sheriff McDaniels, you keep a civil tongue!" Mrs. White was visibly outraged.

"Okay, stay here. If they can't hang a nigger tonight, a Jew will do them just as well," he growled.

The dust from the patrol cars carrying Little Eddie and Etta May swirled around Mrs. White as she reluctantly got into the back seat with Sarah.

Sheriff McDaniels looked in the rearview mirror and reflected his disdain for them both as he roared off into the night.

Chapter Thirty-nine

My Dear Christi,

I don't know how to tell you all this, but I got to tell you because you got to come help. Momma's in jail for resisting arrest and little Eddie done shot Mr. Firman James's grandson. He tried to rape me, Christi, but they don't talk about that none. They just say I let him in and tried to charge him money and Little Eddie is a pimp who killed Mr. James when he wouldn't pay. Christi, it's all lies but nobody listens to my side. You got to come help, Christi. You just got to.

Love, your sister Etta May

Ramon had brought Christi the soiled letter on a silver tray as she sat on the back of her lovely white Arabian stallion, J.C. The horse was a gift from Eduardo for her ability to tame him so quickly. She and Eduardo had just returned from a glorious three-week vacation in Rio and Christi had all but forgotten about the other world she had left behind.

Christi had thrown away the mail from home without reading it. She wished she had thrown this one away also. She resented the other world intruding on her newfound happiness and she felt little kinship with those people now.

"Those people are nothing but trouble to themselves and others," Christi muttered as she started to throw the letter away.

Eduardo sat on Poco and looked at the anger in his wife's lovely eyes. He slipped the letter from her fist and read it. He looked worried. "This is bad. Very bad. Is this true?"

"How do I know?" Christi feigned indifference.

"Christi! This is your mother!"

"Eduardo, I'm not going back there. I want you to send them money. Please! Send them lots of money for good lawyers. That's what we'll do. You can do that for me."

Eduardo frowned. "*Es su madre!* You would send her money?"

"Eduardo, those niggers are always in some kind of trouble. I can't go back there. I'm not like them! I speak Castilian better than you. I beat Carlos at chess and I'm better at bridge than grandmother. I want to go back to Ipanema. I don't ever want to go to Charleston again!" Christi started to spur J.C.

Eduardo grabbed the reins and shook his head. "No! I will not let you abandon your family. This would be a very bad thing to do. We will fly to Charleston tomorrow. I will have my friend Miguel find us the best lawyer in America. But you will go home again!"

Christi pulled the reins from his hands and whipped J.C. into full gallop across the hilly Mexican countryside. "I knew it! I knew it! They don't want me to be happy. I knew those niggers would screw up my life! I knew it!" she screamed into the wind. "I'm not going back to that mess! You hear me, Eduardo. I'll never go back there! Never!"

Eduardo pushed Poco to the limit. Finally he managed to catch up to Christi. He reached for the bridle and succeeded in reining in her mount. Eduardo dismounted his horse, reached up and pulled Christi down.

Eduardo stood her up straight and looked at her sternly. "You stop this talk right now!"

"No! No! No!"

"I understand your fears, *mi corazón,* but you will never enjoy this life unless you face the old life and conquer it. It would work for now, but someday it would come between us. The family is most important. We will go." Eduardo held her firmly in his grip.

Christ shook loose. "Eduardo! Please! Don't make me do it. Please! I could never make you understand."

"Enough of this! There is nothing to understand but that you never abandon family!"

"And what about us?"

"I will be at your side."

"Not after you've seen Charleston!"

Eduardo had never seen such a look of desperation in Christi's eyes. "Whatever it is you fear, you must trust the depth of my love to handle it."

Christi hugged him tightly and kissed him on his chest where a shirt button had come undone. "I'm just so afraid of losing you. I really love you, Eduardo! I really do!" Christi insisted as she held him even tighter.

Eduardo's reply was to hold her and rock her as he comforted her.

The thought of Eduardo seeing her shantytown was too much and Christi pulled away.

"What? What is it, Christi?" Eduardo demanded.

"If I go, I will go alone, Eduardo. That is a world so far removed from ours I hardly remember how it was. I do remember it is an ugly world and I don't want you to see it. Ever!" Christi insisted.

Eduardo pulled away and looked at her sadly. "Do you think I have always been this way? That I have always lived in this glittery protected world? I have seen all the bad things you have seen and more. When I was a young boy I was always hungry and cold. I had nothing. You had more than I because at least you know who your mother is." Eduardo stopped himself.

Christi looked at him in disbelief.

"Maria is not my grandmother. I have paid her well to play the role. She even believes it to be true now. But the truth is I am a bastard child born into one of the worst *bohios* in the world of a mother I never saw and a father I never knew. I was a man at the age of ten. I was a man or I was dead. That was how hard my world was! "

"You don't have to make up things to make me feel better, Eduardo."

"Don't call me a liar. I do not make up such things. But enough of that talk. We must prepare to go to Charleston. After all, I have been there and in many respects it is a lovely city."

"Not my part," Christi mumbled.

She was curious about his past, but his expression told her he would say no more about it.

"Then we will not stay in your part. We will find a fine house in the best part of town."

"Oh, Eduardo, you are so naive. Even with all your money you couldn't buy a fine house in the best part of that town. Your skin is more brown than mine." Christi forced a laugh.

Eduardo looked insulted. "In this you are wrong. I will buy the finest home available in the best part of Charleston and we will have many white servants. This I promise you," Eduardo said proudly.

Christi started to challenge his wisdom but saw the determined look in his eyes and thought better of it. If anyone could break into the Battery, Eduardo would be the one. That thought lifted Christi's spirits.

"It must be on the Battery. One of the homes overlooking the harbor. One of the homes I used to dream about owning. It has to be one of those, Eduardo," Christi insisted.

Eduardo held her tightly and nodded agreement.

"What we were is long past, my love. The position I have attained in this world makes all things possible. Perhaps I will buy the whole damn block of houses and we will fill them all with the *pobrecitos*," Eduardo laughed.

Christi laughed with him as she clung to him tightly. As his laughter waned her thoughts were of home and what might be waiting for her there. "Charleston," she repeated under her breath.

It all seemed so remote to her now. She had purged her mind of all bad memories in order to enjoy her new life. The old memories were vague and disjointed, as if they occurred in another world in another life.

"Charleston," she murmured and her body shivered uncontrollably for a moment.

Eduardo stroked her back gently and held her tighter.

"Do not worry, my love. Tomorrow you shall begin preparing to go home to Charleston. With me at your side the ghosts of the past will not dare to bother you," Eduardo said assuringly.

"Charleston," Christi repeated as if the word was foreign to her tongue.

"Yes, my darling, home to Charleston." Eduardo stroked her hair as a strong wind blew across the hill and carried Christi's letter from home tumbling off into the distance.

Chapter Forty

IT WAS CHRISTMAS IN CAROLINA AND THE DARK GREEN PINES LINED THE coastal highway in thick groves broken by treeless gaps that afforded vistas of the blue-green Atlantic. Some were trimmed with Christmas lights and tinsel. The sight and smell of Carolina pine always reminded Christi of home. She had particularly delighted in decorating a Christmas tree each year and had taken great joy in the Christmas season. This Christmas back in Carolina she felt only apprehension and dread. As she and Eduardo neared Charleston seated in the back of the rented limousine, Christi held Eduardo's hand lightly and he felt her anxiety.

The white limo driver eyed them both suspiciously through his rear view mirror as he watched the ticking meter nervously.

Eduardo saw the nervousness in his eyes. He reached into his pocket and withdrew a hundred-dollar bill. He stuffed it into the driver's top pocket.

The driver smiled and relaxed.

Christi resented the driver's look of derision but Eduardo's gesture proved that green was the color that mattered most.

"It is funny, Christi. I have come here many times on business. I once owned a small shipping company out of Beaufort. Yet today I feel a little bit the stranger," Eduardo mused aloud.

"It's not a nice feeling, is it?"

Eduardo gave her a peck on the cheek. "Everyone was nice at the airport. They seem very helpful but there was something amiss," Eduardo said.

"Eduardo, let's go back home. This is a strange land to me. I'm not the little girl that left Charleston in 1951. That was many years ago. This world has changed so much. I've changed too. It's wrong for me to come back. Momma always taught me about Lot's wife in the Bible. Lot's wife looked back and turned to salt. My Momma taught me to respect the Bible, Eduardo. It's a sin to look back. It says so in the Bible!" Christi insisted nervously as the driver entered South Charleston and drove ever deeper into the blight of shantytown.

"The Bible also says honor your father and mother. That is a commandment. Not to go back is a parable. We will not go back my love, we go forward. Forward to dispel all the ghosts and do this good thing for your mother. And when we do go back home, then you and I will live happily ever after." Eduardo smiled.

Christi looked deep into his eyes. He was not embarrassed by the squalor of shantytown. He still loved her. She was so insecure in this environment, she hugged him dearly.

The driver looked ill.

The shantytown was worse than Christi remembered. Mangy dogs foraged through scattered garbage and small children ran around naked or in rags. The unpaved streets were deep with mud from a recent rain and the shacks that lined it were for the most part unpainted and leaned to the leeward side of the north wind.

Christi knew the shanties were just a cut above some of the *bohios* she recalled from the slums of Latin America. The big difference was that the adult males of the shanty seemed very well dressed and they all seemed to have the longest cars in the world. "These are the downtrodden poor of America?" Eduardo mused as a young black man almost blew the limo off the road as he whizzed by. His engine and radio were at full blast.

Christi started to reply until she saw Etta May, Mrs. White, and Sarah standing on the cracked sidewalk in front of her humble home.

They were all watching the long limo make its way toward them. Christi's homecoming was an event. Word of mouth had heralded her arrival.

In the distance Christi could not see them well. She didn't care. She saw all this as a giant step backward. After the years of struggle she was not going back to the powerlessness of poverty. Christi shook her head and tried to read the impassive look on Eduardo's face. "Please stop the car," Christi instructed the driver who pulled over and stopped.

"Christi!" Eduardo chided.

"See, I told you, Eduardo. This is so embarrassing. It is even worse than I remembered. I don't think the Cuban *bohios* were this bad." She shifted nervously in her seat.

"Driver, please continue," Eduardo instructed.

The driver shrugged and continued on.

"I'm sorry, Eduardo. I'll be alright now. Just stay beside me and hold your nose." Christi shifted nervously.

She pulled her mink wrap secure around her shoulders.

Its extravagant feel made her feel more secure. She partially hid her face in the mink as the limo pulled up in front of the shanty and Etta May stared into the back window.

"Christi?" She looked confused.

Eduardo opened the door and stepped out, pulling Christi behind him.

For a moment Etta May stood open-mouthed, staring at Christi.

Eduardo broke the silence "Allow me to introduce myself. I am Christi's husband, Don Eduardo."

"Oh, Etta May! Yes, it's Christi! How are you, little sister? How are you?" Christi broke into tears as she hugged Etta May tightly.

"Oh, Christi! I didn't hardly recognize you. You look so pretty and elegant. You look just like those white ladies on those magazines. I swear you do!" Etta May bubbled.

Sarah and Mrs. White stood behind Etta May and Christi as they hugged.

Christi could not look directly into her mother's eyes.

"It's good to see you, Etta May. How have you been . . . oh, I'm sorry. Well, I'm here to help. Everything will be alright now." Christi stopped and her eyes met Sarah's.

"I hope so, Christi. I . . ." Etta May stepped back as she saw Christi was looking past her to Sarah.

Sarah and Christi said many things with their eyes before they both broke into tears.

Mrs. White cried openly too.

They both hugged Christi together.

The limo driver looked worried, as the all-black neighborhood gathered around to watch from a distance. He tugged at Eduardo's sleeve.

"Oh!" Eduardo nodded understanding. He pulled out a big roll of bills and paid off the limo driver.

The limo driver looked around anxiously, shook his head in dismay, then jumped into the limo and roared away.

Eduardo watched his bride, her mother, and Mrs. White envelope themselves in kisses and tears.

"Mother, this is my husband, Eduardo De La Cruz."

"Lord, chile! You done got even more beautiful! And THIS is your husband? Good gracious! He's pretty too." Sarah beamed as she reached out to hug Eduardo.

He reluctantly yielded to her bear hug.

"Actually, it's Doctor De La Cruz but he gets embarrassed if you make too much of it," Christi explained.

"Eduardo? Ain't that like Eddie? Why that gives us two Eddies in the family. Welcome to the family, Big Eddie," Sarah laughed.

Eduardo smiled politely.

"What about Little Eddie, Momma? Etta May says it was self-defense. How can they hold him if it's self-defense?" Christi fumed.

"It ain't self-defense if a black shoots a white boy. Eddie's done shot a white boy who's Senator James' grandson. They are going to treat Eddie like he was an adult, that's what." Sarah gritted her teeth.

"But he's just fourteen. They can't do that!" Christi said.

Sarah put her hands on her hips and looked steely-eyed.

"They can do what they damn well please. They make up the law for us as they go. The other white boys, they're going to swear Etta May begged them to come inside. That she tried to get money and when he didn't give it, she had Eddie shoot. Now, ain't that some stuff for you." Sarah shook her head sadly.

"I'm so sorry, Momma." Christi heaved a long sigh of sympathy mixed with relief.

"You ain't done nothing to be sorry about, chile. It's them we got to make sorry for what they's doing to us!"

"And Firman Jr. is into it personally?" Christi looked deep into Sarah's eyes.

"He is that. He lost his old Congress seat from that reapportion thing. They's going to create a new congressional district and he wants it. He believes he can hang my Eddie and get himself elected," Sarah almost cried.

Eduardo pulled out his pipe and lit it as Christi walked alongside Sarah.

Mrs. White tagged along quietly.

Christi shook her head angrily. Her eyes picked up the unusually timid Mrs. White. "I'm sorry, Mrs. White. Eduardo, this is Mrs. White. Mrs. White, my husband," Christi said in flawless English.

Eduardo bowed politely.

Mrs. White curtsied slightly. "Christi, your enunciation is flawless."

Christi responded with a flurry of Spanish, Russian, and French phrases.

Mrs. White was extremely impressed.

Sarah interrupted. "This ain't . . . isn't any time to do this, Mrs. White. We have to get these people fed and talk about what to do about my Eddie," Sarah insisted.

Christi and Mrs. White agreed in Yiddish before they agreed with everyone else in English.

As Christi and Sarah walked and talked, Eduardo pulled Mrs. White aside.

"I want to thank you for tutoring my wife. She speaks well of you. She speaks well because of you," Eduardo kidded.

Mrs. White looked at the beautiful stature and bearing of Eduardo. "It was for such as you I worked so hard. You are what I hoped for her."

"Well, thank you."

"You are a godsend, Eduardo. She will need you now most of all. This is a very good, but strange land. If you like I will help guide you through the darker passages," Mrs. White offered.

"I welcome your advice. Please, give me a short version of what we are dealing with," he said, puffing on his pipe.

Mrs. White looked sad. She watched Christi and Sarah walk away.

Etta May ran down the old oak-lined street and joined them. A hundred pairs of anxious eyes watched the scene.

Mrs. White motioned toward the onlookers. "It will be a watershed. A test case."

"The Civil Liberties Union wants to defend him. A hundred others want to hang him without a trial. I know many good Jewish lawyers. I also know enough to know it can't be a Jewish lawyer. The D.A. yielded to political pressure."

"He charged Sarah with resisting arrest. She did slap Sheriff McDaniels. He charged Etta May with prostitution and accessory to murder. Eddie is to be tried as an adult for first degree murder. Some things have changed here, but nothing has changed so much that Eddie

will go free," Mrs. White sighed.

Eduardo drew on his pipe and thought it all over. "I would not be too sure. What about Harry Feingold, I can have him here tomorrow."

"My God! A New York Jew? The jury would knit the rope."

"I see. I do have much to learn."

"Do you know any good redneck lawyers?" she kidded.

Eduardo smiled knowingly. "My personal favorite is Abraham Lincoln. Since he isn't available, I think I'll fly in Carlton Bennett. He's in the middle of a big deal murder trial, but his client is guilty as hell."

Mrs. White looked impressed.

"Carlton Bennett? He was a Carolina State Senator from this very county. Oh, my. What a coup that would be. Is it possible?"

Eduardo nodded quietly. "I love her, Mrs. White. She is now under my protection as are all that she holds dear. Would you agree to help Carlton when he arrives?" Eduardo said smoothly.

The look of admiration in Mrs. White's eyes was a little embarrassing to Eduardo.

"Yes, of course. I want to help in any way I can. I want to tell you there was nothing in my small efforts that made Christi into the polished lady she is now. I don't know what you did, but it's marvelous, simply marvelous!" Mrs. White said with sincere wonder.

"Neither of us did too much. Most of it was already there. She is a lady of elegance. Always has been and always will be. We're merely bystanders, helping out a little here and there," Eduardo posed.

Mrs. White nodded agreement.

"Nice talking to you. I must join my wife now. We'll talk again soon." Eduardo bowed.

As he left Mrs. White and pressed ahead to take Christi's hand Mrs. White felt despair turn into newfound hope. If Eduardo had looked back he would have seen the deep respect Mrs. White felt for him expressed in her tear-stained eyes.

Chapter Forty-one

CHRISTMAS 1960 CAME AND WENT WITHOUT CELEBRATION AT THE Jones house. Every moment was spent consumed by planning ways to help Little Eddie. New Year's Day began with a sleet shower that passed leaving behind brilliant sunlight making the smallest ice crystal a diamond if just for a short time.

Eduardo awoke early and propped up on his elbow, watching his wife as she lay sleeping. The bright morning sun filtered through the Venetian blind of the hotel window and freckled Christi's face with tiny little suntracks. He marveled at how lovely she was without makeup. Her features were classic and her skin smooth and flawless. Gently, he reached over and kissed her. Christi stirred slightly. He ran his finger down the bridge of her cute little nose. She cracked one eye open. He nibbled at her ear. She shifted away and turned her back to him. He bit the back of her neck playfully.

Christi turned over and growled. "Eduardo, you know I'm not a morning person," she grumbled as she turned onto her back and pulled the sheet over her head.

Eduardo grabbed the sheet and pulled it off of her, exposing her naked body to the freckling sunlight. He licked down and gave her navel a tickle with his tongue.

Christi came up laughing.

"Happy New Year, darling. You, Mrs. White, and your mother talked so late we missed Guy Lombardo."

"Stop it, Eduardo, you know how ticklish I am. Please. Oh Lord!" she giggled.

Eduardo kissed her from her navel the length of her firm stomach until he was between her lovely breasts. Lovingly, he kissed her nipples until they were rigid and she was cooing. He massaged her breasts gently with his warm hands as he kissed his way back down her stomach until he reached her curvaceous thighs. Gently, he took one hand from her breasts and eased it between the legs that she parted with some reluctance. "I told you I'm not a morning person."

"Ah! My love but I am a morning man!" Eduardo whispered as his passion filled him with a desire to do more than make love to her. He wanted to inhale a part of her being. To pull her into his psyche and absorb her essence. To have part of her inside his body. At the height of his desire he wished he were a woman so that she could enter him and he could feel her thrusting deep beyond the physical unto the depths of his soul.

Eduardo lay on his back and lifted her on top of his radiantly vibrant body. Slowly, he let her warmth allow his to blend with hers. He held her closely without moving for a long moment after they had become one. They made love, long, slow, gentle love for a brief eternity until they were rudely interrupted by the telephone.

Eduardo talked with whoever it was in Spanish with increasing excitement as Christi lay beside him, savoring the delicious tranquility of fulfillment.

Finally he put his hand over the mouthpiece and leaped off the bed excitedly. "Batista has left Cuba! El Grande has taken over! The revolution is a success! *Olé!*"

Christi tried but managed only a weak smile.

"It is the beginning of the Latin American nation! Oh, Christi! We must go to Havana and join the celebration!" Eduardo enthused until he saw the sober look on Christi's face. "You do not share this moment with me?" Eduardo looked hurt.

"You know how I feel about that stupid war."

"Yes. It is the one thing that scares me the most."

Christi saw the hurt in his eyes and smiled. "Good for you and them, Eduardo. Does this mean we'll get our money back?" Christi pulled her pillow around her ears.

Eduardo looked a little sad. "This is your true feeling. Is it not?"

"You know that, Eduardo. I'm happy for you. Okay?"

"And Havana?"

"You go! Please! I have Little Eddie to worry about."

Eduardo heaved a sigh of frustration. He threw the phone on the bed. "It's Cosmo."

"Cosmo? How did he find us here? I have nothing to say to him." She started to hang up the phone.

Eduardo grabbed her hand and stopped her. "He is a hero of the revolution. You will wish him well."

Christi had never seen such determination in Eduardo's eyes. She shrugged and picked up the phone.

She held it a long moment before speaking. "Who is this?"

"How soon they forget."

"Yes. How soon."

"Well, no hard feelings, lady. Not today! We did it, Christi! I'm here in the lobby of the Havana Hilton drinking a Cuba Libre . . . in fact, a lot of Cuba Libres. As a reward for services rendered, I have a whole suite here. Would you and the good doctor please come down and join me?" Cosmo burped.

"You're drunk."

"Not yet. But soon!" Cosmo paused. "Hey gal! Get the burr out of your ass! This is a day to celebrate!"

"You do it for me, Mr. Collins." Christi studied the excited look in Eduardo's eyes. "I have some things to take care of here but Eduardo's about to jump out of his pants. I'm sure he'd love to come down."

"That's great! He will be a guest of honor!"

"Bye!"

"No, Christi! Don't hang up. There is someone else here who wants to talk to you," Cosmo's voice trailed off.

"I don't have time . . ."

"He just wants to say hello."

"Who?"

"Hello, Christi!" a drunken Kiki gurgled into the phone.

Christi started to slam the receiver down but found herself unable to move. "Congratulations, you finally got what you wanted." Her lip trembled.

"Yes! I get something, I lose something. It is as you say, bittersweet. Can you forgive this *campesino* and come to Havana?"

He hiccupped.

"No, Kiki." Christi handed the phone to Eduardo, walked over to the window and played with the drawstring of the blinds.

"Kiki, congratulations! Save a Cuba Libre for me. I will be there when we have finished with some important business here. Goodbye for now, *amigo.*" Eduardo hung up the phone and looked at his wife with censure. "Why?"

"Why? Why what?" Christi yanked the Venetian blind cord so hard it zoomed to the top of the window and stuck there at a rakish angle.

"These are brave men who have suffered much. They are also your friends. You pout like a child at this great moment?"

"I said hello."

"You will go to Havana and you will join in the celebration as my wife is expected to do!"

"No, Eduardo. I will not leave Little Eddie."

Eduardo had to think that over. He nodded reluctant agreement.

Christi took his strong hands in hers and kissed his knuckles. "I'm sorry, but I don't have strong feelings either way anymore. I think I'm well," Christi smiled.

"That is why the blind is so crooked." Eduardo looked at the jammed blind and laughed.

Christi looked at the blind and laughed with him. "You wish you had been in the mountains with them. You wish you were at that hotel bar in Havana with them." She teased his hair with her fingers.

"But for love I would have been," he smiled.

"What's this lawyer's name you've hired?" Christi walked back to the window and looked at the sunrise.

"Carlton Bennett, a local boy made good. A very good lawyer, from the size of the fee." Eduardo followed her.

"Why don't you introduce us. He and I can do the beginning paperwork without you. I want you to go down there, Eduardo."

"You were a big part of the reason it was successful, you deserve to enjoy the *fiesta*." Eduardo pulled her close. "I would be gone for only a few days. I do want to see the faces of the *campesinos*. I want to hear their laughter." Eduardo held her tight.

"Just leave me the checkbook and a very healthy account," Christi smiled wryly.

"I have transferred ten million two hundred thousand pesos. If you need more I will get it when I return."

"Then you are going?"

"You said it was alright."

"Yes, but you didn't have to accept so fast."

Eduardo held her face between his strong hands and put his nose against hers in an Eskimo kiss. "I will miss you too much."

"And I will miss you. Buy Cosmo a drink on me."

"And Kiki?"

"Oh hell! Give him one too." She laughed nervously as she held Eduardo very close for a long time.

Chapter Forty-two

CHRISTI WAS VERY NERVOUS ABOUT LETTING EDUARDO FLY AWAY. She hated it when her men went anywhere. It was a feeling she never could quite handle. Her anxiety was eased somewhat by the knowledge of how much it had meant to him. She knew deep down he was just as much a revolutionary as Kiki, and holding him back would be as useless as her try at making Kiki a husband. She held Eduardo very tightly for a long time before she let him board the DC-3. She stood and watched the sky long after the airplane had disappeared from view.

Carlton Bennett had driven her and Sarah to the airport. He broke the gloomy silence on the way back into town. "The district attorney is determined to prosecute Little Eddie as an adult. I don't think we can have that overturned. I believe, as do my associates, the key to the case is breaking the testimony of the two witnesses," he pontificated.

"How come they can do that to my Little Eddie and make my daughter out to be a prostitute? Ain't nobody in this family ever done no such thing. We are churchgoing, Christian people," Sarah grumbled under her breath from the back seat.

"It's unfortunate, but that area does have several houses of ill repute. It is quite open and notorious in that regard." Carlton cleared his throat.

"And she's black," Christi fumed.

Carlton shrugged. "With Eduardo's permission I hired a private investigator to see if he could dig up anything that will crack the two boys' testimony. I do not like the facts any more than you, but they are the sons of the most prominent people in Charleston. I heard their father kicked their butts and scolded them. Now that, that's over they will stop at nothing to keep them clear of an accessory to murder charge," Carlton outlined.

"And an attempted rape charge." Christi grimaced.

"That is the scenario," Carlton agreed.

"They done said justice for all. My little girl almost gets raped and they don't do nothing to them boys yet. I swear, if they don't I'll get me a hickory switch and blister their hides myself," Sarah said, shaking her fist in the air.

"No, Mrs. Jones. Please show some restraint. This is more a political show than a serious trial. We must play politics as skillfully as they do if we are to win," Carlton cautioned.

"Politics? I thought this was a legal affair," Christi scoffed.

"Yes. Your cynicism is well-taken. I must say your husband's travels do not play well in this arena."

Christi had to nod agreement.

Sarah looked puzzled.

"Please understand I tried to tell him going to Havana is not good politically. You read the newspapers. If someone finds out where he has gone . . . well, need I say more?" Carlton looked worried.

"This ain't about Eduardo. It's about my boy!" Sarah insisted.

"No, Mother, it's about black against white."

"I'm glad you understand the political explosiveness of this situation, Mrs. De La Cruz," Carlton grinned into the rear view mirror. "It's black against white and red only complicates it."

Christi returned his stare until he diverted his eyes to the road. "I hope my husband has hired a good lawyer and not a politician!" Christi snapped.

Sarah nodded agreement.

Carlton grimaced, then took on a look of pride. "My reputation speaks for itself. Unfortunately, jurors are local people and we are all political animals. I am a good lawyer who happens to understand the politics of a given situation. I also have a Ph.D. in psychology and make a decent taxi driver. You have three professionals for the price of one."

Sarah looked unimpressed. "I don't care what you is, just get my Little Eddie out of that jailhouse."

"Eduardo says you come highly recommended, Mr. Bennett. I trust my husband's judgment, but I have to admit I'd feel better if you were black," Christi sighed.

"I understand your concern, Mrs. De La Cruz. I promise I will try my best not to disappoint you. Please understand, I am not a right wing zealot nut like the D.A. You do not have to drag me kicking and screaming into the 20th century. I realized a long time ago it was here." He nodded in her direction. "Did you want me to go by the address you mentioned earlier?" he added, winking at Christi.

"Please," she replied as Carlton turned off the main highway into a quiet residential neighborhood with old colonial homes and lovely old oak trees dripping Spanish moss.

After he had gone a few blocks, he pulled up in front of a stately old two-story Victorian house with a "For Sale" sign in the front yard.

Christi turned and looked back at Sarah who was wide-eyed, but obviously uncomfortable.

"Good gracious Lord! I only been in this neighborhood one time before to take care of Miss Phelps when she was dying. What we doing here now, Christi?" Sarah wondered aloud.

"Do you like this house, Momma?" Christi said nonchalantly.

"Good Lord! I ain't got no business liking a house like this." Sarah shook her head.

"Well, you'd better like it because it's all yours now."

"Chile! You telling the truth? Don't fool with your Momma about something like this." Sarah shifted nervously in her seat.

"No, Momma. It's yours. Tell her, Mr. Bennett."

"That's right, Mrs. Jones. Paid for in cash." Carlton beamed.

"Oh Lord! Ain't nobody got that kind of money," she sighed.

"Doctor Eduardo De La Cruz does!" Christi boasted.

"Oh, that man of yorn, Christi! Lord! You done married well, chile!" Sarah put her hands on her face and peeked at the house. "But they don't let no colored folks buy over in this here neighborhood," Sarah wondered.

"Technically you're correct. The ownership papers are assigned to the Mexicali Corporation. I will have those papers transferred to you in a few weeks," Carlton assured Sarah.

"Then they don't know colored folks is moving in here?"

"Well . . . no. It would have been difficult to have announced that at the outset," Carlton equivocated.

"Then I ain't moving in. I don't believe in fooling with people. That's just lying and that's all there is to it!" Sarah insisted.

"Nobody fooled anybody. There was a house for sale and we paid good money for it."

Sarah looked defiant.

"I won't have you living in that damn shanty any longer. Now I'm putting my foot down!" Christi insisted.

"I don't know, chile. It just don't seem right," Sarah shook her head.

"Please do it for me, Momma." Christi paused. "Besides, it's not like they haven't ever pulled any funny business on us."

Sarah had to smile. She finally allowed herself to take a long look at the house. "I guess we do owe them some shenanigans," she smiled.

"Oh good, Momma! Good! Carlton, please get those moving people busy right away. I want the eyes in this neighborhood to start popping before the sun sets." Christi reached over the seat and hugged Sarah.

Carlton nodded as he started the car and drove away, sensing twenty sets of eyeballs peering through chantilly lace and shaking their heads in disgust.

Chapter Forty-three

January 15, 1961

My Darling Christi,

I am sorry I haven't called, but your country has disrupted communications with Cuba. I wish you could have been here, my darling, to see the faces of the campesinos glowing with self-esteem as they marched through the streets. It is, as I told you, very much a Latin American revolution. Every South American country is represented and many are wondering how it might be possible in their homeland.

El Grande has already begun giving the land to the campesinos. There will be five million acres given to agricultural units run by the people. The colonos are no more. All those hundreds of thousands you saw who were without jobs will be fully employed and we will make this youngest of revolutions a marvel for the world to wonder at. I believe, as El Grande does, that history will absolve us for anything we did to obtain this glorious moment.

Christi, I love you so very much. I miss you terribly. I ask that you love me enough to be patient with me. Kiki has asked me to accompany him to Nicaragua. I will not go as a soldier, but as an adviser and observer. I will only be there for four to six weeks. Please don't be mad. I have seen the fulfillment of many dreams I have held a lifetime. I wish to be in on the beginning of this in another country.

I truly love you and it tears my heart to be away, but I cannot return until I do this. I have instructed my accountants to give you whatever money you need for the trial with Eddie. Carlton is the best counsel available. I can do no more in this matter for now. My darling, please try to understand. I will be with you soon. I love you now and forever more.

Eduardo

Christi bit her bottom lip so hard it drew blood. "Damn you, Eduardo! You're just like the rest. I knew it. You Latin macho types are all alike. So go get yourself killed. Just don't write me any more letters! Don't tell me any more lies!" Christi fumed as she sat at the large dining room table of the new house she had purchased for Sarah.

Sarah entered the room carrying a large plate of spaghetti topped with three big pieces of garlic bread. "What's the matter, honey? What is it?"

"I should have never let him go, Momma. I've lost him, I just know it."

"Oh, chile! He wants to go play soldier for awhile. He'll be back."

"No, he won't. That's how I lost Kiki," Christi mused aloud.

"Kiki? Who's Kiki?" Sarah quizzed.

Christi grimaced as she fumbled for a lie. "He was a man I knew in Cuba before Eduardo. It's not important except that Kiki is a wild man and Eduardo is a dreamer. Kiki grew up with guns and killing. Eduardo is a spoiled physician playing at soldier."

Christi heaved in pain.

"Momma, I love him. I don't want to lose him!" Christi hugged Sarah tightly.

"Well, hush, chile! You ain't lost nobody yet. You got to have faith. That husband of yours is a good man. He can take care of himself."

"Faith? Faith in what?"

"Lord! I knowed this would happen when you got around those heathens. They don't read the Bible enough. You got to start reading the Bible and get your faith back." Sarah patted Christi's head.

"Momma! I wish things were that simple." Christi walked over to the big window and looked out over the expansive lawn.

"Momma, can you handle this thing with Etta May and Little Eddie without my help?" Christi mused aloud.

"Why, Lord no, Christi! What you thinking about, chile? You thinking about leaving me here alone with that fancy lawyer and going off to Cuba. Is that what you thinking about?" Sarah put her hands on her hips.

"Yes, Momma. Maybe I was wrong all along. Maybe I should have gone with him."

"Why, chile, you don't even know where he is by now. That letter done took almost three months to get here."

"I know, but maybe I can find Cosmo or someone in Cuba who can tell me. Maybe he told his grandmother. I don't know. I just want to be with him."

"Please, Christi. That trial is due to start in three weeks. I can't handle all that stuff. I need you, honey. Please stay here!"

Christi was about to reply when a large rock came flying through the window, spraying glass all over the carpet and narrowly missing Sarah.

"Oh Lord! See, Christi. I knew they would be coming. We been in this fancy house just a little while and they done started up." Sarah looked frightened.

Christi nodded sad agreement. "Yes, I wondered when they would start."

"We should of never done it! I knew it! I knew it!"

"Just relax, Momma! I'll hire a security guard."

"Well, that's well and good for now. But I ain't staying in this house if you going anywhere else!"

Christi thought it over. "I'll stay, Momma. I'll stay as long as I can, but if I have to go, you'll have to understand,"

"No! I won't understand that at all," Sarah insisted as she looked at the rock.

Christi picked up the rock and threw it back out of the window at the quiet lawn.

Christi did not sleep well that night. Her head was filled with too many dreams of Eduardo lying on the jungle floor with blood all over his body. She frequently stared at the luminous dial on her alarm clock, watching time slowly pass. It read 4:00 A.M. when she heard the screech of tires in front of the house and heard the sound of rushing feet and strained voices.

Hurriedly, she slid out of bed and ran to the window. The upstairs windows were thirty feet off the ground.

It was totally dark outside so she could see very little until two hooded men lit the cross then sped away.

The huge cross burned brightly filling the air with the stench of cheap kerosene. Its eerie glow lit up the inside of the antebellum house casting dark, mocking shadows on Sarah's framed portrait of a white-robed, blue-eyed Jesus.

Sarah and Etta May came screaming down the hallway into Christi's bedroom. The three women gathered together and hugged each other as the fire raged. They did not let go until the last coal from the fire died away.

Chapter Forty-four

AT FIRST THE GLARE OF THE TELEVISION LIGHTS ALMOST BLINDED Christi, but as the interview progressed she was amazed at how comfortable she felt in front of the cameras.

"Do you think this was because you are black or because you have brought in Carlton Bennett to help your brother against the district attorney?" The out-of-state newsman stuck the microphone in Christi's face.

"I believe it's a little of both." Christi looked poised.

"Mrs. De La Cruz, aren't you the wife of Eduardo De La Cruz, the Mexican industrialist?" he probed.

"Yes."

"And where is your husband now?"

"He's in Mexico on business."

"Is it true he was involved with El Grande in the Cuban revolution?"

"No! Eduardo is a businessman," Christi lied with ease.

"Mrs. De La Cruz, they have selected an all-white jury. Do you think you have a chance of winning, even with Carlton Bennett?" The New York newsman held his microphone at arm's length.

"My brother is innocent, that's all I know."

"Mrs. De La Cruz, didn't you go to Mexico because you could not tolerate the racial policies of the South?" Moonbeam Jones the Berkeley newsman sneered.

"No! It wasn't like that at all. It began as a pleasure trip and then I met Eduardo." Christi enjoyed the give and take.

The newsmen looked disappointed.

"Will you return to Mexico to live when this is over?" the Chicago newsman asked.

"No! I rather like it here. Charleston is my home, you know. I love it here." She smiled.

The newsmen looked frustrated.

"You mean you could like this place after all that has happened to you and your family?" Moonbeam Jones looked irritated.

"As I said, the South is my home. Are there no racial problems up

North? Detroit? South Boston?" Christi smiled as Carlton motioned for her to join him in the courtroom.

"Please excuse me, gentlemen, I think the trial is about to begin." Carlton shooed them away.

Christi walked away to the admiring stares of all the newsmen. "I'm sure glad they sent me down to cover this one," a Chicago newsman whistled as the others nodded in agreement.

"If I were a producer I could make that woman a star," another one said so loud Christi could hear.

"Hell! She's not going to help us. She talks like a damn California politician." Moonbeam smirked.

"She'd get my vote!" Several newsmen said as Moonbeam looked ill.

Christi ignored them as she moved to her seat just behind the table where Carlton and Eddie were seated. "This thing is attracting a lot of Yankee newsmen," Christi mumbled to Carlton as he leaned back to talk to her. "This is not good."

"No. You are attracting the coverage. You and the liberal press penchant for finding a cause célèbre," Carlton smiled.

"Can we use them or will their presence hurt our side?"

Carlton grimaced but said nothing.

"How are you, Eddie?" Christi reached out and took her brother's hand.

Little Eddie looked at her with hurt in his eyes.

"Hey, little brother, you just hang in there. We're going to pull this one out," Christi tried to assure Little Eddie.

Little Eddie looked at her a long moment. Finally, the look of hurt became one of trust.

Christi looked at Carlton knowing he had not been able to find a way to crack the prosecution witnesses' testimony.

He was as worried as she when Mike Speer, the D.A., got up to make the opening argument.

"Your Honor, ladies and gentlemen of the jury, on April 17, 1960, Eddie Jones took a shotgun and brutally killed young, athletic, scholarly Firman James III. I will not deny Firman made a mistake many young men make and submitted to the temptations of the siren call of a prostitute but that is not a capital offense."

"Objection, your honor!" Carlton shouted.

"Objection sustained." The judge looked bored.

The D.A. shrugged and continued smugly. "It may be true that Mr. James unwisely entered into a house of prostitution . . ."

"Objection, Your Honor!" Carlton repeated.

"Sustained. Mr. Speer, please refrain from unsubstantiated remarks in your opening statement." The judge almost yawned.

"Yes, Your Honor. As I was saying. Young and foolish Mr. James, the beloved grandson of a distinguished senator, made a mistake that placed him in a regrettable circumstance. A mistake many of us sinners have made in the folly of youth. A mistake and a sin, but not a sin that should have cost him his life. A mistake for which I shall show he was brutally and coldly murdered. Thank you." Mike Speer smiled at the jury.

Carlton Bennett got up from his chair slowly and walked over to the jury box. "Good morning, everyone. How y'all this morning?"

The jurors smiled.

"I knew Mr. James since he was a small boy shooting marbles in sling shots against the grocery store wall. I watched him play football. Now that boy had promise. I swear he did. I liked Firman. He had a pleasant smile and I envied the way he had with ladies. Whoo boy!" Carlton shook his head and paused for effect. "But I also like Etta May Jones and I've known Mammy Jones for many years. You all know her as a God-fearing good Christian woman. Mammy Jones would not raise a daughter to be a, well, you know what Mr. Speer has suggested. Mammy Jones and her daughter Etta May are decent people and I intend to prove that Mr. Firman James forced his way into this Christian home to commit the evil sin of forcible fornication!

"My, it's hard for me to say that word but that's what he did. Firman James intended to rape this young Christian girl and might have killed her had not brave little Eddie Jones stepped in to save her." Carlton looked over at Mr. Speer who looked away. "I thank you for your kind attention," Carlton concluded and sat down.

The judge awoke from his nap. "Mr. Speer, you may call your first witness."

"Your Honor, as my first of only two witnesses I will call, in an effort to make this as expeditious a trial for the taxpayers' sake as possible, Macon Myers," Mike Speer pontificated.

Macon Myers slinked to the dock and took the oath.

"Now, Mr. Myers, we don't want to detain these hard-working jurors any longer than we have to, so just tell them in your own words what happened on the night of April 17."

Macon was nervous a moment until he saw the sympathetic eyes of the prevailing white audience. "Like I told you lots of times before, Firman James and me and Hoskins were just out sort of horsin' around. We didn't mean nothin'. Byron, he bought the beer and stuff. We didn't drink no hard liquor. Firman thought it might be fun to go to shantytown and poke fun at the spooks."

"Young man. This is a court of law," the judge cautioned.

"Yes, sir. I mean the Negroes. I mean, the black people." Macon paused and gave the jurors a condescending smile.

"Well, me and Hoskins went along. We was just funnin' when we saw this young nigra woman standing in a window with no clothes on, waving at us to come on over."

"That's a damn lie!" Etta May stood up and shouted.

The judge slammed his gavel down hard. "There'll be no more of that, Miss Jones, or I'll have you removed from the courtroom," he ordered as Etta May sat down by Sarah and seethed quietly.

"Please continue, Mr. Myers," the D.A. coached.

"Well, like I said, she waved us over and asked if we wanted to . . . uhmmmm . . . can I say what she wanted?"

"Just tell the truth, young man!" the D.A. urged.

"Well, she said she would do it with all of us for ten dollars." Etta May started to get up again but Sarah and Christi restrained her.

"I didn't want to do nothin' like that. Firman had a little more beer than the rest of us and he said he would. Well, me and Hoskins waited at the window while he goes inside. But when Firman gets inside she changes her mind and wants more money. Well, that made him mad and he just yells at her. Then this nigra boy comes in with a shotgun and well he shoots old Firman dead."

Macon hung his head.

"What a magnificent liar," Carlton whispered.

The D.A. put on his best empathetic face. "You saw that black boy seated by the defense counsel shoot Firman James III in cold blood?"

"Yes, sir."

"Firman James was not in any way physically assaulting this

woman?"

"No, sir."

Neither Sarah nor Christi could restrain Etta May any longer.

"You lying bastard!" Etta May jumped up and started to run at Macon but was dragged out of the courtroom by the bailiffs.

Sarah started hitting the bailiffs with her purse and they dragged her out also.

Once there was some quiet the judge, now fully awake, gaveled the proceedings to order. "You may cross examine," the Judge ordered after Mike Speer the D.A. yielded the witness.

"How you doin', Macon?" Carlton cooed.

"Fine, Mr. Bennett."

"Been doing any fishing lately?"

"Yes, sir. Much as I can." Macon beamed.

"Tell me, where did Firman buy the knife he used on Etta May?"

"Well, I think he bought it . . ."

"Objection, Your Honor." Mike Speer jumped up and glared at Macon.

"Objection sustained. Mr. Bennett, that type of questioning has no place in my court. You are hereby warned to skip the theatrics and practice law," the judge warned sternly.

Carlton nodded.

"Macon, let me rephrase that question. Did you see Firman with a knife?"

"Well. No, sir. Sometimes he had a knife when we went fishing, but I never knowed what kind it was," Macon volunteered.

"Your Honor, please instruct the witness to answer 'yes' or 'no' and not to introduce hearsay into the testimony," Mr. Speer objected.

"The witness is so instructed."

Carlton Bennett walked away, shaking his head, then turned and looked at Macon. "How come you didn't go into the house, Macon? You weren't as excited by this naked colored woman as Firman? Didn't you get excited by this young black body glistening in the moonlight? Aren't you as good a man as Firman James?" Carlton challenged.

"Objection, Your Honor. Mr. Bennett's badgering the witness." Mike Speer stopped Macon from answering.

"Mr. Bennett?" The judge raised his thick Irish eyebrows.

"I'll rephrase the question, Your Honor. Were you drunk, Macon?"

"No, sir. Just maybe tipsy, but not stinko."

"You could see everything clearly? You remember everything clearly?"

"Yes, sir."

"Are you sure?"

"Yes, sir."

"Well, Macon, I hate to do this to you but I intend to introduce witnesses that will swear you were falling down drunk. I will also introduce witnesses that will swear you have problems with your memory. Isn't that why you can't hold a good job? Don't you drink so much they call you 'Redeye'?"

"I don't like that name none."

"I understand." Carlton paused to smile sympathetically. "Now come on, Macon, a young man's freedom is at stake here. Do you really remember what happened that night?" Carlton insisted.

Macon tried to look at Mike Speer for help but Bennett moved into his line of vision.

"I remember the best I can, Mr. Bennett. I remember seeing that nigger boy shoot old Firman. I remember that good!" Macon shivered with nervousness.

Carlton started to pursue the questioning but thought better of it. "Thank you, Macon," he smiled as he turned to the judge. "No further questions, Your Honor." Carlton moved slowly back to the table, then sat down.

"If I tried to break him, I would make him a hero to the jury. I'm sorry, Christi, I just don't know right now." Carlton looked over at Mike Speer who was more relieved than gloating.

Byron Hoskins took the stand.

He reiterated, word for word, Macon Myers' testimony. The jury tried to look unbiased. They failed.

Carlton called for a recess.

The judge sensed the desperation and granted it quickly.

Outside the courtroom, Carlton turned away from Christi and her family. He massaged his eyes with his fingers as he wondered what new approach he might take.

Christi did not blame Carlton for the way the trial seemed to be going. Deep inside, Christi had not dared hope for victory.

She had only wanted to do her best for her family. Carlton was the best, but even the advantage of being a respected "local boy" seemed to be of no advantage. Christi had seen the jurors' eyes. They believed Macon Myers. They believed Byron Hoskins.

Etta May held onto Christi nervously. Etta May sensed it was not going well.

Sarah, for the first time in her life, seemed confused and disoriented.

Mrs. White had no lectures.

During the afternoon recess they all sat outside the courtroom in a daze.

Carlton maintained his practiced optimism.

Christi admired him for trying. Eduardo had hired the best. The best was simply holding a bad hand.

Carlton tried to say something. His anxious eyes said it all.

They all moved into the courtroom like a legion of zombies.

✳ ✳ ✳

Fifty miles away, old man Moses Green sat quietly fishing. Old Man Moses had fished the black water of Wateree Swamp for fifty years, as man and boy. He had disdained use of modern fishing equipment and still used the old cane pole his father had given him thirty years before. The fishing was poor this overcast afternoon, but he decided to stay until he finished his last pipeful of tobacco before going home. Seconds after he had made that decision, the old cork took a sharp dive under the water and something almost pulled the pole out of his hands.

"Whoooeeeee! Hot damn! I got me the granddaddy catfish of all time," he hollered for joy as the fish took the line all the way out. By the feel of the heft on the other end of the line, Moses guessed the fish's weight at ten to fifteen pounds. He had told people for years there was a catfish in the swamp that big, but no one believed him. They would have to eat their words now!

Moses delighted as he gradually pulled the big fish to shore.

The catfish's sharklike head broke the black water and wriggled its long whiskers at Moses in anger. Moses jumped up and down for joy as he played the catfish in until it was landed on the bank.

Moses stood and watched the huge fish flap around for ten minutes, then he threw it in his pail and hurried home to show it to his wife.

Annie Green was in the back yard picking some collard greens when Moses drove up in the smoky old truck and came running up to her holding the still-wriggling fish by its gills.

"Lordy mercy, Moses! What you got there?" Annie Green shook her head.

"It's that big one I been telling everybody about. Just look at it, Annie. Lord! We can eat for a week off'n this one!" Moses laughed as he lay the fish on an old clapboard table and began to skin it.

"Well, all I know is that you gonna skin that one yourself." Annie shook her finger.

"I'm happy to. I'm just as happy as I can be to do it." Moses peeled off the catfish's slippery outside skin revealing the fine white meat beneath.

He took his serrated knife and slit the fish's stomach, letting the purple innards spill onto the table. He started to brush them off onto the ground when he saw the small glint of metal. He danced his fingers around in the blood and came up with the pocket knife. As soon as he saw the initials "F. J. III" on the small silver plate he knew the importance of the find.

Chapter Forty-five

THE SECOND DAY OF THE TRIAL CAME AND CARLTON WAS STILL AT A loss on how to approach the defense. He had to break the key witness's testimony, but do it in such a way the jury wouldn't take the opposition side, if that had not happened already.

Christi sensed his frustration but kept her fears from Etta May and Eddie.

Mike Speer opened the second day by calling the police officers who investigated the scene of the crime. They confirmed everything he asked like a broken record no one could turn off.

"There was no knife found at the scene, officer?"

"No, sir."

"I remind the jury that several witnesses have sworn under oath that Firman James III never owned such a knife. Or any knife for that matter." Mike Speer seemed pleased with himself as he continued. "Was there evidence the lady had been attacked?"

"No, sir."

"Did you take an immediate statement from the boys?"

"Yes, sir."

"Did they, while the scene was fresh in their minds, confirm that Eddie Jones had, without provocation, shot young Firman James?"

"Yes, sir."

"Did you or any of your fellow officers see anything, find anything or know of anything that would support the defense counsel's contention that Miss Jones was being assaulted?" Mike intoned routinely.

"No, sir."

"Your Honor, it's really a simple, well-documented case of first degree murder. As I said earlier and I repeat, I do not wish to waste your time or the time of these good people in prolonging this trial. I rest my case." Mike Speer sighed.

Carlton had watched the mechanically precise job the district attorney had done. In a way he admired the way Mike Speer had prosecuted the case. Carlton watched the TV news every night and knew Mike knew every racial code word and how to make sure they were mouthed politely so as not to offend biased newsmen while reassuring the smoldering hatreds of potential voters.

"Would the defense like a recess before presenting their case?" the Judge offered.

"Yes, Your Honor. Please." Carlton shrugged, hoping for a miracle as Eddie looked at him with doubt in his eyes. Carlton did not like that look. He felt very bad as he moved out of the courtroom and took a long walk alone.

Christi, Etta May, Sarah, and Mrs. White walked in the opposite direction and worried.

"You think Eduardo knowed what he was doing when he hired that man?" Sarah asked Christi.

"He's doing the best he can, Momma. He knows that jury probably had their minds made up before they even sat down." Christi broke a twig off an old oak tree.

"Well, it just ain't justice. That's all there is to it. It just ain't justice." Sarah put her arm around Etta May.

"Psst! Psst!"

The noise came from some bushes off to their left.

"Did you hear that noise?" Etta May motioned toward the bushes.

"I shore did and I bet it's some young'un up to no good!" Sarah said as she broke a switch off a hickory tree and stomped over to the bushes. "You come on out of there, young'un, and stop trying to scare folks!" she demanded.

"It ain't no young'un, Mammy Jones. It's me, Old Moses Green," Moses said from deep behind the bushes.

"Moses? What's an old man like you doing hiding in the bushes," Sarah huffed.

Mrs. White started to yell for the police, but Sarah stifled her.

"No, Mammy Jones. I got something to give Christi. But I only give it to her if everybody swears they don't know where it come from. You all swears on the Lord's name?" Moses Green's frightened voice said from the bushes.

"Moses Green, all I swear is that if you don't come out of those bushes I'll switch you!"

"Now, Sarah. You done liked me a little when you and I was young. Folks say Miss Christi has got lots of money but I ain't after that," Moses chided.

"You just get on your way, Moses Green. And I ain't never liked you that much!" Sarah snarled.

"Maybe he's got something important," Christi stepped in front of Sarah.

"Thank you, Miss Christi." Moses said as he stepped out of the bushes and looked at Christi with admiration. "I seen you on that television and you shore do look special!"

"Thank you, Moses. Now what do you have for me?"

"You look better than them folks what is on there tellin' us about the weather and all that."

"That's fine, Moses but we really don't have time for this now."

"Yes, ma'am. I want you to take this. I give it to you because you make me proud to be black. I give it to you to help but you gotta promise me you won't tell nobody where it come from. I don't need no more trouble and there ain't nothing but trouble in this if'n they finds out I give it to you," Moses insisted as he handed Christi something wrapped in a checkered handkerchief.

"Thank you, Moses." Reluctantly she held onto it.

"Ain't you gonna open it?" he asked nervously.

"You want me to open it now?"

"Yes, ma'am!"

Christi peeled back the handkerchief tips and nearly dropped the knife.

Etta May picked it up and almost cried. "It's his knife, Momma! Look at them initials. Those are Firman James' just like I told you!"

Christi looked at it and nodded agreement.

"Oh Lord! Maybe there is God's justice!" Sarah said.

Christi turned to thank Moses but he had already disappeared. "Let's get it back to Mr. Bennett." Christi said as they all turned and hurried back to the courthouse.

Two hours later, the judge tapped his gavel and called the court to session.

Mike Speer had a wry smile on his face and Carlton Bennett tried to look as depressed as he possibly could.

"Mr. Bennett, you may call your first witness."

The judge leaned on his hand, bored once again.

"Thank you, Your Honor. As my first witness, I call Macon Myers,"

Carlton announced as he enjoyed the look of disbelief on Mike Speer's face.

"Your Honor, Mr. Macon Myers has already been excused. He's not even in the courtroom. This is just a delaying tactic by defense counsel. We have already heard Macon's, as well as Byron's, testimony and defense counsel has already cross examined," Mr. Speer objected.

"Mr. Bennett, I call for an Order of Proof. I won't hold up these proceedings while someone locates Mr. Myers unless you can establish his further testimony is necessary and relevant." The judge looked grim.

"Your Honor, I have new evidence that will establish that my client is innocent."

"Your Honor. I understand that Mr. Bennett has to earn his huge fee. But this is merely grandstanding," Mike scoffed.

"Your Honor, this evidence concerns a key element of Macon's testimony. If you will allow me to ask him only three questions, I will establish an 'Order of Proof' or you can excuse him."

The judge pondered the decision for a moment. "Bailiff, have someone round up Macon. You'll most probably find him at the pool hall. Get him here pronto!"

Macon solved the problem by moving out of the crowd standing in a corner of the room. "I'm here, Your Honor. I ain't never left," Macon volunteered.

Amidst a roar of laughter, which the judge stopped immediately, Macon was resworn.

"You have three questions, counselor. Proceed!" The Judge admonished.

"Thank you, Your Honor. Now, Macon, first I want to apologize for calling you back here. I know how busy you are, but there's a couple of pieces missing from this puzzle. I said to myself, I said, 'Why, Macon can help me piece those together.' You don't mind helping, do you Macon?"

Macon wrung his hands. "I don't know, Mr. Bennett. Mr. Speer done said to watch out for you," Macon volunteered as Mr. Speer sighed in agony.

"But he didn't tell you to lie to me, did he?"

"No, sir. He didn't say nothin' like that," Macon chortled.

"Okay, Macon, like the judge says, I'm going to ask you just three questions and that's all. Then I'm going to sit down and this thing's going to be over." Carlton Bennett smiled.

Macon slowly nodded his head, his face more blissfully blank than apprehensive.

Christi looked at Eddie and gave him a confident smile. Little Eddie looked as frightened as ever.

Sarah held Mrs. White's hand tightly.

"Now, question number one. Were you present on the night of April 17 when the alleged murder of Firman James took place?"

Macon looked confused. "Yes, sir. You know that."

"Question number two. Did you see everything Firman James did before he was shot?"

"Yes, sir. You know that too." He looked at Mr. Speer who shifted nervously in his chair.

"Good. See how easy it is, Macon?" Carlton paused. He smiled at the jury as he rubbed his tear ducts with his thumb and forefinger.

Mr. Speer leaned forward with his elbows on the mahogany table, his eyes fixed suspiciously on Carlton Bennett.

The jury perked its collective ears.

Christi, Sarah, Etta May and Eddie leaned forward to hear the next question.

"Well, now, Macon. The third question is . . . well, let's see now, how shall I phrase it. You know, you have to phrase the questions just right."

"Get on with it, counselor," the Judge snapped.

"Ah, yes. Let's see. Macon you say you were there when Firman was shot and you saw everything, right?"

"Yes, sir, I done told you that three times already."

"You were there and you saw everything, but you didn't see this knife?" Carlton pulled the knife from his pocket and held it so Macon could see the initials on the engraved plate.

"No, sir! That can't be! Hoskins said he threw that in the swamp. I swear he done promised me he done that!"

Mike Speer became unglued.

"Objection, Your Honor. Objection! This is highly irregular. The witness is incriminating himself," Mike Speer objected weakly.

"No, he isn't. He's perjuring himself and I want to know why," the judge overruled. "Continue, Mr. Bennett."

"Then you have seen this knife before?"

"Yes, sir. No, sir. I don't know, sir." Macon almost broke into tears.

"Mr. Myers, you have already perjured yourself. I admonish you that if you commit further perjury it will go very hard on you," the judge snarled.

Mike Speer stood up, his face beet red.

"Your Honor, you can't do this. This is self-incrimination. What about Mr. Myers' civil rights?" Mike Speer fumed.

"I'm more interested in the truth right now. Answer the question, Mr. Myers. Have you seen that knife before? The knife I will allow the bailiff to mark exhibit K . . . for the record, Mr. Speer." The judge waived for the bailiff.

"Yes, sir," Macon answered in a barely audible voice as big beads of sweat broke out on his forehead.

"Where did you see it before?"

Macon looked to Mike Speer for support. Mike turned away.

"Firman had it that night. Like that colored girl said. I swear I didn't mean to lie, Your Honor, but my dad and Mr. Speer and everybody done told me to!"

Mike Speer almost fainted.

So did a few jurors.

"That's enough. We will continue this in my chambers." The judge slammed the gavel down and motioned the lawyers to follow him into chambers.

"The court is in recess for one hour. The jury is instructed not to discuss this case with anyone."

Eddie jumped up and hugged Christi.

Sarah, Etta May, and Mrs. White all cried together long before, and long after the judge returned. Long after he declared the charges dismissed, released Eddie Jones and remanded Byron Hoskins and Macon Myers to custody.

Chapter Forty-six

THE LAWN WAS STILL SCORCHED FROM THE CROSS BURNING, BUT there was great joy in the Jones's home for the first time in years. Sarah Jones was so happy she even agreed to have a glass of wine. She spit it out in the sink when no one was looking. It simply was against her nature to drink anything containing alcohol. It had hurt her too much, too many times. Christi delighted in the gathering of family and now that Etta May was exonerated and Little Eddie free she could turn her thoughts to Eduardo. She was deep in thoughts of happy times with Eduardo when she heard the pleasant strains of an Irish tenor wafting through the open living room window. Enos, the newly acquired butler, grimaced as his ears picked up the sound. He started for the front door but Christi grabbed his arm and held him back.

"I'll get it, Enos." She shook her head in disbelief as she slowly opened the heavy wooden door.

"Happy St. Paddy's Day, Christi!" A bubbly Cosmo Collins greeted her as the door swung wide.

Christi tried to shut the door but he put up his arm and held it back. "Now, lassie. I come a far ways to say howdy. You would be granting me that small favor?"

"Do you know how much I hate you?" Christi replied.

Cosmo looked at her with his dreamy Irish eyes. The light that danced in them almost melted away her reserve.

"Yes, I do. And you have good reason to hate me. But we Irish forgive everything on St. Paddy's day."

"I'm not Irish."

"Ah, lassie! Today everyone is Irish."

"You bastard!"

"Yes. Certified. Never knew whence I came. Hardly ever know where I am going."

For a quick, horrifying moment, Christi looked deep into Cosmo's eyes. She probed them to see if he was carrying bad news. She shrugged as she remembered she could never tell anything about Cosmo's thoughts by looking into his eyes.

Suddenly all her pent-up fears and hopes seemed petty. She had been lonely too long to slap him so she kissed him full on the lips. Cosmo almost dropped the fifth of Irish whiskey he was carrying. He broke the kiss and gave her a mischievous grin. "God knows if a man ever knows what you're thinking, Christi!"

Christi pulled his mouth to hers and kissed him full on the lips once again.

For one brief, delightful moment he returned her kiss. Then she shoved him away. "Have you come to tell me I am a widow?"

"What?"

"Where is Eduardo?"

"I don't know. I really don't."

"Then why are you here?"

"Jesus, Christi! You can't kiss a man one minute and curse him the next!"

"Oh? Yes I can. Haven't you heard. I love them and leave them now."

Cosmo chuckled and nodded.

Their eyes met for a brief moment of undying love before they both blinked in denial.

"So how are you?" Cosmo said almost soberly.

"How am I?"

"Let me try again. Hello old pal. Can I come in and visit a while?"

"Why?"

Cosmo did not like the hardness he now saw in her eyes. "It's good to see you, Christi. I was just in the neighborhood. I'll see you later." He turned to leave.

Christi let him walk away for a moment. "Get back here, you miserable scoundrel!"

Cosmo turned. He took a pull from the bottle. He shook his head. "Keep them guessing, right, Christi?"

"I take in stray dogs as well."

"It is good to see you, Christi. Tell me, how do you like my Cuban and Miami Beach tan?" Cosmo asked as he moved directly under the porch light.

The golden brown of his skin made his blue-green eyes sparkle, despite the effects of half a fifth of Irish whiskey.

"Who is it? What's the matter, chile?" Sarah hurried to Christi's side.

She saw the staggering Cosmo and frowned.

"We moved to a respectable neighborhood and we still get drunken bums," Sarah said. She looked disgusted as she stared at Cosmo, hands on her hips.

"No, Momma. This drunken bum is not just any drunken bum. This is Cosmo Collins," Christi introduced as she steadied Cosmo with her arm in his.

Sarah's face turned pleasant. "Cosmo? The man who helped you on that boat?"

"Yes."

"Well, then he's a friend of this family. He can come in but he leaves that bottle outside. You hear?" Sarah insisted.

"Yes, ma'am," Cosmo replied as he entered the large, high-ceilinged atrium. He looked around quickly as he winked at Christi. "A long way from the *Calamaria Princess,* eh, kid?" he chuckled.

Enos relieved Cosmo of the bottle of whiskey and his coat. Etta May and Little Eddie were introduced.

Enos handed Cosmo a cup of black coffee.

"Yes, Cosmo, a very long way. How have you been?" Christi wondered.

"Fine! Just fine. I spent a week at Anita's in Miami. She's in Miami now. She fattened me up on frijoles and peppers. A lot of the old gang is in Miami." Cosmo sounded melancholy.

Christi was worried that he made no mention of Eduardo. If the news was bad she didn't want to hear it now.

Cosmo lifted the coffee cup high.

"Happy St. Paddy's Day to you all," he toasted. The coffee went down hard.

"You mind putting a touch of the Irish in here?" Cosmo offered the cup to Enos.

Enos looked at Sarah, who shook her head.

"We have some cousins in Miami." Sarah attempted small talk.

"Oh, if I had known I would have looked them up. Why don't you give me their addresses and I'll look them up on my way back," Cosmo replied.

Christi watched Cosmo intently for any sign something was wrong. Cosmo looked very mellow. Christi could not take the suspense any longer. "Where's Eduardo, Cosmo?"

"Eduardo? Old Eddie boy? Yep, he's one helluva man. That husband of yours is one helluva man."

"Etta May. Little Eddie. It's been a long day. Both of you go get ready for bed. I mean it," Sarah interrupted Cosmo.

Little Eddie and Etta May grumbled as they went up to bed.

Christi poured herself a tall glass of wine while she waited for them to disappear upstairs.

In whispers Cosmo asked Enos for an Irish coffee.

Enos offered more black coffee.

"We were talking about Eduardo," Christi began when she and Sarah were alone with Cosmo.

"Eddie? He's one good man, alright."

"Dammit, Cosmo! Is he okay?" Christi snapped.

Cosmo sat up stiff-backed on the couch. "Eddie?"

"Eduardo! Come on, Cosmo." Christi leaned forward nervously.

"Yeah! Yeah. I think he's most probably alright. I think so," Cosmo mused aloud.

"You think so? That's it?" Christi asked firmly.

Cosmo looked at Sarah nervously.

"Mother could I talk to him alone for a minute?" Christi pleaded.

Sarah grumped a little but finally excused herself and slowly made her way upstairs.

Moments after Sarah was gone, Christi gave Cosmo a hard look. "I want to know it all. Right now, Cosmo!" Christi insisted. Cosmo nodded agreement.

"With you and me, Christi, I am always the messenger boy. I am always taking the news from here to there to here," Cosmo shrugged.

"Cosmo! Now!" Christi stood up angrily.

"Okay, Christi, Chill out. . . . all I know is I don't know. No one knows. Here, I promised to deliver this note and I've delivered it. Now, maybe I'd better go." Cosmo started to get up.

Christi took the note and pushed Cosmo back down on the couch. She looked at the envelope a long moment.

"To my beloved wife," she read the inscription on the envelope.

It was Eduardo's handwriting.

She started to open it. She thought better of it.

"I've got to go and find a motel, Christi. I'll call you tomorrow before I leave." Cosmo started to get up once more.

"Sit down. I'm not through with you yet. Before I read this, tell me where he is now."

"Now?" Cosmo shrugged.

"The last contact you had. Where was he?"

Cosmo started to be evasive but saw the determination in Christi's eyes.

"Nicaragua or Honduras. Maybe San Salvador. Somewhere in Central America. I swear, Christi. They fight a guerilla war. Always on the run." Cosmo sighed.

"Eduardo, fighting?"

"Oh, yes! He's turned into quite a soldier. You would be proud!"

"No, I wouldn't!" Christi tore open the note. She pulled it out and read:

Love of my life,

If you have this note from Cosmo then I am temporarily out of contact. I do not want you to worry. Kiki allowed me to accompany him on a small excursion to Central America. For security reasons I will not be able to contact you for a while. Please do not be overly concerned. It was the chance of a lifetime to see up close the end result of all the money we have spent. I hope you understand. I love you, now and always. I will be back, I promise.

With all my love, Eduardo.

Christi felt nothing as she placed the note back into the envelope. "I am the single biggest fool in the world."

"Naw! Not even close! Not as long as there is me!" Cosmo offered.

"You didn't make a foolish marriage twice. You hang out with the macho Latin types. You don't marry them!" Christi smoldered.

"The note was bad news?" Cosmo wondered.

"I read the papers, Cosmo. Your hero, El Grande, has failed to export his revolution. You know as well as I do Eduardo is dead."

Cosmo had to look away from her before he replied. "It isn't over yet."

"It is for me."

Cosmo studied the coldness in her face. He did not like the way it eclipsed her beauty. He started to ease out once more.

"Would you leave me alone on such a night?" Christi looked at him with forced tears brimming her eyes.

Cosmo stopped and thought it over. He almost reached out and took her in his arms.

"Christi, it was so hard for me to come here. I promised him I would deliver the note. I have delivered it. Please try to understand how uncomfortable this is for me."

"For you? You bastard! You never think about me! You never have!"

"That's not true. I think of you all the time."

Christi's heart jumped at Cosmo's admission. She knew he regretted it the moment he had said it.

"That was the booze talking. How about some more coffee?" Cosmo looked sheepish.

"Liar."

"Look! I fought side by side with these men. I can't let myself relax with you while he is out there, God knows where." Cosmo slammed his fist into the side of the couch.

"Are you that naive, Cosmo?"

"What do you mean?"

"Eduardo knows about us. Why do you think he asked you to come here?"

"That's easy. We are like brothers, Christi. It's hard to explain to someone who is not in the brotherhood," Cosmo stopped and looked deadly serious. "We trust each other with our lives. That's why I have to go."

"Why hurry? If you miss this revolution there'll be another one along soon enough," Christi said sarcastically.

Cosmo censored her with his eyes. "I've got my reasons!"

Cosmo shook with indecision. For a moment he looked very vulnerable. "Besides it's late. I have to find a place to crash."

Christi did not want him to leave but she would not beg him to stay. "There are fifteen bedrooms in this house."

Cosmo could not hide his amazement. "God! We could barracks an army."

"Have you had dinner?" Christi asked.

"Sort of. I had a poor American imitation of corned beef and cabbage at the pub down the street."

"How long did you wait there before coming here?"

Cosmo looked away. "That burned cross on the lawn. I heard some angry talk at the pub. Are you alright, Christi?"

"Yes. That was the Welcome Wagon. We were supposed to run screaming into the night. Instead we roasted marshmallows."

Cosmo looked at her with admiration. "God! You have guts, lady. No wonder men adore you."

"Does that include you, Cosmo?"

"I sort of hoped I was the one and only." He chuckled.

Christi had to look away from him. She knew that if she did not she would find herself in his arms.

Cosmo moved close. He slowly put his arm around her shoulder. "I know why Eduardo sent me, Christi. So do you."

"Yes . . ."

"It was a noble thing to do but I won't take advantage of it. You understand?"

"Doesn't this brotherhood require you to take care of me if he doesn't come back?" Christi scoffed.

"He is coming back."

"If you believe that you are a bigger fool than he."

Cosmo had to think it over. "I'd better go."

"Shut up. You aren't going anywhere. I'll have Enos put you in the room next to his. He's an old soldier. You can stay up all night telling each other war stories."

"Considering the hour maybe I'll take you up on that offer."

He reached out and pulled her to him. It felt good to feel the strength of his body against hers. Cosmo reached down and took her chin in his hand. He pulled her face toward his and kissed her softly on the lips.

"I'm not a good liar. The truth is I wanted to come here. I wanted to see you. This is all too damn complicated for a simple Irishman. Romance is much too complex for simple men, Christi. War is much easier. I should never have left Vietnam. I made good money just showing peasants how to shoot guns at Frenchmen. I knew that over there I had no possible connection to you."

"I understand."

"No, you don't! I was glad when Eduardo decided to go with Kiki. I was actually hoping he would. I knew what was waiting for them down there. The dictators of Central America aren't about to let Cuba happen to them. They were waiting for Kiki and Eduardo with a well-trained army. Damn! Do I feel guilty." Cosmo gritted his teeth.

Christi held him tight. His arms closed tighter around her. "He would have gone despite you or me. I used to catch him playing at war in the stables. A grown man making machine gun noises and shooting at imaginary enemies. You know what? He wasn't embarrassed when I caught him. Please don't feel guilty, Cosmo. I have a feeling he is alright. He has a way of landing on his feet," Christi soothed.

Cosmo agreed quietly. "That may be true, but there can be nothing between us until we know for sure," Cosmo insisted.

Christi kissed him quietly. "You are a strange man, Cosmo Collins. I love you very much," Christi said as she kissed him fiercely on the lips, a kiss that stirred old feelings.

They broke the kiss a moment. He was about to take her back into his arms when they were interrupted by a loud sound of disapproval from Sarah.

"Momma?" Christi said meekly.

Cosmo slinked down on the couch.

"You have the last bedroom on the right at the top of the stairs, Mr. Collins. You best go there now!" Sarah said firmly.

"Yes, ma'am." Cosmo stood up almost at attention. "Goodnight, Mrs. De La Cruz." He nodded to Christi as he quickly passed by Sarah.

"And you best wipe that grease paint off your face," Sarah snapped, eyeing Christi with contempt.

Cosmo took out his handkerchief and wiped the lipstick from his face as he backed his way quickly up the stairs.

"You don't understand, Momma."

"And I don't want to understand. You get to bed now and I better not hear no doorknobs rattling in the night. You hear!" Sarah scolded.

Christi slowly walked by her mother. "I hear. Goodnight, Momma." Christi gave her a quick kiss.

Sarah waited until Christi had disappeared into her bedroom before she picked up the note, put it down, picked it up again and reread it.

Sarah wondered about many things. She no longer wondered why Mr. Collins had arrived to see her Christi.

Chapter Forty-seven

LITTLE EDDIE JONES SLIPPED BEHIND THE WHEEL OF THE SHINY RED Cadillac convertible. Reverently, he felt the plastic smoothness of the steering wheel and let his body slowly sink into the deep cushioned comfort of the leather upholstery. Little Eddie had never been able to get a job and never had over five dollars all together at one time until today. To celebrate his freedom, Christi had given Eddie a fifty-dollar bill and allowed him to use her car on the promise he would only drive it in the neighborhood. Eddie had no license and Christi wanted no more trouble of any kind with the law.

Little Eddie thought he had died and gone to heaven as he stuffed the bill into his pocket and sat down in the deep cushion of the leather covered front seat. He eased the key into the ignition of the convertible and turned over the big engine that started on the first spark. He gunned the engine a few times delighting in the powerful roar coming from the twin exhaust pipes. He eased the car into the snooty streets of this up-scale Charleston locale and leaned back, grinning at every disapproving eye that watched from afar. He turned the radio up full blast and peeled rubber from every stop sign. He was having such a good time he soon forgot his promise to Christi not to leave the neighborhood.

It was twilight and the late evening sun made the bright red car sparkle even brighter as Eddie, lost in euphoria, slowly made his way to the dangerous streets of North Charleston.

In the living room of the big house, Christi sat on the long burgundy couch and looked at Carlton with a steady gaze. Cosmo stood a few feet away in a corner of the room. "I believe Eduardo is alive in one of their prisons. I don't want to be told how irrational that is, I just want your help in finding him," Christi intoned firmly.

Carlton looked across the room at Cosmo only to find a blank stare.

"Eduardo had a lot of faith in you. You have contacts in Washington. Some of them must know someone who knows the leaders of that country," Christi insisted.

Carlton blew into his fist as he pondered Christi's words.

He nodded understanding.

Not far away, Little Eddie grew more emboldened as time went by and no one had challenged him. He felt almost invincible behind the wheel of the big car as he roared through neighborhoods at high speed. He flew through stop signs, creating many near-miss situations and leaving a line of angry motorists shaking their fists in his rearview mirror. He had never known such a feeling of power and had never felt so alive before in his life.

Inside the house Carlton Bennett cautioned Christi. "You realize Senator Firman James is chairman of the Foreign Affairs Committee. In addition, anti-Cuban, even anti-Latin American, feeling is running high in Washington . . .

"Eduardo, rightly or wrongly, would be labeled a revolutionary and I don't know how much help anybody could give us under those circumstances," Carlton grimaced.

"You're telling me those people up there have all of a sudden stopped liking money?" Christi smirked.

"When it comes to communists, particularly those linked to El Grande, I'm afraid it isn't a question of money. Under those circumstances it's hard for even the liberals to be very liberal," Carlton smiled.

"Stop with the damn excuses! I won't let Eduardo rot in some jail in Nicaragua."

Carlton looked at Cosmo for help.

Cosmo looked away.

"I'm sorry, Christi. I don't have any friends in Washington who can help in this matter. I don't know anyone who has. Maybe the answer is for you to go to Washington yourself." Carlton smiled.

"What?"

"Anyone who watched the coverage of the trial saw what a presence you were on television. The exposure you received made you a local celebrity. The reporters are still buzzing about you. You told me you got several letters from agencies wanting to sign you. You are photogenic and articulate. Why not?" Carlton insisted.

"What are you talking about?"

"You would make a marvelous Congresswoman."

Christi laughed and looked at Cosmo to share her scorn for the idea.

Cosmo looked as if he liked the idea.

"I don't want to hear any kind of crazy talk like that, Carlton. This is serious business," Christi insisted.

"Why is it foolish? I know many people who realize you can't shut blacks out forever. Many of us would like to see an orderly change. We are not all head-bobbing redneck hypocrites, Christi. There is a seat in Congress open you would fill quite nicely." Carlton seemed to become more convinced at the sound of the idea.

"I despise politics . . . and politicians!"

"Precisely. That is your most attractive quality."

"What an idiotic idea. Even if it wasn't, I'm only twenty-six."

"You only have to be twenty-five. There is a man named Kennedy in the White House who is only forty-three. The youngest in history. The people reject many incumbents, I believe, particularly on the basis they are TOO experienced in politics."

"Carlton, I will do anything I must do to get Eduardo back alive. All I want from you is a workable plan to do that. I don't want to hear this Congresswoman crap! Tell him, Cosmo. Tell him what a stupid idea it. . ."

"I think you would make a great legislator. God! Think about it. A bloodless revolution! Why didn't I ever think of that?" Cosmo mused.

"Not you too, Cosmo," Christi chided.

Cosmo's response was to look out the window at the full moon.

The full moon lit up the streets as Little Eddie screamed around the corner of a strange street and pushed the accelerator to the floor.

He was so drunk with the feelings of power he did not notice the pickup truck pull across the road a half-mile ahead and stop directly in his path. Three burly men got out of the pickup truck's cab and moved into the shadows on the side of the road. One of them cocked a .12 gauge shotgun and spit angrily through his teeth in Little Eddie's direction.

Little Eddie saw the truck and his hands froze on the steering wheel for an instant. When he was finally able to turn the wheel he turned it too sharp and the big Cadillac broke into a slide, then a spin that almost caused it to turn over.

Little Eddie fought the wheel hard as the car began to right itself. He thought he was in control when the right fender crashed into the telephone pole and his head bounced off the windshield.

The blow stunned Little Eddie into semiconsciousness. He could feel the blood running down his face. He was too weak to wipe it away.

The plump Macon Myers who stood over him was only a blur.

"Well, lookie here! We got ourselves a nigger in a shiny Cadillac who's done gone and got himself all banged up. Hey, Hoskins, you know anything about first aid?" Macon quizzed as he held the shotgun over his shoulder and laughed.

"Why hell yes I do! You know that mouth to mouth resuscitation? Well, you just put your mouth down close to his and whisper, 'Nigger, kiss your ass goodbye'!" Hoskins chuckled.

Macon put down the shotgun, grabbed Little Eddie by his hair and jerked back his head. "He don't look so uppity now, does he?" he smirked.

Little Eddie was slowly regaining consciousness and nearly fainted when he saw the face of Macon Myers and the mayhem in his eyes.

Macon and Hoskins reached under Little Eddie's arms and dragged him from the car.

Little Eddie could stand but he was wobbly.

"Firman James was a good ole boy. You know he was a friend of mine, nigger?" Macon snarled as Zeke, the most cowardly of the three, eased into the shadows.

"That fancy lawyer and that uppity high-yellow sister of yours got you free and you done killed a white man. Now, you know we can't let that go around here." Macon grunted as he picked up the shotgun and pointed it at Little Eddie.

Hoskins grabbed the barrel. "No, we don't need that. This here poor ole boy died accidentally." Hoskin's eyes narrowed.

"Yeah! Yeah!" Macon's eyes brightened as he turned the gun around and held it by the barrel.

Little Eddie was wide awake now and he tried to run past the three men on his weak legs. He had gone only three steps before the gun's heavy wood stock crashed against the back of his head, breaking his neck and killing him instantly.

As Cosmo watched the full moon he felt a sudden chill. He turned back and looked at Christi. "You should think about it, Christi. I would vote for you, if I could vote."

Christi stared at Cosmo in disbelief. Then she stared at Carlton.

"You two are no help at all. I will fly to Nicaragua tomorrow. I'll find him and get him out myself," Christi insisted.

"No, Christi. That whole country is under martial law. Being an American will give you no special immunity. If they find out you are Eduardo's wife, your life wouldn't be worth a plugged peso," Cosmo spoke firmly.

"Well, I sure am not going to sit here and do nothing!" Christi turned her back on both of them.

"Christi, even if he's alive . . ."

"He's alive!" she interrupted Cosmo.

"Well, I want to believe that too, but I'm not going to do anything stupid and I'm not going to let you do anything stupid until we know that."

"It's not your concern, Cosmo."

"The hell it isn't! I promised him I'd take care of you and I'll do it whether you let me or not. He could be back in Cuba for all we know. Communications are screwed up there," Cosmo insisted.

"Please, Cosmo. I know better."

"No you don't! We know nothing except what leaks out and that is all crapola!" Cosmo snapped.

"I know all I need to know. . . . and for the record, I don't need any-one watching over me!"

"Well, I suppose I should go," Carlton offered.

"You will arrange for the proper papers?" Christi asked.

Carlton looked to Cosmo.

Christi stepped between them.

"I am the one who retains you, Carlton."

"Yes. I understand. If you insist I will arrange for the proper papers."

Cosmo shook his head with concern. "You have no idea what you're getting into, Christi."

"Oh? What if he is sick or dying or in prison? You . . . his so-called best friend . . . just want to leave him there to rot?"

"What?"

"You heard me. Maybe you prefer he not come back."

"What?"

"You heard me."

Cosmo moved to within inches of Christi's face and glared as he pointed to an open window "Yes I did, and if I thought you meant that

I would shove your smart ass through that damn window!"

"Oh, really?"

"Yes! Really!"

Carlton cleared his throat and moved cautiously beside them. "I'll get some people working on it. I advise you to wait until we hear from them. It will take time. Mr. Collins is correct. Communications are all screwed up down there," Carlton offered.

Christi and Cosmo slowly cooled and backed away from each other.

"Just do it, Mr. Bennett."

"Yes. Of course. I will expedite it, but under the most favorable circumstances it will be weeks I'm afraid."

"So, meanwhile, I run for president?" Christi smirked.

Carlton thought it over a moment.

"No. Congresswoman in the new Sixteenth District." Carlton replied confidently.

Christi was impressed by Carlton's confident tone. She looked to Cosmo who had his back to her. She moved to open the door for Carlton.

Carlton paused at the door. "Would you at least talk to Monk Miller, the committee chairman? Would you take it seriously if he told you the party would back you?"

Christi started to laugh.

Carlton looked deadly serious.

"Why sure, I'd talk to the devil himself if it would help Eduardo."

"Good! I'll set up a meeting as soon as possible."

"You do that." Christi almost yawned as she let Carlton out.

She shut the door and moved back into the chilly atmosphere of the living room.

Cosmo still had his back to her. He turned and glared at her then walked hurriedly to the door. He opened it to leave but hesitated.

Christi was considering some sort of apology when Sarah entered the room with a look of horror on her face.

"What is it, Momma? What's the matter?"

Sarah looked at Christi with tears in her eyes and she shook uncontrollably.

"Momma? Momma! Please, what is it?" Christi tried to stop Sarah from shaking.

"My Little Eddie. My Little Eddie done wrecked that fancy car of yours and killed himself. He's dead, Christi! My little Eddie's dead," Sarah cried aloud.

"Oh God! No! No!" Christi tried to hold Sarah but she slipped away.

"I told you he shouldn't be driving no fancy car like that. I knowed it, Christi! We should have never let him do it. Oh, my Lord, we done killed my baby boy!" Sarah sank to her knees and buried her face in the carpet.

Christi knelt down, took her in her arms and rocked her like one rocks a baby.

Cosmo was halfway out of the door. He stopped, closed the door and moved back inside where he lay his strong hand gently on Christi's shoulder.

Chapter Forty-eight

CHRISTI SAT ALONE IN HER ROOM FOR SOME TIME AFTER SHE HAD managed to get Sarah sedated and to sleep. It was funny but she thought she had cried all the tears she would ever cry. As she sat on her bed in the huge room she felt very lonely and a little afraid. The full moon streamed through her window and glistened on all the gold surfaces of the trinkets that filled the room. It lit up her three walk-in closets full of clothes and the long line of shoes she had always dreamed of having.

None of it was any comfort.

Slowly she got up from the bed and went to the closet. Hurriedly she moved aside several boxes until she found the one that held the dress and the crucifix.

She carried the box back to her dressing table and took out the yellow cotton dress.

Quickly she removed her clothes and stood naked in the bright moonlight. She frowned at the slight trace of a wrinkle by her right eye. Reverently, she placed the bent crucifix about her neck and slipped the dress over her head. She walked out into the hallway toward Cosmo's room.

Cosmo lay on the floor in his briefs. He had found the bed too soft for his bad back.

He was fantasizing about Christi when she tapped on his door. Cosmo instinctively started to reach for a gun, then realized where he was. He hid the gun and moved to the door.

"Can I come in?"

"Christi?" Cosmo swung the door wide.

"I didn't mean to wake you," Christi apologized.

"It's okay. I couldn't sleep."

"Can I stay with you a little while?"

"Hey, come on in and stay as long as you like."

"Thank you."

"No! Thank you. Here, sit down on the bed. No I didn't mean that." He almost blushed.

"You really are bashful, aren't you?"

"Well, I don't know about that."

"You are. You're a son of a gun when it comes to fighting, but you're basically bashful. I swear I never realized it until now." Christi smiled and brushed his face with her hand as she sat on the bed.

"Well, maybe I am. Maybe I spent too much time with men to be too good with women. Besides you always did make me a little nervous."

"I'll take that as a compliment."

"I'm sorry about your brother, Christi."

Christi's eyes misted and she sighed hard. "He never had a chance to live." She paused. "Will you stay for the funeral?"

"Sure! Of course." Cosmo choked a little and turned his back on her.

Christi watched his muscles shine in the moonlight as he stood by the full window and looked at the sky.

"I've always loved you, Cosmo. It seems I'm always running to your arms but never staying there."

"I wish you wouldn't talk like that."

"Like what?"

"We don't have the right to talk like that. You saw how your mother looked at us."

"My mother knows I'm married to Eduardo. She doesn't know I love you."

"I asked you not to say that."

"I'm tired of lying to myself and everyone else. If you don't want me to say it, okay, but you can't stop me from thinking it."

"You're just hurting right now, Christi. I wonder if you would like me if we ever met when there wasn't trouble."

Christi had to smile. "Well, you seem to always be there. Doesn't that mean anything?"

Cosmo looked very nervous. "It might if my *compadres* said it was okay."

"Neither of them is alive and you know it."

"No I don't. Not for sure."

"Cosmo, you can send me away by saying you don't care for me but don't try to make me believe I'm not a widow twice over. I've accepted it. Why can't you?"

Cosmo looked astonished. "Man! That little girl I knew has turned into one stone cold woman!"

Christi sat on the bed. "Come over here and sit down by me."

Cosmo looked uncomfortable at the suggestion.

"It's okay. Really!" Christi held out both hands."

Cosmo looked at the sky for a moment before he sighed heavily. He looked at the yellow cotton dress folded around her knees up to her thighs. He moved to the bedside. "That dress? I thought I told you not to wear it. It provokes the sailors."

"Do you think Diego has thawed out yet?"

They chuckled together.

"I don't understand all the things I feel about you. You make me do stupid things. I could have . . . I should have sent the letter from Eduardo by registered mail. I should never have come here. You are the only complication in a life I have tried to make simple."

"I'm glad you came."

"I'm a war lover, Christi. I like the strange sanity of bad guys and good guys getting it on. You and I are looney tunes."

Christi lay back on the bed and thought it over. "I like looney tunes."

"Man, you are something."

Christi looked into his Irish eyes and was pleased to see she could read a glimmer of love "You and your Irish blarney. You've always loved me, haven't you?" Christi challenged.

"You said we wouldn't talk about that stuff!"

Christi stroked his hair. "Maybe you're right. Maybe I should look for a sexy accountant who hates guns."

"You should of never had anything to do with any of us. Okay?" Cosmo clenched his fists and looked angry.

"A little late for that."

Cosmo looked at her with a mixture of love and hurt in his eyes. "You don't get it! It's all fucked up, Christi. I helped put power in the wrong men's hands. I have to tell you this! Kiki, Eduardo and I had this big argument in Havana. El Grande shot some of my best friends. Just took them out and shot them. Just like that!" Cosmo snapped his fingers in disgust. "Just like that because someone claimed they were not true revolutionaries. I really thought this one would be different. I really did."

Christi looked at him with concern. "You, Kiki and Eduardo fought?"

"Yes."

"Men do that all the time."

"No! I almost killed them both!"

Christi was visibly stunned.

"Your husbands are true believers. They still have faith in that strutting Cuban peacock, El Grande! I had to leave before they killed me or I killed them. Now you want to talk about love with a man like me?"

"We said we wouldn't speak of it."

"Go ahead and joke about it. The way things are, Kiki and Eduardo could be victims of their own revolution at anytime. Many of El Grande's staunchest supporters were shot. I was stupid enough to believe in me and my buddies against the world forever. Maybe I'm just plain stupid!" Cosmo looked disgusted.

Christi stroked his neck with her fingers. He stretched in pleasure. Then he stood up and shook it off. "Christi, please try to understand. I helped screw things up. I have to go back and try to help make them right!" Cosmo insisted.

"No! I'll never understand such idiotic thinking."

"Then I'm sorry. There is nothing else for us to say."

Christi nodded sad agreement. "You won't give it up for me? For us?"

"I can't. Not until I try to make it right. I can't tell you much but I can tell you that I and a few friends are going back down there soon to make some minor corrections."

"Maybe you are just plain crazy."

"No! This time there is a brave young American backing this expedition. This time I have the generous help of the American Eagle," Cosmo said proudly.

Christi looked doubtful. "You mean Kennedy? The president?"

"I never said that."

"You need some rest, Cosmo. You really do!" Christi looked into his eyes. Once again they were unreadable.

"I'm sorry I came. I'm sorry I interrupted your life." Cosmo backed away.

"Please, just sit by me awhile. We don't have to say anything. I don't want to know where you are going tomorrow, or the day after. I don't want to know what you will be doing. Please, for a little while tonight, can it just be Christi and Cosmo without any ghosts?" Cosmo sat down on the bed and lay back. He looked at her tenderly. "I liked you better as a frightened little girl."

"That was an act. I was a lusty woman all the time."

"You were a brave one, alright. You've had some life already. You're some kind of woman, alright. Maybe you should run for office like that lawyer said."

Christi smirked. "I will if you will stay and run my campaign."

"I'm sorry, Christi. I really am."

"Then this is it?"

"I think so."

"I see. Then at least you owe me a farewell fuck!"

Cosmo thought it over and looked at her with total admiration. "That frightened young girl would never had said anything like that."

"I told you. I'm not a frightened young girl anymore!" Christi stood up and reached back to find the zipper of her dress. She fumbled for it a moment before her fingers found it. With three quick jerks she pulled it down and the dress fell from her shoulders. She stepped out of it and let it drop to the floor. "I want it hard and deep and all night, buster!"

"Oh my God, Christi! You're so damn beautiful!" Cosmo shivered as he admired Christi's naked body in the silver moonlight.

Christi reached out her hands and scratched his chest with long, gentle strokes.

Cosmo held back. His eyes hungry but wary. "Christi, I'm not staying!" he whispered as his lips fumbled to kiss her.

"I know."

She took his face in her hands and pulled his lips to hers.

They kissed slowly at first. He seemed unsure of what he was doing.

Christi thought it funny and wonderful that he was resisting her. Here was the ultimate test of her powers. If she could bend his will to hers and make him stay, all her other losses would soon be forgotten. "Cosmo, please don't be afraid of me. Touch me wherever you like," she insisted.

Cosmo paused a moment to look at her, then he pulled her warm body against his and she felt his body throbbing against hers. He bit her neck softly and eased the tip of his tongue into her ear. It tickled.

Christi stroked his back and he cooed as he stroked hers in return. She nibbled at his chest and he dropped to his knees, kissing her neck and breasts as he fell.

He threw her back on the bed and stood over her with a wry smile and a huge, throbbing manhood. "Afraid of you, Christi? No! I just never wanted to hurt you."

"Please don't worry about that."

"Are you sure?"

"Yes! Oh, yes."

Cosmo shrugged and started to ease down on her.

Christi held up her hands. She stood up and motioned for him to lie down.

Cosmo looked puzzled.

"I like it on top."

Cosmo nodded knowingly. "You would."

"What does that mean?"

Cosmo shook his head. "It won't work that way," Cosmo insisted.

"Yes, it will. It's so much better for me!"

"You like being in control, Christi?"

"Well, yes."

"No!" Cosmo picked her up and lay her on her back. "Tonight you are the flower that awaits the elusive butterfly."

"Cosmo. Please try it my way."

"Stop it, Christi! You'll scare the butterfly away."

"But I . . ."

"Hush! Trust me."

Christi started to object but his eyes were unyielding as was his rising manhood.

"The butterfly?" she wondered aloud.

"The erotic Venus butterfly, Christi. I offer it to you. You, the rare orchid that brings such beauty to my sordid world."

Christi had to think about it and she didn't want to think about anything. "Whatever, my love. Whatever."

"Are you sure? Once you've had the Venus butterfly you are its captive forever."

"Yes, Cosmo. I understand. Please!"

Cosmo smiled. He stepped back and watched her anticipation

for a long moment.

"What are you doing? Come on?" Christi demanded.

Cosmo hushed her with a finger gently touching her lips.

He paused and gave her a long comforting smile. He stood tall and erect before her and let the moonlight become his theatrical lighting, spotlighting the fleshy stage scene that was soon to carry the most erotic drama.

Then he formed the seductive Venus butterfly with his strong hands.

First he interlocked all the fingers. Then he extended the thumbs, forefingers, and little fingers of each hand to form three "steeples." He moistened his lips, slowly with a long, perfectly formed tongue. A tongue ready to perform the flights of erotica that made it a magic butterfly.

"Behold the elusive butterfly of love. Now I want you to pretend you are a young flower. A bud that has never opened its petals to the world. You are eager to blossom but to do so you must have the magic touch that only this butterfly can bring."

"I'm ready, my love. Do it! Do it!" Christi was eager to get on with the game.

"No! I don't want sex. I want you to let me make love to you."

"I'm here. I'm ready, Cosmo."

"No! I want you to forget everything you've ever felt or thought you new about love making."

"Do we have to talk so much?"

"Just let me guide you to a new place. A wonderful place I think you'll like. Now close your eyes."

"Okay! If you'll get on with it!"

At first Christi seemed to feel nothing. Her eyes closed slightly with the anticipation of pleasure.

As Cosmo's erotic kisses flowed from her navel to her thighs, Christi, compliantly, opened her legs. She looked almost bored awaiting the usual.

When Cosmo did not enter her, she stole a glance at him.

Cosmo looked at her with censure. He closed her eyes with the tips of his forefingers.

Christi closed her eyes—then peeked.

Cosmo stretched the Venus butterfly to the heavens. He bowed before Christi's parted legs in a act of near worship. He paused and sighed hard.

With grace and caring, Cosmo filled all her sensuous places with each "steeple" of the Venus Butterfly. He began to stroke them ever so gently as he flicked his tongue into the most erotic of the zones.

Christi had never felt such simultaneously erotic feelings. She almost wet herself with excitement. His gentle but expert use of his mouth and fingers found places she did not know existed and his hot tongue awakened regions of volcanic passion she had never dreamed of. As Cosmo worked his erotic magic, Christi wanted to scream. She knew if she did, Sarah would come running. Quickly, she pulled a pillow over her mouth and yelled her ecstasy in muffled waves of verbal heat.

Now there was nothing she wanted except for him to never stop. In a brief, blessed moment the last nagging vestiges of inhibition dissolved into infinite ecstasy. Her eyes brightened and her face lit up with every tender stroke of Cosmo's touches.

Her eyes shouted what her mouth could not yell as she exploded into the orgasmic wonder she never dreamed attainable. Finally, she could no longer contain it. She threw the pillow away and let out a primal scream of joy. She broke into tears of relief and shook with excitement for a long delicious moment.

Cosmo looked up and delighted in his accomplishment, and her happiness. They both listened quietly to hear Sarah's footsteps.

They were relieved not to hear any.

Christi reached down and grabbed his hair, pulling his warm lips down on her quivering stomach. "Oh God Cosmo! That is some butterfly." She stopped. "But what about you?"

He touched her thighs softly, then held them firmly as he kissed her hips. His hot mouth moved against her waist causing her to weaken and lie back on the bed.

"I'm so wonderfully weak, Cosmo."

He started to back off. "Then I will wait."

"No! I'm not that weak."

"Are you ready for me?"

"Oh God yes! Cosmo! Cosmo! You are the best of all. The very best after all," she sighed.

Cosmo stood up and let her admire his handsome manhood.

"Cosmo, I have never loved like this before. I have wanted you for so long!"

Cosmo's moved his muscular body into the shadows. He let the shadows hide the final rehearsals for the production he was about to present her.

When he was fully ready to perform, he moved out of the shadows so that the moonlight, slowly, illuminated the scene as curtain rises on a stage.

Christi wanted to leap on top of him but was too mesmerized by the show to move.

Cosmo knelt between her parted legs. He kissed her softly on the lips. "I love you, I have always loved you, and I will always love you," Cosmo said evenly.

Christi looked into his eyes. They confirmed what he had just told her. His firm body was warm and now his kisses delightfully romantic. "You were always my husband in spirit."

They giggled and laughed out loud, tickling each other and playing delicious kissing games before they made long passionate love and, at long last, consummated their spiritual marriage.

Chapter Forty-nine

SARAH'S FACE WAS TEAR-STAINED AND HER EYES RED FROM CRYING AS she sat across the kitchen table and stared at Christi. Christi did not like the look in her eyes.

"Okay, Momma, what is it? If you're mad at me for letting him have the car, I understand. I'm mad at me too," Christi soothed.

Sarah sighed hard, looking at Christi with love.

"That is one thing, but not the main thing. I forgive you for that. You were just trying to make the boy happy. God knows, he didn't have much of that. God knows ain't none of us had much of that." Sarah paused to dab her face with a handkerchief.

"What's the main thing, Momma?" Christi pressed.

Sarah shifted nervously in her chair, looking away from Christi for a moment.

"The main thing is I smell a James in here somewhere. They say it's an accident, but I don't believe it. You just don't beat those people like we did and get away with it."

Christi nodded agreement.

"I don't know how they done it but they done it. That's all I know. They done it to my boy." Sarah fought back the tears.

"Oh, Momma. Don't torture yourself with those kinds of thoughts. Maybe it was just an accident. You're paranoid about those Jameses. You've always hated them, and I never particularly liked them but they aren't that bold."

"Yes they are, chile! That family has done and will do anything it wants in these parts. That's why I want you to run for Congress. It's done time somebody else was holding some power around here." Sarah said firmly.

Christi shook her head in amusement until she saw the serious look in Sarah's eyes.

"There ain't nothing funny about the Jameses. They been doing it to this family so long. Well, it's just been too long. Too much! If you don't run for Congress, I will!" Sarah's sad eyes turned bright with anger.

"Momma, I know you're upset, but there's no proof it was anything but an accident."

"I told you, chile! There ain't no accidents where them Jameses are concerned. I guess you take their side because you are one of them!" Sarah blurted before she could stop herself.

Christi looked at her in disbelief.

Sarah jerked at the handkerchief nervously.

"You mean I act like them? Is that what you mean, Momma?"

Sarah looked contrite. "Get me a glass of that wine you been drinking. I guess it's done time you knowed the truth."

Christi looked at Sarah in total disbelief as she took the bottle of wine from the refrigerator and poured Sarah a glass.

It was only the second glass of wine Christi had ever seen Sarah drink.

Sarah wolfed the glass down in two quick swallows and motioned for Christi to refill it. As she slowly sipped the second glass she began her story.

"I know you heard them rumors and things all your life, but I told you they wasn't true. I lied. God forgive me! But I lied. I wanted to protect you because you were the only truly beautiful thing I got out of this miserable life. But that don't make lying any less wrong. I done it and I'm sorry. Now I'm gonna tell you the whole truth, as long as this wine holds out and God gives me strength." Sarah paused and took a deep breath.

Christi waited with rapt attention.

Sarah blew her breath out hard and looked at Christi with deep affection. "Listen now, this is how it was . . ."

✳ ✳ ✳

As Sarah talked to Christi, her mind drifted into deep remembrance of things long past she had kept locked inside too long. The story she told escaped from the long hidden recesses of her memory in vivid songs of freedom. She could see the bright sunshine of that day early in 1931 and clearly remember the long black-orange kaolin road that lead toward the gleaming white plantation house. The road was lined with thirty-six oaks, eighteen on each side. The sun shining through the oaks cast shades of darkness and patterns of light on the road and the antebellum Gothic house beyond.

The shades of light seemed to ebb and flow as she watched the white-washed exterior of the eight thirty-foot columns that held up the high-angled roof.

Sarah had total recall of how young Firman James Jr. looked that day in her sixteenth year.

Firman Junior could have been melted and die-cast into a stereotype for all southern gentlemen of his era. He was a great grandson of slave holders and the son of United States Senator Firman John James Sr.

Sarah had always liked Firman or "Junior" as he was called by everyone except the help.

He had a winning personality and never seemed to be condescending to the help like his other relatives. If anything, Firman Junior was a little too paternalistic and friendly.

His father, Firman Senior, was always grabbing him by the ear and dragging him out of the kitchen for "wasting too much time" and not letting those "colored folk" do their jobs.

Sarah had heard the term "colored folks" all her life. It was funny, she always thought they were talking about someone else.

Sarah was lucky enough to be brought up to the big house with her mother, Carmella, and lived well because of it. It was a glamorous world to her, one that she watched with detached fascination as a person looking at a glittering stardust night through a kerosene lantern chimney. Young Mister Firman was always extra nice to her from the outset. She did not see anything sinister in his affectionate kidding. She thought of him as an older man, but not that much older. She was a late bloomer and had become a woman at the advanced age of sixteen, only two months before coming up to the big house.

"Carmella, how come you have the prettiest young'uns of all the colored folk? I swear! I never seen so many beautiful black folks in one family in my entire life," Firman Junior bubbled that morning.

Carmella didn't like what she considered idle flattery so she would just mumble a reply when Firman teased like that.

"Now, Mammy Jones, you know I mean it," he would insist as Carmella tried to ignore him.

"Mister James, don't you come round here with none of that flim-flam. There's lots of other pretty colored children. You spend enough time around the girls to know that, I reckon," Carmella would finally reply.

"Well, I just don't believe it. There ain't no prettier ones than yours, and Sarah here is the prettiest of all," Firman insisted as Sarah left the room to hide the embarrassment on her face, as well as conceal the excitement in her heart.

Sarah would always start to blush, until Carmella's large brown eyes fell on her. Carmella's eyes could stop the town clock. Sarah kept silent and always left the room quickly as Carmella cautioned Firman Junior.

Carmella would let Firman Junior go only so far with his nonsense before she would challenge him.

"Mister James, I'm asking you not to bother my children with all that smooth talk. You save all that smooth talk for all those debutantes from Charleston College, now, you hear?" Carmella would scold.

Firman would leave the kitchen laughing and Carmella would shake her head in disgust.

Sarah would watch him until he disappeared up the stairs to his room. He was a handsome man and she enjoyed the flattery. She would have entertained serious, exciting thoughts about him if she had not feared her mother so much. Sarah knew many of her female schoolmates who saw white lovers on the sly. Sarah would not want to do it that way. She would want to dress up and go to a cotillion ball like everyone else. Sarah felt she was just as pretty as any girl Firman Junior brought around and she hated the condescending looks those white girls gave her.

Sarah could not help but notice, as she worked around the house that day, that Firman Junior kept finding ways of taking looks at her. Every time he did she remembered Carmella's scolding and moved quickly away from him. She was glad when it was time to go home because Sarah did not like the unholy feeling those stares gave her. She felt much better as she and Carmella left through the back door and walked down the road toward their home.

The road between the big house and the small three-room shanty where Carmella and Sarah lived was a long winding dirt road lined with huge oak trees, dripping Spanish moss. Sarah loved taking the walk on bright moonlit nights like this one and she skipped alongside her mother, acting much younger than her sixteen years. The night was so bright they did not notice the headlights of the car approaching from the rear until it screeched to a stop only a few feet behind them.

"Well, what do ya know, it's Carmella and Sarah. Well, hot damn, ladies! Don't just stand there, get in and I'll give you a ride home," Firman insisted.

Carmella distrusted young men and automobiles. She firmly shook her head.

Sarah tugged at her sleeve and whispered in her ear. "Please, Momma. I ain't never had a chance to ride in that fancy car and I might never get one again."

Firman picked up on Sarah's interest. "Now, Mammy Jones, you got to get over this here fear of automobiles. Good Lord! They've been around for near to thirty years now. This one here is the latest deluxe model and only one like it in the whole southeast."

"I don't know about that, but I know I ain't getting in it and that's final!" Carmella insisted.

"Then what about your lovely daughter? I'll bet she's not scared." he challenged.

"I don't want my young'uns in them things neither. You know they done killed Mr. Timmons and his wife over on the main road just last week," Carmella wagged her finger at Mister Firman.

"Good Lord, Mammy! Pastor Reheems got killed by lightning standing on his own front porch the same week and I saw you sitting on yours the next day."

"Momma, it's only a little ways to the house, please let me ride! Please! Please! Please!" Sarah pleaded.

Carmella thought it over a long moment. It had been a long, hard day and she was so tired her judgement was impaired.

"Well, you know I let my children have their own minds most of the time when it ain't to do with the Bible or schooling. If she wants to go she can, but you take her straight home now, you hear?" Carmella said.

Sarah ran and jumped into the car's front seat before Carmella was even through giving her permission.

"I will, Mammy, now, please, don't you worry none," Firman assured Carmella. He got into the driver's seat and roared off into the night.

Carmella just shook her head in disgust, already wondering if she had done the right thing.

"Here, Sarah." Firman passed a silver flask to Sarah.

"Oh! No, sir! I can't drink any of this. Momma would tan my hide good if I did that," Sarah insisted.

"Oh, come on now. You're sixteen, ain't that right? A girl of sixteen has got to start deciding what she wants to do and not worry about what other people wants them to do," Firman said smiling.

"I don't know, Mister James. I'd better not." Sarah shifted uncomfortably in her seat.

"Okay, just one little drink. Why this is old Whiskey Dan's best stumphole. Two hundred proof!"

Sarah reluctantly took the flask and pulled a swallow into her mouth. She had once taken a small amount of blackberry wine and she had expected this to be sweet also. Instead it felt like someone had put a hot iron on her tongue. Her first impulse was to spit it out. She thought better of it and finally found the courage to swallow it.

"Now see. That wasn't so bad, was it?" Firman Junior laughed.

Sarah shook her head side to side slowly in a half-yes, half-no, then opened her eyes wide as she realized they weren't on the road to her house any longer. "Mister James, we ain't going the right way,"

"Oh yes we are. It's just around about a little ways. I want to show you the top of Devil's Hideaway. Betcha you ain't never been up that grade!" Firman said as he gunned the big car up the dark red clay road that led to the top of the heavily wooded hill.

"No, sir! That's where the white folks go when they want to . . . to . . ." Sarah choked.

"Want to what, Sarah? You can talk freely around me. Here, take one more drink of this stumphole. It'll help you." He passed it her way.

Sarah was scared, and because she was, the hot whiskey didn't seem so bitter. She took two quick swallows, choking them down. It burned for a few moments, but then almost immediately her anxieties seemed to ease. "Oh Lord, have mercy! My head feels so light, Mister James. Oh, that's powerful strong whiskey. Oh Lord!" Sarah began to giggle.

"See, I told you you'd like it. It just takes some getting used to, that's all. Here, just have one more swallow and you'll be right up with me." Firman Junior encouraged as he patted Sarah gently on the shoulder then rubbed her back with his right hand.

Sarah giggled and lifted the flask, pulling down a real long swallow that didn't seem to burn at all this time and instead had an almost pleasant, welcome taste.

"It's right pleasant after all." Sarah offered as she took a swallow willingly, then handed him back the flask.

Firman Junior tipped it to his mouth and drank so long Sarah was worried about the car going off the road.

They were laughing and drinking together like old friends when Firman Junior pulled the car off the main road onto a narrow trail that led back through thick underbrush which slapped at the side of the car.

"Mister Firman, ain't you worried none about your paint?" Sarah wondered aloud.

"That's the least of my worries. What we really got to worry about is anybody seeing us up here. It wouldn't be good for neither of us if someone sees us up here. You duck down in the seat till I tell you to get up."

Sarah obediently slipped down onto the floorboard and huddled until he finally brought the car to a stop. She almost stopped breathing when she heard his zipper open.

"You can get up now, Sarah. It's okay. Now, come over here and sit by me," he said, patting the seat beside him.

Sarah's mouth was dry and even the heady effects of the strong liquor wore off a little as it became clear what Firman Junior intended.

"Mister James, I think I'd better get home now. Please, sir." She shook as she spoke

"I don't think so. I think what you need is some more whiskey. Then I want to show you something I bet you have never seen." He grinned.

"No, sir. I think I'm going to be sick. Please take me home. Please?" Sarah shook with fear as she saw him reach into his pants through his open zipper.

She almost fainted when he pulled out his rigid manhood and began to play with it right in front of her.

"Good God, almighty! Mister Firman James! You got to take me home now!" Sarah turned her face away.

Firman Junior grabbed her head with his strong hand. He turned her head toward him and pulled her face toward his groin.

"I'm glad you decided that you and me can be good friends. Whites and colored folks don't take the time to be friends like they should. I want us to be good friends, Sarah." He replied forcing her face ever closer to the throbbing one-eyed playtoy that he pushed within inches of her mouth.

Sarah was woozy from all the booze and everything seemed to occur in a haze, like she was looking through gauze at a play acted upon a dimly lit stage. She was so numb from the booze she thought it was a bad dream.

Then he shoved her head hard against his groin and she felt the rigid tip of his manhood press against her right cheek. He tried to pull her mouth toward it but she pushed away.

"No, Mister James, this ain't right!" She tried to get up.

He grabbed her shoulder and held her down. "Now, Sarah, I'm just having a little fun here. Ain't no need to go gettin' all excited," he soothed.

"I done told you, Mister James, my head is so woozy I think I'm going to be sick," Sarah insisted.

He gave her a doubtful look then shrugged. Moments later she felt his hands on her breasts. Before she could react he had her blouse off and forced his warm mouth on her bare breasts. Sarah shivered at first, then tingled from the excitable feeling it gave her.

She was ashamed of that feeling and tried to push him away.

"Mister James, I don't feel so good, can I just lie down a moment," Sarah pleaded.

"Why shore you can, Sarah. Here, I'll get out and you lay right down on this seat," he said as he got out of the car and Sarah eased herself down on the seat.

The night was hot and humid and the smell of honeysuckle permeated the air, making it hard for Sarah to get a deep breath that would clear her head.

It felt good to be lying down and she suddenly felt tired and wanted to drift off to sleep. Her dreamy feelings were rudely interrupted when Firman ran his hand up the inside of her thighs and parted her legs.

She didn't think anything of it for a moment. Then he was on top of her and had her panties in his hand. Before she could decide what to do he had entered her. Before she had gathered the strength to protest he had done his business.

✻ ✻ ✻

Six weeks after Christi was born Sarah took her, wrapped in a new pink blanket, to see Mr. Firman James Jr.

Sarah had not told him she was pregnant. She even lied to Carmella, saying she was raped by one of the Carson boys. Carmella knew better but accepted her grandchild gracefully.

Sarah knocked on the back door of Firman's bachelor apartment in downtown Charleston. It was a cold October night and her knuckles felt rigid from the cold. The thick oak door felt hard as a rock.

Christi's small, perfectly formed mouth blew tiny circles of frost. Sarah delighted in what a good-natured child Christi was. She never cried. Sarah was sure Mister Firman Junior would adore her.

Sarah knew he was drunk the moment he opened the door. His whiskey breath overwhelmed her and she backed off.

"Oh shit! What nigger charity are you begging for, woman?" He staggered, not recognizing Sarah.

Sarah looked past him into the kitchen. There was a half-naked blonde pouring a drink by the kitchen table.

"Who the hell is it this time of night, honey?" the blonde chortled.

Sarah was frightened and mad. "It's me, Sarah Jones. I'm sorry I didn't tell you, I was afraid till now. But she's so pretty, Mister Firman, she's so beautiful. Just look at her. Please?"

"What the hell are you talking about? Now look, I'm sorry, but we have already given to every nigger charity there is." He started to slam the door. He stopped and took a long look.

He stepped back a minute. "Sarah? Sarah Jones? Why you're Mammy Jones's kin." He paused as he looked at the baby and thought it over.

The blonde started to approach him as he staggered backwards.

"Jesus! I don't believe it!" he murmured as he turned and moved to stop the blonde. He said something to her. She look puzzled then indifferent. She shrugged and moved back into the kitchen.

Firman Junior moved outside and slammed the door behind him. "Are you crazy coming here to my front door, you crazy woman?"

"You don't need to be talking to me like that. This is your child for certain!"

"Hush! Hush! Just shut up! Okay. Okay." He took a deep breath and blew it out hard. "Now, Sarah we all understand about these things but this is not the time or the place. You understand?"

Sarah shook her head.

"Look, Sarah, I'm not admitting to anything, but I understand you might have a problem. Now don't worry, there will be some money coming your way. I promise."

Sarah was dumbfounded.

"This is your daughter. I've named her Christobel Harriet after your grandmother and mine. But that's temporary. You can have a say in what to name her permanent."

"Look! Now I've tried to be nice. I don't want any say in this at all! Take that nigger child and bury it. That's the best thing for all of us! Now I'll help you with money but it doesn't mean I admit a damn thing!"

Sarah trembled more from hurt than the cold.

She tried to look him in the eye but he turned away from her.

"Don't turn your back on me, Firman James," Sarah challenged.

He wheeled and glared at her. "Look, nigger! Get your ass out of here before I have it locked up. Here! Here's fifty dollars!" He tried to hand her the money.

Sarah looked at it with contempt. "I don't want your money. This is OUR child and you know it!"

The blonde opened the door and moved down beside Firman. "What the hell is going on, honey? You said it was just a nigger charity. So give her some money and come back inside."

"I ain't no charity!" Sarah bristled.

"I'll take care of it, Margo. Go back inside now!"

"No! Don't go nowhere. Please, miss! Don't go nowhere until you seen Firman's child. You a woman. You help me with this." Sarah tried to push past him.

Firman forced her back. "You goddamn little black bitch! You had your chance to do it right, now you want it the hard way. Okay! You're as good as dead. If you don't leave here now and keep you mouth shut I'll fix it so you won't be able to work in the county or state. None of your relatives will be able to find work here. You understand? Now if you don't want that you leave now," he threatened.

Sarah took the blanket from around Christi's body and held the lovely baby up for him to see. "This is our beautiful daughter. I ain't after no money. I just want you to say she's your daughter. I want her to be a lady of elegance like your daughter should be. That's all, I ain't after no money."

"What's she talking about, Firman?" Margo inquired as she tried to look at the baby.

He pushed Margo back inside and closed the door hard. "I don't care what you're after! I told you, get out of here or I'll call the sheriff, and I mean it! Now, here is fifty dollars. Take it and go. Go now!" he insisted.

Sarah looked deep into his bloodshot eyes, watching as he staggered around. She wanted to cry. She wanted to hit him. She wanted to die.

Finally, she stepped back into the darkness and stared hard at him. "She's your daughter. You can deny it if you have a mind to, but if the good Lord is willing there will come a day when she will be a lady of elegance as she should be. On that day I hope she will deny you 'cause you ain't a fit father for no child! Good night and goodbye, Mister Firman!" Sarah said quickly as she huddled Christi close to her breast and ran off into the night.

Firman Junior stuffed the fifty-dollar bill back into his pocket and shrugged.

The next day Margo made the news known throughout five counties in a matter of minutes.

Carmella was a good Christian woman and she took it all hard.

The Senator sent Firman Junior off to college on the West Coast and saw that Carmella was placed with a family fifty miles away in the Carolina high country. Sarah was hurt that Carmella had agreed to leave the James house, but she was more hurt because it had all shamed her in her mother's eyes.

Carmella never spoke of it and gave Sarah all the love and support a wayward child could hope for.

As Christi grew in beauty and grace, things of the past did not seem so important anymore. Carmella had asked Sarah to forgive Firman Junior and Sarah had tried, but it simply stuck too hard in her craw. It was easy to forgive the hurt she had endured, but Sarah could not forget the way he had turned his back on his child.

So from the time Christi was little until now, Sarah had waited for a proper method to take her revenge. As far as she was concerned, the political campaign meant God had forgiven her and provided a great and perfect vengeance.

✳ ✳ ✳

". . . and that's how it was, chile. I swear I'm sorry to wait so long to tell it all, but I sure feels good now," Sarah sighed.

Christi looked at her in stunned disbelief but could not deny the ring of truth in her words.

Chapter Fifty

FOR A LONG TIME AFTER SARAH HAD FINISHED HER STORY CHRISTI FELT numb. The things Sarah revealed were not a total surprise. She had suspected something was unusual about her parentage because Sarah had never talked about her father. She never expected he would turn out to be the Senator's son. Now she knew why her mother had such a blind spot when it came to that family, and Christi now felt her hurt as well.

Christi got up and moved to Sarah's side. Gently, she put her arms around Sarah's neck and gave her a hug. "Oh, Momma, how you must have suffered keeping this secret so long. I wish you had told me before now. You really didn't do anything wrong."

"I sinned, girl. That's all there is to it. But his denying you is wrong too. I just want to see some justice done before I die. Monk Miller says you got that look what them cameras like. He says you can win if you run for office. It would make things alright somehow if you beat him," Sarah said firmly.

Christi looked doubtful, but she could not disappoint Sarah now. "Of course I'll try, Momma. But it takes more than a camera presence to win elections."

"I know that. It takes a lot of money too. I expect you know how to get that," Sarah said.

Christi chuckled. "I always heard you can buy elections. Well Eduardo has more money than they do. So why not?" Christi kidded as Cosmo came through the door and handed her a telegram.

"This just came. Hope it's good news," he said nervously as he handed it to Christi.

Christi opened it, equally nervous.

The telegram was in Spanish but Christi quickly translated it, sighing noticeably.

"What is it, honey?" Sarah demanded.

"Nothing, Momma. Just a letter of condolence from Eduardo's grandmother," Christi hedged.

"You can't lie to your Momma, so don't try. Now tell me, what does it say."

Christi smiled at Sarah with admiration before she spoke. "Eduardo's phony grandmother is trying to disinherit me. She's convinced the Mexican courts to place an injunction on the estate until Eduardo is proven to be dead or alive. That crusty old bitch most probably has relatives in high places in Mexico. Don't worry, Momma. Carlton will take care of it."

Cosmo looked doubtful. "I never liked that bitch. Excuse me, Sarah," Cosmo said.

"You don't need to be excusing yourself. She must be a mean one alright," Sarah said.

"It would have to come now. What lousy timing. Well, forget Congress. She'll tie up the money so we won't be buying any elections," Christi mused aloud.

"Good Lord, chile! You give up so easy sometimes," Sarah huffed.

"Momma, it was a good idea when I had unlimited money available but until I get it freed I'll bet Monk Miller won't want me for dog catcher," Christi grumbled.

"Not true, Christi. The reasons they wanted you in the first place are still valid. You can charm the warts off a frog. There are ways of getting campaign funds," Cosmo said, nodding in agreement with himself.

Sarah looked at them both quietly. "That's right, chile. What you got money can't buy, but money ain't no never mind anyways. There's plenty of money if you just know where to look. Why, I know where there's enough 'old black money' hereabout to elect you president," Sarah chuckled.

"Old black money?" Christi looked doubtful.

"My Lord, Christi! Don't you know colored folks can't run for anything, anywhere, unless the old black money approves?" Sarah chided.

"Momma, there isn't any 'old black money' or new black money. I brought all the money blacks in these parts have ever seen," said Christi, as she smiled at Cosmo.

Sarah scowled at her. "I don't like your arrogance sometimes. Reverend King wants us to do things peaceful, but I don't have no patience with arrogance like that, chile. Now you're a woman of the world and all that, but you don't know much. There's a lot of old black money around. Big old black money. It's quiet money but that don't mean it ain't there.

"If you think you can get elected anything in Carolina or Georgia without it, you are mighty stupid for a woman of the world," Sarah said, pounding the table for emphasis

"Momma, I'm sorry. If it's there it is very quiet because I never heard of it. Rich and black in the South?" Christi tried not to laugh. "You mean like Levi Smith who owns all those funeral homes. Momma, Eduardo's estate is worth a million times that."

Sarah put her hands on her hips and shook her head. "No, not Levi Smith. Not Hiram Carter, not Heyward Ginn. I mean like Potter Brown who owns Continental Security Life Insurance."

"Who?" Christi almost smirked.

"Listen up, chile! Potter Brown. He don't even live here much anymore. He lives in Atlanta, but he still touches any black thing that moves in the South. You didn't know about Potter, did you?" Sarah looked smug.

Cosmo and Christi shrugged.

"No, Momma. A rich black with lots of old money?"

"Girl, I thought I taught you something. You put down your own people, but maybe you don't think we're your people." Sarah stopped as she saw how those words hurt Christi. "I'm sorry chile. I didn't mean nothing by that."

Christi was too shaken to reply.

"Why is the money so quiet, Sarah?" Cosmo tried to ease the tension.

" 'Cause if a nigger gets too loud whitey is going to find some way to strike him down."

"I see."

"Potter has got insurance companies just like the whites. They think he's just a junk dealer. He laughs all the way to his banks." Sarah held her head up proudly.

"I'm sorry, Momma. I didn't know."

"I know, chile. It's okay."

"How do you know this man?" Cosmo wondered.

"I knew old Potter when he was swabbing out toilets down at the Claremont Hotel. You don't have to call Carlton. If you trust your Momma, maybe you can do it without whitey or that crusty old Mexican woman you talk about." Sarah smiled.

Christi gave Sarah a hug. "There has never been anybody like you ever," she laughed.

"I'll go call old Potter right now," Sarah concluded as she stood up and moved out of the room.

Cosmo tipped his coffee cup in agreement.

Christi looked at him with love.

This time his eyes did not turn away. They waited until Sarah was out of the room before they embraced. More passed between them in silence as they held each other tenderly than in all the words they had ever spoken to each other.

As she held him, she delighted in the feeling that they no longer denied their love—and her heart would have leaped with joy had she not known he would leave soon.

"When Cosmo?" She asked as she broke the embrace and stepped back.

He looked very sad before he replied. "When?"

"You know what I'm asking."

"Yes. I really don't know but soon."

Christi turned away.

"I really didn't mean for any of this to happen, Christi. I can't say I didn't want it, but I didn't want it like this. Eduardo was my friend and yours. You know I have to go look for him," Cosmo whispered sadly.

Christi turned back, her eyes brimming with hurt. "No you don't have to. You want to. Fine! Just tell me that when it is all over we will declare our love openly and honestly," Christi insisted.

Cosmo thought it over. He smiled agreement. He kissed her softly on the forehead. "I will have to join the group in Miami soon. One more time and then it is over. You have really got my senses confused. Part of me doesn't want to go. I have never not wanted to go before."

Christi stroked his hair gently. "What group, Cosmo?"

Cosmo broke the embrace. "Just a bunch of guys who feel betrayed by the revolution and who have friends in jail scheduled for execution."

"Is Eduardo one of them?"

"I hope not."

"Maybe I should go with you," Christi said sadly.

"No. I want you to run for that political office. We're going to need friends in high places."

"Cosmo, that is a pipe dream of Mother's. I have no chance to do that."

"Oh yes you do."

"You're as silly as she is. I want to go to Cuba with you."

"No. I don't want you anywhere near Cuba until we manage to change things down there a little." Cosmo grimaced.

"Sounds like something I've heard before. Tell me, Cosmo, are the *bohios* any less offensive, the children better fed, the people more free and prosperous. If Eduardo and Kiki are dead, did they die in vain?" Christi asked cynically.

"Christi, you know what they wanted for Cuba was good. Maybe I can still help make it good."

Christi looked at him hard for a moment. "God, Cosmo! I should be used to this by now. Men come and go in and out of my life all the time. I really should be used to it. But it's so much worse this time. God help me! I don't want to lose you!" Christi grabbed him and held on fiercely.

Cosmo caressed her gently and silently for a long moment. "I promise you that you will not lose me. I'm too mean to die. I'll be back. I swear it!"

Christi had heard such words so many times before they were almost laughable.

But her heart would not let her do anything but believe them.

"Maybe you should go now," she said without force.

"No. We will have some time together. I want to help you get started on your political career."

"Oh, Cosmo! I told you that is something just to make Momma happy. It's so improbable. So dumb."

"You're wrong, Christi. Kennedy beat Nixon because of television. I think Carlton is right. That camera loves you."

"And you?"

"Me?"

"You don't have to say it."

Cosmo smiled as he tipped her chin up towards his lips with a strong finger. "I love you." He kissed her softly.

Christi reached up and grabbed the back of his head and kissed him fiercely as if it was for the last time.

They broke their embrace as they heard the approaching footsteps of Sarah.

"Chile, I done called Potter and he knows about you. He's going to fix up a meeting with everybody who is anybody in these political things. You are going to run for office. I mean it!" Sarah sounded pleased with herself as she addressed a dubious Christi.

"If you say so, Momma."

"Chile? What is wrong with you? Don't you know what a fine opportunity this is?"

Christi studied the look on Cosmo and Sarah's faces. "Momma I'm not political. I hate politics and politicians."

Sarah fixed a hard steady gaze at Christi. "Don't you want to be helping your people?" The look on their faces told Christi she was fighting a losing battle.

"If that's what you want, I will try."

"No! I want you to have some fire in your gut. If you don't then it won't work for sure."

Cosmo nodded agreement.

"Just give me some time to get used to the idea. Okay?"

"Well, we don't have a whole lot of time. Potter wants to meet Thursday. So you get your head right before then or we won't be going nowhere."

"Okay, Momma."

"Lord, chile! Don't give me that pouty look and don't you be thinking about doing this for me. You got to know that."

"I understand."

"Lord! I hope you do, chile! I hope you do." Sarah shook her head as she left the room.

"She's one headstrong woman," Christi said in admiration.

"Then you get it honestly," Cosmo laughed.

Christi watched him laugh. Laughter lit up his face and his face lit up her life. She reached out and touched his cheek with her long fingers.

Cosmo gently kissed the tips of her fingers. "Oh, Christi, how you take a man's mind off the world. It would be so easy to hide out with you and forget everything else," Cosmo sighed.

"Then why don't you?"

"Because when we finally get together I want no ghosts, no loose ends," he chided.

"Finally together? As in permanent?"

"I will ask you that question when it's the right time to ask it."

"Well, I'll give you a 'yes' now."

Christi insisted as she put her arms around his neck and pulled his lips close to hers.

He looked deep into her eyes and for a moment the mischievous Irish sparkle faded and she saw pure love reflected in his eyes.

"Oh, Cosmo, my delight, my old love, my good love," she whispered just before she kissed him tenderly and long, as if she would never be able to kiss him again.

Chapter Fifty-one

CHRISTI HAD NEVER SEEN FIVE MORE SOUR-LOOKING BLACK MEN IN all her life. They sat behind the long polished table and stared at her with long faces as she tried to look indifferent but poised.

Monk Miller, Regional Party Chairman, sat on one side of her and Carlton on the other.

Sarah sat in the corner beside Cosmo.

There were some small pleasantries exchanged before the room fell eerily quiet. Moments later the room went dark. Just as quick as the room had gone dark, Christi felt the sting of a bank of high intensity klieg lights burning her eyes. Her first instinct was to cover her eyes but something told her that was what they wanted.

She blinked but did not look away.

"Are you a communist?" Le Roy "Icky" Stitson, a mousy little man sitting to Potter Brown's right quizzed.

"A what?"

"A communist. You know. A subversive. A pinko type."

"WHAT?" Christi looked insulted.

"Do you advocate the overthrow of the American government?" Icky smirked.

"Why no! Of course not. What kind of a stupid question is that?"

"It's a very necessary question that requires an honest response," Johnny "Jumbo" Jackson, a portly black man sitting to Potter's left insisted.

All the others at the table nodded and frowned except for Potter, who seemed slightly amused.

"Would you please give us an honest answer, Miss Jones?" Jumbo repeated.

"No! I am NOT a communist. Are you?"

Jumbo smiled thinly a moment. "As a matter of fact we don't belong to any organized political party. We are Democrats."

Everyone thought that was funny but Christi.

"What makes you want to get into politics all of a sudden?" Icky asked tapping the table with a broken pencil.

Christi looked to Monk for help. He looked away.

"Well, it really wasn't my idea. It sort of just happened. If you want to know the truth, I'm still not sure about it." Christi looked at Sarah who was frowning.

"Then why are we wasting our time?" Jumbo Jackson snapped.

"Look! I'm here reluctantly and I don't appreciate this kind of grilling . . ."

"See! I told you. She can't take the aggravation. She'd fold the first time they came at her. This woman does not have the kayhones to do this job!" Icky chuckled.

Christi glared at him for a moment. "*Habla español, señor?*"

"What?"

"I believe the correct pronunciation is cO-hon-Es! Of course that is the colloquial idiom. The Castilian is—well, most Castilians are people of breeding and do not use that term."

"That's what I said! Kayhonees!"

"If I were you I would stick to English. Your Spanish pronunciation sucks!"

"—and she's a smart ass too!" Icky broke the pencil on the table.

"This is exactly what bothers us, Miss Jones," Jumbo broke in.

"I don't understand."

"The Spanish-Cuban connection."

"I see."

"Would you like to address our concerns?"

"There is no 'Spanish' connection. I am as American as anyone here. Just look at me. My blouse is red, my dress is white, and my panties are blue." Christi said and smiled mischievously.

Monk shook his head in admiration.

Cosmo chuckled.

Everyone else, with the exception of Potter, were shocked into silence.

"Well, now. That was quite entertaining. . . . however I suppose the truth remains that no matter your qualifications you really do not want to do this. Is that a correct judgement?" Jumbo Jackson asked.

"I didn't say that. I said it wasn't my idea. But I have seen so much done to people because they are powerless. It seems like a good idea to try to get a little power for our side." Christi smiled.

"Our side? Now, which side is that?" Icky glared.

"Our side. Yours and mine. The black side. The underprivileged. The poor and powerless." Christi was visibly irritated.

"Do you see yourself as black and underprivileged?" Potter Brown asked in a quiet tone.

"I have lived well, Mr. Brown. But I always heard the snickering in the background when I got TOO white. I left shantytown some years ago, but it never left me. If my husband's grandmother gets her way I will be back there soon enough." Christi held her head up high.

Potter Brown looked impressed for a brief moment.

"Do you feel the need for revenge on whitey for the way they treated Sarah and Little Eddie?" Jumbo Jackson leaned forward.

"Yes. But as you know revenge is a dish best served cold."

Potter Brown nodded agreement.

"Maybe this is an opportunity to keep things like that from happening again." Christi was beginning to feel more comfortable.

Sarah smiled her support.

"Christi, I have some reservations that we would be financing a lark. I feel this is an impulse thing with you. It's nothing personal, but we need black people in Washington. Oh Lord, do we need them! But we need serious people who can help us now and for a long time to come." Potter looked very grim.

Christi did not have a quick answer.

Carlton shifted nervously in his seat.

"Maybe you're right. Maybe this was a bad idea." Christi started to get up and walk out.

"Excuse me. Do you mind if I say something?" Cosmo stepped forward.

The panel looked at Monk for direction. Monk thought it over.

"This is Mr. Collins. He is a friend of the family," Monk said more in the way of apology than introduction.

"That's right. He is an old friend of the family," Sarah said.

The panel did not buy it but Potter motioned for Cosmo to speak.

Cosmo stood tall and paused a long moment before he spoke. "I just want to say that I've known this lady a long time and I've seen her grow from a frightened young girl into a mature woman who cares deeply about helping others.

"I've had a lot of experience with politics and politicians. I don't know how long someone as honest and caring as this lady can stomach the type of shenanigans that go on in politics, but for however long that is, you'll have a winner. I think you're lucky to have her, gentlemen," Cosmo offered.

"Thank you, Mr. Collins. If we did not think that we would not be here." Potter paused. "But what do you say, Christi? Is this a serious commitment? If we back you can we count on you to stay with it?" Potter questioned sternly.

Christi looked at Sarah and thought it over. For some reason an image of Father Maldonado asking her to remember the poor flashed into her mind. "Yes."

"Yes?"

"Yes. I want the James congressional seat. The more I seriously consider it the more I REALLY want to do it. I believe I can go to Washington and help the little people. I promised a nice priest who saved my life I would not forget those people. If you want me, you have my complete commitment without any reservations."

"I see. Tell me, Christi, do you think you can win?" Potter mellowed a little.

"Isn't that what we are here to decide?"

"That's no answer," Icky scoffed.

Jumbo chuckled. "My! Quite a political reply for one who disdains politics."

Potter Brown was visibly impressed. "Well, that's a good start, young lady. But what do you really know about the competition? About old Senator James and his son Firman Jr.?"

"I know the James family is behind most of the mischief that occurs in this part of the world. He's no friend of the black people and he was behind the district attorney's attempt to get Eddie put away. I think they have ruled this region long enough. It's our turn," Christi said smoothly.

"What chance has an unknown like this young girl got against anybody?" Icky snapped.

Christi started to reply.

Carlton Bennett stood up and answered for her. "You understand, gentlemen, television has changed the game. She may be unknown now, but a few well-done television spots and the marketing men I have shown her clips to are unanimous. We have a winner."

Icky the grouch looked unconvinced.

"Mr. Bennett may have a point. They say that's how Kennedy beat Nixon. It was a beauty contest. So maybe we run a beauty queen," Potter mused aloud.

"No, Mr. Potter! I won't have it that way. I despise beauty contests and I DO have a brain!"

"My apologies . . . and from what we have seen here today quite a sharp one," Potter said.

"Well, I say I ain't spending one dime on no unknown," Icky grumped then got up and stormed out of the room.

"I must apologize for my friend Icky. He's a little hardheaded when it comes to new ideas, and I must say, you are a very new, if compelling idea, Christi," Potter said as he paused to survey the faces of the remaining men. "I believe we have seen enough to take the matter under submission. Would you give us a few days to think about it?" Potter stood up and extended his hand to Christi.

"Of course, Mr. Brown," Christi replied politely, returning his handshake. She then shook the hand of each man in turn. Sarah beamed with pride.

Cosmo gave her an approving wink.

Christi posed for some quick photographs with the group and endured a personal grilling by each of the men.

She enjoyed the feeling of being treated like an intellectual equal instead of a sex object more than she had imagined. As she watched Cosmo look at her with admiration she felt she was doing the right thing.

Minutes after Christi and the others had left, Potter Brown stood alone by his window and watched as Christi exited the building. He smiled as he watched the hoard of reporters gather around her and the ease with which she handled them.

Potter knew Carlton was right. It was the television age and she was a natural. To wait would be to risk losing her. The decision was a simple one. He felt good about it as he picked up the phone to gather the troops to her side.

On the street outside Potter's window Christi held court with a gaggle of loud reporters. While she continued to answer their repetitious questions she noticed Cosmo slipping more and more into the background.

She began to wonder how much this new life might cost her in personal terms before it was all over.

Chapter Fifty-two

"CHRISTI JONES FOR CONGRESS—A NEW BEGINNING," Cosmo read aloud then folded the brochure into a paper airplane and sailed it across the lawn. Christi was three weeks into her campaign and surrounded by stacks of campaign material.

"You're really enjoying yourself, aren't you?" Cosmo smiled at Christi as they sat on the terrace by the pool and enjoyed a bottle of wine. They said little as they watched the lavender sunset behind the Carolina palmettos cast long shadows on the patio brickwork.

"It's not like I thought it would be. I was nervous about the questions they would ask until I saw them ignoring my answers. Sometimes it's like I could be reciting the telephone book so long as I've got my hair done up right. God, Cosmo! It is just a glorified beauty contest!"

"Carlton says he's excited by the preliminary polls. If it happens like they predict you'll win by a landslide." Cosmo lifted his wine glass in tribute.

"I don't know," Christi frowned. "It's just too easy. It doesn't happen like this." She twirled the wine in her glass.

"Yes, it does. You are a real-life princess and good things come to princesses, even in real life."

"Ah, but this princess doesn't get to win the handsome prince."

"Oh? But no one knows that yet. The ending has not been written." Cosmo winked.

"How would you write the ending?" Christi nervously took a swallow of wine.

Cosmo had to think it over a minute. "They lived happily ever after, of course."

"Of course. Although they are told not to be seen together in public."

Cosmo grimaced. "Carlton just thought that was best for awhile."

"Right! If they find out I'm fooling around with a white man I couldn't get elected dog catcher," Christi scoffed.

"Things are changing but I'm afraid not that fast." Cosmo sighed.

"I don't like sneaking around."

Cosmo picked up a silver spoon and tapped it on the clean white linen tablecloth. "I know. But behind closed doors is better than nothing."

"I'm not afraid of them."

"It's just for awhile and we have to consider Sarah."

"Hell, Cosmo! We haven't fooled her one minute."

Cosmo nodded agreement. "Wonder why she's letting us slide?"

"She's focused on this election. I've never seen her happier," Christi stopped to smile. "God! She'll die if I lose."

"You won't lose. You are a special person, you always have been. There are great things waiting for you. There always were."

"Why don't I believe that?"

"I was raised in a strict Presbyterian foster home and they convinced me predestination is a reality. You will go to Congress and you will do great things and I will always stand a little back in the shadows and watch proudly." He stroked her hand with his fingers.

"No! If I win you will stand on the platform with me when I take the oath. Promise me that or I will drop out now!"

Cosmo hesitated.

Christi looked deadly serious. "You won't be there, will you?"

"You belong to the people, Christi. That television camera loves you more than Kiki, Eduardo, and me put together. It's the damndest competition any man ever had." Cosmo tried to laugh.

"No! You're not getting off the hook that easy. I'll walk away from it right now if you really think like that."

"Tell me, what has Monk Miller got scheduled for you tonight?" Cosmo avoided a direct answer.

"Cosmo!"

"What?"

"I knew it. This damn thing is going to mean the end of us, isn't it?"

Cosmo could not reply.

"That's it! I'm withdrawing right this minute!"

Cosmo gave her a steady gaze. "Walk away from this and you WILL lose me."

Christi studied the firm look in his eyes. She sighed hard.

"You mean that don't you?"

Cosmo nodded slowly.

"Why does this thing mean so much more to everyone than it does to me?"

"Because there is no one else in the world like you and we won't let you turn your back on your destiny."

"Please don't give me that destiny crap anymore."

"Okay."

They fell silent for a long moment studying each other's eyes. Cosmo did not like the serious look in Christi's eyes. He sought to break the heavy mood by playing footsie under the table. They had just finished a swim and their bare feet were slightly damp. Cosmo rubbed her feet dry by sandwiching them between his and rubbing them erotically. Christi rubbed back and they let their toes tease and touch and fondle through childish giggles until Cosmo ran his foot far up her inner thigh.

Christi let his foot come within inches of her bikini bottom. Then she squeezed her legs together so tight Cosmo winced. She let him suffer a moment then parted her legs enough to let his toes touch the bikini fabric and massage her maidenhood for a moment.

Then she pushed his leg away and stood up.

"I think we should have a platonic relationship from now on, Cosmo."

Cosmo gave her a flustered and puzzled look. "What?"

"You heard me. If all we are going to be is friends then no more of that kind of stuff."

"Christi!"

"I mean it!"

Cosmo shrugged. "Okay. But you know Plato was gay and he and Socrates got it on all the time."

"You never take anything serious do you?"

"Come on, Christi!"

Christi glared at him then dove into the pool. She swam quietly for awhile before she got out and toweled off.

Cosmo tried to help her dry but she shunned him. He backed off and shrugged. She popped his butt with the towel.

He turned and smiled as he rubbed his backside. He grabbed the end of the towel and pulled her close to him.

Christi was chilly form the swim and he felt so warm she melted into his arms.

"So? What's on the menu for this evening?" Cosmo broke the stilted quiet.

"Oh? My hectic schedule? Let's see. The Sumter PTA was last night. Tonight I believe it's the Colleton Club."

"That bunch of stuffy old conservatives. God, what is Monk doing to you, throwing you to the wolves?"

"No. He said if I only win over three or four, that's four fewer powerful enemies I'll have. But you're right. He's had me before so many groups I don't remember half of what I said or promised, or anything," Christi frowned.

"It's okay. Just look glamorous and remember how Mrs. White taught you to speak. I bet it drives the rednecks nuts to hear that smooth, articulate language come from your mouth," Cosmo chuckled.

"I say, old chap, they do seem surprised," Christi laughed with him.

Sarah ambled out onto the terrace. "Christi, there's some man named Jerry Barnes on the phone. He says it's something important about Kiki and he won't talk to anyone but you. Who's Kiki?"

Christi looked at Cosmo who looked back with concern. "He's the friend I told you about, Momma. I'll talk to him." Christi hurried to the phone leaving Sarah shaking her head and Cosmo trying to look innocent.

Christi picked up the phone nervously. "Yes, this is Christi Jones."

"The Senator wants to see you Friday night, 8 P.M. Francis Marion Suite of the Flager Hotel. He wants to talk to you about Kiki and a Caribbean vacation. If you aren't there alone, he will talk to the newspapers. Understood?"

"Kiki?"

"Kiki Chevarra the commie, Mrs. Chevarra!"

Christi started to deny Kiki, but the voice was too convincing. "I'll be there," Christi said weakly as she hung up the receiver, cursing loudly at an empty wall. Slowly, Christi walked back to the terrace and tried to look cool.

Sarah had already gone back into the house and she was glad to be alone with Cosmo.

"So? What is it?" Cosmo demanded.

"Can't hide anything from you. It's someone from Senator James's staff. I wondered when they would start fighting dirty."

"I guess the latest poll shook them up. They suggested they knew something about Kiki. I'll have to go find out what." Christi looked despondent.

"You didn't admit anything?"

"No, I just agreed to a meeting but I have a feeling they know something. Eduardo had all the paperwork buried, but I have a bad feeling."

"Bullshit! They can't prove anything. They know just enough to shake you and that looks like what they did. A very easy victory, I'd say," Cosmo chided.

Christi took a deep breath and blew it out hard. "They called me Mrs. Chevarra. If they know that then they know I was married to one of El Grande's men. They know I helped in the Cuban revolution. God, Cosmo! They will ruin me and embarrass Sarah!"

Cosmo took her by the shoulders and held her firmly in his strong hands. "Don't you give them an easy victory. Little Eddie's soul would not rest easy if you did that. We'll find out whatever it is they know and we'll deal with it then. Until then we'll stay cool, okay?" Cosmo said firmly.

Christi smiled thinly as she nodded in agreement. Cosmo released his grip and tossed her hair playfully. "Who is the meeting with?"

"I imagine one of the Senator's men. I don't believe the Senator will be there himself."

"Have you ever met this Senator?"

"No. He lived on another planet. My kind does not meet his kind."

"Your kind? Christi, the De La Cruz fortune could buy and sell the Jameses. You're the uptown people now."

"The De La Cruz fortune is tied up in court. That old bitch is trying to have Eduardo declared officially dead and my marriage annulled. I can't lose this election, Cosmo. I need to get to Washington and have the power to fight for what is legally and morally mine," Christi said angrily.

Cosmo looked pleased as he watched her anger. "That's it. They're trying to take everything you have away. Get real mad about it. Get mad enough you'll fight them hard enough to win. Good, Christi! Anger is good!" Cosmo insisted.

"Anger won't change the facts if they have some proof."

"We don't know if they have anything but bluff. Until we know that you are still going to win it. I knew you were a winner the first day I saw you," Cosmo smiled warmly.

"Me? You mean that skinny, frightened little girl? Oh God, Cosmo! Did that ever really happen? How strange, I seem to have fond memories of that terrible time. I must be losing my mind," Christi sighed as she leaned against his firm chest.

Cosmo gently folded his arms about her.

"I need you to stay with me through this fight. I won't win it without you Cosmo. I don't want to win it without you," Christi insisted.

Cosmo's silence was not the answer Christi wanted.

"You are leaving soon, aren't you? Dammit, Cosmo! Every time I need someone they leave me. Why not you? Especially you. Why should the love of my life be any different from any of the others?" Christi snapped as she broke his embrace.

"You know what I have to do. I've already missed more of the training than I should have. I must be in Miami in three days, but I will be with you in spirit and I'll be back."

"Well, that's just not good enough, Mr. Collins. When and if you get back I most probably won't need you. What good is it to love somebody and not have them when you need them? You might as well not have them at all. Just go! Get the hell out of my life!"

Cosmo started to reach for her.

Christi pushed him away.

"Okay! Okay! If that's the way you want it!" Cosmo stepped back.

"That's damn well the way I want it!"

"Well, okay. God, what a bitch you turned into!"

"Yeah, well it takes a real bastard like you to know that."

"Goodbye, bitch!"

"Goodbye, bastard!"

Cosmo turned and walked hurriedly across the lawn and down the street, out of her view.

Christi wanted to call him back but her wounded pride would not permit it. After he was gone from sight, she sank slowly into a tree swing that hung from a big oak. Slowly she began to swing herself to and fro gradually picking up speed and enjoying the childish freedom of the swing until Sarah called to her.

Chapter Fifty-three

To help her forget her fight with Cosmo, Christi became more and more involved in the campaign. All day Friday she attended meetings and made appearances, all the while trying not to think of Cosmo or the meeting with the Senator and failing to do both. As eight o'clock approached Christi made her way alone to the hotel. She was strangely at peace as she made her way to the room to meet with the Senator.

Once there, she boldly opened the door and stepped inside. Immediately her eyes fell on the white mane and dour face of Senator James. He wore the most sardonic smile Christi had ever seen. She wanted to turn and walk out of the room, but she was determined not to give him the satisfaction.

"Sit down. Please be comfortable," the Senator offered.

Christi sat down and surveyed the room. The Senator was flanked by his son, her opponent Firman Jr., and three other well-dressed white men.

"Would you like some coffee or anything before we start?" the Senator offered.

"No, Senator. Thank you anyway. If you don't mind I would like to make this as brief as possible."

"Yes. I see. Interesting. You are a businesslike woman. I respect that. You are quite a remarkable young lady also. I've seen a few straw polls that show you running a close race with my son for that penny-ante congressional seat. Not bad for an unknown."

"My polls show me well ahead. Mine must be correct or I wouldn't be here, would I?"

The Senator smiled wryly. "Well, maybe so, maybe not. I just had to get a close-up look-see at the person causing all the ruckus in my little corner of the world. I must say as a man I like what I see. As a taxpaying citizen, well, that's a different matter altogether," he said coldly.

"It's not your corner of the world anymore, Senator. It belongs to everyone on the street. Now, what is it you have to tell me?" Christi demanded.

"My, ain't she the uppity one? They sure do get pushy fast these days. Long before they've paid any dues they want to be a full member of the club. No, by God, they want to be president of the club," the Senator fumed.

"My people have paid double dues for two hundred years and I've come to get my membership card," Christi challenged.

"Well, you look here Ms. Jones, or Mrs. De La Cruz or is it Mrs. Chevarra?" the Senator sneered.

Christi was caught off guard for only a moment. "My married name is De La Cruz. My husband Eduardo has contributed generously to your party. I have a canceled check to your last campaign for $20,000. Am I here to collect a refund?"

The Senator looked like he was going to have a heart attack before he regained his composure. "Yes. Mr. De La Cruz is a good solid citizen." The Senator paused to gloat. "As good a citizen as Kiki Chevarra is a communist!" The Senator leaned forward, anticipating her answer.

Firman Junior stood behind him fighting off a grin.

"Is that supposed to mean something to me?" Christi fought to stay cool.

"Oh! I think so. Let's say, for openers, it's the name of one of El Grande's captains, his brother and some say his right-hand man. Kiki Chevarra is a Marxist, a red, a commie revolutionary terrorist of the first rank. A man who, according to our records, married one Christobel Harriet Jones. Ever hear of her?"

The Senator's eyes sparkled with delight.

Christi had only seen the Senator before in pictures, or on TV. He looked bigger than life in those media spots. Here he looked short and old and more pitiful than foreboding. Far from being intimidating, she found him sadly amusing.

"That's funny. I read somewhere that Kiki had never married," Christi replied.

The Senator looked a little irritated. He shuffled some papers he had in front of him.

Christi tried not to look at the papers.

"A mere technicality, my dear. In the eyes of the church he never was. In the eyes of the civil authorities he still is and we've got the documents to prove it." The Senator wanted to see her fold.

"Poor Kiki. He must be awfully confused," Christi looked nonchalant.

"Smugness does not become you, young lady. You married Kiki Chevarra in Cuba on July 25, 1951. You lived with him before and during the terrorist assault on Moncada Barracks. Later you helped El Grande launch his revolution. I've got it all! I've got it all right here and you're one dead politician. Do you understand that?" The Senator stood up, laughing in triumph.

Christi had to fight hard to maintain her composure. His mocking laughter made her strong. "No, I don't. I don't know what you have and I really don't care. I'm Ms. Christobel Harriet Jones, or if you prefer, Mrs. Eduardo De La Cruz. And if you want to try something with him, you'll find out what power is, Senator," Christi bluffed.

"Oh? Well, why don't you try and contact him and tell him to come meet me. I'll wait. How long do you think it would take to get a hold of him? Ten years? Twenty? How about forever?" the Senator smirked.

Christi had to wonder what the Senator knew. The look in his eyes and the tone of his voice hinted that Eduardo was dead. "I will contact him when I need him. I see no reason to do that now."

"Oh? Why not? Because you believe truth and justice will prevail? Is that why? You dumb, silly little woman. You foolish woman. Don't you know it's muscle and information that wins elections. It always has been that way and it always will be. Women are too stupid to know that. That is why they should stay home and leave politics to men where it belongs.

"God made man in his image and everything was good until you damn women were made. We would all be fine if you bitches hadn't taken that apple off the tree and eaten it." He paused and sneered.

Christi almost leaped for his throat. "You old fossil. I'll bet you were in Eden to see it!"

"Scoff if you will but it was a woman's disobedience and lack of respect for authority that began mankind's fall from grace. Now, I'm telling you to pick up that apple and put it back on the tree."

The Senator picked up an apple from a fruit bowl sitting on the table and threw it at her.

It rolled to a stop right in front of her.

Christi ignored it. "You, Senator, are a dinosaur and you don't know it. All your life you have been in the forefront of every backward move-ment, keeping my people down has been your lifetime work. Well, that's over, no matter what happens to me. That's over! If I don't stop you and yours, somebody else will. You're so narrow-minded you can't see the writing on the wall. I'll fight you and a lot of other good people will fight you. Yes, I believe truth and justice can win, and I'll prove it."

The Senator laughed. Then stopped and looked at her with un-bridled hatred. "You won't be proving anything. What you will be do-ing is notifying the press you are withdrawing from the campaign for personal reasons."

"I don't think so. I plan to be busy pulling rotten apples off of decay-ing trees."

The Senator huffed, turned red and popped a small pill in his mouth. He took several labored breaths before he spoke. "Enough! Just shut your mouth woman and listen! You are withdrawing immediately and furthermore you are going to support my son Firman Junior here. You will state that even though you don't agree on everything, you think he will make a fine congressman. That's what you're going to do!" The Senator turned red on every visible patch of skin.

"The hell I will!" Christi snapped.

"The hell you won't! If you don't I'll see that not only does informa-tion concerning your commie past get to the media but a lot of other information that will make you look like a two-bit whore. I'll have you laughed out of the state and maybe even deported along with that nigger-loving Irishman you are currently cohabitating with, as well! Now, how is that for power?"

In her mind Christi knew he could do most of what he threatened, but her heart would not yield. "I'm not withdrawing and I would never endorse that wimp of a son of yours. I don't care what you try to do about it. It doesn't matter about me. If you hurt Mr. Collins, he knows some people who will cut your jaded old heart out and feed it to you while it's still warm. Now, how about that for power?" Christi stood up and turned to leave.

The Senator shrugged. "You've got until twelve o'clock tomorrow to clear your head and make the right decision. Think it over carefully. Twelve o'clock, you hear?" the Senator shouted after her.

Christi paused and started to reply. The apple he had thrown at her was only inches from her hand. She picked it up and threw it back.

The Senator ducked as it hit the floor harmlessly.

They all laughed behind her back as Christi walked out into the night, shaking with anger and fear.

Chapter Fifty-four

CLOTHED ONLY IN HER YELLOW COTTON DRESS, CHRISTI WALKED the streets of Charleston in a cold midnight Carolina rain. She wandered aimlessly past the usual brace of drunks who made obscene catcalls she did not hear. She ignored the policeman who started to say something but let her alone. She wandered past the nice townhouses until she found herself walking on Bee Street in the heart of old shantytown.

She noticed her old shanty was now empty and up for sale so she wandered inside, cold, wet and shivering.

The tired old floors creaked even under her light weight. The old boards, brick and mortar smelled of decay and the roof leaked from big and small holes. The big ones formed irregular pools that ran themselves out in large cracks in the floor. The small ones dripped drops that fell in slow motion before they were quickly absorbed into the thirsty old wood. Lightning cracked in the distance and seconds later the thunder rolled in classic baritone sounds that made her wonder if the original Frankenstein was playing next door.

There was an old soup can on the floor. She kicked it away before she sat down on one of the few dry spots and pondered all that had happened.

It was a very strange feeling. She did not want to cry, but she did not want to laugh. She simply did not want to feel anything. She wanted to drive the unpleasant feelings away with a total denial of her senses.

If only she had not left Mexico City and J.C., her white stallion, and Henri, her tutor, who would not allow her to do anything that was not graceful, and Eduardo who did not know how to think mean, ugly thoughts.

She wondered about Kiki. She wondered if he ever really loved her. She felt numbness when she thought of Eduardo. She blamed Kiki for taking him away from her.

A huge raindrop hit her on the head as she smiled at the thought of Cosmo.

She loved Cosmo, but she knew he was a hopeless wanderer. She doubted he truly loved her. Cold reality told her she had never had the slightest chance of keeping him. "What a damn fool for love I've been," she chided herself.

"So why should you be different than the rest of us?" Cosmo's voice broke into her thoughts.

At first, she thought it was a dream. She turned to see him standing in the doorway. "Cosmo?"

The rain had soaked him through to the skin.

The small shafts of moonlight lit the sparkling raindrops that rolled off his muscular frame. His eyes sparkled through the gloom. "Sarah was right. She thought you might come here." Cosmo moved beside her and tenderly put his arms around her.

Christi looked at him, caressing his face with her long fingers. "You bastard!"

"Certified. But yours."

"Sarah? She told you about this place? She knew I would be here?"

"Your mother is one savvy lady. We all go back to a place of security when we're troubled." Cosmo kissed her forehead gently as the rain trickled down his face. "Oh? So where do you go?"

"I'm still looking for such a place."

Christi thought it over. "I don't even know where your home is."

Cosmo grimaced a moment then shrugged. "It was a small shanty in Belfast. Not too different from this place."

"I'm sorry."

"Don't be. There is nothing for me there now. This will do fine. Can I share this hiding place with you?"

Christi laughed. "My grand palace? Sure. You get the south wing. It has a view of Mrs. Parlor's chicken coop."

They laughed together and shared a sweet kiss. Christi broke the kiss and looked contrite. "Cosmo, I'm sorry I called you those names."

Cosmo shrugged. "You don't have to apologize. In name calling we're even."

Christi took a long moment to study his face and make sure he was really there. "Will you be disappointed with me if I drop out of this stupid political thing?"

"I'm on your side. But a lot of people who care will be disappointed."

"I know. I would like to beat him, Cosmo. Not for anybody else.

Just for me. I would like to beat him just for the thrill of it. Just to see one of my kind in that big leather chair. God, Cosmo! If I could see him running around in panic wondering where the power went, it would be so delicious!"

Cosmo pulled her close to him and she felt warm against him in the cool dampness. "And why can't you?"

"They know about Kiki. They know about Eduardo, and they know about you." Christi shivered.

"So?" Cosmo shrugged.

Christi pulled away and stared at him.

"So? So they're going to paint me as a pinko terrorist spy! President Kennedy might be young, but even he doesn't like Cuba."

"No, he doesn't. You let him and me take care of Cuba. I have a new respect for American politics. Monk Miller is some kind of guy. Do you think Potter Brown and his people are idiots? Let me tell you about a very lovely trump card. Do you want to hear something that will make the sun come out in this midnight rain?" Cosmo asked, holding her even closer.

Christi looked confused. "Cosmo, I really can't take any more intrigue. Please," she begged.

"No, nothing like that. They had their men digging and we had ours digging. They dug up a big hammer. They did good, alright. It would have been real good, but our men did better," said Cosmo smiling.

"What are you talking about?"

Christi snuggled closer to his warm body.

"Christi, Eddie's death wasn't an accident."

"I should have known it. I did know it, Cosmo. I did!" She shook her fists in rage.

"Monk Miller had some people inside the coroner's office. It seems old Firman Junior had the coroner cover up the fact Little Eddie was hit in the back of the neck by a blunt instrument. He wasn't killed by the car's windshield."

"What?"

"Monk has signed affidavits from a guy named Zeke Daniels who will swear in court he saw Macon Myers hit Eddie with a shotgun barrel. The Senator paid to have it covered up."

"Can we prove that?"

"We have him on obstruction of justice, accessory after the fact, all that good stuff. Monk has it all documented. He's waiting for you at the big house. You should trust people who love you, Christi. You were never alone, sweetheart. A lot of good people want to see you elected." Cosmo kissed her softly.

"Cosmo, that's too good to be true! You mean I've got that crusty old son-of-a-bitch by the balls?"

"They're in your hands, all you have to do is squeeze," said Cosmo grinning.

Christi squeezed both her hands into tightly clenched fists. "I'm to meet with him at noon tomorrow to concede." She paused to savor the thought. "Instead let's hang him high and let him twist slowly in the wind." Christi was exuberant.

"You're beginning to sound like a politician already," said Cosmo glumly.

"God! Please stop me if I get to sounding too much like one! But for awhile I want to be one and a good one."

"I can see."

"It's so exhilarating to have a powerful man like the Senator in a corner. But most of all I want Firman Junior's hide. It's what my mother has waited for all my life." Christi exclaimed.

Cosmo looked slightly puzzled. "Firman Junior is a wimp. He's just the old man's puppet. More to be pitied than feared."

"No! He must go down as hard as his father!"

Cosmo looked curious. "Is there something I should know?"

"No. It's just that Momma has never liked him. I'm not sure exactly why," Christi started to lie.

Cosmo looked at her affectionately, then he frowned. "Christi, don't bullshit the troops."

"What do you mean?"

"I've known Firman Junior is your father for some time," Cosmo said sympathetically.

"It seems everyone knew about it except me." Christi sounded disappointed.

"I think with the Senator and his son, 'father' is merely a biological term, Christi. Don't let it influence what you have to do," Cosmo added.

Christi nodded agreement. "It's funny. I wanted to know him for so long and I look at him and feel nothing but contempt."

Cosmo nodded and stroked her hair gently.

"I just don't like anybody thinking they're better than you and me. I got used to the idea of not having a father a long time ago. I'm too old to get sentimental about it now. I just want him to feel a little pain for Sarah's sake," Christi said evenly.

"If Firman Junior loses this election, he'll lose a lot of friends and a lot of prestige. It will hurt him bad. You can bet on that." Cosmo paused. "Are you sure you are alright with that?"

"Yes! I have no feelings for him! None! Most of all, I want Momma there when we meet to tell him what we know!" Christi shivered with delight.

"Well, tell me how much good news you can take at one time," he challenged.

Christi looked timid for a moment. "A lot. All you have. Please drown me with good news."

"Okay, how would you like to see Garbo again?"

"Garbo? Garbo is dead."

"Nope. He was hurt real bad. He's been in and out of hospitals for years."

"Why didn't you tell me before now?"

"He was crippled and he swore he would never let you see him that way. He took his first steps last week and wants to show off for you." Cosmo beamed.

Christi's eyes welled with drops as big as the rain that fell on her shoulders.

"God, Cosmo! Garbo is alive. That's wonderful."

She buried her face in his muscular chest and hoped the moment would never end. A chill in the air brought her back to cold reality and she knew it would end soon.

Christi gave him a teasing kiss then leapt to her feet. She started to move out of the room. She stopped in a doorway where the moonlight shone behind her illuminating her curvaceous figure as if the yellow cotton dress was not there. "Come here, young man. I have something to show you.

Cosmo stared at her moonlit body before he replied. "Oh? And what might that be, young lady."

Christi did not reply as she disappeared into the bedroom.

Cosmo followed. Once inside the door he saw her sitting on an old bed that, fortunately, was not beneath a leaky part of the roof.

"This is my old bedroom," Christi said.

"I see."

"This is where it all began."

Cosmo nodded.

"I used to lie here at night and dream that a knight in shining armor would come and take me away from this dreary place."

Cosmo looked at his rain-soaked clothes and chuckled. "Would a slightly wet version do?"

Christi thought it over. "Why don't you get out of those wet clothes, Sir Collins?"

Cosmo smiled as he looked at her sitting on the bed in her yellow cotton dress. "Do you remember I told you not to wear that dress. It's much too revealing. It might give men the wrong idea."

"You mean those awful men on this ship might want to despoil the flower of my virtue?" Christi asked as she hiked the dress until she revealed her smooth, partly open thighs.

"Oh, yes!" Cosmo was visibly aroused.

Christi invited him beside her with a wicked look.

Cosmo hesitated then moved to her side. "God! What a woman you have become!"

"I became one the last night you made love to me."

"I don't know about that. I think it was always there."

"Will you stay this night, brave knight?" Christi's mood became more somber.

Cosmo's answer was to stroke her hair gently. "I think that can be arranged." Cosmo kissed her softly. "After I get back from Cuba we will we will have many nights."

Christi sighed hard and gave him a sober look. "Will you go back to Santiago, Cosmo?"

Cosmo stroked her back with his strong, warm hands. "It's not for sure. There is some talk it will be Playa Giron. You remember that beach?" Cosmo said quickly.

Christi half-nodded.

"That's where old Pancho had his fish stand. Playa Giron is just off the Bay of Pigs!" Cosmo laughed.

Christi snuggled into Cosmo's arms. She tried not to remember Pancho, Kiki, Eduardo or anything painful. She had a strange premonition she would not see Cosmo after tonight. She turned her face toward his and let him kiss her softly on the lips.

She shivered with pleasure. He took her face in his hands and brought her lips to his again and teased at kissing. It made her back muscles tense then quiver with pleasure. She grabbed him and held him tightly around the waist.

Christi drew up closer as the night seemed to get colder. "At least for tonight, no more talk of Cuba?" Christi put her finger on his lips and hushed him.

Cosmo smiled and nodded.

Christi held him so tight he found breathing difficult.

Slowly Cosmo broke her grip.

"It was dumb to hold on so tight. I'm sorry, Cosmo," she said, stroking his face.

"No, it was nice. I know how you feel. I know how I feel. I don't know what to do about it. Don't you think I want to stay?" Cosmo pulled her close again, holding her quietly.

"Not enough," Christi replied.

"No! That's not it. We are both so damn strong-willed we won't let anyone else have any control because that's just the way our world operates. I've loved you since the first night I saw you come through the door on the *Calamaria Princess*. I just don't know what to do about it and thinking about it makes me real crazy."

"You don't have to run, Cosmo. I'll let you be in charge."

"No you won't! You aren't about to let anyone else be in charge, Christi."

Christi pursed her lips into a mock pout. "Oh? What about the other night?"

Cosmo had to smile in fond remembrance. "That was wonderful. Let's let it go with that thought. Okay?"

"Will I ever see you again, Cosmo?"

"Of course! I would not go unless I believed in my heart I would come back. I cannot live with the thought of never seeing you again."

Christi pressed her head hard against his chest. "You do what you have to. We will make it right with everybody and then, someday when everyone is satisfied, we will satisfy ourselves. I have to look forward to someday having you with me forever, or I don't want to go on," Christi insisted.

"Someday soon." Cosmo took and deep breath and let it out slowly.

The rain was pouring through the leaky roof. It was cold but they did not feel it.

"I will live for that day!" Christi shivered.

"As will I," Cosmo swore quietly.

They said nothing else as they held each other tightly for a long moment.

Christi broke the spell by nibbling on his ear. "Sir Collins, would you protect me this night from the evil men who would deflower me?"

Cosmo looked gallant. "Of, course, fair lady. I will protect the flower of your virtue with my life."

Christi gave him a mischievous look as she stood up and slipped out of the yellow cotton dress. It fell to the floor and she stood naked in the moonlight before him.

"I do not ask you to risk your life, good sir. I am ready to be deflowered. I ask only that it is done by the magic butterfly of love."

Cosmo smiled as he stood up and took off his wet clothes. He lifted her up and lay her back on the old bed. He moved into the stage lighting cast by the admiring moon. He formed the magic butterfly of love with his hands.

Christi lay back and sighed in anticipation as he eased in between her parted legs.

"Tonight the butterfly flies all night long!" Christi insisted.

"Oh, my! Can this be done?" Cosmo wondered in mock outrage.

"You better believe it, Buster!" Christi said as she watched the butterfly slowly descend upon her.

Cosmo hesitated until she shivered with anticipation. Then he gently descended the butterfly toward her waiting bloom.

Without her mother around to eavesdrop, Christi relaxed and let her inhibitions vanish. She began moaning in ecstasy the moment the butterfly parted the petals of her flower.

She locked her legs around Cosmo's neck, netting the butterfly in a nectar-filled web.

She screamed in unbridled shrieks of passion all through the night. It was not until dawn that she released her hold and let the butterfly flutter away.

Chapter Fifty-five

WHEN CHRISTI AWOKE COSMO WAS GONE. ONCE AGAIN SHE was without the man she loved, but this time she felt hopeful. She made herself believe Cosmo would come back. After all, he was indestructible. Meanwhile, she would do all she could to gain a position to help him and the others.

The walk home in the bright morning sunshine that followed last night's cleansing rain was more hopeful than melancholy. Once at home she prepared to meet the Senator. As she did she promised herself she would win her confrontation with him for Little Eddie's sake, and if not for him then for Sarah.

That thought made her strong as she entered the room at the hotel to meet with him once again.

This time the look on the Senator's face more strained than condescending. Christi looked at Monk Miller and he nodded. She knew the Senator had been told of their findings. She only wished she had been the one to tell him.

As Christi and Sarah sat across the polished oak table from him and her father, Firman Junior, and a few of the Senator's cronies, she felt much more at ease than she had during their first meeting. It was his turn to rotate on the spit and Christi was determined to enjoy it.

The Cheshire grin on Sarah's face meant she was going to enjoy it as well.

As the Senator read over the copies of the documentation Monk Miller had given him earlier, he seemed to age another ten years. Finally he stopped, removed his glasses and stared first at Sarah, then Christi. "I suppose you think this changes things." He tried to be assertive.

"No, I don't THINK it does! I know it does!" Christi said.

He tried to laugh her off.

Christi retained eye contact.

He threw the documents across the table. "We have documents also. Mr. Collins knows the power of my Senate Select Committee on Subversion. I understand he's even done a few jobs for us. Aren't you and he cohabitating?" the Senator probed.

"My God! What an archaic word, Senator. Mr. Collins is on retainer to the family as a consultant."

The Senator smirked and guffawed. "Yes! And we all know what he consults in, don't we?" the Senator jeered.

Christi smiled thinly as she waited for the Senator to look at her. "Are you adding peeping Tom to your other perversions, Senator?" Christi said calmly.

The Senator's face turned beet red. "I don't need to peek to know what goes on with you and Mr. Collins, or any of your other lovers. Your reputation precedes you and there is no way a whore like you is going to Congress! So take your forged documents and get the hell out of here!"

Senator James stood up and glared at Christi.

Christi refused to rise to the bait.

Sarah could not restrain herself. "You crusty old bastard, don't you call your granddaughter a whore!" Sarah glared back at him and Firman Junior who looked chagrined.

Christi had never seen Senator James so unraveled. "My God! Sarah Jones, are you still holding onto that old lie," he finally stammered.

"It ain't no lie, but now I have seen what I have seen, I wish it was. I don't want to know nobody who's kin of yours. But I just once want you to acknowledge it before God and man." She paused and glared at Firman Junior who cowered in the corner. "Just once and we'll say no more about it," Sarah insisted.

Christi tried to reach for Sarah's hand to calm her down.

Sarah shook her off and leered at the Senator and his son.

"I think we're getting off the agenda here." Monk Miller tried to interrupt.

"You sit down and hush, Monk. This is old unfinished business between me, the Senator and his yellow-bellied, mealymouthed son who . . . God forgive me . . . knows the truth." She sighed hard and gave Firman Junior a stern look. "It's past time you 'fessed up Mister Firman James Junior. Or maybe I go to them newspapers and say I want one of those blood tests!"

Firman Junior moved deeper into the shadows.

"Isn't the death of my grandson enough for you! Isn't the denigration of his name enough? Do I have to legitimize your bastard daughter as well?" Senator James growled.

Sarah started to come across the table after him, but Christi restrained her.

"What about my Little Eddie? You done had him killed and I'm going to see you brought down for it!" Sarah pounded the table with her fists.

Senator James was visibly shaken by Sarah's ire. He turned and glared at his son.

"Step up here, boy!" He paused and pointed to a Bible on the table. "You come here and put your hand on this Bible. You look Sarah Jones in the eye and you tell her that daughter of hers is no child of yours. You swear before me and God that it is all a lie. You hear?"

Slowly, Firman Junior moved out of the shadows. Meekly he put his hand on the Bible. He could not make eye contact with anyone.

"Well! Say it, boy!" Senator James insisted.

Firman, Junior started to speak. As he did his eyes met Christi's. For a brief moment there was a hint of sadness in his eyes. Then he turned and bolted from the room.

"Good God Almighty! I swear that boy is none of mine!" Senator James sat down hard in his chair.

"He's got enough gumption to know not to swear no lies on the Good Book!" Sarah said.

"That don't mean a thing except he's a coward. That is no new revelation to me." Senator James sighed hard.

"I know you to be many things, Mister Senator James but you ain't no heathen. You know the truth. God knows you know the truth." Sarah shot back.

Christi moved in front of her and stood between her and the Senator.

"I think the point is that no one here is the virgin of the snows, Senator. We're sort of like America and Russia. We don't like each other but we both have the potential to destroy each other. I suggest, as they say in Congress, 'we go along to get along,'" Christi said coolly.

The Senator chewed hard on an old cigar. His eyes looked weak and tired as he replied, "What you have is a lot of maybes. Maybe you could prove something and maybe you couldn't. I'm not so sure I wouldn't like to see you try." He paused and tried to appear senatorial. "But I'm a reasonable man. I figure you to lose this election anyway, so we'll just say we have . . ." He paused to smirk. ". . . a Mexican standoff. You know what a Mexican standoff is, don't you, *señora?*" he needled.

Christi did not flinch, she eyed him with a steady gaze. "Yes, that means I have yours gripped just as tightly as you have mine. But I think it would hurt you a lot more if I squeezed than if you did," she said evenly.

The Senator shifted the cigar in his mouth. He looked more irritated than contemptuous. He picked up two apples from a fruit bowl and gripped them tightly before he rolled them softly onto the table. They stopped rolling just before they reached Christi's side.

"I sure have to say old Eve didn't have nothing on you. My, if you had been in the Garden of Eden, you'd have eaten the whole damn tree. Just watch yourself, woman!

"You will be allowed to play the game at this level for a time. But don't ever think you're really somebody. Don't make that mistake!" he snapped just before he got up and moved toward the door.

His obedient hacks followed respectfully and fearfully behind.

Christi watched him go without comment. She grinned to herself as she heard the Senator berating his son all the way to the elevator, telling him the Congressional seat had been his last chance to make something of himself.

Playfully, she picked up one of the apples and polished it with her hand.

Sarah and the others gathered around her, congratulating her on her victory over the Senator.

Christi was not so sure. Yet she didn't care. Never before in her life had she felt so alive.

The best sex she had ever had barely matched the feeling of euphoria that accompanied her battle over power with the Senator. Maybe old Franz was right after all. Maybe power was the ultimate thrill. It was a feeling Christi knew she liked too much and would have to deal with— but not just now.

For now she would enjoy the feeling to its fullest and worry about its excesses another day.

Chapter Fifty-six

THE CAMPAIGN WAS EASY. WITH A BALANCE OF POLITICAL TERROR on both sides, Christi became the issue. Cosmo was right, the television cameras loved her and she loved them.

Poor Firman Junior looked like an emaciated Howdy Doody on camera. He tried to raise phony issues, but no one listened to the issues. They asked inane questions like whether she was going to accept the Hollywood contract she was offered, or whether she had a private hairdresser.

She did not see most of the slick commercials Monk Miller made that presented her as an expert on the issues. Christi resented them because she felt deeply about everything, yet the professionals advised against saying much about anything. She was prevented by her advisors from making any comment beyond several well-thought-out convoluted statements that seemed to say a lot but said little. She let them run this campaign their way, but she knew that the next time it would be her way.

When it was over and she had won, she felt happy and depressed. As she looked at the smiling faces of her supporters, she was sad Cosmo's was not among them.

On election night, there was no news from Eduardo or Kiki. In the midst of the most glorious moment of her life she found herself alone.

She was winning an overwhelming electoral victory and was literally surrounded by a sea of well-wishers, but nowhere among them was a man she loved. She wanted to shout for joy and yet she wanted to cry. Instead, she had to make a happy statement to the people who had worked so hard for her. She walked up to the microphone and looked out over the crowd.

"Christi! Christi! Christi!" they chanted.

Christi waved her hand high in a victory salute. With ninety percent of the precincts reporting, she had an overwhelming lead. She watched the big television screens as Firman Junior gave a conciliatory and complimentary speech of defeat.

Sarah and Mrs. White hugged each other as Christi became misty-eyed. The crowd "oohed" and "aahed." They believed it to be sentiment over the remarkable upset victory she had obtained. They had no way of knowing it was because, although she had attained all the elegance and power any woman could ever know, she did not have the man she loved to share it with.

The crowd watched her a moment as she brushed back the tears. She took several breaths and sighed. "I'm so sorry, I'm so sorry. God knows I don't want to be labeled a sentimental, emotional woman," Christi whispered hoarsely into the microphone.

The crowd went into a frenzy of adulation. Christi had never heard such a roar of approval.

She turned and looked at Mrs. White and Sarah, who stood directly behind her.

"Momma, Mrs. White, I am now a lady of elegance and a woman of power. Do you think out there somewhere, you could find a man who would love me?" she asked bitterly.

Mrs. White and Sarah looked at each other and at Christi. They both embraced her.

"Now, chile, every man and woman out there loves you. You done good! All our hopes and dreams, they have come true. We all here, black and white is proud of . . ." Sarah paused and looked at Mrs. White ". . . all of us are proud of you this day!" Sarah insisted warmly.

Mrs. White nodded approval. "Yes, all that work, Christi. All those extra lessons. They have paid off. You are here now. Here where you always belonged."

Christi did not dislike Mrs. White, she had just outgrown her. Christi wanted no more elocution lessons. She did not want elegance or power, she wanted love. She wanted to her soul not to feel so completely alone among this multitude of people.

"Mrs. White, I appreciate all you have done for me, I really do. But I tell you tonight, amidst all this," Christi waved her arm at the crowd, who increased its level of cheering, "I would rather be in the arms of a man who loves me than here tonight," Christi finished.

"I understand, Christi. But having them both, I believe, would be the desirable goal." Mrs. White looked pleased with herself.

Sarah looked puzzled. "My Lord! Ain't nobody who gets anywhere near all they want."

"I know, Momma. I'm just tired. That's all."

Sarah looked doubtful.

"Lord, chile! You don't have to do this if you don't want to. Maybe I done a bad thing. I wanted it so much. I'm sorry, my darling. If you want to tell these people you don't want this thing, then as God is my judge, I am beside you," Sarah said sincerely.

"No, Momma, we can't ever again do just what you and I want. I'm new at this, but I know that. I'll work the other stuff out." Christi tried to chase the melancholy from her eyes.

"Good Lord! What have I done? I wanted so much for you I didn't think about nothing else." Sarah sighed.

"It's okay, Momma."

"No! I just wanted that arrogant man to say, 'this is my daughter' but he ain't never gonna say that. I should have knowed it all along. I'm sorry I pushed you so hard. I hope God will forgive me." Sarah fought back tears.

Christi embraced her dearly.

They hugged each other tightly as the crowd cheered wildly.

Mrs. White slowly slipped into the shadows and enjoyed a brief moment of joy for her small part in this triumph.

Christi shook off her sadness and slowly turned back to the crowd. They hushed almost immediately. It was a good feeling to watch them anticipate her moves. Franz was right about power. It was a heady feeling to be enjoyed. Christi put the microphone to her mouth and made an impassioned speech the crowd did not hear, they cheered so loudly.

In a small room at his commando training camp in South Florida, Cosmo packed his duffel bags as he watched her victory on television. Since Christi was the first black woman to hold that congressional seat it had made her local election a national television event.

Cosmo knew he was looking at a rising star.

He was already late for his meeting with the Cuban expatriates in Miami but he really did not want to go. Instead, he wanted to sit there and look at her as long as possible. He also wondered at his particular form of madness. How he loved her. How he yearned to even the score with El Grande. The only thing close to his love for her was his hatred for El Grande. His rational mind told him that seeking his vengeance would risk never holding her again. Yet something deep in his heart, whispered there had to be another time that would be their time. To avoid such emotional conflicts Cosmo had dodged romantic entanglements all his life. He had tried not to love her. He had always known that was impossible. Christi was the only woman he had ever known that could make him forget, for a time, the thrill of combat and consider the more subtle dangers of domesticity. He was mad at himself for the perceived weakness of hesitating to join his comrades-in-arms. He had known that hesitancy to be deadly when the guns started firing.

Cosmo took a deep breath, blew it out hard. He took one last long look at her vibrant, dazzling image until it faded to a dumb commercial. Quickly, he turned off the television. "Hey, old lady of elegance. Damn I love you!" he whispered quietly to the darkened screen as he closed his duffel bag and wept.

Chapter Fifty-seven

My Dear Christi,

Congratulations on your victory. I received the news a few days late here in Mexico City.

I must say you have renewed my fundamental faith in the power of status. When I said I was representing Congresswoman Jones, the doors that Eduardo's phony grandmother had tried to shut began to swing open. They are falling all over themselves to court our favor. I'm sure it is just a matter of time and the right amount of money placed in the right hands before I can tell you your husband's fortune is safely back in your hands.

I will now begin to press the search for Eduardo. He was last reported to be in the jungles of Nicaragua with one of El Grande's lieutenants. I assume there is no limit to the expenditures for this endeavor.

Congratulations again. I am extremely proud of you.

Carlton Bennett, Attorney at Law

Christi read Carlton's special delivery letter with a smile. Eduardo said he was the best and he had proved it twice now. She wondered where Eduardo was and if he was alright. Deep in her heart she had a special place for him. He had given her many of the best years of her life and she recalled them fondly.

But today, her day of victory, she longed for Cosmo and felt deeply the emptiness of a great victory without someone special to share it with.

She refused to be melancholy for long. This was a day to be enjoyed, but how to enjoy it?

Washington was warmer than Christi thought it would be this January morning. She had brought her favorite furs but felt they would not be appropriate for her first day in Congress. She had fretted for several weeks over what to wear. Nothing in the boutiques had pleased her and she felt strongly about being feminine without being a source of laughter from her male colleagues.

As she sat in her new Washington apartment and looked across the eleven open suitcases, she censured herself for overpacking. It had taken two bellboys two trips to bring up all her stuff. She had tipped them generously but had seen the condemning look in their eyes. Maybe they were right. It was excessive for one person and with it all she had nothing to wear.

She looked out the window toward the Capitol and smiled as she opened the last small suitcase. She paused and smiled as she saw her yellow cotton dress neatly folded all alone with a silk ribbon around it. Tucked in place by the ribbon was a note. She opened the note and read:

My darling baby girl!

Your Momma loves you more than you will ever know. She wants you to do right by all the people back here counting on you.

Don't you let all those high faluting people up there turn your head. If you ever start thinking you better than anybody, you put on this dress and you remember where you come from and who it is that really matters in this world. God bless you and keep you.

Love, Sarah

Christi wiped a trace of tears from her eyes and lay the note aside. She picked up the dress and looked at it. She almost laughed at its lack of elegance. For an instant she thought of wearing it. She quickly dismissed the idea as too sentimental. Pants suits were the rage. A dark pants suit was dignified and considered appropriate for the occasion. After all, she was now Congresswoman Christobel Harriet Jones, the first black Congresswoman from South Carolina.

She must never do anything that wasn't dignified.

"Oh God! Would that get a laugh!" she thought to herself. She imagined herself walking into that august chamber with all those censuring eyes just waiting for her to make a false step. She had to take that walk into the mostly male, almost lily-white sanctuary alone. She had to walk past the Senate chambers and the Senator James's grinning face. She knew he would see she got the coldest reception possible.

It was a little scary to realize she had to do that all alone.

She smiled as she thought about the TV men being there. She liked them and they liked her. Monk Miller said she got more free TV coverage than all the candidates he had ever worked with. That thought made her happy.

There would be television cameras there and they made her feel good.

Christi was never alone when those lights were on her.

She felt bolder as she picked up the yellow cotton dress. As she held it, a thousand bittersweet memories flooded her mind. Suddenly it occurred to her that to deny that dress was to deny her heritage. Worse, it would let the forces of snobbery she had so despised win.

Without hesitation, she slipped it over her still curvaceous body. She checked her coiffure and makeup. A slow smile spread across her face as she spied the bent crucifix on the dresser. She fixed it about her neck. "Well, Kiki, if you could see me now."

She was interrupted by a knock on the door. She opened it to find it filled with Garbo's huge bulk.

"Garbo!" she squealed in delight, throwing her arms around his neck. "Cosmo said you were well. Oh, you look so good!"

"You are still the most lovely one, Miss Christi. You make me proud to be black," Garbo stuttered, looking embarrassed.

"Oh, Garbo! I'm so glad you're alive. But how did you get here?"

"I can walk now, Miss Christi." He walked with a slight limp. "Almost," he added.

"That's wonderful! It is good to see you."

"Yes, this is good."

They exchanged a quick embrace.

Christi broke the embrace and looked around his huge bulk. "Is anyone with you?" she hoped.

"No, ma'am."

"I see." Christi could not hide her disappointment as she took him by his huge hand and led him into the room.

"I bring you this letter and this gift." Garbo held out a letter and a small box.

Christi took them from him. She took one more look around hoping Garbo was not alone.

Garbo saw her look and looked sad. "I'm sorry, Miss Christi. They won't be coming."

"Yes. I understand." Christi turned away a moment. "So tell me, Garbo what have you heard of Kiki and Eduardo?"

"There's not much to say about that, Miss Christi. Lots of bad things is going on down there."

"Then he's already gone?"

"Ma'am?"

"Nothing. So! It is so good to see you. I'm so glad you made it!"

Garbo gave her a steady gaze. "Yes, ma'am. He's done gone. I was supposed to go to Cuba with Mr. Collins but he said I have to protect you. I was happy to come, Miss Christi."

"I'm so happy you came. At least I have one of my favorite men with me." She smiled as she put down the box and opened the letter.

She was afraid to read it at first. Finally she let herself read:

Christi,

Writing letters is harder than kicking ass. This is the third letter I've written in my life. The other two were forced at gunpoint. I am so happy for you. I wish I was there, but if you are reading this then Garbo is there and he's the best man I've ever known. He will watch over you while I am away.

We launch our mission soon. When it is over I should be in a position to press the search for Eduardo, but if I find him I don't know if I'll tell him where you are. I was always jealous of him. He gave you all the things I wished for you and could never give you myself, and he could quote Shakespeare besides. Anyway, I know you won't be alone as long as you have those TV reporters.

The first time I saw you on TV I knew you would be a superstar.

Well, I've got to polish my boots. Can't look bad at inspection. Take care and remember, don't ever think you're forgotten by this man. If you fall the slightest bit I'll be there to pick you up. I mean it! Wherever I am, my heart will be with you for as long as I live.

Cosmo

Christi was in loud, heaving tears before she finished the letter.

Garbo stood by helplessly.

Finally Christi's tears turned to laughter and Garbo's eyes brightened.

"Garbo, if you ever see me with a man who has a cause, please do me a favor and shoot me on the spot." Christi grinned, drying her tears.

"Oh no! Miss Christi. I know you're just funnin' me. Right?" Garbo wondered.

Christi did not reply, leaving him to wonder, as she moved to clean up her face and prepare for her swearing-in ceremony. When she was finished she walked back into the room to find it empty.

"Garbo?" she wondered aloud.

Seconds later the door swung open and Garbo looked inside.

"You okay, Miss Christi?"

"Yes. Yes, thank you, Garbo."

"I'm right outside the door. You just call and I'll be here." Garbo said.

Christi nodded as Garbo closed the door.

Moments later she moved to her dressing table. As she did, she spied the box that Garbo had brought. She picked it up and opened it. It was a shoe box and inside was a pair of black high-strap shoes. Shoes that matched her dress perfectly. There was a small note in one of the shoes.

Christi picked it up and read:

From all the men who love you.

There was no signature, leaving her to wonder.

Chapter Fifty-eight

CHRISTI HELD HER HEAD HIGH AS THE HEELS OF HER NEW SHOES clicked down the long marble halls of Congress. The critical eyes of some of the men in dark blue suits did not faze her. She politely accepted the hands of the many people of goodwill who gathered around and congratulated her as she walked toward the chambers that held her seat.

Garbo walked a few steps behind her and Sarah and Mrs. White ambled close behind.

The TV cameras led the way.

It was a totally delicious feeling.

It was funny how Cosmo had been right. She was never lonely when the TV lights were on.

"Ms. Jones. Can you tell us how it feels to be the first black Congresswoman from the deep South?" A New York TV man quizzed.

"Congresswoman? That takes some getting used to," she smiled.

The TV man looked starstruck.

"What about Senator James? Do you expect to run for his seat when he retires in two years?" a Georgia reporter asked.

"My! I just got here. But you know me, I never close off any options," she winked.

"That yellow dress . . . and THOSE shoes, Ms. Jones. Do you think that's a little too flashy for these halls?" Julia Barrows, a catty Beverly Hills reporter, probed.

Christi paused and looked her in the eye. "Why no, this is my wedding dress, Miss Barrows," she grinned.

Garbo pushed several paparazzi away as Christi approached a group of senators with old Senator James standing with folded arms in the forefront.

She started to pass him without comment and proceed to the House, but the TV cameras and salivating reporters would not allow it.

"Ms. Jones, would you like to comment again on a possible run for the Senator's seat when he retires?" a Carolina reporter asked.

All the mikes jammed into her face.

Christi tried to wave them away.

Garbo pushed a few aside before she held him up.

Senator James moved in beside her and tried to steal some camera time. He was mostly ignored and his reddened face showed his ire.

"Oh? This lady is after my seat already? I'm not yet cold." The Senator smiled benignly into the cameras. "Well, I've decided to run again and not retire. I'll let my senatorial district decide if I'm too old to run against this charming young lady. I know I'll have an uphill fight, but I'm used to being the underdog," Senator James chortled.

Christi was incensed at his smug condescension, but she had learned a lot about politics in a short time.

She looked his way and nodded politely. "The Senator has served the people well. I have no designs on his seat. I hope he enjoys long life and is able to run for several more terms." Christi offered her hand to the Senator.

He was obviously irritated, until the camera lights turned on his face.

"Why, thank you, and good luck on your first term, Congressman."

"Congresswoman, if you please, Senator," Christi corrected.

"Yeah. Whatever," the Senator shrugged and started to move away.

The TV men turned off the lights.

Christi reached into her purse and pulled out a brightly polished apple. "Senator?" she called after him.

"Yes, woman?" he turned and snarled.

Christi bit deeply into the apple then held it out to him. "Want a bite?"

Senator James looked like he was going to have a heart attack. He snarled something unintelligible then stormed off.

Christi savored the delicious fruit long after the Senator had vanished in the distance. In that moment all the hardships she had endured to get here seemed more than worth it and she was as content as she had ever been. Moments after the Senator was gone, Christi suddenly felt nauseous and had to sit down.

Garbo looked concerned but she motioned him away and moved quickly to the bathroom. Once inside, her stomach still churning, she felt strangely wonderful. There was a new warmth deep inside and a good feeling in her spirit that quickly overcame the nausea.

She put her hand to her stomach and smiled. She knew she had been irregular but was too busy until now to know why. An inner sense told her she was pregnant and that realization gave her a peace she had sought all her life. She was to have Cosmo's child, and in that knowledge was the real fulfillment of all her dreams. For a time she would be a lady of elegance AND a woman of power.

Whatever the world demanded of her she would give it for a time.

But in the end, she would be Cosmo's wife and the mother of his children and that would be enough—for now.

The End

Other books from OZ Publishing

Order your autographed copies today!

THE JOSHUA TRAIL TRILOGY

Volume One: *Six Notch Road*
Volume Two: *The Joshua Trail*
Volume Three: *A Season of Reckoning*

A YELLOW COTTON DRESS

Name _____

Street _____

City _____

State & Zip _____

	Price (U.S. dollars)	Number Ordered	Total Amount
Six Notch Road	$16	_____	_____
The Joshua Trail	$16	_____	_____
A Season of Reckoning	$16	_____	_____
A Yellow Cotton Dress	$16	_____	_____

Shipping & handling included

TOTAL _____

Fill out this form and send with your check to:

OZ Publishing
P.O. Box 1349
Sacramento, CA 95812-1349

Or call toll-free 1-888- 668-0744

Other books from OZ Publishing

Order your autographed copies today!

THE JOSHUA TRAIL TRILOGY

Volume One: *Six Notch Road*
Volume Two: *The Joshua Trail*
Volume Three: *A Season of Reckoning*

A YELLOW COTTON DRESS

Name _____

Street _____

City _____

State & Zip _____

	Price (U.S. dollars)	Number Ordered	Total Amount
Six Notch Road	$16	_____	_____
The Joshua Trail	$16	_____	_____
A Season of Reckoning	$16	_____	_____
A Yellow Cotton Dress	$16	_____	_____
Shipping & handling included			
		TOTAL	_____

Fill out this form and send with your check to:

OZ Publishing
P.O. Box 1349
Sacramento, CA 95812-1349

Or call toll-free 1-888- 668-0744

Printed in the United States
27830LVS00004B/37-54